sweetshop OF DREAMS

A NOVEL IN RECIPES

JENNY COLGAN

Cover design by Stephanie Gafron/Sourcebooks
Cover images © Arx0nt/Getty Images

Published by Sourcebooks Landmark, an imprint of Sourcebooks
P.O. Box 4410, Naperville, Illinois 60567-4410
(630) 961-3900
sourcebooks.com

Originally published as *Rosie Hopkins' Sweetshop of Dreams* in 2012 in Great Britain by Sphere, an imprint of Little, Brown Book Group. This edition issued based on the paperback edition published in 2014 by Sourcebooks Landmark, an imprint of Sourcebooks.

Library of Congress Cataloging-in-Publication Data is on file with the publisher.

Printed and bound in Canada.
MBP 10 9 8 7 6 5 4 3 2 1

a word from jenny

Her name was Mrs. McCreadie. Do you remember the name of the lady who ran your sweetshop? They tended to come in two flavors: nice and rounded or grumpy kid-haters you couldn't believe ever chose this line of work, complaining about sticky coins and glaring at you if you looked like you might touch anything.

Mrs. McCreadie was in the first group, always ready with a smile and a gentle hand on the scales that would round up to your ten or twenty pence worth, not down. It was such a treat to go in there, marveling at the colors and the choices, the big ten-pence piece growing hot and grubby in your tightly clenched fist as you weighed your options—long-lasters or delicious melt-in-the-mouths? Expensive chocolate or cheap chews?

Then, with the fashion for things retro and handmade, they started to return. When an old-fashioned sweetshop opened just up from where we were staying in London a year or so ago, my husband and I were very excited about it (we are shamelessly enthusiastic consumers of our own children's party bags—as yet they have absolutely NO idea that the things you are given when leaving a party contain anything more than a whistle and a small bouncy ball). We took the children up there and, in the manner of Ozymandias, said, "Ta dah! And you can choose ANYTHING you like!"

Our poor children, brought up with the absolute nonsense that passes for sweets where we live in France—small hard jellies, horrible chews that you can't get the paper off—and the nasty salt licorice my husband gets sent from his homeland of New Zealand, just gazed around, confused, completely unaware of the treasure store that surrounded them.

Flumps, jelly beans, cola cubes (black AND red), humbugs, sherbets, toffees, caramels, nougats, rocks, and éclairs stretched up to the ceiling as far as they could see. Our eldest, five years old, looked around, slightly panicked, for a long time then, very quietly, pointed at a plain licorice pole and said, "I'll have that, please," whereupon the three-year-old, whose sole aim in life is to replicate, as far as possible, every precise detail of the existence of his elder sibling, went, "ME TOO, AH WAN THAT." My husband and I looked at each other, shrugged, bought them the licorice, then splurged on half the rest of the shop and guzzled it walking up the road in a way that couldn't possibly have imparted any meaningful life lessons.

And every penny chew, every blackjack, every highland toffee is a direct path, a running track to childhood. (Honestly, what was my mother thinking? Although in fairness, as an ardent sweetie fan herself, she suffered terrible damage to her own teeth as a child and was extremely vigilant about ours. She does, though, think the severe sweet limiting we practice on our own children is going to come right back around and bite us once they get old enough to think for themselves, which may yet turn out to be the case.) It is also a path to comfort, and sweetness, and sharing, or not. I remember, once I hit my grim secondary school, the anticipation of sharing a Twix with Gillian Pringle while hiding from the horrible kids on the back stairs was about the only thing that could get me through the day. I haven't eaten a Twix since.

By contrast, when I got a little older, about to leave school and go off to college, getting invited to parties and beginning to feel freer and happier, I went through a period of basically existing off crème eggs.

(And staying a size two, back when a size two really WAS a size two. And teenagers think they've got it tough!!) I do still love a crème egg.

I remember the excitement of my first American friend being sent three huge bags of Hershey's Kisses, which we binged upon, the little silver sweetheart wrappers littering our chilly dark dorm room in Edinburgh. I thought Hershey's Kisses were just about the most sophisticated things I could imagine. And I can measure my first trip to America in the flaking of Butterfingers and melting into Reese's Peanut Butter Cups on the everlasting Greyhound bus.

And now? Now I have moved to a country that has almost no interest in sweets at all; otherwise, they wouldn't wrap them like they do (in cheap paper that sticks to the surface, so you invariably get a mouthful of candy flecked with wrapping). There's only one brand too.

France, where I live for my husband's work, is the country of patisserie, of cakes that float like air, of pastries and mille-feuille and macaroons and schoolchildren who, when I make a tray of tablet, a type of crunchy Scottish fudge, for "tastes of the world" day, gather around me to tell me solemnly that it is *trop sucré,* a fact that is hard to argue with a recipe starting, "take one kilo of sugar..."

But I do miss them. Chocolate limes—what a perfect combination of flavors that is. I can eat Edinburgh rock till I've burned off the roof of my mouth. My plan, before I get really old and have to start worrying about pulling out one of my teeth, is to eat as much toffee as I can. If I ate as much fudge as I could, they would have to take me to the hospital in one of those reinforced animal ambulances. After knocking down a wall. My grandmother, and this is true, ate nothing but sweets from the day she retired, as a *staple diet*. And she reached a ripe old age.

So this book is a way of channeling my affections really. It is my homage to the sweetshop; to Star Bars and Spangles and refreshers and licorice allsorts and jawbreakers and Hubba Bubba and Saturday mornings and playtime and friendship, and all the Mrs. McCreadies of this world; to all those who are kind to nervous children when they have only pennies to spend. And I've included (because, I'm afraid, I just can't help myself) some of my favorite recipes, for coconut ice, marshmallows, tablet, and peanut brittle. The smell of syrup gently thickening in the kitchen on a chilly afternoon is my idea of heaven. I have been reminded to warn everyone, even though obviously you already know, that especially if you're cooking with children, boiling sugar is very, very, very hot. There you go: I have fulfilled my health and safety commitments!

Anyway, in the manner of a wine waiter at a fancy restaurant, I consider this book best enjoyed with a large bag (paper, ideally pink and green faded stripe with a serrated edge) of sherbet lemons and an epically large mug of tea.

Then brush your teeth!

With very warmest wishes,
Jenny

In 1932, the Milky Way appeared in the U.S., followed by Mr. Mars Jr.'s invention, the Mars Bar, in the UK in 1933. In 1935, the Aero; in 1936, Maltesers; and in 1937, the Kit Kat, Rolos, and Smarties.

In music, the equivalent would be the golden age of Bach, Mozart, and Beethoven. In painting, it was the equivalent of the Italian Renaissance and the advent of Impressionism at the end of the nineteenth century; in literature, Tolstoy, Balzac, and Dickens…

—Roald Dahl

soor plooms

• • • •

This is a Scots term that translates as sour plums but in its original language imitates exactly the contortions of your mouth as soon as you pop one in.

More of an endurance exercise than a treat, this is a hard candy of exquisite, roof-of-the-mouth-stripping, bitter intensity; the occasional rush of sweetness comes as a blessed relief. Near-impossible to bite and still maintain an entire set of teeth, they are therefore the ideal purchase for the pocket-money-strapped child as, number one, they last forever and, number two, they are something of a rarefied taste and therefore require less sharing than other sweets.

Downsides include being a choking hazard, their bright green color, which renders them very visible to teachers, and their density—a correctly trajectoried *soor ploom* can knock out a dog from forty feet.

Rosie put the very peculiar book down. She was in any case sitting near the front of the bus, hopping up every now and again anxiously, trying to peer through the grimy windows. Why was the countryside so dark? Every time they left a tiny village with a few streetlights in the little, single-decker, green-painted bus with ripped, ancient leather seats—it looked like it should have been retired years ago—it felt like they hit a great sea of blackness, a vast wall of nothingness looming out of a few scattered remnants of civilization.

Rosie, a city girl born and bred, wasn't used to it at all. It was sinister up there. How could people live amid so much dark? She pictured the bus, the only point of light for miles around, trundling up and down hills, the only mark of civilization before what seemed to be a great, endless night. The few people who had joined the bus in Derby—old ladies, mostly, and a couple of foreign-speaking young men whom Rosie took to be farmworkers—had all gotten off ages ago. She'd asked the bus driver, who had an enormous beard, to tell her when they got to Lipton, but he'd grunted at her in a noncommittal way, which meant that now she was hopping up and down nervously every time they entered a village, trying to figure out from his head movements whether it was this one or not.

Rosie stared at her reflection in the dark window of the bus. Her dark curly bob was held back with hair clips above a button nose full of freckles. Her large, soft gray eyes were probably her best feature, but now they looked worried, lost, and anxious. A large suitcase sat above her in the ancient luggage rack, feeling irrevocably heavy, reminding her that there was no easy route back. Other people's lives, she thought to herself, were meant to be full of excitement, of a feeling of lightness and freedom. Hers was just baggage. She checked her phone to ring Gerard, but there was no signal.

The bus chuffed and coughed up another endless hill into nothingness. Rosie had thought England was a small country, but she had never felt so far away from everything she had ever known. She glanced anxiously at the bus driver, hoping he remembered she was still there.

• • • •

That last day at work, though. Really, when you thought about it, her mother couldn't have chosen to ring at a better time.

"Where the HELL is that sodding bedpan? What the HELL is going on here? What do you think you're doing?"

The young doctor didn't look more than about twenty years old, and absolutely terrified to boot. He was covering his terror by being aggressive; Rosie had seen it a million times before. She rushed to his side—every other nurse had disappeared from view—and he was trying to help an old lady who appeared to be reacting to the lancing of a particularly unpleasant boil by peeing the bed at the same time. Which would have been fine, but Rosie had only been on the ward ten minutes, and no one had bothered to give the agency auxiliary even the most cursory show-around. She didn't blame the staff nurses—they were up to their eyeballs—and there were different agency nurses in every day.

So she had tried to unobtrusively change sheets, bring water to those who needed it, take lunch orders, do the tea round, empty the bedpans and sharps boxes, and generally help as much as she could without getting in anyone's way, even though she'd worked a twelve-hour day in a different hospital across town the day before and was still absolutely exhausted. She was always too terrified that the agency would take her off their roster that she never turned any job down.

Meanwhile, the very young, rather posh-looking doc was getting positively hosed with pee and pus, which might, Rosie tried not to think, have been funny under different circumstances, but as it was, she managed to dart to another elderly patient and grab a large cardboard bedpan just in time, knocking it in front of the doc to catch the remainder like a doubles tennis player.

"God," said the doctor rudely. The old woman, in pain and upset, started to cry. Rosie knew the young doctor's type. Straight out of medical school, he had barely met a real patient before. He had spent years in nice lecture halls, being treated like the crème de la crème by friends and family for being a student doctor, and he was now getting his first unpleasant wake-up call in the real world—that most medicine was looking after the old and the poor, and very, very little was performing dramatic lifesaving operations on fashion models.

"There, there," said Rosie, sitting on the bed and comforting the old lady, who was a shapeless bulk beneath her humiliatingly open hospital robe. It was a mixed ward, and the young doc hadn't even pulled the curtains properly. Rosie did so now. As she did, she heard the shrill tones of someone who she could identify even at this distance as the head nurse.

"Where's that bloody agency nurse? They turn up, hide out drinking coffee all day, and make twice the wage of everyone else."

"I'm here," said Rosie, poking her head out. "I'll be right with you."

"Now, please," said the head nurse. "There's a mess in the men's loos you'll need to sort out. I'd put on some gloves, if I were you."

It had been a long, long, long day, not helped by getting home three hours after Gerard to find that, nonetheless, the breakfast dishes were still on the table, next to the huge pile of mail, and he barely turned around from grunting with a mouthful of pepperoni pizza and *Grand Theft Auto*. Their little flat needed a window opened. And, Rosie thought with a sigh, probably the sheets changed.

Frankly, the chances of her changing another pair of sheets today were very, very small.

• • • •

So dark, Rosie thought, trying to make out shapes behind the streaky glass of the bus window. It never really got that dark in East London, where she'd grown up. The streetlights and the cars and the hum of the noise of the traffic and the people and the police helicopter... then when Mum had left for Australia, she'd moved to St. Mary's, the hospital in Paddington, where you were never far away from sirens and people shouting and thronged streets. She thrived on living in the city, had always adored London, its shiny side and the dark side she stitched up on a regular basis coming in through emergency or postsurgery. She'd even liked the shabby nurse's lodgings she'd lived in, although buying her own place with Gerard had been…

Well, it was grown-up, she supposed. It wasn't quite what she'd expected—she hadn't remembered the meeting where she'd volunteered to do all the housework, but he did earn more money. And the fact that it was so tiny, with no prospect of a move on the horizon.

Still, that was adult life, wasn't it? And she and Gerard were settled now. A bit too settled. But settled. She could, it was true, do without all her girlfriends eyeing her deliberately when that Beyoncé song played. They'd been telling her for ages that if he didn't put a ring on her finger by their second anniversary, he wasn't serious and in it for the long term, and she had closed her ears and chosen not to believe them—Gerard was cautious and safe and didn't make big decisions lightly, and that was one of the reasons she liked him.

But still, at the end of that long, long day, when her mother had called, she couldn't lie to herself that she was annoyed, cross, and feeling cheated, backed into a corner, and emotionally blackmailed—and a teeny-tiny part curious.

• • • •

Their last night had been sweet and sad all at once. "It's only six weeks or so," she'd reminded Gerard.

"Yes, so YOU say," he said. "You'll be round-the-clock caring from now till the end of time. And I shall stay in London and waste away."

Gerard rarely looked like he was going to waste away. Round of head and tummy, he had a cheery countenance, like he was always on the verge of a laugh or a joke. Or a sulk, but only Rosie got to see those.

Rosie sighed. "I wish you'd come. Just for a bit. A long weekend?"

"We'll see, we'll see," said Gerard. He hated any change to his routine.

Rosie looked at him. They'd been together so long now she could barely remember when they first got together. He'd been at her very first hospital; she was just out of a nearly all-female nursing college and dizzy with excitement at the thrill of having a little money and a job. She'd hardly noticed the little jolly pharmacist, who turned up occasionally when drugs were late or rare or urgent and always had a quip, although she'd noticed he was kind to the patients. He'd made silly remarks to her, and she'd dismissed them as standard banter, until one night he'd joined them on a work night out and made it clear that he was actually a bit more serious than that.

The other, more experienced nurses had giggled and nudged each other, but Rosie hadn't minded about that. She was young, she'd had some pink wine, and she was open to new experiences. At the end of the night, when he offered to walk her to her Tube stop then tentatively took her hand, she suddenly felt alive with possibility, excited that someone could be so clear about how much he fancied her. She'd often found that kind of thing confusing before, crushing helplessly on men she didn't have half a chance with, ignoring chaps she later realized she might have had potential with.

Rosie often felt that she'd missed a meeting every other girl in the world had had when they were about fourteen about how boyfriends and girlfriends actually worked. Maybe the PE teacher had taken everyone aside, like she did with the period-and-BO talk, and briefed them thoroughly. This is how to tell who fancies you. This is how to talk to a guy you like without making a complete idiot of yourself. This is how to politely leave a one-night stand and find your way home. It was all a bit of a mystery to Rosie, and everyone else seemed to find it so easy.

Meeting Gerard at twenty-three seemed like the answer to her prayers—a real, proper boyfriend with a good job. At least it would get her mum off her back for once. And right from the start, he'd been keen. She was a bit taken aback to learn he was twenty-eight and still lived with his mother, but hey, everyone knew how expensive London was. And she enjoyed, at least to begin with, having someone to look after; it made her feel grown-up to buy him shirts and to cook. When, after two years, he suggested they get a place together, she'd been absolutely delighted.

That had been five years ago. They'd bought a tiny flat that they both felt too tired to do up. And since then, nothing. They were, if she was totally honest, in something of a rut, and perhaps a little separation might just…she felt disloyal for even thinking it. Even if her best friend Mike was always rolling his eyes. But still. It might just shake them up a little bit.

• • • •

The bus driver grunted. Rosie jumped up, reaching for her bag, and followed his beard, which he'd nodded in the direction of a tiny pinpoint of light, far away. Rosie realized this must be the village and that they must be at the top of a big hill. Cripes, where were they, the Alps?

• • • •

That day at work, Rosie had been wondering over the pepperoni pizza box for the thousandth time how she could expand Gerard's diet—she liked to cook, but he complained that she didn't make anything just like his mum did, so they ate a lot of takeout and frozen dinners—and thinking about her job.

She had absolutely loved working in the emergency room as an auxiliary nurse. It was busy and exhausting and sometimes emotional, but she was never bored and always challenged, occasionally ground down by the challenges of working at the sharp end of the National

Health Service, but often inspired. She loved her job. So of course they closed the unit. Only temporarily, then they were going to reopen it as something called a Minor Injuries Unit, and she was offered the chance to stay on for that—which didn't sound very exciting—or relocate, which would mean a longer commute. She'd suggested moving to Gerard, but he wanted to be close to his own hospital, which was fair enough. Even though an extra bedroom, maybe a little bit of outdoor space might be…Gerard didn't like change though. She knew that about him.

So, in the meantime, she was doing agency work, filling in for sick or absent auxiliaries wherever she was required, often at only minutes' notice. It had a reputation of being easy money, but Rosie knew now that it was the opposite of that. It was a grind—everyone used the agency staff to do all the absolutely worst, crappiest jobs that they might ordinarily have done themselves. The traveling was murder, she often worked double shifts with no days off in between, and every day was like the first day at school, when everyone else knew where things were and how everything worked and you were left scrabbling behind in the wake, desperately trying to catch up.

Then, that day, the phone rang. "DARLING!!!"

Rosie's mother, Angie, still, after two years, found it difficult sometimes coordinating telephone calls from Australia (there were only twenty-two years between them, so sometimes she was Mum and sometimes she was Angie, depending on whether Rosie felt like the younger or older person in the conversation). Early in the morning was usually best, but sometimes Rosie caught her mum and her younger brother Pip at the thin end of a long afternoon's barbecuing and beer-drinking in the sunshine, and with the children yelling down the phone too. Rosie felt sorry for them—she'd only seen Shane, Kelly, and Meridian once, and they were constantly forced to make conversation with their Auntie Rosie, who as far as they knew or cared had a huge wart and gray hair. It was tricky to chat. But now—Gerard was having his dessert, a large bowl of Frosted Flakes—wasn't a bad time at all. She picked up the phone.

"Hi, Mum."

Four, Rosie had found herself recently thinking darkly to herself. Four. That's how many of her friends had met someone and gotten married during the period she and Gerard had been dating, before they'd even moved in. And she'd ignored every single alarm bell. She'd been twenty-three when they'd met; young and carefree, it seemed now (though at the time, she'd been desperate to meet someone). Looking at it now, from the wrong side of thirty, the idea that all that time and all that love might not be leading anywhere sometimes gave her vertigo.

Rosie had heard them all talk about the good life down in Oz, the swimming pools in the back gardens and the lovely weather and the fresh fish. Her mother, whose patience was constantly stretched by Pip's three children and whose unflattering opinions on Gerard (not Gerard himself—he was perfectly pleasant—but his seeming unwillingness to marry, provide for, and impregnate her only daughter, preferably all by last Thursday) she rarely hesitated to share, was always trying to persuade her down under for a year or so, but Rosie loved London. Always had.

She loved its bustling sense of being in the middle of things; its people, all nationalities, jumbled together on the crowded streets; exhibitions and theater openings (although she never went to any); great historic monuments (although she never visited them). She just had absolutely no desire to give up her life and move halfway around the world, where, she was sure, cleaning old people's bums was much the same and cleaning her nieces' bums for free would just be thrown in.

"Darling, I have a proposition for you."

Angie sounded excited. Rosie groaned mentally.

"I can't work down under, remember? I don't have the qualifications or the points or whatever it is," she'd said.

"Ha, oh well, who cares about that," said her mother, as usual as if there were no connection between her dad leaving and her failing half her exams that year. "Anyway, it's something else."

"And I don't want to…nanny."

According to comprehensive emails from her mum, Shane was a thug, Kelly was a princess, and Meridian was developing an eating disorder at the age of four. And since she'd moved in with Gerard and they'd gotten a mortgage, Rosie hadn't been able to save even the tiniest bit of her salary. She couldn't afford the ticket in a million years.

"I don't think so. Mum, I'm thirty-one! I think it's time I stood on my own two feet, don't you?"

"Well, it's not that," Angie said. "This is something else. Something quite different. It's not us, darling. It's Lilian."

fudge

• • • •

The fact is that fudge (and its northern, crunchy variant, tablet) appears to be an addictive substance that should be handled with extreme care. Overconsumption will result in illness and premature death.*** There are those who say that one should eat a tangerine or other citrus fruit when one first starts to become nauseous, thus freshening the digestive system and allowing it to consume yet more fudge, but they are pushers and enablers and should be avoided. Fudge should also be eaten in private, as the ideal method of consumption (inserting three large pieces into the left hand, right hand, and central areas of the mouth simultaneously then allowing them to warm and melt there) is considered impolite in many societies. Here are acceptable flavors for fudge: none. Are you talking nonsense? Fudge as a flavor is one of the most divine creations in the pantheon of human endeavor. Would you color in a Picasso? Would you add a disco beat to Fauré's "Requiem"? No? So keep out the vanilla and, heaven help us, raisins. There is a time and a place for a raisin. It is called "in the bin." As for Bailey's fudge, it is an aberration of a level undreamt of…

***if consumed daily by the pound over several decades

1942

Lilian Hopkins charged over the meadow slightly nervously, shadows lengthening from the golden haystacks on the other side and the gently waving avenue of elms. She wasn't sure if young Isitt's bull was in his shed or not, and she didn't want anyone to see her running. He was an easygoing old thing, everyone said so. She just didn't like the way he blew smoke out of his nose and swerved unpredictably, that was all.

Her heart sank as she saw a familiar outline sitting on the stile, smoking and openly staring at her, and she picked up her skirts crossly. He didn't put out an arm to help her up, which was annoying, because if he had, she could have made a remark about his impertinence, whereas this was actually rather more impertinent, but she certainly wasn't going to point that out.

"Excuse me," she said, lifting the pail. "I need to get on."

Henry didn't budge an inch.

"I think I'd like to watch you climb over the stile."

"You will do nothing of the sort," said Lilian, flushing.

"Why were you walking so strangely out there anyway?"

"I was not."

"You was. I saw you."

"Well, stop spying on folks then."

"I don't spy on folks," said Henry infuriatingly. "Anyone walks that strangely over a field, half the place is going to notice. You're not scared of young Isitt's bull?"

"No!"

Henry smiled, then his face changed to sudden shock. "Oh, here he comes now, right galloping fury."

Lilian leaped up toward the stile and spilled half the contents of her pail. "Where?"

But Henry had nearly toppled back off the stile with glee and, chuckling, headed off down the lane toward the village, leaving her crossly in the empty field, climbing the stile alone and muttering to herself about rude herd boys all the way to the shop.

• • • •

He was in on Saturday too, while she was serving, the children in with their ration cards and tightly clutched twopence. They liked to take their time to choose, marveling at the glass jars reflecting the light through the small windows, the colors of the humbugs and the twisted golden barley sugar. The young farm men would come in, sleeves rolled up, showing off burned brown arms and ruddy necks, scrubbed and shaved for the village dance, spending their wages on the velvet-trimmed heart-shaped boxes for their sweethearts. At sixteen, Lilian felt it was well past time for her to find a sweetheart. Not one of the village boys though, with their mucky boots and teasing. Hugo Stirling, the largest farmer's son, perhaps, when he came back from college. He was the handsomest boy in the village. She smiled wryly. By the time he got back from York, it wasn't very likely he'd be looking for a shopgirl. More likely Margaret Millar, whose father owned the next farm over. It would make much more sense to join up the land, even if Margaret had one eye that looked at you and one that looked at the floor—she had even worn a pair of spectacles that hadn't improved a thing—and was always trying to put her hand on her forehead like you wouldn't notice anything. She always wore the most expensive dresses and told everyone how much they cost and how her mother had had them made up for her in Derby, rather than going to Mrs. Coltiss's like everyone else.

Lilian sighed. Derby. There were jobs up there, lots of them. Cotton and munitions and all sorts. Or even down south to London, where her brothers had gone, though that was a bit too much, even for her. Her father didn't like the idea of it, couldn't bear the idea of her living away in rooming houses somewhere; he'd rather she stay and look after the shop, but she'd said just because the other three had grown up and moved away and hadn't stayed looking after the shop, he needn't start thinking he could pin it on her.

"I was looking for some kind of shop service," came the teasing voice intruding on her dreams. "But I can see I've come to the wrong place."

Lilian blinked and looked up. Henry was standing in front of her, a rough white shirt on. He looked unusually nervous.

"Um, half a pound lemon drops?" he asked, as an old lady browsed beside him and two children bickered on the floor.

"Have you your coupon?"

Henry looked shifty. "Um, no. Thought you might slip me a couple, you know."

"Of course not," said Lilian without giving it a second thought. "I would never do that."

In fact, Lilian, and her father too, had found it impossible not to slip a tiny piece of toffee or the odd gobstopper to some of the poorer village mites. But she certainly wouldn't be telling him that.

"No," said Henry, rubbing the back of his neck. "Well, that's all right. I don't really like lemon drops." He glanced around. The old lady had left, and the two children were engrossed in their bickering. "I only wanted to ask…um, would you like to come to the dance tonight?"

Lilian was so taken aback she instantly felt her face pinken up. Henry's eyes darted around, seeing her confusion.

"Uh no, of course. It doesn't matter," he said, backing away from the counter. "It's not…"

"But…" Lillian pulled herself together and tried to find the words. A bit of her would have liked to humiliate him, the way he made her feel when he cheeked her in the street or pointed and nudged his mates when she saw them all together. But the look of embarrassed anguish on his face made her change her mind. "Um, my dad probably won't let me go."

"You've left school, ain't you?" said Henry, a touch sullenly. All his usual techniques when he liked a girl had come to nothing, which was unusual for him—most girls liked the wide smile and his curly brown hair, but this one thought she was a cut above, obviously. Probably waiting for an airman in from Loughborough to swank around town with.

Lilian hesitated, and they looked at each other. Then the two squabbling children leaped up from behind the counter.

"Treacle toffee!" shouted one triumphantly, waving his penny in the air. The other looked like he'd been made to give in sullenly and stood to the side. Both watched very carefully as Lilian measured out the thick, sticky shards, making sure to make the packet come out to an even number. The first child held the bag in triumph as they marched out of the shop. By the time Lilian had closed the cash register, Henry had gone.

• • • •

2012

Rosie shook her head and turned another page of the book. *Sweets: A User's Manual, by Lilian Hopkins* was inscribed on the front, along with the insignia of a small press. She glanced out of the window again. The bus showed no signs of slowing down or stopping, so she wasn't feeling quite as nervous just yet.

There were lights dotted here and there around the valley now, tiny pinpoints that must be farms, surrounded by great oceans of blackness. And was that a tiny street down below? The light had a faintly odd glare to it. As she craned her neck to have a better look, the bus turned a hairpin bend around the hill and everything disappeared once more.

"Is it nice, Lipton?" she ventured of the bus driver, then again in case he hadn't heard her. The beard grunted slightly. She guessed that was all she was going to get. Then, to her surprise, he turned around.

"What you doing here then?" he announced gruffly.

"I'm…I'm visiting someone. And maybe staying for a little while. Relax a bit."

"By yourself?"

"Yes," said Rosie crossly. This wasn't 1953. She didn't need it pointed out that she was by herself. "I'm just going to relax and have a look at the local countryside."

The bus driver snorted. "Seen the forecast, have you?"

Rosie never bothered reading the weather forecast; she just checked whether the Tubes were running.

"Of course," she replied stiffly, as the bus finally creaked its way along the main street of the village. It seemed perilously small to Rosie, with a few shops, a pub, a grocery store, and not a soul to be seen, even though it was only eight in the evening.

The bus driver continued up the little street then trundled to a stop, ringing a bell and shouting loudly, "END OF THE LINE! ALL CHANGE! ALL CHANGE, PLEASE!"

"It's okay," said Rosie. "It's just me on the bus."

"Just checking," said the bus driver. "I'll be back here in three days. Pick up?" Rosie glanced out toward the pub and back toward the now darkened shop.

She swallowed then braced herself and her heavy suitcase.

"Not sure," she said, stepping off the bus and onto the quiet pavement beyond.

• • • •

"Lilian?" It had taken her a while to even think of who Angie could possibly mean.

"Great-Aunt Lilian?" said Angie. "You remember?"

Rosie looked into the fruit bowl. As usual, they were running out of apples (which she liked), but there was a heap of bananas (which Gerard said he liked) going moldy. Rosie squinted into her memory.

"The lady who smelled of Parma Violets? With all the sweets?"

"Yes!" said her mother triumphantly. "I know. She started you off."

Rosie's love of sweets was a long-running family joke. Even now, she was rarely to be found without a bag of fruit pastilles or rhubarb and custards around her person. She said it was for the patients, but all the nurses knew it was Rosie you went to if you needed a quick pick-me-up in the middle of the afternoon. "Oh goodness!" said Rosie. She did remember, when she and Pip were children. An old lady—she had seemed very old to them then; it was hard to imagine she was still alive—who would occasionally visit and bring mounds of slightly out-of-date sweets with her: Edinburgh rock, hard candies, humbugs, and gobstoppers. She and Pip would stuff themselves silly then lie around groaning and feeling completely green while their mum heaved a sigh and said she'd told them so, Lilian, don't bring them so much, and Lilian had sniffed and said maybe she should raise children with some self-control. They hadn't seen her much after that. But she'd never gotten over the excitement of the rustling paper bags, the light dustings of sugar, the sticky, fruity smells.

"Wow! I do remember! It was rubbish, having a relative who ran a sweetshop but we never got to go there. Is she still alive?"

"Rosie!" said Angie reprovingly, as if she'd been popping in to visit Lilian every week for the last twenty years.

She was Angie's aunt, the spinster sister of Mum's beloved da Gordon, who'd never lived outside the village in Derbyshire her family came from, for reasons completely uninteresting to an eight-year-old who'd just overdosed on licorice allsorts.

"She must be a hundred," said Rosie absently.

"Mid-eighties," said her mum. "Definitely getting on a bit. Although she was always one of those spinstery women who look old from about forty. Not that you'll be like that," she added hastily. Rosie hadn't actually been thinking that at all, but it was nice of Angie to give her a complex about it. Since Angie had moved to

Australia, she'd gotten into aqua aerobics and bleaching her hair and wearing Lycra pastels and having a deep tan, which had the odd effect of making her look simultaneously much older and much younger than fifty-four.

"But she still writes. And she sent sweets for the monsters, even though you know how sugar exacerbates Kelly's asthma and chocolate sends Meridian quite hyper."

Rosie started boiling up the kettle.

"But why are you telling me this, Mum?"

"Well," said her mother. She paused. This wasn't like Angie at all, who if she needed something tended to usually holler about it.

"Here's the thing."

"Mmm."

Rosie had a sudden premonition this might be like the time Angie tried to get her to diagnose Kelly over the phone. Only a bit worse.

"The thing is, Rose. She's in a spot of bother. And you're the only one in the family who..."

Angie left the sentence unfinished. She didn't have to finish it though. Rosie felt instantly cross.

"Who what? Who doesn't have a job? Who doesn't have any children? Who doesn't have a husband to look after?"

Rosie knew what people thought about her. It was a very sensitive spot. Why did she let her lovely mum always wind her up?

"Okay, calm down," said Angie. "Darling, you know I didn't mean it like that. But..."

"But what?" said Rosie, conscious that she sounded like a truculent teenager. So Angie explained.

• • • •

"So of course you said no."

Rosie had bought Gerard an ice cream immediately. She saw to her pleasure that the kiosk also stocked flying saucers. She loved the interplay between the tasteless exterior and the sharp hit of sherbet inside them and ordered them immediately. It was only the promise of ice cream that could force Gerard out on a Grand Prix day, even a glorious summer Sunday like this one. He really wanted to stay inside with the curtains drawn and watch cars racing around a track then play a computer game that involved cars racing around a track.

Rosie wanted to tell herself not to worry, she had absolutely loads of friends she could go and visit by herself, but the problem was that over the last year or two, those loads of friends had all started popping out kids like there was some terrible shortage of babies in London, and they would either be having "family time," which sounded gruesome, or they'd be at some horrible gastro pub trying to eat a relaxing meal while mopping up vomit, growling at each other as to who was the most tired and who had changed the last diaper, trying to get a forkful of food in their mouths while jiggling a baby frantically, and talking about how either it was the greatest thing ever or the worst thing ever and often both at once. Rosie liked babies, she really did, but by the time her new parent friends got around to asking her how she was doing, it was almost always given in the form of "So, when are you and Gerard going to have one of these?" and she'd gotten absolutely tired of brushing aside the question. Gerard wasn't tired of brushing it aside at all. He liked to say, "Ha, Rosie's already got one big kid to look after," then laugh. Heartily.

"Where's my Butterfinger?"

"I didn't get you a Butterfinger," said Rosie, trying not to look at his ever-growing paunch. It didn't matter, she told herself. She wasn't a model, was she? Everyone got older.

"Hmm," said Gerard. There was a pause. "I wanted a Butterfinger."

The more Angie had explained it to Rosie—there had been several phone calls and a long and emotionally punctuated email—the crosser and more hemmed in Rosie had felt.

The situation was this: Lilian, who had been apparently happily living a quiet life in a sweetshop in Lipton for several thousand years, had suffered a bad fall and needed a hip replaced. Whereupon it had turned out that perhaps she hadn't been living a perfect life after all, and there was almost no money left, that it looked like the shop wasn't even open, and there was no one to look after her, and as she hadn't ("selfishly" snorted Angie, and Rosie had reproved her at once) had any children, it fell on the rest of the family, which couldn't be Angie or Pip in Australia or Angie's brothers who were retired or point-blank refused, and all their kids had families of their own—yes, all of them, Rosie was delighted to learn. In short, Lilian needed to be cared for and put in a home, and her shop and the attached house needed to be sorted out and put on the market and sold to pay for the aforementioned home. And was there a single unemployed nurse in the family?

("I'm not single, I'm not unemployed, and I'm not a nurse. I'm an auxiliary nurse," Rosie had retorted. "Apart from that, spot-on.")

"So," said Rosie to Gerard. "Here are the reasons I can't go. And you have to listen to all of them and not just say 'you're being very selfish, Rosemary' hundreds of times like everybody else has."

"Hmm," said Gerard, trying to pretend to be listening.

"Number one: I live here, and I'm looking for a new job of my own.

"Number two: summer is in full swing and I don't want to miss lots of cool outdoor stuff.

"Number three: I don't know anything about running a shop or selling a shop or any kind of business at all.

"Number four: if I wanted to be an unpaid nurse, I'd still be doing my old job, ah ah ah ha.

"Number five: I don't even know this woman. What if she has dementia and starts knocking me around?

"Number six: she's Angie's aunt. She should do it. I've only met her twice.

"Number seven: I don't want to. I'm not sure that's going to cut it. Anyway. Lots of good reasons. That don't make me a really selfish person."

"You forgot number eight: me," said Gerard, who had already nearly finished his ice cream cone and was looking thoughtfully at the van.

"No, I didn't," said Rosie. "But you, I figure, could look after yourself for a few weeks."

In fact, though she wouldn't have admitted it under torture, Rosie had kind of thought, given that Gerard had come straight from his mum's house to their own flat and seemed to treat it very much the same way, that the one positive thing to come out of this might be, she had been slightly wondering, if a few weeks doing his own laundry and paying the bills by himself might not be so bad for him. Angie told her off all the time for babying him, which was hilarious, because Angie babied Pip so much she'd actually moved right across the world to work as his unpaid maid, whereas Rosie sometimes felt lucky if Angie managed to remember her birthday. That would have been the only positive side of such an arrangement. If she was going to go. Which she wasn't.

"So what did she say to that? To your list?"

They were walking down the South Bank together on a sunny spring Sunday, clutching their ice creams and flying saucers—Gerard had explained he needed another one because he didn't get a Butterfinger the first time around so it was wrong—and looking at the artists and the people out promenading, riding bikes, and pushing strollers. On the riverbank in London, Rosie leaned against the railings over the river. Boats full of tourists were going up and down, taking snapshots. The view was incredible: the Houses of Parliament and Big Ben, all the way around the curve of the river to St. Paul's Cathedral. Bathed in golden late summer light, the city was stunningly beautiful, full of young families enjoying the day, young, beautiful couples in matching sunglasses heading toward art galleries, and happy groups of Italian teenagers whacking each other with their rucksacks. Rosie felt as she sometimes did in the prettier parts of town: so happy to be a part of it, to be a tiny cog in the buzzing, brilliant wheel of their city.

"Well," said Rosie.

Gerard sighed. "Oh, come on. You're not being soft?"

"Well, it is family..."

"Did Angie kick your arse?"

"It's not about being soft," said Rosie. "It's about...well. I'm only agency at the moment. And it's family."

"Hasn't she got any kids of her own that can do it?" said Gerard. "It's not very fair that it's you. You don't even know her."

"I know, but..."

"Did you even give her the big, long selfish speech with all those number things in it that you just gave me?"

Rosie felt like an idiotic wimp. Her mother was always telling her to be more assertive with Gerard (or "the ring-dodger" as she liked to call him). Gerard was always telling her to be more assertive with her mother. Ironic, as he still called his mother "Mummy," and they had lunch there every Sunday because Rosie couldn't possibly make roast pork as well as his mother could, which Rosie had to agree with, as she could rarely spend two hours perfecting crackling. Although just one day off every now and again would have been nice, and especially if they'd been having a tricky time and Gerard had slept through his work alarm because he'd been up all night playing *Portal* or he'd spent the holiday money on sneakers, she had to sit there every seven days and listen to the usual litany of what a genius Gerard was and how brilliantly he'd done at school and how much everyone always liked him and how successful he was. At first, Rosie had found this endearing, how close they were, mother and son. Now, she wasn't too sure. Gerard's mother's subtext always seemed to be "With me, he is perfect. Don't you dare ruin it." And Gerard would sit there, refusing to eat his vegetables—at thirty-six!—basking in the admiration. The most easygoing of men, the one total no-go area for teasing was, undoubtedly, his mum.

"Well, I know, but I have the training, and no, she never got married or anything."

"Oh. Lesbo," said Gerard.

"No, I don't think so...well, maybe. But I think she was just—Christ, she must be ancient. I think she was just one of those women when all the men went off to the war and got killed, and then there was nobody left."

"Did she get really fat and spotty on all those sweets?"

"I don't know," said Rosie. "I don't know anything about her. Except she needs help and I'm her..."

"Lackey," said Gerard.

"No, I mean relation-wise."

"Yeah, what even are you?"

"I'm her great-niece," said Rosie.

"Great-niece?" said Gerard, daubing her on the nose with ice cream. Rosie laughed but wiped it off, still thinking.

"You never know," said Gerard. "Maybe she's got thousands in a box under the stairs and she'll make you her heir."

"Ha," said Rosie. "That's right, someone in our family with money. Hilarious. Anyway, I know for a fact she doesn't, because that's why I'm going: she's had to run that crumbling old sweetshop for ages, miles after she should have retired, and I think if there was a big box stuffed with money, she might have used some of it to get hold of a nurse and get herself into a decent home."

"Mmm," said Gerard. "But how long for?"

Rosie shrugged. "Well...I mean, I can apply for jobs, obviously, while I'm up there. But I need to get a buyer for the shop, find her a home, check she's all right, then sign over something to a lawyer so the money from the shop goes straight to the nursing home. With a little bit for me for expenses, Angie says, to pay for my time. There's a house with the shop, so it should be a bit of cash if I can sort it all out."

"That sounds like shitloads of work," said Gerard. "In the middle of bloody nowhere? With some old bag who doesn't know you from Adam and will hardly pay you anything."

"I know, I know," said Rosie, sighing. "What could I do? You know what Angie's like."

"She lives in Australia," said Gerard. "What's she going to do, attack you by satellite phone death ray?"

"I know, I know. Maybe I should try saying no again. Will you come visit me?"

"No chance! I'm allergic to the countryside, and they don't have KFC."

"You're teasing."

"I'm not. You'll see. You'll hate it up there. What do you know about the country? You were born and raised here. What are you going to do when you're surrounded by, I don't know, cows?"

"I'm not going to be a vet," said Rosie, cross that Gerard was so dismissive of her adaptive abilities. "Anyway, I don't think I have much choice."

"Can you ride a horse?"

Rosie shook her head. "No one said anything about riding a horse."

"Have you ever TOUCHED a horse?"

Rosie, after another pause, shook her head again.

"Oh well, I'm sure you'll be totally fine and fit right in."

"I'm not going up there to make FRIENDS," said Rosie. "I'm going up there to do a rubbish, lonely, boring family job. With maybe some money as a bit of an incentive when I'm done. Then come back in five minutes."

"What if you fall in love with the countryside and never want to come back again?" said Gerard. "I'll have to pine away without you."

"Ha," said Rosie. "We'll get a wee farm with some lambs to gambol about."

Suddenly, completely against all her better instincts, she had a swift vision: of little dark curly-haired children running around a farmyard, feeding chickens and running about with dogs. She quickly reminded herself how much poo animals produced.

"You never know," she said. "We might be natural country lubbers."

Gerard gave a theatrical shudder. "You'd never get me up there in a hundred years," he said. "I don't think so."

"Oh God. I know," said Rosie. "It's going to suck."

"And you're going to miss the summer! Sitting out in pubs and drinking pink wine and lovely evenings and loads of parties and fun." Gerard pouted. "Don't go."

"But a little bit of money," she said. "If I got a couple of thousand from the sale of the house… I mean, we could even think about moving. Into a bigger place. Big enough for… I don't know… It'll be quiet."

She found her heart beating faster even as she said it. Maybe she should go for the unselfish reasons. But a little bit of spare cash to punt them up the ladder a little bit…maybe it was just time for the two of them. Together. When she got back from this stupid bloody thing. To bite the bullet and go for it.

"I think they're making ice creams smaller," said Gerard, once more looking unhappily at his extra cone. "I'm sure of it. They whack the prices up and put less in on hot sunny days. Stands to reason."

He eyed her up.

"You've said yes already, haven't you?"

And that was the end of that conversation.

licorish

• • • •

Modern language seems to think it can change things willy-nilly for utterly no reason. Licorish is a perfectly adequate word that also manages to onomatopoeically sum up the constituency of a thick black sweet in your mouth. Licorice is French, and we know where that ends up—in crème de marrons and macaroons and all sorts of other unpleasantness.

The push for modernity in the sweet industry—or, as our vulgar cousins would term it, "candy"—is entirely unnecessary since the very first refining of sugar. Sweets do not need dragging into the twenty-first century. Unlike the bastardization of the humble potato chip into more and more repulsive flavorings, a decent bonbon is timeless, a work of art, and few more so than the licorish, an endlessly permeable substance capable of forming whorls, twists, strings, cords, and the like.

For those whom the dark, complex flavorings of the fruit of the licorice roots and aniseed flower are too overwhelming (not all sweet appreciators can be connoisseurs), it comes too in adulterated form, notably (see subsection 41) the allsort, the bootlace, and, possibly its crowning achievement for nonpurists, the sherbet fountain.

Lilian Hopkins hated staying up late. It gave her more pain than she could let on, and it made the day seem so terribly, terribly long—it didn't help her sleep any later in the morning. Her internal clock had been stuck at 6:30 a.m. for a very long time now. And they showed such rubbish on the television, which was in any case hard to see no matter which pair of glasses she had on, so she normally listened to the radio at full blast—it was company—and read her magazines and wrote in her notebook with her elderly Parker pen and tried to ignore the aching in her hip until it was a reasonable hour to retire to bed and try not to think about how she was going to get through another day tomorrow.

But tonight was different, of course. Tonight, the girl was coming. She'd always had a soft spot for little Angie, her brother's kid. She'd been so blond and funny and spunky and full of life and had ended up pregnant barely out of her teens, two babies, dad long gone, and she had rolled up her sleeves and gotten on with it. The two women had exchanged letters (Lilian always sent sweets) for years, and it was a sadness to both of them that Lilian hadn't managed to get to know Angie's children. She'd never married herself, but it was hard to leave the shop, and she'd never learned to drive and was quite frankly frightened of London, and between the kids being at school and Angie working and all of them trying to keep their heads above water, the dreams they'd had of Hopkins holidays up in the beautiful Derbyshire countryside had never quite materialized. And they grew up so fast.

So to meet Rosie again after all this time...well, she wasn't quite sure what to expect. A bit of a slacker, she suspected. Angie had said she was nursing trained, so maybe she could help her out with everything. Since the operation...well. There was no getting around it. She was finding it very difficult. Anyway, she didn't think this Rosie could help. She didn't seem to be making much of a go of it. Perhaps she was a bit of a party brat. She hoped Rosie wasn't expecting too much. After all the bright lights and noise of London, she was going to find

Lipton very quiet indeed. She couldn't think of a single thing to do with her, or even what you said to a young person. It had been a while. She looked at the clock. Another five minutes till the bus got in. She would say her hellos. And then perhaps this girl wouldn't mind helping her to bed.

You would have had to have tortured Lilian before she would let you know she'd been sleeping in her chair.

• • • •

1942

If it hadn't been for Ida Delia Fontayne, it seemed unlikely that Lilian would ever have given Henry a second thought ever again. Although he had lingered…a young man, even an infuriating one, asking her to a dance wasn't something that happened every day. Lilian was too thin for the current fashion, too pointy of nose and elbows and knees to be considered one of the village beauties, like Ida Delia Fontayne, whose thick blond hair and round blue eyes and soft high bosoms drew the eyes of every man in the village up to Lord Leyton himself, it was rumored, and didn't Ida know it. Mind you, she'd been a general showbox since Miss Millet's schoolyard, always in charge of the games, elbowing out shy, caustic, wiry-haired Lilian, fluttering her eyelashes at teachers, the vicar, or anyone even passing likely to show favor. They'd even been best friends when they were little; Lilian's father thought she was adorable and would let her have an extra piece of fudge or two, and Ida Delia caught on to the wisdom of this arrangement and started inviting Lilian to her birthday parties, or to play dominoes, or summer hangouts around the swimming hole.

At first, scrawny Lilian, with no mother and three big brothers and no knowledge of fashion or Hollywood film stars or lipstick, felt out of place and awkward. But as they grew older, Ida Delia took to

Lilian's sharp, funny tongue and clever ways with schoolwork (handy for copying homework), and for a time, they were close. Then adolescence had begun in earnest, like a winnowing of who the boys liked and who wasn't going to quite make the grade, and Lilian could tell, as Ida Delia started announcing loudly how embarrassing it was being measured up for a brassiere then getting the same bus home as the vicar, that their friendship might not survive the dawning interest from the lads of the town, and she had been entirely correct. Ida Delia had palled up with Felicity Hayward from the neighboring farm, whose russet curls and bright green eyes made cows out of boys all the way to Hartingford, and left Lilian with Margaret, who didn't always look directly at you. Margaret was fun enough, but Lilian hated the idea of friendship being traded as a commodity and could neither forgive nor forget.

Lilian liked to think that since she'd started working for a living and living like a young lady, she was less bothered by the likes of Ida Delia Fontayne, or so she thought that summer until ten seconds after she saw her walk down the main street side by side with Henry Carr, laughing uproariously at one of his jokes. Lilian knew Henry wasn't anything like as funny as that. Mind you, nobody was as funny as the way Ida was going on. She held up her shopping basket and smiled at them politely, but inside, her guts were twisting furiously. So you ask someone to a dance one day, and then the next you're up and down the high street with the town flirt. That was clearly how it worked. Lilian was amazed to find how worked up she was about someone she didn't even like. It was just bad manners, that was all, that was getting her riled.

"Miss Hopkins," said Henry.

"Hello Henry," said Lilian, as coolly as she could muster. Ida obviously wanted to stop and show off her prize.

"Henry and I were just heading the same way," she said, flicking back her elegantly permed hair that, as she never tired of telling everyone, she had to get done up in Derby at Gervase's as nowhere else could quite get it right. "It's a shame you missed the dance on Saturday—such fun!" She turned to Henry. "Lilian's not really one for the dancing—do you remember that school dance when she tripped over the refreshment table? I thought I'd die laughing."

Lilian waited for Henry to laugh cruelly along with Ida, but surprisingly, he didn't; he merely nodded and smiled, almost sympathetically. Well, she didn't need his sympathy now. She hadn't, she remembered, had it at the time. She'd been thirteen years old, just after she and Ida Delia had gone their separate ways, and it was the school's summer dance. Her brothers—Terence, Ned, and Gordon—had teased her ragged around the table. Well, Gordon had; he was always a bit of a rascal. Terence tried to tell him off and tell her off for dressing loosely—Terence was born a prig, always had been, and thought he was in charge.

Gordon, the youngest, little (he had been born early; that was what had done for their ma), always the joker, was carrying on about how Errol Flynn would be all over when he saw that dress, and Lilian had colored and told them to shut their holes. It was only Neddy, sweet Ned, the middle child, whom Lilian absolutely adored—blond and handsome, sweet and dreamy—who had told her not to worry; she looked absolutely beautiful. And he had made her feel like a princess, right up to the point where she had tripped over the stupid tablecloth in front of everyone and drenched herself with punch.

Henry Carr had laughed every single bit as hard as Ida and her cronies and everyone else, as the juice had run down the old-fashioned dropped waist dress a cousin had passed down to her. Ida, of course, had been taken to a dressmaker for the occasion and had worn a neatly cut dress with a full skirt. It was a beautiful dress, and its pale blue color had set Ida's cream skin and wide eyes off perfectly.

Lilian, in dated hand-me-downs, taller than nearly every other child her age, had felt awkward enough to begin with, even before she'd tripped. Henry had been in the corner with the older boys, guffawing mightily.

"I must get on," she murmured in the street, banishing the memory while feeling the color rise once again in her cheeks, and Ida raised her eyebrows and waved gaily. Just once, Lilian glanced back at Henry and was shocked to find him also looking after her. There was something in his nut-brown eyes that, for once, wasn't mockery or teasing, but something else. Something that, however much she wanted to fight against it, suddenly seemed to make her heart jump and flutter on the wind.

• • • •

2012

Rosie thought about Gerard as the bus lumbered on. He'd always been around, but she'd only really noticed him after Mum took off. He'd always had a friendly word for the nurses on his rounds, but they'd mostly just humored him, his round cheery face and chubby cheeks making him more "aww" material than the latest hunk in radiology.

But then Rosie had gone with her mum to Heathrow that dank miserable November Monday morning with an insane amount of luggage and kissed her good-bye, and her mum had asked her one more time if she wouldn't consider joining her and Pip in the sunshine, and she had almost—almost—wavered and changed her mind. But she was halfway through her training, had settled in, and was making her own life now. It didn't stop her feeling completely and utterly alone though. She never really saw her dad, and it tended not to be a great experience when she did. He tried his best, but as he explained when drunk, family life wasn't really for him. Why Rosie was meant to find this useful, she had no idea.

When the cherub-faced Gerard had popped up on Monday

morning as she checked on Mrs. Grandle's fluid levels and asked her if she was all right, he wasn't to know that he was the first person to ask her. Her best friend Mike was on late shifts so she hadn't dared wake him. And Gerard, a kindly soul, was genuinely concerned when pretty, bubbly Rosie burst into floods of unexpected tears.

"Hey, hey," he had said as she explained. "It's all right. Come have a coffee on break. God," he said with some force, "I don't know how I could cope without my mother."

This remark had proved to be somewhat prescient.

But his kindness and his sense of fun had helped things along a million. He had introduced her to silly things and helped her rediscover her love of sweet things; he had the dietary habits of a let-loose five-year-old. They had fun eating pick and mix candies at the movies, and every Friday, she would find a treat in her locker—a walnut whip or a little bag of rock. It was sweet and very cute, even if it hadn't done much for her waistline.

"Is that it?" Mike had said, a bit snippily, frankly, when they were discussing it in the pub. Hospitals were very small places, without secrets, and everyone knew everyone else's business. "I just thought he'd asked out absolutely everyone else and they'd all said no."

"That's not true," Rosie had protested. "He's really nice when you get to know him."

This was true. He was funny and kind and seemed keen. The idea of someone she already knew, with a steady job, rather than someone she bounced off of on nights out, was beginning to appeal a bit—after all, she wasn't getting any younger. She explained this to Mike, who rolled his eyes and continued to talk about Giuseppe, who made his life a living hell, but it was worth it because of the heat of their unbelievable passion.

"But what about when that dies down though?" protested Rosie. Passion wasn't everything. The last time she'd felt unbelievable passion, it was for a drummer in a failed rock band who'd given her scabies.

"I'll just provoke a fight," said Mike, getting up to get another bottle of wine.

"But don't you yearn for the nice quiet simple things in life? Someone to come home to every night? Being settled?"

Mike shrugged. "Do you?"

"Well, maybe a rest is as good as a change," said Rosie, pouring out the wine. "Maybe I'd like things just to be nice and calm for a while, no one yelling their head off about moving to Australia."

And they had been nice and calm—a little too nice and calm, perhaps, but Rosie put that to the back of her mind. Not earth-shattering. Not fast-moving. There were no massively romantic declarations, no ring. But then, Mike and Giuseppe went through a fortune in crockery. So nothing much had changed in two years. Until now.

• • • •

The first thing Rosie noticed about Lipton was that it was possibly the quietest place she had ever been. The main street of the village was completely deserted even though it wasn't long after ten o'clock. There were only a couple of streetlamps, old-fashioned lanterns that lit up a pub, a large, square stone house that looked like it might be the doctor's office, a post office, and a couple other small businesses Rosie couldn't see. Over the tops of the opposite buildings, blocking out the stars, loomed the great dark shapes of the Pennine hills at which she'd just gazed from the bus. A huge, fat harvest moon sat low in the sky, silvering the landscape. Somewhere, far away, Rosie could just make out the hoot of an owl.

After Paddington, with its brash neon and sirens and fast-food joints and late-night trains and street-thronging hordes, Rosie felt as if she'd been picked up and set down again a hundred years ago. She turned around slowly, picking up her suitcase, almost scared to make a sound. There seemed to be no lights on in the buildings at all. It was rather unnerving.

Rosie had printed out a map from Google as to the whereabouts of her aunt's house, but it quickly became clear from the size of the place that there wouldn't be far to go.

The cottage was absolutely tiny, like something out of a fairy tale. It really did have a thatched roof with a dormer window and smoke coming out of the chimney; it looked like someone ought to be sculpting it onto a plate or lighting it up to use as a tacky Christmas decoration.

"Hello?" Rosie yelled nervously.

"All right, all right," came a cross voice. "I'm not deaf."

There was a pause, then came a shuffling noise, and then, after some wrestling with the doorknob, Lilian opened the door.

• • • •

The two women regarded each other. Rosie had been expecting a very old lady; Lilian had been old when she had been a child. Instead, and particularly in the murky light, she was greeted by a bowed but still slender figure with a severely cut bob, wearing what seemed to be a maroon chiffon dress and full makeup.

Lilian in return had been expecting a young girl, not this curly-haired, rather weighed-down-looking, fully grown woman with bags under her pale green eyes. She remembered little Rosie as a pretty, sparky thing, always putting her dollies to bed and tucking them in and staring at her bag, shyly, too polite and nervous to ask if she had any goodies within.

"Hello," said Rosie.

Lilian eyed up Rosie's shoes. They were flat and clumpy and covered in mud. She wondered if she could ask her to take them off. But that really would be getting off on the wrong foot.

"You'd better come in then," she said.

Rosie followed her over the threshold, noticing as she did so the terribly pained stiffness in her aunt's movements. Inside, the room smelled beautiful, of a warm, flowery beeswax. Through another set of beams was a little sitting room, toasty warm with a wood-burning stove flickering away very merrily in the grate. The mantelpiece was entirely covered in framed photos, many old, but without a fleck of dust. Rosie surmised it was Lilian herself, and she had clearly been something of an extraordinary glamour-puss in her younger years. Rosie admired a beautiful '50s shot of her, framed in black and white.

"Is this you?" Rosie asked.

"No," said Lilian. "I'm creepily obsessed with someone who looks a bit like me." Rosie glanced at her to figure out if this was a joke. Lilian's face gave nothing away.

"So," said Rosie, looking around. The living room was tiny. Her enormous, mucky bag seemed to be cluttering the whole place up. Lilian sat herself down in her armchair carefully, as if her bones were made of glass.

"Thanks for having me to stay!" said Rosie cheerfully, as if she was a houseguest and not someone with her heart set on getting in, completing an unpleasant job, and getting out as quickly as possible.

Lilian sniffed loudly.

"I daresay you don't want to be here any more than I want you here."

Lilian spoke in a posh accent with a touch of the local flattened vowels. She sounded very different from Rosie and her mother. Angie's dad, Lilian's big brother, had left Derbyshire long ago to make his fortune in the big smoke. It hadn't quite worked out like that in the end. It occurred to Rosie, sitting herself down on an immaculately cozy floral sofa, that maybe they were the downwardly mobile end of the family.

Rosie squirmed at the rudeness.

"No, I'm thrilled," she lied. "It's like a holiday in the country."

"What, forcing me out of my home?"

There was an awkward pause.

"Mum just said maybe you needed a bit of help," said Rosie gently.

Lilian sniffed. Rosie took this to mean, correctly, that Lilian did indeed need help but couldn't bear to admit it.

"Well, the local doctors are no sodding use."

"How did you break your hip?"

"Practicing for the ice dancing finals."

Suddenly Rosie felt tired. It had been a long day, and she and Gerard had been up late the night before. Although when Gerard had said he was going to be busy, a tiny worm in Rosie's head questioned once again why he didn't just come up for the weekends. She wasn't in Swaziland. Why did she always have to do everything?

She looked around again at the cozy room. Lilian had been born in this cottage. Never married, just focused on the business and stayed in the same village all her life. It seemed so strange.

"Do you get to London much?" she asked, knowing it was a stupid question as soon as it came out of her mouth.

"Well, obviously David Niven telephones me when he's in town, but apart from that…"

Lilian suddenly stopped herself. It wasn't this girl's fault she was getting older and everything was packing up, and it was the most irritating, frustrating thing she could possibly imagine with absolutely no bloody hope of getting any better, and then seeing this frumpy thing bounce in to look after her who obviously didn't have the slightest clue what an incredible luxury it was to hop on a London train whenever it took your fancy, hopping hither and thither without a care in the world, who thought you were just a broken toy that needed packing somewhere neatly out of the way.

"Hmm," said Lilian. "Are you hungry?"

Rosie wasn't, really. She'd eaten three enormous and vastly overpriced sandwiches on the train to give herself something to do apart from staring out of the window, worrying about Gerard, and wondering whether she'd come back to London and he'd meet her at the railway station and suddenly jump down on one knee and she'd have to pretend to be surprised and make her face look all wide-eyed and appealing—she'd have to remember to put on extra makeup—and everyone around them in the station would smile and maybe even clap, like in a movie or something... Yes. That was definitely and absolutely what would happen. Then she'd opened her eyes. Gerard didn't even like getting down on his knees to tie his shoelaces; he made old groany noises.

Lilian glanced backward toward a door that obviously housed the kitchen. It occurred to Rosie that she might be very hungry; if she wasn't mobile, it was a bit of a mystery as to how she was feeding herself. The house was very tidy; how did she manage that?

"You could make tea..." Lilian said. "Only if you want some. It's easy to find everything."

Rosie turned to her. There was a lot less hostility in her tone.

"Okay," said Rosie carefully. "Yes, actually, I'm really hungry. While I'm in there, can I rustle you up something?"

"Oh, hardly anything for me... I eat like a bird," said Lilian defensively, willing the girl to hurry up. She was desperate for a cup of tea; her arthritis meant she could no longer lift the kettle.

Rosie stood up and headed into the tiny, immaculate kitchen. Ornate old-fashioned tins lined up on the white surfaces, labeled flour, sugar, tea. Unfortunately, they were all empty. Next to the kettle—the old-fashioned kind, which stood on a gas burner—there was a half-empty box of loose tea, a chain sieve-looking thing, and a flowery teapot covered in a knitted cozy. Rosie stared at it for a while.

Once she'd figured out how to light the gas, which flared up with a "pop," she peered into the kitchen cupboards. They weren't empty. But what she found surprised her. Instead of bread, pasta, and cans of beans, there were packets and packets half-empty of sweets. Rainbow stars and jelly fish and cola bottles and blackjacks, Minstrels and

Maltesers, highland toffee and great slabs of Fry's chocolate cream, soft little flying saucers and jelly flumps, twists of rhubarbs and custards, Wham Bars and chocolate éclairs and wrappers Rosie couldn't even identify. She opened up drawer after drawer, but it was the same story everywhere: jelly tots and jelly beans, lemon sherbets and fizz bombs, bubble gum and Parma Violets.

No wonder her great-aunt's bones weren't healing well, Rosie realized. This stuff was pure poison. But if it was too hard for her to lift a pan, too difficult to cook every day… She went back into the sitting room to announce that, starting tomorrow, she would go shopping and start cooking for them both, only to see her aunt snoring tiny baby snores, head nodding onto her chest, in front of the dying fire.

"Lilian," she said, quietly at first, then more loudly. She suspected Lilian's claims of not being in the slightest deaf were probably a little overstated, and she was used to working with the elderly. "Lilian. Lilian. Come on. Let's get you to bed. We'll eat better in the morning."

Leaning heavily on Rosie—she weighed about as much as a child—Lilian let herself be led into the neat, small bedroom at the back of the house. Once there, Lilian pretended to be half-asleep, and Rosie let her professional nursing training take over as she efficiently found a nightgown and helped the old woman change and toilet. Pretending to be asleep meant Rosie didn't get a thank-you, but she decided on balance it might be best for both of them if it stayed this way. She looked at the tightly packed white bedspread. It didn't look like it had been pulled back for a while. There was nothing else for it. Carefully, Rosie bent down—bending from the knees, not the back, as her nurse manager must have yelled at her a million times—picked up the old lady, and tucked her into bed, as cozy as a child, as Rosie placed the tea on the side table, mixed with cold water in case of scalding.

Something came out of Lilian's mouth that might have been a thank-you, or just a sigh of relief, but the comfort and happiness of lying down in her own bed for the first time in weeks was simply too much: Lilian was overtaken almost immediately by the first good sleep she'd had in a long time.

Rosie came back to the sitting room and looked around, counting the doors, and wondered where she was to go. Surely she wasn't going to have to sleep in front of the fire in that tiny sitting room. Suddenly, even with the sound of the kettle cheerily whistling in the kitchen, she was feeling mind-achingly tired. She checked her phone; there was almost no signal here, and she had no messages. She texted Gerard quickly to say good night, but the message took a long time to get through and he didn't reply. He was probably at the pub with his mates Joe and Ise. She would have liked to have said good night to him.

Opening random cupboard doors, she found, finally, a pull-out wooden ladder fixed to a trapdoor above. Was there something else up there? Surely Lilian would have mentioned it if she didn't have a bed.

The fire was dying down behind her, and the dim lights made it hard to see her way. Rosie gave up looking for a light switch and tentatively felt her way up the ladder. At the top, the trapdoor opened into a space so dark she couldn't see a thing, except a dormer window with a clear view of a starry, starry night and the omnipresent dark shadows of the hills beyond. Gradually, as her eyes adjusted, she made out the shape of a double bed, just under the lowered eaves. Her whole body relaxed. Sleeping on a sofa would have been a bit much. Hopping down, she extinguished the lights, popped into the loo, and hauled the bag she thought was most likely to contain her pajamas upstairs, punting it on her shoulders. Unable to find them, however, she just slipped off her trousers and her bra, snuck under the heavy duvet and thick, crisp, heavy cotton sheets that were, like in Lilian's room, so tightly tucked in she couldn't move any more than a swaddled baby, glanced briefly at the moon through the open curtains, and just as she thought, "I must get up to close those curtains," somewhat to her surprise, Rosie fell into a deep, deep sleep.

Nobody is saying there is anything wrong with a Crunchie. The Crunchie is a fine, fine feat of well-balanced confectioner's engineering and has been for nearly one hundred years. Malt balls are another matter best left between you and the forty-five minutes it will take to scrape the residue from your mouth after you finish a packet, this calorific expenditure presumably leading to their advertising slogan as to their being slightly less heavy than other brands.

But honeycomb toffee—pure and eaten by itself, that delicate, friable, crumbling pop of sharp, yellow sweetness that cuts in the mouth then vanishes, as if by magic, to nothing; the satisfying tearing of the granules without the softness of chocolate getting in the way or cushioning the blow. A truly excellent solo honeycomb toffee bar can make you feel like you are eating your way through the rocks of Elysium. And it truly is the lighter way to enjoy… itself.

1942

You could hear the screaming all the way down the street. It sounded like one of Caffrin Stirling's pigs being slaughtered but grew nearer all the time. Lilian, in the middle of stocktaking, scrambled down the steps, wiping dust from her forehead, and charged out into the middle of the street.

It was a very strange sight. Henry Carr, white as a sheet and with a look of holy terror on his face, was carrying a small girl, kicking and screaming as if the devils were after her. Lilian recognized her as the young Lady Henrietta Lipton, only daughter of the manor house, and breathed in sharply. Everyone else on the road on the quiet Wednesday afternoon, mostly the elderly, stood and stared, but Lilian didn't think twice and ran out into the middle of the road.

"What on EARTH have you done now, Henry Carr?" she cried, taking the young girl from him. "Hush, hush there," she said, as the little girl took no notice and continued to screech and twist herself furiously.

"There's no one at that damn doctor's," said Henry, his voice trembling. "They've all gone to market. She just came into my yard. I was working down at the end yard."

Lilian looked over the child. From her foot protruded the end of a snub-nosed nail. She winced and looked at Henry. They both knew what that meant.

"Come in, come in," she said and led them through to the back of the shop, where a tiny area had a running water tap and antiseptic under the sink.

"Where was Gerda Skritcherd?" Lilian asked in a fury about the child's nanny. "She's only a mite."

"She was there," said Henry, looking shifty all of a sudden. "She's run up to the house to fetch Charlie."

Lilian turned on the tap.

"Is there a girl in this town who can keep her eyes off you then?" Without waiting for an answer, she turned around to Hetty.

"Now, little miss," she said, trying to sound strong and practical, even though she felt anything but. "We have to do something very important. Something you're going to have to be big and brave for."

The little girl's screaming, which had quieted down at the sound of Lilian's voice, transformed into nervous jerky breaths. Lilian looked at Henry.

"Can you take her arms?"

Henry looked as though he'd rather cut off one of his own, but he came forward. The little girl flinched as he held her, then, as quickly as she could, Lilian took out the nail and washed the area with watered-down bleach. The little girl screamed the place down, but Lilian was relentless. Lockjaw haunted the countryside. And neither of them felt like explaining it to the manor.

Finally, the wound glistening red and raw, Lilian reckoned they'd done enough and bound the area up in a freshly laundered handkerchief. The little girl's sobs started to quiet and lessen, and Lilian held her close, arms clasped tightly around her neck. Lilian rather enjoyed the little clawed monkey hold, the fresh scent of the child's hair.

"Are you feeling better?" she asked gently. She glanced up to find Henry, the color starting to return to his cheeks, once again looking at her in that peculiar way, and instantly she started to blush too.

"BE-AH LILYIN," said the mite, already perking up enough to start eyeing up the rows and rows of sweetie jars on the walls. From the young lady of the manor to the lowest back row urchin, there wasn't a child in town who didn't know Lilian and Mr. Hopkins. Lilian smiled.

"Would you like to choose a sweetie for being such a brave girl?"

Hetty nodded enthusiastically.

"She wasn't brave at all," said Henry.

"And you weren't watching her. And neither was that Gerda, flashing her eyelashes at you. They're stuck on, by the way."

Henry looked confused.

"Those eyelashes."

"Oh," said Henry, as the little girl reached up for a large red lollipop. "Really? And aren't you going to ask her for her coupon?"

"'Thank you, Miss Hopkins, for helping me with the child,' is the sentence I believe you were grasping for there, Mr. Carr."

Charlie, the butler from the big house, threw himself around the wooden framed door, closely followed by a sobbing Gerda. Lilian handed over the bandaged, happy child, proudly showing off her lollipop and attempting to babble her adventures to anyone who could listen, and they watched the party head off.

"I hope she doesn't lose her job," said Henry.

"I hope she never looks after your children then," said Lilian, regretting immediately, as so often, the sharpness of her tongue, as Henry looked wounded.

"You're not much for the second chances, are you, Miss Hopkins?" he said a little sadly. Lilian swallowed hard, wondering if he was going to ask her to the dance again. Because, sure as eggs were eggs, she was going to say yes this time, and she wouldn't care what the other girls in the village would say for once. She turned her face toward him, shining and full of expectation, but he had already picked up his cap and was heading for the door.

"Thank you, Miss Hopkins," he said formally and left Lilian openmouthed, scouring the sink viciously, thinking that the Gerdas and the Idas of this world had all the fun while she did all the damned work.

• • • •

2012

Rosie slept late the next morning, and she awoke not to a chiming alarm clock or the sounds of the buses wheezily groaning to a stop outside her window or, worst of all, the clattering of bottles being emptied out from the night club next door at 4:00 a.m. This was bad enough when it woke her; worst of all was when she'd been lying awake for so long wondering about the future that she heard them carting them out.

But here the only sound was a faint rustling and birdsong, twittering happily somewhere. The room, with its open curtains, was bathed in soft, golden light, and she sat up to take in her surroundings for the first time. Wiping the sleep from her eyes, she breathed a sigh.

The room was plain and bare, but in fact Rosie rather liked it like that. Whoever had converted it had done a beautiful job. It had a plain, whitewashed wooden floor covered in thick patterned rugs, with two walls a very pale blue and the other two wallpapered in very tiny blue flower print. Her large antique sleigh bed was covered in a thick white duvet and had two white wooden bedside tables on either side, both with candlesticks and white candles. A small wooden door led to a compact, white en suite bathroom, another to a built-in wardrobe, and there was a slightly incongruous baggy, big pink armchair in the corner of the room.

There were two dormer windows looking over the front of the house. Jumping up and peering through them, Rosie saw that they pointed toward a field full of sheep, the green gorse of the hills, and beyond, miles and miles of blue-washed sky.

On the other side of the room, above the trapdoor, a further single tiny window high in the wall looked over into Lilian's back garden. It was exquisite, bordered by a picket fence and neatly laid-out hollyhocks and wisteria predominating. It wasn't a large garden, but it was extremely neat, with gravel paths meandering here and there between high-tied rose bushes and sharply clipped hedges. One corner was laid out with vegetables (Rosie wondered about this; Lilian certainly didn't seem to be eating any of them), one to herbs, and at the very end, where a small wooden gate led out onto yet another field, there were two huge apple trees, full of russets, growing intertwined with one another to form a bower. Tiptoeing to lean out, Rosie thought she could hear the dreamy buzzing of summer bees among the lilacs. Well.

Rosie had never been anywhere like this before. A garden like this, spilling into open land. Of course, it just didn't happen in the city, or certainly not in the parts of it she knew well. Rosie took a deep breath, inhaled the scent of the garden, the dark-green gorse smell of the hills, the underlying flavor of the earth. She felt as if something was missing; there was no underlying thrum of traffic and motion and trains rumbling beneath the earth or planes cutting through the sky. Just this peace. Shaking her head, she washed and dressed, feeling, for the first time, a tiny hint of excited curiosity about what the day might bring.

Downstairs, there was no sign of her great-aunt. Rosie peeped her head into the bedroom, but the old lady was fine, just fast asleep. Sleep and good food—what Lilian needed more than anything, Rosie surmised. She could work on the second one.

She crept back upstairs and picked up the phone. "Ange?"

"Aw yih?"

"Mum! Stop that. You're not Australian."

"Darling, I have a natural facility for accents. I just pick them up. Are you there?"

"Of course I'm here. What did you think, I was going to say I was coming then fly to the U.S.?"

"No need to be so touchy! Were you always so touchy?"

Rosie took a deep breath and managed to avoid saying anything sarcastic about being plucked out of your life and sent to the back of beyond to babysit a grumpy geriatric because everyone else was too busy having barbecues by the swimming pool and drinking beer from a little bottle and saying yih.

"Never mind," she said.

"Did Gerard drive you up and settle you in?" said Angie in a conciliatory tone, which unfortunately failed almost completely in its goal.

"No," said Rosie. "I got the bus. I didn't mind," she lied.

Angie didn't say anything. "Well, okay!" she added finally. "Why don't you go out and explore?"

Rosie had actually been considering staying in bed till Lilian got up, hiding with her book and enjoying a rare chance to sleep in on her own that wasn't punctuated by the sound of Gerard playing *Grand Theft Auto* at ear-shattering volume, but her mum was insistent.

"Go on," she said. "Lipton's nice. I used to spend a lot of time there as a child. Get your bearings. Introduce yourself."

Rosie rolled her eyes.

"I'm not 'introducing myself.'"

"It's a village; they'll expect it. They'll find out who you are anyway. Everyone gossips nonstop."

"Well, they'll have nothing to gossip about with me."

• • • •

Rosie decided to follow her mother's instructions anyway; there wasn't a sound from downstairs. She wondered, thinking about the tidily made and unused-looking bed, exactly how much sleep Lilian had been getting lately and figured she'd better leave her to it. Plus she was absolutely starving and didn't want to stomp around the tiny dollhouse kitchen.

So she tidied up the sitting room; put a load of laundry into the prehistoric twin tub—how on earth had Lilian managed to look so dapper when laundry must have been agony for her?—changed into a floral frock, a denim jacket, and the patterned rubber boots she'd bought four years ago in an attempt to be hip and go to Glastonbury, which had ended very badly indeed; left a note for Lilian and the door on the latch; and stepped out into the morning.

• • • •

1942

When she first saw them, she couldn't quite believe it. Four weeks' worth of ration cards, pale pink cardboard, neatly lined up in a row.

"What's this?" she asked coolly, convinced he was buying an enormous box of chocolate for another girl.

Henry looked pink. "A large bag of caramels, please."

Blinking nervously, Lilian climbed carefully up the little stepladder, conscious of his eyes on her. It was a ravishingly beautiful day outside, and the shop was empty so early.

She filled the bag with the sweet, shining, fudgy caramels. No one took her responsibilities more seriously than Lilian. Her father had made it very clear that, in times of hardship, they absolutely couldn't be seen to be taking more than their fair share. He had seemed so grave when he had said it, asking for their absolute trust on the issue, that Lilian hadn't had a sweet since. Surrounded by them all day, most of the time she didn't miss it too much. She didn't even usually eat caramels, had always liked to get more for her money, something with a bit of crunch in it.

The pink-striped bag was bulging by the time Henry put down his sixpence. "There you are," she said. Henry didn't pick up the bag.

"They're for you," he said.

Lilian stared at him. "What do you mean?"

"Your friend told me they were your favorites."

Ida Delia, thought Lilian. Ida Delia would even tell a fib about something as stupid as that.

"Are they all for me?"

"They are," said Henry, blushing. "Unless you'd like to share one."

Lilian looked at him, half-shocked, half-giggling, as her father dinged into the shop.

"Come on, Lils," he said. "Get a shuffle on." He looked up.

"Hello, Carr," he sniffed quickly then grabbed the bag. "These yours, are they?" By this time, Henry was puce and he looked at her in horror. Lilian's father pressed them into his hands.

"Well, come on, young man, we haven't got all day. There's a war on, you know. You DO know?" he said with the slightly serious air of a man who had three sons fighting, looking at a perfectly healthy young man who had the time to wander around eating sweets.

Lilian looked at him, waiting for him to announce that he'd bought the sweets for her. But poor Henry looked completely torn. Such an enormous gesture; he might as well ask for her hand. His face looked totally panicked. This wasn't what he'd expected at all.

"Umm, well," he began. "I'd like to…"

Mr. Hopkins had already started examining the ledger. Henry glanced at Lilian, who couldn't help him at all but just looked at him like a big-eyed, panic-stricken mouse. He couldn't read it at all. Was she terrified he was going to say something in front of her father? Had he misjudged the situation entirely? She hadn't even looked cheerful that it was caramels; were they even her favorites at all? He felt a horrid dull flush creep over his face.

"I'll come back for these later," he said then turned around and left. Neither of the Hopkins said good-bye. Lilian's fingernails were tightly dug into the palm of her hand.

"What an odd fellow," said her father eventually then wondered why his daughter was pushing past him into the house. He'd never understood her mother either.

• • • •

2012

First off, Rosie stopped at the little shop next door. The front of it was ancient, and the windows, which were mullioned glass, could really do with a proper scrubbing out. The wood frontage was painted a kind of fading burgundy, but although the building was pretty, the paint was flaking, and the swinging striped sign outside—Hopkins's Sweets and Confectionery—was gilded but tired-looking. Inside, Rosie could just about make out jars of this and that, in a slightly higgledy-piggledy order, and lots of jelly snakes sitting out in a huge dusty box. It didn't, she thought, look terribly appealing. In fact, to her horror, she realized that it wasn't open at all, that it clearly hadn't been open for a long, long time. Lilian had been fooling everyone for what looked like years.

Rosie winced. This was going to be, she realized, even more of a pain in the arse than she had been expecting.

A little clock in the window indicated that it opened at 10:00 a.m., but even as Rosie stood there, little lines of boys and girls wearing smart blue uniforms with ties under their sweatshirts were wending their way down the road, walking in pairs or sitting upright in large Land Rovers, obviously heading for the little schoolhouse Rosie could just make out at the other end of town. She shook off her horrible sense of foreboding and decided to follow the flow and see where she ended up.

The cottage and the shop sat on the western end of the main street of Lipton, a mismatched collection of thatched cottages, a doctor's office, lawyer's office, dentist, several feed stores, a clothing store that featured some extraordinary mother-of-the-bride outfits that Rosie, belying her hunger, spent several moments staring at, wondering what type of person could be in need of a huge jade, silver, and violet-striped formal jacket with shoulder pads and large paisley flowers embroidered down the front for two hundred and seventy-nine pounds. The clothing shop next to that sold jodhpurs, quilted jackets, and waterproof trousers. Rosie wondered where the nearest shopping center was, then figured out it was probably at the other end of that two-hour bus trip. She mentally ran through her wardrobe. Since she and Gerard had moved in, though, she had just gotten so comfy. Maybe that was why Lilian still dressed so formally, because she had never found anyone she could relax with. A perfect night for Rosie these days was takeout food, a bottle of wine, and a movie, her head tucked under Gerard's arm, lying on the sofa they'd bought together at IKEA. That was perfect happiness to her. Okay, so Gerard teased her about wearing her old pajama pants and slippers around the house and asked what had happened to the hot young thing he'd met at the hospital, but this was what contentment looked like. She thought about Lilian's smart appearance, though, and wondered for an instant if this might just be complacency.

Rosie made a mental note of the right kinds of high-calorie foods to bring back for Lilian. She wondered how much she would balk at eating peanut butter, but it was worth a shot.

She wandered past a bank, the post office, a large grocery store that looked like it stocked just about everything in the world, an electrical store that proudly boasted that it still fixed toasters, a large old-fashioned pub called the Red Lion, and, unexpectedly, a very chic little restaurant with wooden benches and a chalkboard menu. Streets ran off the main road, all heading upward out of the valley, with houses dotted more and more sparingly up the hills till you got to the farmland.

There was no doubt about it, Rosie thought. It was definitely pretty. She popped into the bakery and said a cheery good morning to the woman behind the counter, who smiled back. She looked pink and exhausted. Must have been up early, thought Rosie, wondering if the sweetshop shouldn't be open early too. There was a queue out the door of children buying doughnuts for the break-time snack and what looked like farmers and laborers stocking up on pies and sandwiches for lunchtime. She chose a cheese and onion pasty and bought a cup of tea from the vending machine and took it outside. The tea was horrible. Next to the war memorial, there was a green wooden bench, and from there she had a good view of the little town coming and going around her. A dapper young man with a briefcase bounced up the steps of the doctor's office with a large set of keys; a rather chubby-looking vicar emerged from the beautiful, square-topped Norman church across the road and looked around confusedly. A postal worker wearing shorts and riding an ancient-looking bicycle freewheeled down one of the hill roads. The children shouted and dawdled and raced and hopped up the hill to the schoolhouse; the Land Rovers—it seemed to be the only type of car allowed around here—nudged through the narrow road, followed by a truck containing a large and mutinous-sounding flock of sheep. By the pond on a small patch of green outside the church, two geese honked loudly back in response. By the time she saw the two large ladies on horseback, Rosie was half expecting Ms. Frizzle to arrive from somewhere. She phoned Gerard.

"Hey," he said. He sounded groggy.

"What are you doing?" said Rosie in mock annoyance. "I've been gone five minutes, and you're already having big celebration nights out about it?"

"Course not," said Gerard easily. "Just me and the lads, you know. Friday nights out. Like the old days. Plus I've got to eat somewhere."

"Hmm," said Rosie.

"So how's the old witch?"

"She's very rundown, a bit weak...and a grumpy old witch."

Rosie said this to make Gerard laugh, but she felt a bit disloyal as she did so.

"She managed to make two rude remarks about my shoes as soon as I walked in the door."

"What, those big Cornish pasties you wear?"

"Don't you start." She paused. "No, she's all right. Just lonely I think. Sad."

"What's it like?"

"Well," said Rosie. "Well. It's a bit weird-looking. And there isn't a Starbucks."

"OH. MY. GOD," said Gerard. "You won't last the week. Have you been arrested and charged with witchcraft yet?"

"No," said Rosie. "But nobody has met me yet. Do you know they have a vicar?"

"God," said Gerard "Watch out for him. They're always the worst pervs, vicars."

"That's your medical opinion, is it?"

"No," said Gerard. "Scientific fact."

"It's pretty," said Rosie. "You'll like it. You should come visit."

"I will, love, I will," said Gerard, stifling a yawn. "But first, I think I have to get to Starbucks."

• • • •

However pretty the scene, and however many people gave her inquisitive looks—which was odd, since in London, nobody ever looked at you at all; you could have two heads for all anybody cared—before too long, her pasty was finished and her tea had been poured in the bin. Rosie was beginning to feel a bit like she was in London again, spectating on people's lives—other people's happy, perfect lives, which always looked so effortless from where she was standing. When she got to the point where she was working out whether the mothers escorting their infants to school were older or younger than she was, she decided something had to be done.

Although a couple of clouds were gathering in the sky, it was still a lovely summer's day. Larks were circling, and beyond the gray stone buildings opposite, the deep, rich, brown, loamy fields were beginning to be plowed. A tractor trundled up a little road toward the gentle hills in the distance, and hedgerows marked out the sprawling fields. It was lovely. Rosie decided to explore. She knew she should be getting back, making plans, sitting down with Lilian, and figuring everything out. This idea was not appealing. A quick walk around, just to familiarize herself with her surroundings, that was what she needed. That would be fine.

She passed by the tiny, traditionally redbrick primary school with hopscotch drawn out in the playground. After the sign thanking people for driving slowly through Lipton came a long avenue of trees without a sidewalk. Fortunately there was little traffic, and Rosie marched along the ditch side, remembering as she did so how highly uncomfortable rubber boots were to wear for any length of time and feeling her feet begin to sweat. Then she turned onto a side road that was little more than a track. Here, mud tracks left by farm machinery had plowed up the earth, and she found herself sinking into deep trenches. It was harder to see the fields from out here, and as she continued on down the long, solitary track, just the quiet cries of birds sounding in the distance, Rosie began to feel her optimistic mood drain away, particularly as the wispy clouds she'd noticed earlier clearly changed their minds and decided to start massing grayly above her head. Rosie started to wonder where she was going. In all senses. But she trudged on, turning onto smaller and smaller tracks, sometimes covered in trees, sometimes barely a path, before popping out onto what seemed like a road again.

After about half an hour, she reached the crest of a small hill but turning around realized she could hardly see back down; the clouds were closing in much more quickly than she'd expected. Just at that moment, the first drops started hitting her head, and she realized that (a) she didn't have an umbrella with her, (b) she couldn't remember which way she had come and now she couldn't see it either, and (c), she was wearing her shaggy H&M shearling, which, while stylish and relatively forgiving to her lumpy bits, was also made of thin wool and thus, if the rain got any heavier, was going to prove totally and completely useless in about five minutes' time.

The rain got substantially heavier.

"BUGGER!" shouted Rosie out loud at the sky, hoping this would make her feel better. It did, but not for long. Where was she? Where the hell? She took out her phone. Of course, there was no signal. Who would need a signal out here, cows calling in home-delivery grass?

The sky was nearly completely black; you could see so bloody FAR in the country. She certainly could see far enough not to get her hopes up as to the weather changing in the next five minutes or so.

Rosie had never wished to see a Starbucks more fervently in her entire life. "Bollocks, bollocks, bollocks!!"

Rosie felt rivulets of rain starting to infiltrate the collar of her shirt and dribble down her back. There were droplets in her eyelashes. Her boots might be keeping the outsides dry, but stray raindrops were still finding their way inside and down her socks. Rosie started wondering seriously if it might be possible to drown. Didn't cows drown if they looked at the sky or something?

She turned around. She had to guess a route, and if she did, it would be downhill. She'd come uphill, hadn't she? Hopefully, she'd be going down the same hill…and not, for example, the other side of a different one that led into a crevasse or a ravine.

Rosie realized she was shivering now. She couldn't believe it had turned so very nasty so quickly.

Suddenly, in the distance, she caught sight of a set of headlights. Her heart leaped. She'd be saved! It must be the farmer! Maybe he'd caught sight of her out alone on the wild moors on a mad day and was coming to rescue her! And he'd take her back to his lovely farmhouse kitchen, and his rosy-cheeked wife would have a plate of scones and… she put her hand out to wave down the car as it swept down the muddy lane. Dazzled by the lights, it was hard to see who was at the wheel. The car, a dirty white Land Rover, failed to slow down, even as Rosie pushed herself more out of the shelter of the trees to wave her hands wildly. For her troubles, the car spat out a large fan of muddy water all over her jeans and down her boots and continued on its way. Rosie had the impression of an angry-looking face at the wheel.

"You PRICK!" she yelled after it. "You've left me here to DIE!!!"

At this, the brake lights of the car went on, briefly, and she thought that it might be slowing down, that he'd had a rethink. But after a couple of seconds, they went off again, and the car continued on its way down the hill, the opposite road to the one Rosie had been about to take.

"Karma is going to TOTALLY bite you," she screamed. She was so wet now that it didn't really matter at all. She marched out into the middle of the road.

"I hope toads eat through your electrical wiring and a BADGER gets in your bed. A toe-eating badger. And that your car suddenly explodes for no reason. Without you in it, because I am a GOOD PERSON, unlike YOU, you DICKWAD. But with ALL YOUR STUFF IN IT, like your camera and your computer, but when you ring your insurance company, they DON'T BELIEVE YOU, because you are so OBVIOUSLY A JERK. In a LAND ROVER."

Rosie was so absorbed in bringing down curses on the head of the vanished car that she hardly noticed when two lights appeared behind her and another Land Rover skittered to a sudden, horrified stop.

A late-middle-aged, very tall woman alighted.

"What the HELL are you doing in the middle of my road?" she shouted.

Rosie wiped the rain out of her eyes and lowered the fist she suddenly realized had been angrily raised.

"Umm…well, I got lost."

"Where are your clothes?" barked the woman, who was wearing a Barbour jacket and an enormous deerstalker hat. Her boots were dark green and had a rubber tie at the top, Rosie noticed. No flowers at all.

"Umm, I got wet."

"You're going to get hypothermia in about a second. Where are you going?"

"Lipton."

"Well, you're facing completely the wrong way... Get OUT of my road!" Rosie jumped to one side, completely intimidated.

The woman hurried back to the car then looked up again. "You're not…you're not a vet by any chance?"

Rosie shook her head. "No."

"No, of course not. What was I thinking? Look at what you're wearing..."

The woman shook her head. Rosie finally realized she was extremely distressed. "Why? What's the matter?"

"Bloody...bloody vet's an hour away, operating on a horse in the next valley along. I'll need to get to the next town over... It's my dog..."

Rosie peered into the back of the Land Rover then clapped her hand to her mouth. Staring at her with wide, unblinking, terrified eyes was a large golden retriever. That wasn't what caught her eye though. Sticking out of his abdomen—grotesquely, spread-eagling his paws away from it—was a huge coil of barbed wire.

"Christ," said Rosie.

"Quite," said the woman. "So if you could get out of my road and out of my way..."

Rosie shook her head. "How far is the next town?" she asked.

"Forty miles."

"That'll take too long," she said.

"I know," said the woman. "That's why we're following the doctor. But I don't know if he can manage on his own."

"The *doctor*?"

"Do you have any better ideas?"

Rosie shook her head. The idea of a doctor trying to help the poor beast in the back...it was crazy. On the other hand...she definitely, definitely needed a lift back into town.

"Umm, you know I'm a nursing auxiliary," she said quickly, not stressing the "auxiliary" part.

"You're a nurse?"

"...auxiliary," said Rosie quietly. The rain showed no sign of letting up. But she had held down heavy patients before, helped with catheters, held paws...well, hands. "I might be able to help," she said.

The woman revved the engine. "Get in then," the woman said brusquely and took off with a squeal of brakes in the mud before Rosie had even closed the door.

Rosie patted the dog's head. "There, there. You're going to be all right. I just need to wash my hands, then we'll make you feel all better, yes?"

The dog whined slightly in response, his eyes glassy, which worried Rosie. She knew it was better when patients were crabby; it meant they still had a bit of life left in them.

"Hurry up," she said, but the woman in front was already driving through the rain like a maniac.

• • • •

Back down in the village, which turned out to be over a completely different hill from the one Rosie would have expected, the sky was dark and the streets were empty. The practice was locked up—there obviously wasn't a surgery every day, and it had been closed that morning when Rosie passed by—but the white Land Rover that had sprayed her earlier was parked haphazardly along the side of the building, and a side door was open. It was peculiar—the office had obviously at one time been a rather grand house and still had a fully laid-out garden, including a shed.

Rosie barely had time to notice this before the woman was opening the trunk and the two of them, as gently as possible, started to lug out the huge dog.

"What's his name?" said Rosie.

"It's Bran," said the woman, her voice choking. "Oh Bran, darling."

Holding open the door with his elbow, his hands in the air obviously newly sterilized, was a tall man, trying to wipe a large mass of hair off his forehead with his other elbow. It wasn't a very elegant maneuver.

"Hurry up," he was shouting, glancing around.

The women followed him in, and he let the door clang behind him. "If Hywel finds out about this, we're screwed," he said as they followed him down a small passage to a utility room at the back of the building.

"Did you stop to pick up a hitchhiker?" continued the man. He spoke very quickly and helped them lay the dog out on his back.

"She SAYS she's a nurse," said the woman.

The man looked impatient and unconvinced. "ARE you?"

"I'm a nursing auxiliary," said Rosie.

"Do you know what you're doing?" he said to Rosie shortly. Fortunately, Rosie had seen this kind of thing before in the emergency room, many times. It was just a stab wound, she told herself. To a dog.

"How much do you think he weighs?" she said back. The doctor was already trying to fill up the syringe with anesthetic.

"Forty-five pounds? Fifty-five?"

They both glanced at the woman, but the sight of Bran stretched out and whining piteously was clearly too much for her, and she dissolved in tears.

"Let's say fifty-five," said the man. "We don't want him waking up and biting us."

Rosie went around to the back of the dog's head and made soothing noises while she held his paws apart. The man looked very tentative indeed as he stood over the animal with his needle. Bran chose this moment to wake up and suddenly growled, writhing and howling and twisting his body in agony. As soon as the doctor tried to hold down one paw, another would writhe free, and he couldn't stay still enough to get the injection in. The woman had gone to pieces completely.

"God, Jim really picks his time to go foal a bloody horse in Carningsford," the doctor muttered to himself. Rosie, almost without thinking (although trying her best to avoid the bite-y end), clambered up onto the table and, as she had been taught to do with violent drunks and drug addicts, held down the dog's thrashing paws in a wrestler's hold, which allowed the doctor to practically kneel on the bottom one. The woman let out a howl, but quickly the doctor seized a scruff of the dog's neck and smoothly sent the needle deep under the animal's muscles.

After a few seconds, the creature started to relax. Rosie checked his breathing and took a quick glance at his pupils before nodding at the doctor and releasing his front paws. The woman was still standing there, half in shock, trembling and agape.

"Hetty, do you want to go wait in the waiting room," said the man. It was an instruction, not a question. "You," he said to Rosie. "Get scrubbed in. You're going to have to hold the area for me."

Rosie boiled up catgut at the same time as the doctor selected the right fine instrument and crouched down, starting to carefully coax out the wire. They both watched, breathlessly, as he extracted pieces of metal.

"Stupid old fence," said the man. "It's rusted to nearly nothing."

"Are you going to get it all?"

The damage, though painful, didn't seem to be too deep, as he drew out the last poking piece, spiked with blood. The man shrugged.

"He can go and have an X-ray...at the veterinary hospital...tomorrow. But we need to get this little lot sewn up. An infection in there could be very nasty."

Once the stomach was stitched up, with a large amount of antibacterial powder, they could both relax a bit, and Rosie stood next to the doctor, passing over the catgut and the scissors as he made a very tidy job of the rest of the dog.

"You're good at that," she observed at one point. "I've worked with some right butchers."

"I always liked it," admitted the doctor. "I miss a bit of the wet work in general practice." He let a smile cross his face. "I'm Moray."

"Like the eel?" Rosie said then immediately felt like an idiot. "Sorry."

"Don't be," said Moray. "I use it as a diagnostic tool. If you don't say 'like the eel,' then you're obviously suffering some form of mental distraction or injury."

"Oh," said Rosie, feeling herself go pink. She noticed he needed the stitch trimming and did it unconsciously.

"So, what—a veterinary nurse just suddenly appeared at the right moment out of the sky?" said Moray.

"Oh, no," said Rosie, pleased he thought that. "No, no. I'm a real nurse. Well, not really. I'm a nursing auxiliary. Or at least, I was."

Moray raised his eyebrows.

"Well, that was lucky," he said. "It got really hairy just there before the anesthetic. Don't know what we'd have done without you. Do you have a name, Nursing Auxiliary, or are you just going to vanish off on your magical rain cloud?"

"I'm Rosie," said Rosie. "Do you do this kind of thing a lot?"

"Almost never," said Moray. "Actually, never. You?"

Rosie shook her head, and they smiled at each other as, slowly, the dog started to stir just a little.

"I don't know how I'm going to get all this hair out of here," said Moray. "This isn't going to go down well."

And sure enough, when Dr. Hywel Evan, head of practice, rolled up forty minutes later, after a telephone call he had completely failed to understand in every way, he was frankly amazed to find a dog on the utility room table, out for the count (Moray and Rosie had in fact slightly overestimated the anesthetic, despite the giant weight of the dog), and his most junior doctor and a total stranger putting on a large bandage while a woman cried tears of relief in his waiting room.

Moray turned around just as he entered.

"I think we got it all," he was calling through to the waiting room. "But probably worth an X-ray and a checkup just in case."

Rosie saw Dr. Evan, who had a face like thunder. "Hello?" she said tentatively.

"Who the hell are you?" he demanded, a corpulent, comfortable-looking man in tweed.

"Oh," she said, her face falling. After the adrenalin of their dash to the doctor's office, it finally sunk in to Rosie just how many illegal things she'd done in the last forty minutes.

"Oh," she said again. "Oh dear. Oh dear. I'm so sorry…it was just…"

Dr. Evan looked from the dog to Rosie to Moray to the dog again. "You…you brought a DOG in here?"

"Nothing else to be done, sir," said Moray respectfully. "Jim Hodds is over the other side of the mountain in the middle of a tricky foaling. Perforated abdomen. He'd have died, sir. And fortunately, this young lady happened to be passing and proved the most excellent nurse."

Dr. Evan spluttered.

"That is ABSOLUTELY and CATEGORICALLY not ALLOWED!"

Rosie moved back toward the table and tentatively rested her hand on the dog's head. To her astonishment, the dog lifted his head a tiny amount and gently licked her hand. Despite the amount of trouble she was currently in, she couldn't help it. She was delighted.

"Hey, boy," she said softly, her voice trembling.

Moray's face broke into a smile. "Hey, old fellow!" he said. "Look at that, Hye."

"Well, I can't…I can't believe this," said Dr. Evan. "Do I need to call the police?"

"Do you need to call the WHAT?" came a loud imperious voice suddenly, and the woman strode into the consulting room.

"He's stirring," said Rosie.

The woman rushed over and put her hand to the dog's muzzle, and he tried out another tentative lick. "Bran," said the woman. "Oh, Bran."

She briefly buried her face in the animal's neck. Dr. Evan watched in disbelief.

Then she turned to him.

"Hye Evan," she said. "Your young doctor and this strange girl just saved my dog's life. They were MAGNIFICENT."

There was a long pause.

"Lady…Lady Lipton," stammered Dr. Evan. Rosie's eyes opened wide with shock.

A lady! Well, that was a stupid reaction, obviously. But even so. Maybe that's why she kept insisting that it was "her" road. Because it was.

"Amazing. You are SO lucky to have this young man at your practice. I shall tell everyone so."

"Umm, but…" stammered Dr. Evan.

Lady Lipton nodded at Dr. Evan. "I'll pay you for the medicines, of course. Without these young people around, it would have been a very different day indeed. You know, it's not the first time I've been to this office and found nobody here."

Moray and Rosie looked at each other and grimaced. "You'll still need to get him X-rayed," warned Moray.

"I certainly will," said Lady Lipton. "Well done, Hye. Nice to see you take on somebody competent for a change."

Dr. Evan spluttered.

"I'll send Mrs. Flynn down to clean up. Now, please, Moray. Could you help me lift my darling boy back into the car?"

• • • •

Moray snuck off after helping Lady Lipton with her big woofer. He wanted to find the girl—what was her name again?—and thank her, because he had no idea if she was just passing through. It had taken him a while to realize what was peculiar about her, then it finally struck him that she had been completely and utterly soaking wet.

"In 1932, the Milky Way appeared in the U.S., followed by Mr. Mars Jr.'s invention, the Mars Bar, in the UK in 1933. In 1935, the Aero; in 1936, Maltesers; and in 1937, the Kit Kat, Rolos, and Smarties. In music, the equivalent would be the golden age of Bach, Mozart, and Beethoven. In painting, it was the equivalent of the Italian Renaissance and the advent of Impressionism at the end of the nineteenth century; in literature, Tolstoy, Balzac, and Dickens...

"Never mind about 1066 William the Conqueror, 1087 William the Second. Such things are not going to affect one's life. But 1932 the Mars Bar and 1936 Maltesers, and 1937 the Kit Kat—these dates are milestones in history and should be seared into the memory of every child in the country."

So said none other than Roald Dahl, and he should know and, in fact, gets the last word on just about every single sweet-related issue out there.

So take that, you smarty pants "one square of 90 percent cacao dark chocolate with chili taken with a glass of Château Pétrus 1978" brigade, and bugger right off.

Here are the facts: the more rarefied and bitter you take your chocolate, the less you actually TRULY like and appreciate the stuff. The chocolate you grew up with—mass-produced, high fat and sugar, low in cocoa—is one of the many, many things that made Britain great. Along, of course, with Roald Dahl.

If you truly are a chocolate snob, then the great mass-market bars cater to you too, with the most exquisite, classically, perfectly balanced fusion of chocolate-based mint flavoring: the Fry's Chocolate Cream (plain, in the navy-blue wrapper). If this peak of delicate, sweet, and ever-so-slightly sharp, mouth-melting infusion of happiness, class, and flavor does not assuage your snobbish taste buds, then you're doing it wrong. May I therefore commend to you an alternative volume entitled "Being Pointlessly Snotty and Showing Off: A User's Manual."

It took the adrenaline wearing off for Rosie to realize just how wet she was. That and stepping out into an afternoon as clear and blue as the morning when she'd left Lipton. What on earth had the weather done? Had it been an entirely topical downpour? As she dripped up the road toward Lilian's house, she felt it was unfair that so many faces turned toward her to stare. Didn't they know they lived in a mad bloody climate?

Lilian was pottering about in the house looking worried when she arrived but desperately trying not to show it too much.

"What happened to you?" she said. "I thought you'd turned around and gone home. Which you can do whenever you like."

Lilian wondered if she'd been too hard on the girl before. Although she did look absolutely atrocious.

Rosie didn't mention how close she'd come to pledging to go home alone on the hilltop.

"There was a storm! I got drenched!"

"Well, this is Derbyshire, darling, not the Balearics. Run yourself a bath and get a proper coat."

Rosie put the kettle on and ran her fingers through her hair. Without wanting to get anyone in trouble about having a dog in a doctor's office, she mentioned in passing that she'd met the local doctor.

"Hye Evans? That fat old fool," said Lilian. "That man couldn't diagnose a nail sticking out of your leg if you turned up with a nail sticking out of your leg, saying, 'Doctor, I just accidentally hammered a nail into my leg.' And trust me, I should know."

"Umm, no, the other one."

Lilian's eyebrows went up. "Were you quite so damp at the time?"

"What do you mean?" said Rosie.

Lilian glanced very briefly at the glamorous portraits of herself as a younger woman but didn't say anything. Rosie sniffed and marched upstairs to run the bath, trying not to look in the bathroom mirror at her hair, which had widened to twice its normal size, like a loaf of bread rising by a stove.

"I have a boyfriend, you know," Rosie said from the top of the stairs.

"Boyfriends, schmoyfriends," said Lilian. "I don't see him here."

"I'm going to make you lunch," said Rosie. "And you are going to eat it. And then you're going to get out of that chair. It's not doing you any good."

• • • •

"Okay," she said, coming down warm and dry forty-five minutes later. She only had one sweater. That she probably needed to rectify. Lilian was still sitting in her armchair, listening to Radio 4 and staring into the fire. Rosie was tempted to join her, but she was here for a reason.

She heated up the thick vegetable soup she'd grabbed from the grocery store, ignoring the looks and whispers of the other shoppers at her dripping state.

"Eat this. And the bread."

"This is DRIPPING with butter," said Lilian, looking distasteful.

"It is," said Rosie. "And if you don't want me to make you eat two slices, I'd get on with it. Unless you want me to dissolve it in milk."

Lilian made a face but started in on the soup. As she did so, she felt a little start of worry; how long had it been since she'd had hot food? Hetty popped in and heated something up now and again, but even Hetty complained about her not having one of those new oven things that heated up things so fast. Lilian didn't trust the idea of them, and anyway, she'd always gotten along fine without.

"We need to get you a microwave," said Rosie. "You know. If you want to keep living here."

"Ugly things," murmured Lilian. "So many modern things are so ugly." Rosie tried not to take this as a personal slight in some way but didn't quite know how to manage it.

"Have you really lived in Lipton all your life?" she asked, amazed.

"Well, I've traveled," said Lilian crossly. It was none of this girl's business. "I've been to York…Scarborough of course…Scotland once."

"London?"

"I have NO idea why the entire world seems so fixated on London," said Lilian. "I thought it was absolutely crammed full of unspeakable people, incredibly noisy, and totally filthy."

Rosie grinned.

"It is," she said. "All of those things. That's what makes it so amazing."

"Well, if you like hooligans, I suppose."

"Didn't you ever want to travel any further?" said Rosie. "New York? Paris?"

"Not particularly," sniffed Lilian. "I know what I liked. And I had the shop. And I might go still."

A silence descended, and the atmosphere grew stiff. Neither of them could quite say it. That there was no "still." That what Rosie was here to do was not going to result in any trips to Paris. Lilian sniffed and turned away, refusing to touch any more of her lunch.

Afterward, Rosie insisted on examining her aunt's hip. Lilian would have liked to have refused but realized she was in no position to do so.

Sure enough, the wound was a little nasty and sticky around

the edges, but nothing Rosie couldn't sort out without too much trouble. Lilian for her part was a bit more impressed than she let on at Rosie's cool hands and efficient manner as she changed the dressing. After that, Rosie figured there was no point in pussyfooting around any longer.

"Let's have a look at the business then."

Lilian looked guilty. "Well, since I hurt my hip..."

"It's fine," said Rosie. "Honestly. I've seen it." There was a silence. "But didn't you ever want to just sell up before? Retire? Go see Paris?"

Lilian's expression turned absolutely mutinous.

"You retire," she said.

Rosie bit her lip, hard.

"All right," she said. "Can I have the keys?"

With some difficulty, Lilian picked up the large set of ancient brass keys from the top of the mantelpiece.

"Come on then," said Rosie. "Let's go and have a look."

• • • •

The key twisted reluctantly in the old lock on the red-painted wooden door with nine panels of beveled glass. With a horrible squeak, Rosie managed to click it around.

"There's a knack to it," murmured Lilian.

"Oh yes?" said Rosie. "What's that then?"

"You get Rob the butcher to do it."

Rosie shook her head in disbelief, pushing over stacked mail on the mat. "I can't believe this has been going on for so long," she said. She moved into the middle of the tiny shop and turned around 360 degrees. The last rays of the day were picked out through the tiny windows.

"Wow," was all she could say.

First off, there was no denying it. The place was filthy. There were cobwebs in the corners. The windows were so dirty the sun had trouble picking through at all. Things were toppled over, gray and crumpled. The antique till still had shillings and pence on its ancient keys. The scales, burnished and at an awkward angle, stood there as if the last seven decades had hardly touched them. It was a museum.

And there, too, inside, every square inch of the little shop was covered—in sweets, in posters, in things Rosie hadn't seen for years. There were little tins of travel sweets and jujubes, neatly piled up in pyramids; great glass bowls full of striped candy canes tied with bows; huge slabs of dark red Bournville chocolate and neatly stacked alternating boxes of Dairy Milk and Black Magic. On the very highest shelves were the most enormous, elaborate boxes of chocolates, in red velvet heart-shaped boxes with huge ribbons, completely covered in dust.

An old ladder was attached to sliding rails, like at a library, to allow the higher sweets to be removed from the shelves. Then, like an old apothecary's shop, the back three walls were lined with shelves that held great glass bulbous jars filled with every imaginable sweet: neat pastel chunks of Edinburgh rock; haphazard slabs of peanut brittle; bright green gobstoppers and sharp pink little wrapped packets of Hubba Bubba; chocolate frogs and ladybugs; dolly mixtures and rainbow drops and cough sweets and bouncing, fat pastel marshmallows; and four different flavors of sticky, icing-sugar-coated Turkish delight. And tucked neatly by the old-fashioned black pop-up till, the classics, in neat and tidy rows: Mars Bar, Kit Kat, Aero, Fry's Chocolate Cream, Crunchie, Twix. Oddly, the smell wasn't too terrible; a sweet mustiness, rather than a horrible decay.

"Are there mice?" said Rosie first off. "I bet there are mice." She looked around. "Wow," said Rosie again. "I can't believe you don't get burgled all the time. I mean, how long…"

"None of it's worth much," said Lilian. But Rosie, taking in a deep breath below the layers of dust and atmosphere of neglect, begged to disagree. In the few available bits of space between the displays hung old posters—a little girl in a purple-furred coat for Fry's, suggesting boys drink more milk by eating chocolate; a very smartly turned out little boy playing cricket for Cadbury's; and a beautiful wartime dolly bird suggesting a Mars Bar was a meal in itself. The posters represented the great triumvirate of British chocolate making.

The floor was an old black-and-white linoleum that had been worn smooth by generations of children beating a path with their farthings, their sixpennys, their ten pences, their pound coins, clutched stickily in excited paws, eyes darting everywhere to decide what would be best, terrified of making the wrong choice.

"But this is—I mean, it was obviously absolutely amazing in here at one time," said Rosie. "It's fantastic."

"Shows what you know," said Lilian. "It's all done. And anyway, it's not what kids want these days. They don't want gobstoppers anymore. They want great big, super large bars of Dairy Milk that you buy in six packs from the supermarket. They want family packs and super-sharers and liters of cola and hot dogs and nachos, whatever they are. Sweets are boring and old-fashioned. No one is interested anymore."

Rosie looked around. "I can't believe that's true." Her eyes caught something at the back of the shop. Her face lit up.

"Are these…sweetie cigarettes?" she said. "I haven't seen these for years. You're not allowed to sell them anymore. Lilian, why didn't you throw away all this stock?"

Her aunt looked cross but stoic.

"Sweets keep for a long time. I'm coming back to the shop."

"Mmm," said Rosie. She hadn't realized things were quite so bad. This wasn't just from Lilian's operation. The shop had obviously been like this for a long, long time, and Lilian had been completely unable and unwilling to tell anyone that she could no longer cope.

"These aren't even LEGAL anymore!" said Rosie. But she couldn't help opening the cigarette packet and inhaling the sticky candied scent of the little white sticks with the pink ends.

"I used to love these," she confessed.

"You'll pay for those," said Lilian.

"I will," said Rosie. "What are they, nine pence?"

"I was still getting some tourist trade," Lilian was saying, looking around her as if confused as to whether she was still open or not. "Some chocolates around Valentine's Day. But the children have moved on."

"But this could be…I mean the fact that it's all unchanged."

"Well, nothing much good happens in the world of sweets. Everything they invent now actually tastes worse than the old stuff. It's the children I feel sorry for," grumped Lilian. "So I saw no reason to change."

Rosie looked at the ancient cash register. "How did you use this?"

"Well, you just got used to it," said Lilian. "Decimalization was terrible for the children though. It made their sweets more expensive. It just did. It was a terrible thing. I definitely think they should go back. Idiot politicians."

"I'm not sure that's going to happen," said Rosie. "But on the plus side, keeping the till may have been a smart move. You know, this kind of thing is really fashionable."

Lilian looked almost flattered.

"Well, good things never go out of style," she said.

"No," said Rosie. "They never do. You know, adults like sweets too."

"You don't say," observed Lilian dryly, as Rosie realized that, completely without thinking about it, she had stuck a sweetie cigarette in her mouth.

"Ha! I don't even smoke," said Rosie.

Suddenly there was a ting as the little brass bell above the shop door rang. Both the women turned around, Rosie slightly guiltily.

It was the woman with the dog. Or rather, Rosie supposed, Lady Lipton.

"Coo-eee! Lils, DARLING. You have to hear about this

extraordinary new girl in the village. You won't BELIEVE what she did with Bran..."

She sounded like a different woman.

"Oh, who is it?" said Lilian eagerly. "Is she awful?"

Rosie rolled her eyes.

"Hard to say," Lady Lipton said then finally realized who else was in the room. Completely unperturbed, she simply outstretched her hand.

"And here she is. Hello. Have you bought a proper coat yet? We're predicted four days of rain, by the way. Which either means nine or none at all. Lils, I stuck the groceries in your kitchen. Don't tell Malik. I got Mrs. Cosgrove to pick me up some bits at the store in Carningsford. Man cannot live by the grocery store alone. Now, let me tell you the whole story."

So Rosie had to stand by as Lady Lipton told the entire thing to Lilian, leaving out the parts where she'd been hysterically upset about her dog and had to leave the room, but laying it on quite thickly about Rosie careering about in the rain wearing a bikini.

"And that terribly smart young doctor managed to save the entire thing. Wasn't that wonderful?"

Not wanting to point out that she'd helped, Rosie busied herself by examining the rest of the shop. Not that there was much more to it, but the store room revealed itself to be a knocked-about treasure trove of Gold Bars, Wham Bars, caramels, chocolate éclairs, sherbet lemons, and, to Rosie's overwhelming excitement, an enormous jar of chocolate limes. Chocolate limes were her absolute, absolute favorite thing, yet she probably hadn't thought of them for years. Now all she wanted to do was scoff a dozen of them. And if that was how she felt, she wondered, surely other people would feel the same...would want to taste something again, something that had made them feel happy and loved and cared for as a child.

For her and Pip, it was Friday mornings, and their mum would give them twenty pence to choose what they wanted for school breaks. Rosie had the hazy idea you weren't allowed to take in sweets for school breaks anymore. That seemed a shame. She and her best friend Daniela would plan Fridays all week. One would get one thing and the other would get another, then they would solemnly split the bags absolutely exactly between them. If there was an odd number, they would offer it up to their teacher, Mrs. Gilford, who had bright yellow hair and wore lots of blue eye shadow and was, Daniela and Rosie were entirely convinced, actually a princess in disguise. Mrs. Gilford would always smile politely and, when they explained that they were trying to be fair, would always take the sweet with heartfelt thanks and a bright pink lipsticked smile. Rosie, now she came to think of it, never remembered seeing Mrs. Gilford eat one.

She did remember, though, how the feeling of being nice to their teacher and being praised for their generosity would stay with her all day, long after the fizzle of the sherbet bombs mixed with the heavy fondant of the orange creams had faded from her tongue.

Rosie poked her head out of the store room. She wanted to know what that woman was nattering to her aunt about. Plus, she couldn't help it. She was slightly fascinated. She'd never met anyone with a title before.

"Do you live in a big house?" she asked, not realizing how rude it sounded till it had come out of her mouth, almost like an accusation. Lilian laughed in a way that sounded like she was trying to excuse her gauche London scruff of a niece, which made Rosie feel a bit hot and prickly.

"Well, that very much depends on what you think of as 'big,'" said Lady Lipton, busying herself with something on the counter. Rosie correctly ascertained this to mean "yes, ginormous."

"Doesn't it get freezing?" Both the women stared for a moment. Then Lilian burst out laughing.

"It certainly does," she said. "That's why Hets is down here all the time."

"It most certainly is not," said Lady Lipton. "I'm being charitable."

Lilian snorted.

"You're being cozy. Look at her," she ordered me and lifted the edge of the woman's Barbour jacket with her stick. Underneath was a gigantic man's pullover, patently ancient, and the holes in the wool showed evidence of another underneath.

"And it's only September," cackled Lilian. "You wait till February; she'll be camping out in her front room."

"You overheat your house dreadfully," said Lady Lipton. "It's not good for you."

"She's strong as an ox," interjected Rosie, who'd already witnessed Lilian hurling logs onto the fire that afternoon.

"Apparently I'm as strong as an ox," said Lilian. "And she's a nurse. She ought to know."

"Auxiliary nurse," said Lady Lipton, and Rosie made a quick note not to underestimate her. "And what exactly IS an ox?" she added.

"It's a gigantic cow. A boy cow," Rosie said, flushing, with a sudden stab of panic in case it was the one where you cross a donkey and a mule.

The two women laughed at each other.

"Well, enjoy your stay," said Lady Lipton, sweeping out.

Rosie watched her go. "Well," she said. "After I saved her dog and everything."

Lilian chuckled. "Oh, that's just Hetty's way," she said.

"Ugh," said Rosie. "I hate it when people say, 'Oh, they're just like that.' If someone is rude and not very nice, they shouldn't be like that, instead of everyone else having to make allowances just because they're Lady Snot-a-Lot. Anyway, she needn't worry. I won't be going near her stupid road again."

Dolly mixtures, like chocolate buttons, are often considered a training sweet, to be discarded when the adult teeth arrive. This is a shame; taken together, or separately, dolly mixtures are a fiendishly clever mix of jelly, pastes, and the highly covered—and coveted—cube sweet, coming in purple, reddish pink, or green (green being the least popular, of course). The natural resilience of the cube, when taken with the softer fondant of the layered rectangle, the inner tube, and of course, the sugared jelly, combines to form an entirely satisfactory trinity, together or separately. Although the advent of the "giant" packet (and the encroaching hegemony of those filthy *Name Deleted*, all future reference to whom has been removed on legal advice) has mostly been a bad thing, producing sweet exhaustion, obesity, and a cudlike, bovine chewing without tasting in front of 42-inch televisions pumping out garbage twenty-four hours a day, ruining our children and all future generations, here an exception can be made.

In the case of dolly mixtures, the move to the larger packets, or indeed anything that reminds the more mature sweet buyer of their delicate, balanced triangle of excellence, can only be commended as a good thing.

1942

Lilian's father looked at her with a quizzical expression on his face. "So just a night out with your friend, is it?" he asked, poking at his bacon and eggs. They kept a few hens out the back still like most people, supplementing their rations, and the vegetable garden had been there as long as the cottage itself.

Lilian looked again at the little pot of rouge Margaret had given her. She wasn't exactly sure what to do with it. Sometimes she thought life had dealt her an unfair hand, not just in losing her mother—there were plenty of motherless and fatherless children among her acquaintances—but in having three big brothers and no big sisters, meaning there was barely anyone to give her the merest hint of feminine insight. She could talk to Neddy about just about anything, but not boys. Terence was far too straitlaced, and Gordon was a grub, that much was obvious.

Her friend Margaret tried to help, but Margaret was daft as a brush and boy-mad and only wanted to get married and kiss, and Lilian was never quite sure whether to follow her advice or not. She dabbed a little on her cheeks.

"Ah, now you look like you've been hauling in the fields all day," said her father, realizing as he did so it was exactly the wrong thing to say to his only daughter, sharp, clever Lilian, whom he loved dearly but didn't even pretend to understand.

Lilian sniffed and pulled down last year's sprigged cotton dress. Its sleeves now looked dated, and the waist was dropped too low to show off her pretty figure; she looked like a stick, she thought, all up and down. Still, at least Margaret could do her hair. And sure enough, here came Margaret now, clattering along on her bicycle, her hair tightly lacquered and her bright eye shadow and dress as tight as modesty allowed, almost disguising the slight cast of her eye. Margaret never mentioned her eye, but she hated her front snaggletooth and would often spend the entire evening talking with her hand directly positioned in front of it. Despite this, she was funny and loyal and daft, and Lilian loved her.

"Come on, you," said Margaret. "Let's be having you."

"Well, you look like you're going to kill them fellas tonight," said Lilian's father, who found Margaret much more the type of straightforward girl he could get a handle on.

Margaret giggled and squeaked at him and told him to hold his tongue, heating up the rollers by the fire and imprecating Lilian to sit still, even when the smell of singed hair was rising up through the little kitchen.

Lilian tried to sit still, but she couldn't deny the truth—that since last week, she had thought of little else but Henry Carr. Suddenly, everything she had found irritating about him—the teasing, the cheek, the hanging around the shop—now that it had stopped, she found she missed it beyond reason. The idea of him walking out with Ida filled her with horror. Gerda had not, in the end, been sacked, but she had been demoted and was keeping her head very low in the village. But tonight, maybe tonight, with her new hair…maybe Henry would look at her again the way he'd looked when they'd patched up Hetty. And this time, she would hold his gaze and toss her lovely black hair, and…

"Darn it," said Margaret, who loved American movies to distraction.

"What?"

"Never mind."

"What?"

"It smells like that farrier fire we had last spring in here, do you remember?" said her father. "Those horses screamed like the very devil."

"What are you DOING?" said Lilian, scrambling to her feet and trying to see her whole head in the very small mirror that hung in the hallway.

Margaret unsuccessfully tried to hide a small ringlet of burned-off curls behind her mauve dress. "MARGARET!"

"I'm sorry!"

"You've ruined it!"

"I didn't mean to!"

"But it's ruined!"

"There, there girls," said her dad, laughing heartily, and suddenly, as if on a whim, he took out the bottle of Johnson the butcher's homemade rhubarb wine he kept for special occasions.

"Come on," he said. "Let's have a glass. Celebrate two lovely girls going out to have a good time."

"One of them half-bald," said Lilian crossly. This was a disaster.

"And no messing about, you understand? If you have to dance with a chap, I want someone nice, local, good family. None of that seasonal Derby mob."

The girls blushed bright red, and Margaret let out a haw-haw peal of laughter as they waited, nervously, until it was time.

There was a large group of young men down for the harvest, hence the dance. Margaret giggled immediately, her hand in front of her mouth. Lilian rolled her eyes as if to indicate that all that was beneath her, trying her best not to betray that she did, indeed, have her heart set on finding a nice young man. Just a very specific one, that was all.

Her father poured them all a small glass of wine. He knew other fathers worried about their daughters, but if anything, he wished he could worry more about Lilian. And with three sons in the war—they'd said Gordon didn't have to go, could stay and mind the shop, but his headstrong youngest son was having none of it. He had enough to worry about. But he knew it wasn't easy for her, the last one left behind and the only girl. When the boys came back on leave and told their stories of the big cities and the shows and the lights, he felt sad for Lilian, stuck here with the shop. But what else could they do? A living was a living, even in wartime. Still, she could do with a bit of fun. She wasn't a daft piece of stuff like Margaret, or a sly little piece like Ida Delia Fontayne, but she was a decent sort, and he'd like her to meet a decent chap. *Before the war took 'em all*, he thought glumly and drained his glass.

Feeling warm and jolly and just about over the hair incident, Lilian and Margaret set off on their bicycles toward the village hall, Lilian's heart rattling against her chest, her cheeks flushed without the need of makeup, eyes sparkling. The summer air was warm for once, clear and gentle, the stars just starting to come out overhead. Even missing a hank of hair, Lilian felt as close as she ever had to beautiful.

• • • •

2012

Rosie was determined to start the next day afresh. She smiled at her aunt, who was coming to the table and trying not to look overcurious about the porridge with wild honey, full cream, and fresh blueberries Rosie had made for her. "Lilian," she said, "did you ever take legal advice about Haribo?"

Lilian looked shifty.

"I can't talk about that," she said, pursing her lips, and sat herself down. "What's this?"

"It's to..." Rosie nearly said "fatten you up" before realizing that was unlikely to go down well.

"It's the fashion breakfast," she said. "It's what the models eat."

Lilian sniffed. Today she was wearing a cerise shift dress with a bright red scarf tied at the neck. It could have looked a bit peculiar, but with Lilian's silver hair nicely done at the back, it actually looked rather chic.

"Where did you get the cream?" said Lilian.

"Umm, the grocery store," said Rosie.

"Well don't. The Isitts have a perfectly good dairy farm just down the road. Just don't get put off..."

"Put off by what?"

"Never mind," said Lilian. "That's where you go. It's two miles out the village, turn left, down the hill. Can't miss it. Milk too. Take the empty bottles back."

"You want me to walk two miles with empty milk bottles?"

Lilian raised her eyebrows.

"No, of course not. You can take the bike."

"Hmm," said Rosie. "Well, there's a problem with that."

Lilian made her step out into the bright golden morning. (Rosie didn't trust it, though, and was leaving nothing to chance. Although the shops in town seemed to sell only those waxed jackets, they'd begun to look increasingly attractive in light of how her H&M shearling was bearing up, i.e., not at all, and it still smelled damp from the day before. Plus, she was, as she reflected, absolutely broke.) Rosie followed Lilian out behind the little cottage and into the dreamy garden.

"In there," said Lilian, indicating a small shed. Just the walk into the garden had puffed her out.

"Seriously?"

Lilian just nodded her head toward the door, and Rosie finally did as she was bid, heaving and straining to open the rusty bolts.

Inside was a huge, black metal spider of a thing, weighing a ton. Rosie popped her head back out.

"You're not serious," she yelled.

"Are you here to help me or not?"

Rosie hauled it out. It was the size of a small tank. She maneuvered it out and leaned it against the wall. They both stared at it.

"What is it?" she asked finally.

Lilian looked at her in consternation. "That's my bike!! I'm going to let you use it. It's not that I can't because of my hip or anything. It's just that I don't want to."

The bike was very old, black, with a huge basket up in front. It looked like something the witch rode in *The Wizard of Oz*.

"Yes, well, there's only one problem with that. I can't ride a bike," Rosie protested.

Lilian's substantial eyebrows shot up. "You *can't*?"

Rosie metaphorically backpedaled furiously.

"Well, of course I can… I mean, I did when I was younger. Obviously."

Rosie wasn't sure her mother occasionally taking her and Pip to the park and sitting and having a flask of tea and a cigarette while they wheeled their secondhand bikes around then dumped them to play on the climbing frames really counted.

You couldn't really ride your bikes on the roads where Rosie grew up—well, some kids were allowed, but not them—and you couldn't ride them to school or they'd get stolen, so Rosie had never really gotten in the habit. Who thought success in your adult life would depend on whether or not you could ride a bicycle anyway?

"You know," said Lilian, "you're in luck. I'll get Jake Randall around. He fixes bikes for the kids in the village. I'll send him around when we're done, and he'll fix it up for you pronto. He'll do anything for some highland toffee."

Rosie sighed and headed back indoors again.

"I'm supposed to be looking after YOU," she said as a parting shot.

"You will be," retorted Lilian. "When you pick up the milk and cream. And do notice which of us is wearing pajamas in the street… Hello, Vicar!" she called out to the passing man in the dark suit. Rosie scampered up the stairs.

• • • •

And there wasn't even any point, Rosie thought, in getting dressed up today, given the horrible job of emptying out the shop, so she was steeled for the arched eyebrows by the time she came back downstairs in her old jeans and a fleece, her bouncing black curls forced up in a floral scarf. Lilian glanced over.

"So Angie says you have kind of a boyfriend?" she inquired as Rosie filled a large bucket with soapy water and grabbed a scrubbing brush from under the large white butler's sink.

"Why did I ever think you were a quiet, frail old lady when you used to visit us? You're actually really nosy."

"Because," said Lilian dramatically, "I only ever came to your house in London when I was recovering. From adventures."

"What sort of adventures?"

"I'm not just an old lady who runs a sweetshop, you know."

"Well," said Rosie, "tell me about them."

"I'm afraid not," said Lilian, picking up the empty breakfast bowls. Rosie noticed Lilian's had been scraped clean. "It's nearly time for *The Archers*."

"Well, I won't have time to tell you about Gerard then."

"Gerard? What kind of a name is that? Sounds very modern."

"Yes, amazingly the man I'm going out with isn't a hundred years old."

Lilian looked expectant.

"Well," said Rosie, "he's little and cute…"

"Sounds like a squirrel," sniffed Lilian.

"He's a pharmacist," said Rosie.

"Not a doctor then?"

"No, it's completely different," said Rosie, not revealing that Gerard had never quite gotten over applying and failing to get in to medical school. "It's a really responsible job. He's really good at it."

"Putting bum cream in paper bags?" said Lilian.

"If you're going to be rude, we don't have to talk at all," said Rosie. "In fact, I want to get started anyway."

Rosie picked up the heavy brass keys from the sideboard.

"What are you doing?" said Lilian suspiciously. "Get started on what?"

"One of the things I came here to do," said Rosie in a tone that, on the wards, would brook no arguments. Her mild-mannered mother and brother had always wondered aloud where she'd gotten it from. Rosie was beginning to figure out the answer. "Sort out your shop."

• • • •

Lilian had a radio in the shop too, and Rosie retuned it from Radio 4 to Radio 1 and hauled out a roll of huge black garbage bags. There was nothing for it; a lot of this stuff simply had to go. There wasn't a dishwasher in the little cottage, so she was going to have to wash out all the glass jars by hand too, and they weighed an absolute ton. Still, thanks to a strict matron and a steady training program at St. Mary's, if there was one thing Rosie knew how to do, it was scrub things down, ideally so thoroughly that every germ within a five-mile radius would run cowering in terror. The sun shone again through the grubby windows, making her job easier, as she could spot every line and every smear, every age-old fingerprint and trodden-in line of treacle or caramel. She started at the top and worked down, lining up all the glass jars, sampling everything and checking for sell-by dates; any chocolate with white spots was thrown out instantly.

She washed the dusty old shelves with lemon cleanser till they smelled and looked fresh, blew the dust off the top of the vintage, huge boxes of red velvet chocolates, and decided that although their contents were past saving, she would wash down the boxes and keep them for display purposes. Their classic styles were hard to find these days.

Likewise the tins of travel sweets with vintage images of exotic places printed on the tops, of the Côte d'Azur and great train journeys through the Alps. With a little bit of a spit and polish, they would make a lovely display, and if someone actually did want some travel sweets (although Rosie tended to think that the idea of giving sweets to someone with motion sickness had rather gone away with the amount of vomit doing so tended to produce), she would order some in and stock them through the back.

After all, she was meant to be selling this place as a going concern. But actually, the previous night, a thought had struck her. Rather than get rid of everything and sell a soulless concern, what if—what if—she returned Hopkins's Sweetshop to its glory days *just as it was*, almost like a museum, keeping all the original fixtures and fittings. After all, they were all still here.

Rosie had been so excited by this that she'd leaned out the window at the top of the house (you could just about get a signal) to call Gerard, who said he was at his mum's watching *Midsomer Murders* and could they talk tomorrow, so Rosie called Angie, who'd said to do what she liked as long as she sorted it all out, so Rosie was feeling rather left alone with her idea. But she still thought it was a good one.

Before she got started on the windows, she took a packet of chocolate caramels and a glass of water—she wondered about how her aunt would feel about their installing a coffee machine somewhere. The village, in Rosie's opinion, could be improved about twenty times by the simple installation of a Starbucks. She sat down on the large gray stone step on the pavement to polish up the original brass scales and watch the world go by; a couple of smart-looking ladies clopped by on horses with shopping bags in their hands. Rosie wondered what it would be like to go and get your shopping on a horse. Probably less awful than having to go and get it on a bike, she reflected gloomily, watching the horses clip-clop down the road. One of them stopped to have an enormous poo. The ladies completely ignored it happening and continued chatting on regardless. There was no doubt about it, the countryside certainly was different, Rosie reflected. She watched down the quiet cobbled road as they continued on their way then picked up her scrubbing brush again.

"What's this?"

The voice was snappy with a heavy local accent. It did not sound happy. Rosie looked up, squinting in the sunlight. It was hard to make out the silhouette of the man standing over her, but from what she could see, he was bald and exceptionally thin.

"Hello," she said, scrambling up. "I'm Lilian Hopkins's niece. I'm here helping her out with the shop."

The man took a step back. He wore little round glasses and had peculiarly red lips, which he licked, quickly and nervously, displaying a sharp little tongue and extremely white teeth that glinted obtrusively. Rosie wondered if they were false. He wasn't as tall as Rosie had thought from the step; when he wasn't looming over her, they were about the same height.

"What do you mean, helping her out with it? You mean you're going to reopen it?"

"I haven't decided," said Rosie, staring at him. What was with his tone? This wasn't even any of his business. She thought people were supposed to be nice and friendly in the countryside and that it was London that was cold and unwelcoming. Well, not so far. "We'll see..."

"Well, I don't like that," said the man. "Best thing that happened to this town, that place closing down."

What kind of weirdo is happy when a sweetshop closes down? wondered Rosie.

"Roy deBlaine," said the man. He didn't extend his hand for a shake, more kind of waved it in her general direction. "Town dentist."

"Oh," said Rosie, understanding. "Ah. Hah. Well."

The man peered in the windows, unsmiling.

"Actually, I would have thought a sweetshop would have been good for business?" Rosie risked a joke, but the man didn't smile.

"It's a bloody disgrace," he said.

"Umm, it's only sweets," said Rosie. "I think you'll find the grocery store sells the same kind of stuff. Except they sell lots of fizzy drinks too. Which are far worse."

Roy deBlaine looked at her with the expression of a man who understood far more of the sufferings of the world than she would ever understand.

"It's a bad business," he said. "A damn bad business."

"We'll promote good dental hygiene," promised Rosie suddenly. "We'll put signs up reminding children to brush their teeth after eating a sweetie. And we sell small portions. And we'll sell chewing gum!" She suddenly remembered one of the chapters in her aunt's book was entitled "Why Chewing Gum Is Death." "Well, maybe not chewing gum. But we'll be responsible!"

She realized as she said this that she wasn't actually meant to be opening the shop up again the way she wanted it, just readying it to be sold.

Roy deBlaine sniffed. "Nobody cares," he said. "Nobody cares about the infants with rotting mouths howling and dying with agony. For *sweets*." He hissed the last word, as if it pained him even to say it.

Rosie shot him a look.

"Would you like me to fetch my aunt?"

Roy deBlaine backed off.

"No. Oh no, no, don't do that. No."

And he walked off down the road, muttering. Lilian had painfully come to the door to see what the commotion was.

"Was that that swindler Roy deBlaine? That scrubber. Worst dentist this side of the Pennines. Not that I would know," she added proudly. "I never go."

"You never...LILIAN!" said Rosie in despair. "Anyway, I told him we'd promote good oral hygiene. And maybe sell chewing gum."

"NEVER," said Lilian, turning on her heel and slamming shut the door. Rosie sat down again. "Get back to bed," she tried calling out feebly to her armchair, but without much luck.

• • • •

Rosie returned to her scrubbing rather crossly after that. She wasn't here to make enemies, and really, how passionately could one fight against a sweetshop? They weren't pretending to be healthy. It was a place for treats, for somewhere to come excitedly clutching your pocket money, to look forward to. They didn't pretend to be selling orange juice that turned out to be full of preservatives and sugar or making healthy frozen dinners that turned out to be full of saccharine and salt. They sold honest-to-goodness, up-front sweets, wrapped up in pink and green paper bags… Rosie realized suddenly that she'd drifted away and that she had taken on the shop's identity as hers. She didn't even know what type of bags they used. Those were the bags she used to get in Mrs. McCreadie's shop, on the corner of Blackthorne Road. She wondered where you bought them wholesale. Then she told herself off. She was just here to help out for a little bit. Set her great-aunt up. Obviously she would never again be up for a whole day serving behind the counter, but clearly all her marbles were there. If the shop could pay its way and make a little extra that could pay for a bit of care for her aunt and someone to run the business, then everyone would be happy.

"Penny for 'em," came a gruff voice. She looked up, squinting in the sun, and was greeted by a friendly smile, showing off strong white teeth.

"You Lilian's girl?" he said, his strong country accent made thicker by a very deep voice. Rosie scrambled up, suddenly slightly wishing she wasn't wearing crappy old trousers and a fleece of all things. Maybe she could take off the fleece. Then she remembered that underneath it, she'd pulled on her very faded Race for Life T-shirt, which had breast cancer written all over it. Maybe not.

"I'm Jake," he said, holding out a strong, calloused hand. His hair was the color of straw, some bits lightened by the sun; his face was a walnut brown, the kind of brown that came from working outside all day, not lying by a swimming pool wearing flip-flops. The area around his eyes was creased, but his eyes shone out of them, a very bright blue. "Something about fixing a bike?"

• • • •

By the shed, Rosie watched him work—he had the bike upside down and was gripping the front wheel between his legs as he did something to the gears. She wondered if she could pop off and put some lipstick on.

"Want a cup of tea?" she asked.

"No, you're all right, ducky," said Jake.

Rosie didn't even notice her arriving, but suddenly Lilian was at her elbow. "Enjoying the view?" said Lilian, chuckling to herself.

"Did you do this on purpose?" said Rosie.

"Yes," said Lilian. "But I thought you'd have washed your hair."

"I know," groaned Rosie as Jake flipped over the heavy bike as if it were nothing, pausing only to push a muscled arm through his heavy straw hair. "Oh well, I'm sure he's horrible."

"Jake's a pussy cat," said Lilian firmly. "He does all the…I mean he VERY OCCASIONALLY helps me out with the heavy lifting."

"All right, Mrs. Hopkins?" said Jake, glancing up. "Don't you ever oil this thing? It's as stiff as a badger's gate."

"What does that mean?" asked Rosie. Lilian told her to be quiet.

"Thanks so much for fitting us in," said Lilian in a nice voice Rosie hadn't encountered before. "I know you're busy. We'll sort you out with some peppermint ice."

Jake rolled his eyes. "Tell me about it."

"Bad as ever?"

"She's a…she's a…"

Jake looked like he was about to say something harsh. Then, as if realizing he was in the presence of two ladies, he checked himself.

"Okay. Here you go. Good as new," he said, righting the bike and holding it up by the seat.

• • • •

1942

The village hall was wreathed in smoke under the lights and perfume, mixed with a hint of illicit alcohol and sweat, and absolutely packed with people, young boys and giggling young girls. There were the boys down to work the harvest and the land girls, whom the local girls roundly shunned, seeing them, with a certain level of accuracy, as competition for the few remaining menfolk. Lilian had tried to chat to them in the shop—she found them fascinating, with their confident ways and various accents—but they kept themselves to themselves. There were soldiers home on leave from all the towns around and an overheated atmosphere engendered by the warm night and the transient population. Lilian felt not just the excitement of looking for someone she desperately wanted to see, but also the sense that she rarely felt of being young and free, not tied down—although, of course, she was, in so many ways. For the first time in her life, it felt, she was walking into this hall without knowing every single person in there. With all the seventeen-year-old confidence she could muster, she felt that this just might be the most important night of her life.

Margaret was in flirt overload, her eye wandering furiously, as they parked their bikes and sidled in. The noise level was overwhelming; on the raised platform at the end, the band members were perspiring in their cheap shirts to keep up with the dancers, who seemed hell-bent on squeezing as much fun and entertainment out of the night as they could, as if they couldn't predict when the next one would be.

Lilian paid for the small ticket at the door and left her cardigan on her bicycle. She might not be wearing the most fashionable dress, she noted, but it was light and cool in the hot sticky room, and her shoes weren't smart with a heel, but they were comfortable. If, of course, anyone asked her to dance. She was almost too scared to scan the room, just in case he wasn't there, and kept her head down as she followed Margaret to the fruit punch stand. Hanging out by the punch was a good place to start and figure out who was where; it was at least better than immediately giving yourself up to being a wallflower, like Merry Foxington, whose pimples were so awful Lilian was extremely impressed she'd come out at all and made a mental note to go and say hello.

Clutching their paper cups nervously, Margaret and Lilian smiled at each other—which was about all that was possible through the noise—and looked around. This was definitely an unusual night for Lipton. The uniformed men were sitting down, looking handsome, with a couple of girls around them, it seemed. They were laughing with each other and playing the big men, telling stories about bravery, and beating ten men, and skirmishes in the sky and at sea. On the opposite wall, eyeing them up, were the harvest boys, those too young to enlist, the traveling groups who fought for no one, and the farmer's boys too important to go off to war. They were sunburned, not smartly dressed in uniforms, and looked awkward. There were no girls crouched around them. Lilian sensed there might be trouble later.

Out on the dance floor, the dresses of the girls shone like parachute silk; there was not much around, but they had made the best of what they had. Cyan blue, primrose yellow—the girls flashed and twirled around the floor to the enthusiastic farmers' band, who were doing their very best Glenn Miller with a double bass, a banjo, an oil drum, two trumpets, and a harmonica. They were laughing overexuberantly, tossing back (Lilian noticed bitterly) perfectly coiled hair, as the Brylcreemed boys threw them about the floor, showing off their moves, sweating and nervous too.

"We have to get a date," whispered Margaret in a state of high excitement. "We have to tonight. I haven't seen so many men since we went to the parade."

Lilian didn't answer. She wasn't interested in too many men. She wasn't interested in being whisked off by a navy man from Scarborough or toyed with by an officer down from Harrogate slumming it. There was only one boy, one mop of unruly nut-brown hair, one pair of laughing nut-brown eyes, who was of the faintest interest to her.

Suddenly, she saw him at the other end of the hall.

• • • •

2012

Rosie looked at Jake the bicycle fixer and did her best to smile at him. She didn't want a bicycle as good as new. She didn't want a bicycle at all.

"I've replaced the tires, oiled the chain, fixed the brakes, and raised the seat…no disrespect, Mrs. Hopkins."

"None taken," said Lilian, sitting on the sun chair. "It is RIDICULOUS that I keep getting shorter. The most appalling design flaw. Among the many, many shocking design flaws that accompany the act of getting older."

She shook her head.

"Still, I'm sure this is being passed into good hands," said Jake. That, Rosie was not sure about at all.

"Well, thank you," Rosie said, hoping Jake would simply leave the bike against the shed, stay for a cup of tea, then when she needed some of her aunt's precious milk supply, she could just call a taxi.

Jake was still standing there.

"Well, let's be having you then. I haven't got all day."

"Oh, well, I'm going to…in a minute…"

"Come on, I need to see if the seat is the right height."

He shook the bike in what was obviously meant to be an encouraging fashion. Her heart in her throat, Rosie slowly stepped forward. This bike was huge and weighed a ton. She held it up to herself tentatively.

"Well, this seems FINE," Rosie said brightly. "Thank you SO much."

"Come on, lass," said Jake again. "Let's be having you."

With a sigh, Rosie threw up her leg and tried to get up on the seat as if she was getting on a horse, all the while conscious of his eyes on her. Once mounted, her feet only just touching the ground, Rosie set her feet to one of the pedals, telling herself fiercely that everyone knew that you never forget how to ride a bicycle. Obviously this motto was probably invented on the assumption that you'd properly learned how to ride one in the first place, but still. Taking a deep breath, Rosie hopped up on the seat and pushed the pedal forward.

In her defense, she nearly made it. She pitched and wobbled and almost, almost, got going, and would have too, if she'd remembered to put her other foot on the other pedal before starting to move, rather than flailing about with her right leg, trying to find it.

As it was, Rosie did a graceless soar across the right-hand side of the handlebars straight into the flower bed, hitting her right shoulder before twisting and landing, winded, on her back, staring at the tiny clouds puffing across the sky.

There was a long silence.

"Miss, would you like a hand?"

Jake's friendly face loomed over her, but actually, for the moment, Rosie felt she was almost more comfortable lying in the flower bed.

"All right," Rosie said finally, standing up and shaking herself like a dog. Her shearling coat was not bearing up to this country life very well. Rosie looked down regretfully at the flower bed.

"Sorry about your lovely flower bed," Rosie said sadly, twisting her shoulder around to check for pain, but it was more her pride than anything.

Lilian sniffed. "I don't know what Angie was thinking of, not teaching you to ride a bicycle."

"She was mostly thinking of us not being squashed to smithereens beneath the wheels of an enormous truck," said Rosie, conscious of being very pink in the face. Lots of her curls were escaping from the floral scarf that was meant to be holding them back.

"I'll just go call a taxi," Rosie mumbled. Jake and Lilian looked at each other and burst out laughing.

"That's right, darling," said Lilian. "You'll find it just beside the Fortnum and Mason, opposite le Caprice beside our National Gallery. There's a whole rank of them. And some unicorns."

Jake smiled uncertainly and glanced at his watch.

"Look," said Lilian, "Jake has to get back. Go cycling with him. He'll help you out."

Rosie rolled her eyes, but with the sense that this day was getting away from her, she allowed herself to be led back to the bicycle. This time, Jake held the end patiently, disregarded her complaints, and made her go a little way then a little further, until finally Rosie turned her head behind her and realized that she was moving and he wasn't holding on to it at all! And it felt amazing; the wind blew in her hair as she started to pick up some speed.

"Easy now," yelled Jake, but Rosie couldn't believe she'd never wanted to do this. Riding a bike was GREAT! Confidently, Rosie took the alleyway at the side of the house. She hadn't, though, realized it was on a downward slope and, being concrete instead of grass, moved very quickly. Before she knew it, she was charging out in the street, completely unable to help herself.

Thankfully there wasn't any traffic coming down the road at that particular moment, but marching down the street was the young doctor from the day before, carrying a heavy leather bag. Rosie attempted an insouciant wave and smile as she sailed past, but that did nothing other than make her wobble alarmingly and cause a slightly concerned look to cross Moray's face.

Still watching him, Rosie didn't realize the bike was continuing to move, and she was about to hit an enormous rut on the other side of the road, where the cobbles ended and the mud began. Swerving to avoid it, she managed to get back onto another road that led downhill via the rutted road toward something marked Isitts' farm, past fields of cows that regarded her as she passed by. She was moving faster, Rosie realized, then faster still, as the inexorable momentum of the gentle downward slope made the bike pick up speed, with brakes that seemed to be doing nothing, her legs flying out, until all she could see in front of her was a gigantic barn and a gray stone farmhouse, looming ominously in front of her. She had only seconds to think how embarrassing it was going to have to be for her mother when Rosie was killed cycling into a wall on the second day of her new life and to wonder in passing what Gerard would say in the eulogy at her funeral. She wondered how much he'd regret not asking her to get engaged before she'd left London and also thought that it really was time to make a will, not that she had anything but debts to leave to anyone, but to specify absolutely and beyond a shadow of a doubt that her mother was getting nothing for insisting she move out to the ridiculous countryside solely in order to get killed.

At the last moment, her adrenalized survival instincts finally kicked in, and Rosie twisted the handlebars to the left, heading around the side of the house through, to her utter horror, a perfectly levelly maintained vegetable patch, with rutabagas and potatoes sprouting in neat rows. She swerved again, now finally losing speed on the level, until she ended up behind the barn, managed to turn a 180-degree semicircle, and inelegantly let herself fall sideways, breathless, into a gigantic pile of straw in the middle of the Isitts' farmyard.

Staring at her from the side of the house were a stern-looking old woman and an old man who was leaning heavily on a walking frame. Both of them had their mouths open. Rosie tried to smile politely, as if crashing into someone's farm was something she did every day. Her head hurt, and she felt a bit stunned, and her elbow had really taken a knock, even if it was in the straw. Suddenly, Rosie was overwhelmed with the desire to burst into tears. Instead, she seized on absolutely the last of her reserves of being-brave-moving-to-a-new-town, half smiled (it hurt), and said, "Hello."

The woman did not smile.

"What the 'eck are you doing?" she said, folding her arms and looking down at Rosie.

Rosie was so fed up she was on the point of saying, "I'm from MI5, checking for sniper activity," when the sound of two sets of running footsteps pounded around the side of the barn. She squinted and raised her head and suddenly thought how much, however embarrassing a time she was having, however disheveled and frankly unwell she appeared, she suddenly didn't feel like an almost-engaged cohabiting type of person at all. Instead, she felt a bit squeaky and slightly giggly. Because, after dimly noting the noise of a car coming to a screeching halt outside, there, both looking very concerned and out of breath, stood Jake and Moray.

• • • •

Rosie sat up as carefully as she was able, checking herself for broken bones. She could anticipate some pretty awkward bruising on her upper arms, never her favorite area at the best of times. She realized she was under the scrutiny of four people—and a cow.

"Umm, two pints of semi-skimmed?" she said shakily, picking a piece of straw out of her head.

"Din you SEE what she did to Pa's vegetable patch?" shouted the woman. "Din you SEE?"

The man didn't look as upset as his wife. In fact, he didn't seem too put out at all. He scratched his head.

"I'm really sorry," said Rosie. "The bike...must have malfunctioned."

Moray crouched down.

"Well, you're certainly making an impression," he muttered as he peered professionally into both her eyes with a tiny flashlight. "How many fingers am I holding up?" he asked her, and Rosie realized that she was actually quite dazed because she wasn't focusing on his fingers at all; she was reflecting on how his eyes were a very unusual mix of blue and green, which probably meant she was concussed or something. Definitely.

"Umm. Four," she said, snapping back. "Definitely."

"And are you drunk or under the influence of any substances..." he asked with a slight moue of amusement around his mouth.

"Is that an offer?" Rosie found herself saying before clutching her hand to her head in horror. "Sorry. Sorry. It's been a big couple of days."

"So can I take that as a no?" said Moray, helping her to her feet.

"Tragically, it is indeed a no," said Rosie, brushing herself down. She smiled. "You are the worst bicycle teacher ever," she said to Jake, who was standing in the corner, looking anxious.

"Why didn't you brake?" he asked. "No, hang on, why did you throw yourself off a hill? This isn't skiing."

"Well, I couldn't brake, could I? I'd just have gone arse over tit."

"Into our vegetable patch," said Mrs. Isitt fiercely. "Oh no, you couldn't, you've already ruined it."

"I am very sorry about that," said Rosie. "I really am. I'm new here."

Mrs. Isitt flared her nostrils with a harrumph that made Rosie wonder if a horse had wandered into the barn.

"While I'm here," said Moray, "Peter, let me take a look at that hip."

"It's fine," said Mrs. Isitt.

"Yes, well, I'd still like to take a look. In passing," said Moray. "Seeing as we have no further casualties."

"Apart from..."

"Yes, yes, the vegetable patch."

Rosie was still blushing from saying something so stupid to Moray, but Jake came up beside her kindly, asking, "Would you like me to get you the cream?"

Rosie smiled gratefully. "I wouldn't want to face Lilian without it." Jake steered her toward the barn door.

"You've got that silage to move," said Mrs. Isitt huffily as he left.

"Yes, Mrs. Isitt," said Jake. "I'll just sort this out."

Rosie followed him obediently. "You work for them?"

Jake shrugged.

"Times are hard," he said in a tone of voice that said he didn't want to talk about it anymore, so Rosie followed him quietly out into the dairy, a large, bare, concrete place.

"It smells funny," she said.

"So do you, to a cow," said Jake. "You get used to it."

"I don't think so."

"Well, where are you from?"

"London."

"London! I've been to London!"

"How did it smell?"

"Terrible," said Jake. "Of frying grease, and noodles, and sweat, and the exhaust from those great ruddy buses."

"Mmm," said Rosie. "And takeaway coffee and Mexican food, and strange hair products and outdoor cigarettes and incense sticks and hot pavement..."

"Yes," said Jake sternly. "Ugh."

Rosie smiled as Jake picked up two plastic-capped water bottles, went to a large silver metal vat, and ladled them full of dense, freshly churned cream.

"No charge today," he said. "But bring back those plastic bottles or else Mrs. Isitt will have my guts for garters. And she will too."

Rosie nodded her head. "But how do I get back up the hill?" she asked. Jake laughed.

"Get a pedal on, girl," he said.

"That is simply not possible," said Rosie severely. "You are kidding."

"Fine," said Jake. "I'll send the helicopter."

"JACOB!" came a shrill voice from outside the barn. "Are you getting on with that silage?"

"I have to go," said Jake. "Bye now!"

And he left Rosie standing there with her foaming bottles of cream, feeling more than a little dazed by the country life she'd expected to find so dull.

• • • •

The bike was absolutely fine, and someone had picked it up and propped it on the side of the barn. There was no one to be seen. Rosie looked longingly at the Land Rover parked outside the austere-looking farmhouse, but there seemed to be nothing else for it. She deposited the milk in the ancient wicker basket at the front and started to push the heavy machine up the steep muddy track.

It took forever. At one point, she was almost tempted to get up and try to ride again, but as soon as she did so, she wobbled horribly and started to slip down the hill backward, so she gave up and recommenced trudging. It was a lot longer to get up than it had been to get down, and at some point, she looked around and appreciated the view of the neat, patchwork fields of the Isitts' dairy farm, the cows roaming the green fields, eating in preparation for their evening milking, and a couple of fields away, a brown and red field being plowed up by a tractor. It is beautiful, thought Rosie, but as she stamped, red-faced, embarrassed, hot, and cross, she didn't care how it looked. All she wanted was a transit card, a Tube station, and a sit-down in a coffee shop. To run into someone who didn't appear to already know all about her. She glanced up the hill. Miles. Dammit. Bugger. She was boiling hot and incredibly thirsty and incredibly pissed off and sick of being a laughingstock, and…

She hardly heard the Land Rover pull up beside her till it

honked, loudly. "Okay, okay," she said, trying to pull the bike off the muddy ruts to the side of the road. "I'm moving! I'm moving! Bloody hell."

Moray leaned out of the window. "Need a lift?"

Even though she would have liked nothing better than to tip the damn thing onto the path and leave it there, Rosie shook her head reluctantly.

"I have this gigantic bike," she said.

"Yes, umm, I can see that," said Moray. "Sling it in the back."

Sure enough, the Land Rover was about the size of a truck. Rosie tried to fling the bike in casually, but the damn thing swung around and knocked her on the shin. Swearing, she manhandled it in upside down, taking the milk out and putting it by the side.

"BUGGER," she shouted.

"Tell me," said Moray when she clambered into the front seat. "Are you always either soaking wet or covered in mud?"

"Have you always lived in a world of rain and mud, even when everyone else followed the industrial revolution and moved?" said Rosie. "Look, it's clouding over again."

This was true. Ominous black clouds had appeared out of nowhere. "How do they even DO that?" Rosie complained.

Moray glanced at her as they continued bumping up the pitted track.

"Why ARE you here?" he asked finally. "Is this some kind of alternative to prison?"

"Yes," said Rosie. "Well, I think so. It's not easy coming to stay somewhere new."

"No," said Moray. "No. It isn't."

"Everyone just thinks I'm some kind of city type who knows nothing about country ways."

"Is that mud on your nose?"

"I don't care," said Rosie crossly, looking to change the subject.

"I'm going home soon." Then she thought back to the farm. "How's that old man doing on his hip? He didn't look too happy."

"Week five," said Moray.

Rosie squinted. "He should be moving better than that. He's mobile, but he's obviously wincing."

Moray glanced at her again.

"I agree. I think that old witch…ahem, I mean, his wife…is forcing him back into stuff he's not ready for. Jake obviously helps out, but I think she's pushing it too far. A little exercise is good…"

"Like digging a vegetable garden," said Rosie regretfully.

"Hmm," said Moray. "But I think she's got him on full-time hoofing, and it's not doing him any favors."

"No," said Rosie. "Maybe if you drew up a plan? One of those ones on really official-looking paper that mentions the word 'insurance' or something? Those are always handy. And have a word with Jake, see if there's some way Mr. Isitt could LOOK like he was working without actually having to move the wrong way?"

Moray raised his eyebrows.

"That might work," he said, pulling up in front of Lilian's house.

"Hmm," said Rosie. "Thanks for the lift."

She got out of the car. Moray jumped out and helped her with the bicycle.

"Thank you," said Rosie. "Now I shall take it into the garden and ceremoniously burn it."

Moray smiled.

"Actually," he said, "if you like…it's always useful to have a nurse's eye around the place. We have a district nurse, but she's quite frightening and marches about looking for things to vaccinate…well, anyway. If you like, I could take you out on my rounds tomorrow. Show you around a little bit. To say thanks for your help yesterday. And for, well, inadvertently getting me to check in on Peter Isitt. He wouldn't come to the office in a million years."

Rosie thought about it.

"Okay," she said. "Will I get absolutely soaking and mucky?"

"Not normally," said Moray. "But seeing as it's you, I expect so."

• • • •

"What's this?" Lilian said, pushing at her soup with her spoon.

"It's more vegetable soup," said Rosie firmly. "With plenty of cream from the top of the milk. And eat plenty of bread. Good bread."

"I would rather," said Lilian, in a dignified fashion, "have a tutti-frutti."

"Well, you can't," said Rosie. "You need to get your strength back. I think we need to get back to work on the shop. Formulate your way ahead when I go back to London."

"Hmm," said Lilian. "And when are we starting? Tomorrow?"

"You're not starting at all. You're getting your strength back."

"And you? Tomorrow?"

"Uh, no, not exactly," said Rosie. "Actually, umm, the local doctor asked me to go with him tomorrow. To, er, show me around. Show me how nice it is here."

Lilian's eyebrows shot up.

"That young whippersnapper. Hmm."

"What hmm?" said Rosie. "It's nothing. He's just being friendly. Well, that wouldn't matter anyway. He's not after me. He's only ever seen me covered in soil. It's just friendliness, that's all. And I have a boyfriend."

"So you say," said Lilian.

Rosie chose to ignore her.

"You'll get yourself a reputation in the village," said Lilian, thickly smearing butter on her bread.

"I think I'm doing that already," said Rosie.

"I think you are too," said Lilian primly. Then they lapsed into silence once more.

You would have to be very ill indeed to consider a lozenge any kind of a treat.

"Come home if you don't like it."

Rosie couldn't believe Gerard had another hangover. He sounded a bit surly, not at all like himself. She'd really wanted to touch base with him just to reassure herself. She had been startled by how daft and girlish she'd been yesterday when Moray and Jake had been helping her up and wanted to get back in touch with the man she really wanted and her real life, which wasn't all mucky and covered in cow. But she'd woken Gerard up on his day off, and it didn't sound like he was best pleased to hear from her.

"You've only been there a few days."

It sounded like he thought she was whining at him continuously, rather than the truth—Rosie had never lived anywhere other than the city, and neither had Gerard. She might as well have moved to Timbuktu. She wished he could be just a little bit more supportive.

"So…so you can't come up this weekend then?" she said, hating herself for sounding like she was begging.

Gerard sighed. "Let me see," he grunted, desperate to get off the phone and get some sleep.

Hanging up, Rosie felt very alone. She and Gerard hardly ever had a cross word, or so she thought. Maybe, it struck her now, they just hadn't been paying attention. She wished he would just propose to her, so she could stop panicking about all this kind of thing. Feel secure. Now, she felt she was careering around the countryside, covered in mud, without a clue what she was doing. She hadn't even had the chance to tell him she was off for the day with a handsome doctor on his rounds, so there.

Dimly, Rosie wondered if Moray thought this was some kind of a date. He wouldn't, surely? Although of course she'd arrived on her own, and she wasn't wearing a ring…just in case, she would have to disabuse him. On the other hand, if he was telling the truth and it was just a professional hand, then that would be the most embarrassing thing ever and probably quash any hopes of them becoming mates…she decided to play it by ear. And at least stop dressing like a bedraggled lamb.

She was going to look pretty and elegant and friendly, but not sluttish or desperate. Outside, it was partly sunny, partly cloudy, but if it was at all wet or messy today, Rosie was determined to stay inside the car. Making interesting conversation with a new friend. Who happened to be pleasingly tall and have a calm manner and a rather naughty smile. But that wasn't important either, and of course she hadn't even noticed. She sighed.

"Lilian, do you have an ironing board?" she called downstairs.

"Are you making yourself up to look cheap?" came the imperious tones. Rosie's new soft diet didn't seem to be softening up Lilian's tongue any, Rosie noticed.

"NO!"

"Well, darling, of course I have an ironing board. Do you know what it's for?" Lilian had been sitting in her chair, daydreaming.

• • • •

1942

The center of the hall was, if anything, even hotter, and at first, among the bright, red, excited faces and sparkling eyes, Lilian wasn't sure she was going to be able to spot him. Margaret was waving gaily and smiling at people she even vaguely recognized, sipping her punch and whispering that she thought some of the hay boys had brewed their own beer, and should she try to get some for them. But Lilian said nothing and had gone stock still, for there, in the far corner, not dancing but engaged in what was clearly some very serious chat, were the two heads, one curly and brown, one blond, a particular, thick, corn-colored shade that Lilian would never like in her life.

Lilian found herself clinging on so tightly to her cup that her knuckles turned white. She felt a furious flush start at her chest and climb up her neck to the very tips of her ears; her entire body felt so suffused with burning heat that she was sure she must be attracting stares. The noise and chatter around her suddenly sounded like so much squawking of birds, and her chest tightened up and made it difficult to breathe. At that exact moment, Henry Carr looked up and saw her stricken face. Not exactly expert in the moods of women, he wondered what was wrong with her. Then, when he tried a cheery smile and received nothing in return, he wondered if it might be something else.

"I'm just going out…to get a breath of air," Lilian managed to gasp to Margaret, who was already entertaining the affections of a young, very short soldier who had teeth not dissimilar to Margaret's.

"Ooh, are you going to get the beer?" said Margaret. "Get some for us, will you?"

The young man smiled at her agreeably, but not before Ida Delia had marched up to the party.

"Lilian," she said. "Are you all right? You look very high colored." Her voice was dripping with fake concern. "It's not Henry, is it?"

At that exact moment, Lilian knew that Ida Delia had set her cap at Henry exactly because she knew Lilian liked him, that it had greatly increased his attractions for her. And what Ida Delia wanted—like the lovely green print dress, with its tiny bird motif all over it—Ida Delia got.

"I mean, there's nothing wrong? It's just every time you see us together, you seem to go all queer!"

She laughed a little tinkly laugh that sounded like someone crushing glass. "Henry! Come say hello to Lilian." Ida waved a hand in a way that implied that Henry was devoted to her, following slowly to her whim.

"I'm just going out to get some air," Lilian managed to choke out again, her eyes stinging.

Henry grinned at her optimistically. "One dance?" he said.

Just then, the ramshackle band struck up a fast-moving jitterbug.

"Oh no, I can't," said Lilian, covered in humiliation. She had waited for him, was expecting him…but there was Ida Delia, smothered in the perfume she insisted came from Paris, her perfectly ringleted blond hair set tight against her forehead. She barely disguised the look she gave Lilian as Henry asked her to dance but covered it well.

"Yes, you should dance with him," she said to Lilian in a superior manner. "He's a very good dancer. Could teach you a thing or two."

The sound of ownership in her voice was so distinct, Lilian immediately fell back to the pecking order at school, when everyone took their cue from Ida all the time. Almost unable to say no, she let Henry take her by the hand and lead her to a tiny uncongested spot in the busy dance floor. Young red-faced soldiers still in heavy tweed trousers were jitterbugging furiously, desperately trying to chat up young ladies who were enjoying the unusual situation of being outnumbered for once.

Instead of attempting all the silly new moves, Henry simply took her in a dance hold and led her around, nimbly bouncing around the floor. Ida Delia had been right; he was a good dancer. Lilian gradually found she was letting her body relax, letting him lead her wherever he wanted to go.

Emboldened, he attempted a spin or two; she flunked the first one but managed the second and suddenly felt herself swept up in the music. They hit every beat, and as Henry bent her back, both of them laughing into each other's eyes, she forgot, for possibly the first time in her life, to be self-conscious, to worry about who was watching, to think about anything other than the person regarding her, twirling her around the floor as if it was the Christmas ball at the great house (which she had never visited, of course), rather than the Lipton scout hall and social club on a chilly Saturday evening with a crowd of demobilized happy military boys. The brash bare bulbs overhead dissolved to shimmering chandeliers, the tin cups next to the punch to crystal goblets full of the finest wine, the plank walls hung with tapestries and plush thick curtains, and her skimpy, dull dress became a full, swinging gown. And her partner was the handsomest, kindest, most charming prince she had ever imagined.

As the dance ended, their hands lingered, unwilling to let go. Ida Delia, of course, was there, clucking over them like a mother hen.

"Well, there you go," she said to Lilian. "Did you enjoy that? I told you he was a good dancer."

She slipped her hand through his arm like she owned him.

"Now come on, get me a drink," she whispered to him. Henry looked at Lilian askance. Lilian was confused. After the way they'd danced...he wasn't going to let Ida Delia just grab him off, was he?

• • • •

Henry was confused. This girl was all over him. All he wanted to do was dance more with Lilian. But even as he looked at her, she was retreating with that anxious look on her face again. When they'd danced, she had glowed; she had looked straight at him, and it had felt...well, it had felt like nothing he'd ever felt before. But now she looked awkward, uncomfortable, like she didn't want to be there with him at all. Even now, she reversed into a table full of half-discarded cups—and suddenly upended it, without realizing.

Ida Delia erupted into high-pitched peals of laughter. Henry leaped forward to clean up the mess of the collapsed table and hush the expostulations of the soldiers who'd been sitting there. But Lilian, horror-struck, looked at the catastrophe, turned around, and fled.

• • • •

Outside, in the quiet and the coolness of the air, Lilian marched to the end of the field, past the already paired-off couples, breathing in deeply the fresh meadow grass and honeysuckle until she reached the fence at the far end. When the music of the band had fallen far behind her, the smoke had left her nostrils, and she could hear the lambs calling for their mothers in the hills, she grabbed onto the wire and waited for her heart to slow down. She felt, for the first time, unbelievably and dramatically stupid.

The mess, the fuss. He must think she was such a fathead. Going all gooey over one dance then making such an idiot of herself. Looking at the huge stars dripping from the sky above her head, she cursed herself over and over. Then, even though she hated herself for doing it, she turned around. Just in case. Just in case he had seen her, and understood, and come after her. Like David Niven would have done.

There was nobody there. Not even Margaret. Lilian rubbed furiously at the ridiculous rouge she had painted onto her face, vowed never to come to a dance again, and went to find her bike.

By the time Henry had calmed everyone down and finished clearing up the spilled punch and gone into the field to find her, she was gone.

• • • •

2012

Rosie presented herself for inspection, her pretty dark curls washed and hanging loose around her face, with mascara and a touch of blush to try to give her the pretty pink glow she was still waiting for the countryside to bestow on her. She was wearing a black sprigged skirt with opaque tights and a black sweater.

"Can't you girls wear a bit of color?" sniffed Lilian. "SO much more flattering to the skin. Look at me, for instance."

It was true; today Lilian was wearing a lilac top underneath a very pale pink pinafore with heavy silver jewelry. It should, Rosie reflected, make her look like a four-year-old. Instead, the effect was charming.

"You look lovely," said Rosie. "Not sure it would suit me, though."

Lilian harrumphed as a hearty voice yelled out "View hulloooo!" and pushed through the back door without knocking. It was Hetty.

"Oh good, you're up," she announced, looking around expectantly and taking off her gloves.

"How cold was it last night?" asked Lilian.

"A three-dogger," said Hetty, incomprehensibly to Rosie's ears. "Stick the kettle on, will you, toots?"

Rosie belatedly realized this meant her and jumped next door.

"Rosie has been getting up Roy's nose," said Lilian by way of conversation.

"Oh good," said Hetty. "I don't hold with dentists anyway. Ridiculous bourgeois convention."

Rosie peeked her head around the door. Sure enough, Hetty had long, strong-looking yellow teeth, exactly like a horse.

"Nothing wrong with the teeth God gave you. When are you opening up?"

"Well, our Rosie has got herself a date today, so she can't work," said Lilian mischievously.

"I have NOT," said Rosie, feeling her face go hot as she waited for the kettle to boil up. "And you're not having tea, by the way; you're having hot chocolate. And a peanut butter and banana sandwich."

"I don't eat American things," said Lilian. "They were too late entering in the war."

Rosie rolled her eyes and ignored her.

"It's that young Doctor Moray," said Lilian to Hetty. "Taking her out in his car."

"And you accepted?" said Hetty, looking amused.

"Yes!" said Rosie, suddenly cross. "Because it's not 1895, and because I'm not fourteen. So you can mind your own business!"

Hetty and Lilian exchanged another look.

"No," said Hetty. "Obviously you are not even vaguely like a fourteen-year-old."

Rosie stomped back into the kitchen to finish their drinks.

"Of course," said Lilian, her voice carrying effortlessly through the cottage's thick stone walls. "You know why he's asking her?"

"Oh yes," said Hetty cryptically. She harrumphed. "Well, I wish them luck with that. But—and I know she's your niece—but really. I don't think so."

"Why not?" demanded Rosie, furiously pink as she set down the tray. The women looked at her as she came back through.

"Talking to us again, are you?" said Lilian.

"Oh, you'll find out," said Hetty, just as they heard a car horn honk outside.

"Tell me!" said Rosie, cutting up Lilian's sandwiches into small pieces. Although she always protested about the food, Rosie had noticed, she did tend to scoff the lot when Rosie wasn't around.

"Well, I shall just wish you good luck," said Hetty. "I wonder if you can succeed where so many others have failed."

"Are you going out like that?" demanded Lilian. "You can't." Rosie was just wearing a large cardigan.

"Oh, darling, you'll catch your death."

"It's lovely outside! It's summer!"

Hetty sighed. "You are never going to get the hang of this, are you?"

"And I look nice."

Hetty shook her head then picked up her huge waterproof raincoat with the flaps that came off the shoulders and made her look like a particularly hefty, ruddy-cheeked velociraptor.

"Here, take this. I've got the stockman's in the car."

Rosie stared at it.

"I can't take that."

"Course you can," said Lilian. "It's going to be pouring by eleven. You'll be drenched through."

"I need a new coat," muttered Rosie to herself.

"Yes, you DO," said Hetty. "But until then, this will be perfectly adequate."

"NO!" said Rosie, struggling, but resistance was useless. Hetty forced her into the enormous overcoat, which smelled of hay and dog. Rosie caught a glimpse of herself in the mirror above the fireplace. She looked like a murderous fisherman.

"I'm sure I'm…"

"Not a word," said Hetty in a regal voice that brooked no argument. Was she, Rosie found herself wondering, actually in charge? Were you legally obliged to do what the lady of the village said? She'd have to check up on it.

"Off you go now!"

"And tell us everything when you get back!" pealed Lilian, who was obviously finding all of this hilarious and the arrival of Rosie clearly some huge entertainment package on a par with DVR.

• • • •

Moray stared at the figure emerging from the cottage with that same twitch of amusement around his mouth. Rosie wasn't sure whether to find it charming or irritating.

"I'm sorry," he said, leaning against his Land Rover with his arms folded. He was wearing a well-worn tweed jacket that looked slightly too big for him, a checked shirt, and a green tie. "I was looking for a new girl. You, it is clear, have been here for generations."

"Shut up," said Rosie. "It was Lady Lipton's fault."

"That's her coat?" said Moray. "She IS grateful we saved Bran."

"It's a loaner. Can I take it off and put it in the back?"

"If you like," said Moray. "But it's going to hose it down in about forty minutes. You may want to keep it close by."

"But it smells absolutely horrible."

"Does it?"

"You are such a country lubber! Of course it does! Look!"

Rosie picked out a piece of hay from the pocket. Moray glanced at it. "Oh look," he said. "A Tube ticket."

"We don't have Tube tickets anymore," said Rosie loftily.

"Oh yes? Have they stopped charging for ramming you in like slaughterhouse cattle and making you stick your nose in a stranger's armpit for two hours a day?"

Rosie didn't deign this as worthy of response. "So, what's this in aid of then?" she said.

"Well, I thought you might like a ride-along," said Moray carefully. "Show you a bit of the town and so on."

"So you won't be needing my professional opinion?" said Rosie, smiling. "What happens around here anyway? Goat bites?"

Moray raised his eyebrows.

"Well," he said. "Let's get the morning calls out of the way first."

They popped in on a heavily pregnant young woman who didn't have a car and who demanded to know if Rosie had children. When Rosie said she didn't, she ignored her after that.

Then they went to see Anton Swinley, who had hurt his back in a truck-driving accident six years before and since then had made it his life's ambition to become Britain's fattest man. He had fallen well short of that, but he still had various medical conditions, not least of which was unpleasant skin, that were a lot easier to cope with when two people were doing them.

Moray looked at her, a tad guiltily.

"I've brought you lunch for later," he said.

Rosie looked back at him. "I hope it's not pork scratchings," she said quietly but readily put the rubber gloves on.

"Ooh," Anton was saying in a wheezy voice. Next to his bed was a large respirator that helped him sleep. "You're going to reopen that sweetshop! I really love Lily's sweetshop. Chocolate caramels... fudge squares..."

"Hmm," said Rosie, scrubbing away. She didn't mind at all the unpleasant jobs—they were part of life. Bodies were bodies, and someone had to do it. She did, though, slightly mind the slightly hunky doctor, who'd started at the bottom end, having to see her in such unromantic circumstances. Obviously she wasn't looking for a man. Obviously not; she had a perfectly lovely man waiting at home. A perfectly lovely man, she tried to ignore a voice in her head saying, who seemed to have been out drinking till all hours since the second she'd left and started crashing at his mum's. A perfectly lovely man who'd been very happy to move into her flat and pay a monumentally tiny amount toward the mortgage she'd manage to fix at the right time while seemingly using it as a crash pad to go out with his mates and...the man she loved, she told herself firmly. The man she loved, in the flat she loved, in the city she loved, where her future lay, firmly planned out ahead.

On the other hand, it would be nice to know, whatever Lilian and Hetty appeared to think, that it was possible for her to be perceived as an attractive woman, someone you might want to take out on a date. When she'd seen Moray, tall, handsome, humorous, leaning on his car that morning, her heart, however much she tried to deny it, had skipped. Just a tiny bit. Just a tiny bit to show there was a tiny flicker of life in her yet. Just because she was taken, she told herself, didn't mean she was dead.

Plus, it hardly mattered. It seemed, though, more than likely that if you fancied someone, you probably wouldn't take them on a first date to scrub down a morbidly obese man's fungal skin folds. Yes. Pretty unlikely. She'd been out of the game for a while now, but it was unlikely to have changed that much. So. Nothing to worry about at all. So she should try to stop sneaking peeks at his eyes, to see if they really were that color.

"Doesn't your health visitor have a word with you about how many sweets you can have?" Rosie asked.

Anton and his wife, a surprisingly petite woman, both shook their heads. The fact that she was petite was slightly less surprising than that he had a wife at all, thought Rosie. Maybe the man shortage was even worse than she thought.

"A health what?" said Anton.

"Someone who could maybe discuss the effects of your, ahem, lifestyle choices on your health outcomes," said Rosie.

Anton and his wife looked at one another for a second.

"Well," said the wife tentatively, "we watch those fat TV shows, don't we?"

"Yes," said Anton, nodding his head, which was oddly stretched by all the bulbous chins coming out underneath it. "Yeah, we do. All of them."

"But you don't think to do any of the things they say?" said Rosie.

"Oh yes," said Anton.

"Yes," said his wife. "We're going to fill in the forms. They come and give you a haircut and all sorts of things."

"Well," said Rosie. "Even if you don't actually get on the shows, I'm sure there're plenty of other useful tips you could take from them."

"Oh, I'll get on the show," said Anton proudly. "I had four bacon sandwiches this morning. Four! That should do it."

Rosie shot a look at Moray, whose face betrayed nothing.

"But if you followed what they say about fruit and vegetables and exercise, you wouldn't need to go on the show! You could live your life much more easily instead!"

Anton looked confused then looked at his wife and back at her again.

"Are you going to have those violet creams when you open your shop again?"

Rosie looked surprised. "I hadn't thought of it. Do you think there's much call? They're a bit out of fashion these days."

"Not with me," said Anton proudly. "I love my crèmes, don't I, love?" His wife beamed proudly. "Violet are the best, but I'm not that fussy really. Coffee. Raspberry."

"I bet you do well at Christmas," said Rosie. "Loads of people hate them."

"I know," said Anton. "It's my party trick, you know."

"What is?"

"I can tell you which Revel is which…without even touching them!"

"Wow," said Rosie. "Maybe we could get you down to the shop to do that!"

"Hmm," said Anton.

"No, I'm serious…if you manage to get yourself together and walk down, we'll have a display event and people can bet against you. It'll be great."

Anton's eyes lit up.

"That WOULD be great. I could hustle them a bit, just to get them started. Mix up a peanut and a raisin."

"Which is a rube's error," said Rosie seriously.

"Right…"

Moray harrumphed, and as they finished up, handed over various large bottles of emollient creams with instructions to Anton's wife to lay them on properly.

"This is the only cream I want you anywhere near," he said pointedly.

"Is it worth giving you this for the bath?" he said, looking critically at a large white bottle of bath salts. The woman shook her head.

"Me in a bath!" said Anton. "They'd never get me out again! We'd need to get the fire brigade in! From the zoo!"

He and his wife started to chuckle. They were still giggling as Moray and Rosie left the house, which did smell of bacon.

Moray took the hilltop road. "So we see one patient who's eating himself to death and you suggest he eats more?"

"I did not, I think you'll find, suggest anything of the sort," said Rosie. "I dangled a carrot. Okay, a carrot made of icing, but nonetheless. I have tempted him with something that involves getting out of the house. And getting out of the house is the first step on this. Trust me. I've worked on bariatrics. I've cleaned stuff out of crevasses I thought were starting a new civilization."

Moray shot her a look.

"Okay," he said. "Maybe you can be OCCASIONALLY useful when I'm not digging you out of ditches."

That still didn't sound much like a date, Rosie thought. Useful wasn't a word you used about a date. It was a word you used about a stapler. No. Good. Best to put the whole thing behind her.

"It's hard," said Moray. "I can't yell at Anton. We are the whole support team out here," he said. "But we're not the police. It's not illegal."

"That's what we used to say when they brought in the same drug addicts four times a week," said Rosie. "Of course, drugs ARE illegal, but the same principle applies. Do what you can, keep moving on. Patch and dispatch."

"Are you sure you want to open a sweetshop?" said Moray. "Because you still sound a lot like a nurse to me."

"Do you know how many people turn up at sweetshops covered in blood?" asked Rosie pleasantly.

"Almost none?" ventured Moray.

"ALMOST NONE. With a small subsection of skinned knees.

Anyway, I'm not opening up a sweetshop. I'm selling a sweetshop. VERY different."

"And then you're going back to all the drug addicts and the Tube tickets and the mess and the people, are you?"

"It's a wonderful town."

"Mmm."

• • • •

Up higher and higher the Land Rover clung to the road, effortlessly cresting the switchbacks and steep gradients. Now the clouds had cleared away, Rosie could get a proper look around at where she'd ended up. At the very top of the crags, Moray stopped suddenly. From a boulder by the side of the deserted road, Rosie could see for miles to her right and behind her; on her left was the top of the hill.

"Spot of lunch?" asked Moray, and they both got out of the car.

There was no denying it: it was stunning up here. Obviously there were people down there, working and plowing and shouting at Jake and so on—but up here, the sepia autumnal light was broken with weak beams of sun. Shadow and light passed through the valleys and over the softly rolling moors, all divvied up by ancient stone walls, making it look like a gently shaded eiderdown, the oranges and greens and browns merging into one another through the bushes and the trees.

Sheep were dotted around here and there, but all Rosie could hear was the caw of a circling bird; in fact, Rosie felt as if she were seeing the landscape the way a bird would see it, without human concerns. Except that over in the far corner, tucked under a set of hills just next to a forest, like a beautiful woman wearing jeans and a white T-shirt, as if out of politeness not to dazzle the rest of us, was a huge, magnificent mansion. It was full square, with a tower on each corner and all manner of twiddly bits over its millions of windows, as if just waiting for Mr. Darcy to roll up. It was extraordinary.

Rosie realized that the landscape she was looking at, although it felt entirely natural, was in fact totally sculpted—a lake just there, where it could be seen from the house, an orchard of fruit trees, and of course acres and acres of the land that no doubt belonged to whoever sat in that pile, or had, once upon a time. It had been designed by men, which didn't make it any less beautiful. It was like something out of a fairy tale.

Sitting down, Rosie slowly felt all the stresses of the morning, and her new, temporary, awkward life—that her life partner had seemingly no interest in—slowly melt away. Silently, Moray held out a package of waxed paper. Inside was thick, white crusty bread, filled with rare, cold roast beef and a smear of mustard, thick with black pepper, with sliced and salted tomatoes on the side and a bottle of water.

"I picked them up in town," he murmured.

Rosie thanked him, opened them up, and stared out at the view. She felt peaceful—peace and quiet and a place to rest the heart. It was lovely. Rosie was not going to let anyone else bring her down. She took a photo on her phone and tried to send it to Gerard. No signal. Of course not. Rosie found she was pleased.

"This is gorgeous."

"Well, say what you like about Phyllis, she does make a good sandwich," said Moray.

"No, I mean, this…all this."

Rosie indicated the brown and green and gold of the world beneath her feet and pointed to the mansion. "Is that…is that Hetty's place?"

"Do you mean Lady Lipton?" said Moray, sounding amused.

"Umm, yes," said Rosie. "I probably will go back to calling her that now I've seen it. How could you LIVE there? There's, like, a million rooms. You'd never get your wireless to stretch, for starters."

Moray smiled.

"I think she only lives in a little bit of it. Rents the rest out for weddings and film shoots and so on. She opens it up from time to time; the gardens are pretty spectacular. Plus she has to, I think. Costs a fortune to run. She's probably poorer than you."

"I'm not sure that's possible," said Rosie, heaving a sigh.

"What?"

"Oh nothing. I just…I just need to get it together to sell the shop. Quickly."

"Well, that'll be good, won't it?"

"Yes," said Rosie. "Yes, it will." She looked at the big house again. "Wow. Is it just her?"

There was a long pause.

Then Moray changed the subject. "I wonder, can I ask you something of a favor…my next patient."

"Aha," said Rosie, brushing down her hands. "Man, that was an excellent sandwich."

"Mmm," said Moray. For the first time, his effortlessly confident demeanor seemed to wobble a little bit, and he looked slightly unsure of himself.

"Are you trying to bribe me with sandwiches?" said Rosie.

"Mmm," said Moray. "My next patient. He's proving a little… intractable."

"I don't know what that means," said Rosie. "Has he got a gun?"

"I don't think so," said Moray, then looked worried, as if this thought had just occurred to him. "I hope not. God. No. No, definitely not."

"Uh oh," said Rosie.

"He's just…he keeps refusing treatment. And all three of us from the office have been up and he hasn't really wanted to see any of us. And we're just irritating him now. So I wondered if…possibly…a fresh face might clear the way a bit."

"What's wrong with him?"

Moray looked to be handing over a thick file of notes then stopped himself. "Well, I can't give you these," he said.

"No," said Rosie. "Just tell me."

"Actually," said Moray, "why don't you tell me what you think? Once you're inside, just tell him we're going to take a look at it then call me."

"There's no mobile phone signal up here," said Rosie.

"No, CALL me. 'MORAY!' You know."

Rosie swallowed. "I'm not sure about this. Is he violent?"

"No!" said Moray. "No, no, nothing like that. I'm sure. No. No. You're very brave," he said. "I saw that with Bran."

"Am I in more or less danger of being bitten?"

"It's just five minutes," said Moray. "Till we get through the door."

"Or I get shot."

Moray looked at her. "I promise, I wouldn't ask if we weren't...a bit desperate." They got back in the car.

Just over the crest of the hill, where the sun disappeared and the temperature in the car seemed to instantly drop several degrees, was a tiny lane. Who on earth would build a house up here, Rosie wondered. She'd noticed the farm houses tended to be down in the valleys, to protect them from the harsh winds that blew through the region in the long, dark winter months. Well. It was obviously someone who really did NOT like their neighbors.

There was a long drive through a heavily wooded track, blocking out even more light. Rosie began to feel a touch of excitement; perhaps, like the great house down below, this was something else out of a story. It felt like anything could be at the end of the tunnel of trees: a fantastical castle, a great waterfall, a giant beanstalk.

Instead, as the Land Rover cleared the canopy of trees, Rosie found herself looking at the road ahead that led straight to the side of the cliffs. At the end, perched right at the top, and absolutely deserving of its name, was Peak House.

At first glance, Rosie thought it was indeed from a fairy tale—the giant's castle. It was a flat-fronted edifice of gray local stone; it missed being beautiful by its forbidding aspect. It was a little too large, with rows of sash windows, unlit, facing into the late afternoon, where the sun was already leaving and a chill wind starting to blow. Rosie made a mental note as she stepped out of the unheated car to buy one of those really unattractive down-filled parkas that would make her look like a waddling penguin—but keep her warm—as winter approached. Moray smiled gratefully.

"You just stay there and enjoy yourself," said Rosie, starting the long walk toward the front door.

"You just get us in the door," said Moray. "With your exceptional charm. I'll be, uh, right behind you."

Rosie stuck her tongue out at him and trudged on. It was a long way to the huge front door; once red, it had faded badly in the weather. The entire building looked a bit rundown, in need of some care and attention. There was a huge bell, a proper old-fashioned clanging one, by the side of it. Rosie couldn't be meant to pull that, could she? Tentatively, she knocked. There was no answer.

He could be very deaf, of course. Many of her more elderly clients were. "Hello?" Rosie tried tentatively, then louder. "Hello?"

Nothing. There was nothing for it. Biting her lip, Rosie pulled down on the huge bell. The ringing erupted; in the silence of the high hills, it was deafening. There was no response. Inside, Rosie started to feel a tiny bit worried. This did happen on the job of course—sometimes old people, left alone too much, with no friends or relatives still living close by, simply fell asleep in their armchairs and never woke up again. It happened all the time. The older nurses who came to give lectures would tell them horror stories—of bodies fused to sofas, of terrible decomposition. It couldn't happen to her though; Moray wouldn't let that happen. Surely. She glanced behind her, but the Land Rover, parked underneath a tree, was almost completely out of sight. But, Rosie thought, looking up at the big house again, shadows lengthening over the valleys, if it was going to happen anywhere, surely it would be up here, far from anywhere…

Telling herself not to be so stupid—it was just a stupid, spooky, old dark house with possibly a dead person somewhere in it and no mobile connection—Rosie slowly pulled at the door. Sure enough, it was open. So it wasn't the case that they'd just popped out for a pint of milk. The door creaked as if auditioning for a part in a horror movie. Rosie sighed. In her head, she could hear Mike sarcastically saying, "Yeah, Rosie, now go down to the cellar, and watch out for the ax," and she tried to tell herself to calm down. But the sight of the unlit corridor in front of her—dusty wood parquet on the floors and old Victorian pictures on the walls—did nothing to still her heart. Rosie sniffed, tentatively. There was no scent in the air apart from a little dust. Well, that was something. Unless, of course, it was a skeleton already.

"Get a GRIP," Rosie said to herself, then out loud, "HELLO! HELLO!!!"

Nothing. Rosie took a step into the building. She could hear the blood pounding in her ears.

"HELLO!"

The first door on her right revealed a large sitting room with two high-backed chairs around a fireplace. There were books on a shelf and pictures on the wall, but apart from that, no signs of human habitation at all.

Rosie closed the door and reversed back into the hall. Stepping forward again, she nearly screamed when she realized she had caught sight of her own reflection in a large, dull mirror.

"Jesus," Rosie said. This was ridiculous. Rosie marched forward as quickly as she could, past the staircase and on toward the back of the house. The kitchen was always the warmest, so that was the most likely place for anyone…or thing…to be. Anyone.

Rosie pushed open the door quickly, loudly and too forcefully, until it crashed into the wall. Facing away from her was the silhouette of a man, sitting stock still. All the breath twisted out of her body and Rosie gasped. As she stared at the form in front of her, suddenly it twisted around quickly and let out a high-pitched yelp of its own.

"GRRRAAAAARGH!"

For a second, they stared at each other, absolutely paralyzed with fear. Finally, some oxygen made its way to her brain, and Rosie managed to understand that she was looking at (a) a person, (b) a living person, (c) quite a young person, not entirely ugly, as it happened, and (d) he was wearing headphones.

As her brain computed this, the man, looking shaken, took the headphones out of his ears.

"Who the FUCK are you?" he said incredibly loudly. "And what the HELL are you doing in my kitchen?"

8

While all sweets are not born equal, there are many on the layered shelf that perhaps escape the attentions given to the more flashy of the species—the attention-seeking bumblebee stripes of the humbug, or the actual experience of pain that accompanies a red devil or a Wham Bar.

Take, for example, the refresher. It may seem nothing to you, a passing fizz or a consolation prize for when one's pocket funds fail to rise to the challenge of a Toblerone. But the refresher is, in itself, a work of art.

Marvel at the colors: that delicate duck egg blue, the palest powder pink, lemon sorbet, and eau de nil. Wonder at the hours of effort and experimentation that went into balancing the light sugar crunch with the faint but never intrusive fruity fizz upon the tongue. Admire the smart 1930s art deco striped packet and font, which has never needed to be changed or improved upon in its lifetime. Whoever dreamed up and invented anything as beautiful and wondrous as a refresher, which has given so much joy to so many, really deserves a statue.

Rosie was shaken up; there was no denying it. She gave the man a Paddington Bear hard stare, but it had absolutely no effect on him at all—he was still staring at her furiously.

"Oh," he said finally, his voice at a more normal register now he was used to his headphones being off. His eyes fixed on her bag. "What are you? Some nurse?"

"I'm not 'some nurse,'" Rosie said, trying to recover herself. She'd had a very bad fright, at the end of an extremely long couple of days, and was finding it hard to control her emotions. "I'm here to help. And I stood outside in the cold for half an hour ringing your bell, actually."

He glared at her. "Why didn't you come around the back door?" he asked, indicating a glass half door at the back of the kitchen.

"Because I'm not looking for a job as a new under-housemaid," Rosie said. "I didn't know where your back door was. What, you'd rather I go stampeding over your garden, or your hallway?"

There was a pause.

"You're very grumpy for a nurse," said the man eventually.

"Auxiliary nurse," said Rosie.

"Oh well, that explains it," said the man sarcastically.

"And you yelled at me," Rosie said, justifiably, she felt.

The man rolled his eyes. "I reserve the right to yell at anyone who materializes in my kitchen. You're lucky I didn't throw a golf club at you."

"Yes, that's what I feel right now," Rosie said. "Really, really lucky."

They looked at each other.

"I'll just go get the doctor."

"That idiot?" said the man. "Fuck off."

Rosie raised her eyebrows and stuck Moray's bag up on the huge, scrubbed wooden kitchen table. She'd brought it in for him just in case.

"Okay," Rosie said. "Let's take a look at you. Stephen...can I call you Stephen?"

"As opposed to what—Patricia?"

Rosie looked up at him. He hadn't moved out of the chair to greet her. Behind him, leaned up against a kitchen range that was blazing merrily—it was substantially warmer in here than it had been in the rest of the house—was a walking stick. He had very broad shoulders and a large head with a thick brush of black hair. His brows were currently furrowed, but it was easy to follow the lines in his forehead and see that this was often his expression. His eyes were a surprisingly bright blue, given the blackness of his hair. He was sitting upright, and she noticed that his left leg was set out at a stiff angle, held away from the rest of him.

"So it's your leg," Rosie said, taking out her blood pressure cuff.

"Good work, Sherlock," said Stephen. "Actually, it's fine. Don't worry about it. I don't really need anyone to come in anymore."

"Really?" Rosie said. "What happened to you then?"

Stephen snorted.

"You can tell YOU'RE new around here."

"How are you finding getting around?"

"I'm entering the Olympic gymnastics," said Stephen. "Honestly, I'm fine. Tell that horse's arse Moray he can stop these visits."

Rosie gave him a look.

"Could you make me a cup of tea, please?"

"No," said Stephen rudely.

"Well, could you get me a glass of water, please?"

"The glasses are in the cupboard behind you."

Rosie stared him out. With a heavy sigh, eventually Stephen pulled himself out of his seat. Rosie watched him closely. His arms were heavily muscled, Rosie noticed. It was patently obvious how he was getting around, and it wasn't by using his leg. One leg was significantly thinner than the other. Stephen lugged himself to the cupboard.

"It's all right. I've changed my mind," Rosie said. Stephen looked at her crossly, but it was with clear relief that he dropped himself back into the chair.

"Are you going to let me take a look at it?"

"No."

Rosie made some notes rapidly on a piece of paper.

"What are you writing down?"

"Well, I'll need to tell Moray we're going to need a plan for when they have to do the amputation."

"What are you talking about?" said Stephen. "It's fine. It's okay. I'm okay."

Rosie put the pad down with a sigh. "You're nowhere near okay," she said. "You won't even let me see it, you won't put weight on it, I see no evidence you're doing your physical exercises, and you're clearly depressed."

"I am not depressed."

Rosie was too quick for him and snatched up his iPod.

"Leonard Cohen. 'This Mortal Coil'?"

"So that's what they teach you at nursing university? Diagnosis by pop music?"

Rosie looked around. The kitchen was clean and tidy, at least, and a lingering scent of toast was in the air.

"Who's feeding you?"

Stephen shrugged. "Mrs. Laird comes in."

Rosie made a mental note to track down this Mrs. Laird. "And she thinks you're all right, does she?"

Stephen looked as if the thought hadn't crossed his mind. "I suppose. She normally doesn't bother to wake me."

"And apart from that, you're here all alone?"

"I like it."

Rosie glanced out of the large kitchen window. There were views right across the darkening valleys, down to the great house below.

"Lovely views."

"Hmm," said Stephen.

"Which is why you were facing the other way when I came in."

"Look, Nursey, I don't mean to be rude, but could you go now, please?"

"I am—AT LEAST—going to check your blood pressure. You've certainly raised mine."

Rosie came around and took his left arm, which was extremely muscular. The band would hardly fit around it. Rosie fumbled a little as she did it, nervous around his truculence and aware that she was off her turf. He was wearing a pair of baggy cord trousers that were patently too big. Stephen said nothing, sitting as still as a statue. Rosie was peculiarly aware of him so close up.

Rosie checked the dial. Ninety over sixty. Low. "Well, that's fine."

"Thank you, nurse," said Stephen.

"What about eating?"

"Fine."

"Physio?"

"Yeah, yeah, yeah."

"Sleep?"

For the first time, when he paused, Rosie glimpsed a crack in his armor. His voice, which before had sounded confident, if peeved, faltered a little.

"Uh, I…"

Rosie waited him out. When he finally spoke, his voice sounded hoarse. "I never sleep at all."

Rosie looked at him then marked a few more notes on her pad.

"What's that for?"

"You'll see," Rosie said. She packed her kit away.

"You're going now?"

"Yes," Rosie said.

"Good."

"But I'm coming back."

"Don't."

"Well, either I'm coming back or the ambulance is, when they have to take that leg off after all because of neglect."

Stephen looked her straight in the face. "Nurse…"

"Rosie," Rosie said firmly.

"*Rosie*," said Stephen firmly. "You know nothing about neglect. Believe me." Then he picked up his iPod again, clicking it around and around like a sullen teenager and refusing to look at her again.

Rosie looked him up and down for a few minutes. Then she felt in her pocket and withdrew a large pink-striped paper bag of cola cubes she'd brought with her from the shop in case they met any recalcitrant children. Clearly, she had. She left it sitting on the table.

• • • •

Moray was hovering anxiously outside the car. "Can I come in?"

"Umm, probably not," said Rosie.

"But you were in there for ages!" said Moray.

"Did you think he'd shot me with his gun?"

"No! But you have done better than anyone else has. Better than me, better than Hywel."

"I didn't really get anywhere," said Rosie. "His blood pressure is low though. Unhappily so."

"He let you take his blood pressure?"

"Sorry, I know I shouldn't have."

"No, no, that's fine. That's great."

Moray lapsed into silence as they bumped down the hill with the Land Rover's headlights on full beam. Rosie reflected on what she'd just seen. This Stephen Mannering was obviously in all kinds of pain, only about 20 percent of it physical, she reckoned, but the most crucial was getting someone in to take a look at that leg.

He couldn't be up there all by himself, could he? Who lived like that? Where was his family? His siblings? His girlfriend?

"What HAPPENED to him?" she asked out loud.

"God knows," said Moray. "Turned up with an injured leg, missing notes, and an absolutely furious refusal to engage with anyone anywhere who might possibly be able to help him. Something about a military hospital."

"So?"

"If you ask me," said Moray, pulling onto the main street again, "I reckon the silly bugger blew himself up by accident and is too embarrassed to tell anyone."

• • • •

"Are you making kissing noises?" Rosie asked crossly. "You can't make them very well."

"My teeth hurt," said Lilian grumpily. She was sitting on the sofa and most annoyed to be disturbed from her nap. Sleeping these days was her favorite thing. In her dreams, she was always as strong as a horse and there was nothing wrong with her. And she knew, deep down, that having an afternoon nap would keep her up at night, but she couldn't seem to do anything about that either.

"So how was your date? Are you going to get him on your side to get me committed to a mental institution?"

She couldn't help it; she was interested in this girl. Determined and awkward, she reminded her of Lilian herself. Although, of course, they'd been very different in ages. But still. There was definitely something there. And she didn't think much of this fella in London who hadn't bothered to drive her up or phone the house to check she was all right, who hadn't put a ring on her finger or as much as sent a postcard. She didn't think much of him at all.

"Do you want to go to a mental institution?"

"All those old people's homes are mental institutions."

"I'm sure some of them are lovely," said Rosie. "And I'm sure they don't all serve lollipops for supper."

"You'd think, at the end of someone's life, you'd get a chance to eat some sweets and enjoy yourself," grumbled Lilian, "without being pestered every five minutes."

"Yeah, yeah, yeah," said Rosie. "Now eat your banana and honey. How can that not be sweet enough for you?"

Lilian stuck out her tongue like a small child. "Bleurgh. I hate do-gooders."

"I'll get over it," said Rosie.

"And how was your day out with the young chap?"

"Ha," said Rosie. "It's nothing like that at all."

"Oh no?"

"Well, put it this way," sighed Rosie. "It wasn't the worst thing in the world that I was wearing that bloody horse coat."

• • • •

Rosie couldn't shake it, lying in bed that night. For the first time since she'd arrived and everything had been so strange and new, she wasn't absolutely exhausted, collapsing as soon as her head hit the pillow. It was as if her not-a-date with Moray had sent her head bursting, because now, ludicrously, she found she couldn't stop thinking about Stephen Mannering. She wondered if that was just what people did up here. Where life was more old-fashioned, maybe they just had more of the stiff upper lip. Look at her great-aunt. So bottled up, so cross. Obviously a bit of a beauty in her day, there was no way she hadn't had intrigues, hadn't had romance in her life. But did she ever mention it? Did she ever talk about her life, or even think about it? Never. It was all locked away, and she had thrown the key away decades ago, and if this boy didn't sort himself out, the exact same thing might happen to him.

There was still no mobile signal. Rosie cursed then remembered that there was a telephone next to her bed. It was a lovely old thing, and she'd assumed it was just an ornament, but as she picked it up, she could hear the hum.

How, she wondered, had people ever been able to be bothered to dial all these numbers? It took half an hour, because her fingers kept slipping off the keys. Finally, she got through, and it rang. And rang. And rang.

She tried another number.

"Yes?" said Mike. She could tell straightaway this wasn't a good time. Giuseppe was muttering crossly in the background.

"Don't tell him it's me," she said quickly. "He hates me."

Mike snorted. "He hates everyone. Because you hate yourself! PERCHÉ TI ODIO!" he hollered away from the phone. The flood of invective continued, only slightly muffled.

"Umm, yes?" he asked.

"Never mind," said Rosie quickly. "Ehm, just…have you seen Gerard about?"

There was a tiny pause. Rosie assumed Giuseppe was performing rude gestures behind him and paid it no mind.

"Well, yes," said Mike eventually, with a tiny shade of reluctance.

"Oh," said Rosie. "Ehm, how's he looking?"

"You really want to know?" said Mike warily.

"Yes," said Rosie, suddenly feeling fearful. "What is it?"

"Well, okay," said Mike. "But don't say I didn't warn you."

"What?"

"He was looking…" Mike searched for the words carefully. "He was looking…ironed."

There was a long silence. Rosie sighed.

"Oh," she said.

"I know," said Mike, to the accompaniment of a door slamming. "I know."

"I can't…I mean, I really thought…"

"I know."

"I can't believe he's moved back in with his mum. I JUST LEFT."

"She's got him tucking his shirts back in."

They were both quiet. Mike loved Rosie and didn't want to rub it in by talking about it.

"Sometimes," said Rosie, "sometimes I wonder...if he can't look after himself, he's never going to want to look after me, is he? Or..."

The silence continued.

"I'm sure he was just hungry," said Mike optimistically.

"Yes, for fish fingers and beans done just the way he likes them with lots of ketchup in front of Formula One," said Rosie. "Bollocks."

Mike started to get a bit twitchy.

"Listen, I'd better go after Giuseppe...you know what he's like."

"He's a crazy person," said Rosie. "But at least he doesn't live with his mother."

"She's even worse," said Mike. "Chin up, sweets."

• • • •

The next morning, still cross, Rosie took to scrubbing with a ferocity that would have surprised Angie very much if she'd seen it, taking down the removable shelves and washing them, removing every sticky smudge and trace, until they were restored to a slightly paler version of their original red-painted selves. She threw away boxes and boxes of sweets (hiding the garbage bags from Lilian) that were past their best, including toffees, a very iffy-looking Marathon bar, and some radioactive-looking Wham Bars (she did eat a packet of Spangles herself very quickly just for the nostalgia rush), and swilled her bucket of suds repeatedly. The hard manual labor, accompanied by the radio, actually worked a little to up her mood; the day was warm and fine, and about lunchtime, she was considering trying to figure out where Moray had bought that sandwich when she heard a noise and turned around. Coming up the road into the village was a large party of people, starting with a coach pulled by horses and a huge hub of people around it. Rosie wiped her face, which was a little pink, and stood up to get a better look.

It was a wedding party, most of them walking into town, surrounding the coach and horses. In it sat a girl, her dress long and elegant, like a thirties tea dress, and long blond hair tied back simply with flowers. She was very, very young to Rosie's eyes, early twenties, her face pink with unusual amounts of makeup and biting her pink lips with nervous delight. She sat between her parents: the father bald and wearing a ridiculous top hat, his forearms a dark hazel, his belly barely contained by his gray waistcoat, his face one huge smile; and the mother, anxious-looking in fuchsia. Two little flower girls lay on the floor of the open coach, like white posies, their ballet-shod feet wriggling gleefully in the air, their bouquets discarded. Nobody seemed perturbed or was telling them off. Behind, Rosie could now see, was a smart Rolls Royce, traveling very slowly, obviously containing grandparents and older members of the party. And all around were laughing, happy people: some older, teenaged bridesmaids, looking self-conscious and smoothing down their dresses; young men with stiff collars over sunburned necks and new haircuts; fat ladies in big floral dresses; older men with hip flasks; and lots of other children, some from the wedding party, some obviously just there to join in the parade.

People came out of their houses to watch and shout good wishes, car horns honked, and the bells of the church tower at the other end of town started to ring out. Lilian emerged too, slowly and stiffly, leaning on a stick. Rosie was absolutely delighted to see the stick. Accepting that she needed help was Lilian's worst problem by miles. "Look at this," said Rosie.

Lilian looked at the procession, but her dark eyes seemed misty and unfocused. "Yes, well, weddings. Overrated. Waste of time, most of the time."

"What do you mean?" said Rosie.

"Nothing," said Lilian petulantly. "Waste of time, that's all. Waste of everybody's time."

• • • •

1943

They all got their call-up papers in the end, all except the eldest sons, the ones who'd own the land. They got to stay, though many of them didn't want to, managing the land girls, the elderly workers, the itinerants. But nearly everyone else was off, one by one, household by household.

Margaret, too, was off to Derby, going to build munitions in a factory, boy crazy and half mad with excitement at rooming with other girls and at last getting out of her family house, where, as the eldest of six, she rarely had a moment to herself.

"You should come," she implored Lilian. "You must! You know, there are bands playing every night of the week and the forces boys through all the time. It'll just be parties and dancing, and we'll be earning our own money too."

Lilian couldn't admit she wasn't tempted. With the harvest over, the village had simply seemed to shut down, to get smaller and quieter as the pickers moved on and the men all left to go to war. It felt like she was there by herself, tending what felt very much, at the age of seventeen, like a broken heart.

She'd seen Henry and Ida together, of course. That was how it seemed to be now; the girl wouldn't let him alone for a minute. She'd pasted on a cheery smile when she'd seen him, and he'd looked confused then been dragged away. He didn't come in the shop for sweets anymore, she noticed. She missed him hanging around and teasing her about her wild hair and the freckles she detested. Still. That was then. She worked hard, sat up late at night puzzling over the accounts, organized the coupons, weighed and measured, and smiled all day at the little ones counting out sticky pennies, occasionally smacking a dirty, roguish hand that might sneak up over the slabs of peanut brittle that were placed temptingly on the very bottom shelf.

Yes, she was tempted. She didn't want to follow another year doing this, with no friends left in town, nothing to do, no more dances or parties. Nothing, really. And her brothers had spoken so often of the delights of the big city. So she told Margaret she'd think about it, which Margaret immediately took as an exuberant yes and started planning how they would room together and found her a job at the same factory, and with the bounciness of youth, Lilian found that she did have something to look forward to after all.

That was before the telegram.

Her father was not a tall man, but that didn't matter so much; he had always been so strong in himself, had never stopped or broken down when they'd lost their mother, or when he had to raise a girl and three boys by himself, or when war had broken out, although he had certainly been concerned—he remembered the last one. The worry and strains of the boys being away, the shop only just paying its keep—all of these things, Terence Sr. handled with a bad joke and a smile, lighting a cigarette and carrying on.

But not today. When Tom, the wireless boy from the post office, was going through town on his bicycle, hardly anyone could look at him, waiting till he had passed before they turned their heads to see which direction he was headed, sighing in relief when it was not their road or track. Tom hated his job with a passion, and as soon as he turned seventeen and could pass the medical, he was going to join the air force and fly planes, he had decided.

Lilian hadn't even noticed him stop by, busy in the higher reaches, looking for a box of jellied fruits for a young man on leave to give to his sweetheart.

Everyone else, she had been thinking that morning, still wrapped up in herself and seventeen and heartbroken. Everyone else had a sweetheart except for her. And she never would, unless she left this place.

She popped over at lunchtime to have some dinner with her da, to find him, unusually, sitting at the kitchen table. He wasn't moving or smoking, which was most unlike him. He didn't even turn his head when she entered.

"Da?" she said. When he didn't respond, even on the third time of asking, a cold grip of fear clutched at her, and she realized there was a feeling worse than seeing Henry Carr with Ida Delia at the dance. Far worse.

She spotted it immediately without quite realizing what it signified—the ripped envelope, the typewritten sheet. Taking a deep breath, she felt herself go suddenly faint and, conscious she was wobbling, grabbed onto the back of the seat then sat herself down, feeling her vision narrow and her head grow dazed.

"Da," she said again, but he still hadn't heard her. There was only one thing left to know—which? But she didn't have to even read the telegram to know. Of course she knew. It wouldn't be Terence Jr., so steady and thoughtful like her father, responsible, mature, considered. And it wouldn't be Gordon, the youngest, who was a rascal and a troublemaker, who always managed to get himself out of any sticky situation with a bright grin and a hop and a skip and usually some black market goodies. There wasn't a German alive who could get the better of Gordon.

"Ned," she said, as sure of anything as she'd ever been. Sweet, dreamy, easygoing Ned, by far the most handsome and laziest of all the boys, adored by his teachers, petted by the girls, slow to move and respond but with a smile and a kind word for everyone. It could only be Ned.

And sure enough it was. Blown up by a mine on a road. They found out later from a man in the platoon that he'd stopped to pick everyone some apples. So typical. So like him.

Everything in Lilian's life came before and after the telegram.

It amazed her constantly later that something as ridiculous as worrying what another girl thought about her could ever have caused her pain, could ever have mattered, even for an instant. She would never again care what anyone else thought, what anyone else saw. Because when you knew what life really was, what pain and tragedy could do to a person, then the pettiness of life fell away and no one could tell you what to do, not really. Because anyone could go, anyone could die. And it didn't matter how good they were, how brave, how decent, how kind. Because Ned had been all of those things, and it didn't save him any more than it saved any of the rest of them.

"Da," she said again in a blur and, not sure her legs would hold, found herself suddenly on the floor, hugging his legs like she had done as a tiny child. And just as he had done then, without words, he put his hand on her hair, stroking it as her tears soaked through his trouser leg, stroking it over and over again, his confused brain moving in circles, trying to comprehend, trying to manage this piece of new information—that he had lost his darling, darling boy and he was never coming home.

Lilian and her father never spoke of her moving to the city again. By contrast, neither Terence, who took advantage of soldier's tickets after the war and went back to college and became a successful accountant, nor Gordon, who moved to London and wheeled and dealed and eventually fathered four children, including his beloved youngest daughter Angela, could ever face living in Lipton again, with the constant echo of the boy who did not come home.

• • • •

2012

Lilian seemed to come back to herself.

"Oh this," said Lilian. "It's Farmer Blowan's daughter. Taking up with a Romany man. He wasn't happy about that to start with, but he seems to have gotten over it now."

Rosie watched fascinated as one of the children ran up to the coach with a huge knotted wreath of corn. The horses were stopped as the bride took it with grateful thanks, queen for a day, and handed it to her mother, who put it down with care. The little girl practically curtsied and ran back to the side of the road to be congratulated by her own mother.

"A Whitsun wedding," smiled Lilian. "Should be lucky."

"She hardly looks old enough to be getting married," said Rosie, striving to keep the bitterness out of her voice. Watching the scene under blue skies...she would like something like this.

Lilian shot her a look. "What about you?" she asked her. "Are you and your chap going to tie the knot?"

"Hmm," said Rosie. "We like things just how they are, I think."

"Do you?"

"Yes," said Rosie. "When I'm not here looking after invalids..."

"Oi!"

"We have a lovely time. Not tied down...we've got our freedom."

"Oh yes? What do you do?"

"What do you mean?"

"With all your lovely freedom. What do you do?"

"Well, we go to the pub," said Rosie, feeling a bit uncomfortable. "And, you know. Out. To the movies."

Actually, they hardly ever went to the movies. Gerard thought most modern movies were rubbish, which was true, and Rosie didn't like teenagers talking and texting and chucking stuff about, which seemed to be allowed these days and made her feel really old.

"But mostly we just like being in and being together," she said, conscious again that actually staying in did not, in current form, seem to be the kind of thing Gerard liked to do at all, seeing as he'd hared off to his mother's and was out on the town every night.

"You'll meet him soon," said Rosie. "You'll like him." She hoped this was true. Lilian didn't seem to like a lot of people.

"Hmm," said Lilian. "Well. Anyway. She's twenty-two."

"Hmm?!" said Rosie. "Wow."

"How old are you?"

"Thi…umm, why does that matter?"

"It doesn't," said Lilian serenely. "Not at all."

"Twenty-two is ridiculously young to be getting married," said Rosie, thinking there wasn't much point in explaining it to Lilian. It wasn't as if she were likely to know anything about it.

"Good luck!" she called to the bride who passed. Many of the children gazed at her with frank curiosity. Obviously there weren't that many strangers in Lipton, especially not ones who appeared to be fiddling about with a sweetshop.

Impetuously, Rosie turned back into the shop and grabbed a box of cherry lips that weren't past their sell-by date but certainly looked a bit bashed. Running back out, she threw handfuls of the sweets into the crowd and watched the people laugh as the children dived and pounced on them, happy shrieks renting the air.

"Thank you," mouthed the bride, and Rosie couldn't help but smile back as the coach moved on. Lilian was giving her an old-fashioned look, but she steadfastly ignored it. "It's marketing," she hissed out of the corner of her mouth. "That's right, opening up again soon!" she said bouncily out loud.

The party moved on, and Rosie watched them go, her thoughts far away, until she became aware of a presence at about knee height. She looked down into a very serious face with an old-fashioned haircut and steel-rimmed spectacles.

"I think you should know," said the small boy, "I didn't get any sweets."

"Well, you weren't fast enough then, were you?" said Lilian. "You'll know better next time."

The boy and Rosie regarded each other.

"I can't bend down in case I lose my glasses," explained the boy carefully. "Well, Mummy thinks I lose them. Actually sometimes they are knocked off. On purpose. By bad boys."

"That sounds terrible," said Rosie, meaning it.

"Yes," said the boy in an accepting way of the fact of the world having bad people in it. "Yes, it is."

"Well," said Rosie. "Here is a sweetie for you. And do you have any brothers or sisters?"

The boy shook his head.

"Oh. That's a shame. Well, would you like a spare one to give a friend?"

"My friend isn't allowed sweets," said the boy. Rosie had an idea of what the boy and his friend might be like.

"Okay," she said. Then she crouched down and whispered, "Would you like to eat his?"

The boy's already magnified eyes widened. "But I don't want the dentist to come get me," he said.

"Okay," said Rosie. "Just the one then."

"Yes," said the boy hesitantly. "I think that would be best. Thank you very much for having me. Good-bye." He scampered off down the road.

"What a peculiar chap," said Rosie.

"Some academic and his hippy wife," said Lilian scornfully. "They've pampered the bloody life out of him, poor booby. He has a terrible time of it."

"That's awful," said Rosie, genuinely sympathetic. "Well, I like him. What's his name?"

"Edison," said Lilian. "Short for Edison. Have you ever heard anything more ridiculous?"

"Ooh, I rather like it," said Rosie.

Lilian peered over her shoulder through the shop door. "Scrubbing up, are you?"

Her tone was less peevish and sarcastic than usual.

"Yup," said Rosie proudly. She'd covered a lot of ground today. "And I'm doing an inventory."

"What's that?" said Lilian, absentmindedly picking up the box of flying saucers and turning around to go back indoors.

"It's...never mind," said Rosie. "And I'm going to need to see your accounts!" she yelled after the elegantly departing figure, who did nothing apart from wave a bony hand in response.

• • • •

Several hours later, with Lilian napping again and the shop clean as a whistle, the sun streaming in through the newly immaculate mullioned windows, Rosie looked around her with some satisfaction. Then she glanced at her watch. It was only three o'clock, and she wondered what to do. Sighing, she decided she'd better go out and explore.

There was no way it was going to rain, she decided. The coat was frankly doomed, and Hetty's mud duster was just going to stay right there until Hetty came to get it or it crawled back to its owner. Or better, Rosie thought, as soon as she learned to ride that bicycle, maybe she'd ride up to the big house and deliver it personally.

Her mobile rang. She squinted at the unfamiliar number. "Hello?"

"Nurse Rosie?" came the amused sounding tones.

"Moray!" she said, pleased. "What are you doing? If it's catheterization, I'm really incredibly busy."

"Nothing QUITE that exciting," said Moray. "Actually I was going to ask you another one of those special favors."

• • • •

The little road to Peak House looked more fairy tale than ever, with leaves littering the pathway leading up to the flat stone house. Moray didn't park out front, of course, but led the car around the side, honking the horn loudly.

"That'll sort him out if he's got headphones on," he said. Then, getting out of the car, he shouted loudly, "Medical! Medical! Now use the kitchen door."

"Why is everyone so frightened of this guy?" said Rosie, taking the prescription pills Moray had written out, as well as the page of strict instructions.

"I'm not FRIGHTENED of him," said Moray. "Apart from the fact that he shouts a lot and has a gun."

Rosie raised an eyebrow at him.

"I'm not, honestly," said Moray, laughing. "Trust me. I did my training in Glasgow. Very little scares me."

His face turned more serious for an instant.

"He's one of my patients and I'd like him to get well. And it seemed the other day that you might have been getting through to him. I.e., he spoke to you."

"Rudely," added Rosie.

"Yes, but that's more than anyone else has had in a long time. I just wanted to borrow your skills."

"You're a flatterer."

"Plus, I think it was a good move with the sweets."

Rosie smiled. She had a box of little fruit salads with her, and she'd only chewed four so far, Moray two.

"Fine," she said. "If you swing by later and see Lilian. I know she won't make appointments, but she really does need checking out."

Moray shook his head. "It's amazing, you know. I become a doctor to help people, and not one solitary bugger wants me anywhere near them."

A sudden silence fell, in which Rosie felt an overwhelming urge to giggle.

"Okay," she said finally. "I'm going in. And I'm armed." She held up the fruit salads.

Moray smiled. "You're a brick," he said.

Rosie shook her head. "Just what girls love to hear," she said in response. "Keep the engine running."

• • • •

Rosie went straight up to the kitchen door and hammered loudly.

"SWAT strike!" she yelled, then realized immediately that shouting something like that was possibly at best tasteless and at worst dangerous for someone who used to be in the services and wasn't anymore, so she simply tried the handle.

"Stephen? We're here to check up on you."

She needn't have worried about the noise. At first, she got the shock of her life. A man was lying with his head on the table, thick hair flopping over his forearm. Rosie started forward.

"STEPHEN?" she repeated again, and with a jerk, the figure moved, and the head rose from the table.

"Gah?" came out. Clearly completely disoriented, he stared at her through bloodshot eyes. His face was bleary and unshaven, and there was a half-empty whiskey bottle sitting next to him with a dirty glass on the wooden kitchen table.

"Now, now," said Rosie, suddenly overcome by a wave of sympathy for this young wreck of a man. "What's this?"

The apparition blinked at her then rubbed at his bristle. Practically, Rosie filled him a glass of water at the sink—it was freezing cold—and handed it to him. He drank it in one gulp, and his eyes gradually began to focus on her.

"Stephen Mannering," said Rosie. "This is getting out of hand."

Stephen sighed.

"Oh GOD. What do I have to do to get people to leave me alone?"

"Your physiotherapy exercises?" said Rosie tartly.

Stephen looked at her. "Are you the one who's just turned up in the village, can't ride a bike, and is flirting with all the local men?"

"I have no idea why they say the countryside is a hotbed of gossip," said Rosie, huffing. "And I am NOT flirting with all the local men."

"Maybe that's why you're in my kitchen," said Stephen wonderingly.

"No, it is not. I'm in your kitchen because I have some antibiotics for you and I need to make sure you take them."

"How will that work then?"

Rosie took a look at the whiskey bottle.

"How often is that going on then?" she said softly.

Stephen stared at her challengingly.

"Why? Planning on what to haul me off for first—leg rehab or booze?"

"I'm sure I can find somewhere that'll do both," said Rosie. "You won't like it."

Stephen held her gaze for a long time. His eyes were very dark and direct, and the shadows underneath them contrasted with his too-pale complexion and black stubble. Rosie didn't care. She looked around. Once again, the kitchen was tidy, with one plate in the sink and only the empty glass out.

"Mrs. Laird looks after you," she observed. "So obviously SOME help is okay."

"What are you here for again?" said Stephen. "Is this some volunteer program for nosy people who like to be annoying?"

"What would you care?" said Rosie. "Just drink another bottle of whiskey. That will make it all go away."

Stephen breathed a heavy sigh and glanced longingly at the kettle.

"Would you like a cup of tea?" said Rosie.

"Are you going to make me make it?"

Rosie weighed up the options. Ideally, he ought to make it. Anything that got him moving around right about now was a good thing. On the other hand, the chance to talk to him a little, find out what was going on, might be best.

"I'll make it," she said finally.

In fact, Stephen had to get up to go to the bathroom. She pretended to be busying herself at the sink, but instead was watching him like a hawk out of the corner of her eye. He was very thin, even though his frame was big—she felt, suddenly, like she should be feeding him up, like Lilian. His navy blue T-shirt was hanging off him, his flat stomach visible as it flapped up. But though his torso looked young and taut, his gait was like an old man's. It was pitiful to see.

Ten minutes later, the tea was brewing nice and strong in a brown pot, and Rosie had found fresh milk, an untouched box of eggs, and an unopened packet of bacon in the fridge. She lit the stove (which took a couple of tries—the gas popped alarmingly, and Rosie was only ever used to electric burners), located a frying pan, and started to cook up what she decided to call brunch. Stephen descended to find the kitchen warm and smelling good. Rosie turned around to see him scrubbed and looking a lot better in a clean T-shirt with wet hair.

"That's better," she remarked.

"What on earth are you doing?"

"I was hungry," said Rosie. "I'm eating your food. You are quite at liberty to attempt to perform a citizen's arrest."

Stephen sniffed.

"And is that all for you? Is that how you keep your sweetshop-based figure?"

"Can we keep the personal remarks to your health, please?"

"Sorry," said Stephen, looking a bit sheepish, as if he'd overstepped the mark and knew it. "There's nothing wrong with your figure. In fact…"

"Ahem," said Rosie.

There was a silence while Rosie dished up two plates. They smelled wonderful. The bacon hadn't been in a packet but simply wrapped in wax paper. Rosie wondered if it was from a pig he actually knew. That would have made her feel a bit awkward, until she started cooking it. It smelled heavenly. Rosie set down two huge earthenware mugs just filled with strong tea. She'd added sugar to Stephen's. In her experience, everyone liked sugar in their tea really. Anything other than milk and two lumps was just a nod to passing convention. She saw Stephen look at it, weighing up his need to be ornery and difficult against his obvious hunger and a bit of a hangover.

"It's all right," she said. "I won't tell anyone that you lowered yourself to actually eating. I'll tell them you wouldn't talk to me and turned away and went boo-hoo in a corner."

"Is that meant to shock me out of my latent depression?" asked Stephen lazily. "Congratulations. You're clearly an eminent psychiatric genius. Why didn't I think of that?"

"No, it's meant to get you to eat your breakfast," said Rosie, putting out some ketchup.

Sighing heavily, Stephen sat down, carefully not favoring his injured leg. Once again, Rosie found herself desperate to take a look at it. He was being so stupid and bloody-minded about it, as if ignoring the problem would make it go away. And it was so pointless and attention seeking. She wondered idly if this was what having children was like as she put her hand on his fork.

"But first," she said, handing over the antibiotic.

"More pills?" groaned Stephen. "You came all this way just to give me more pills?"

"No," said Rosie. "I came for your wit, charm, and conversation. Now, do I have to make my arm into an airplane?"

Stephen looked longingly at his breakfast. "No," he said.

"Are you sure?" said Rosie. "Bbbbbrrrmmmm...bbrrm..."

"Stop it! Shut up!"

At first, Rosie thought he was joking with her then she realized, somehow, that he was genuinely distressed. He pulled himself together to say, "Could you stop that noise, please?" then quickly and without comment swallowed the pill and started to eat his breakfast, shoveling it in like a man who hadn't eaten properly for a long time.

Rosie sat back, staring at him. There had been genuine anger—no, fear, of course. Anger was just fear made loud. About what, her pretending to be an airplane? That was daft. And serious too. He needed help.

They sat in silence eating, Stephen's ears a little pink as he cleared his plate at rapid speed then sat back, swallowing his tea. Nothing was said till Rosie finally said, "Thank you, Rosie, for the delicious breakfast."

"Thanks," mumbled Stephen, who had gone completely into himself again.

Rosie picked up the pills.

"One three times a day with meals," she said. "I'm going to talk to Mrs. Laird and make her pop in every five minutes if I have to."

"Please don't do that," said Stephen. "I need some time to myself." Rosie thought that was the precise opposite of what he needed.

"And you have to finish the packet," she said. "If you don't, it's pointless, and it makes antibiotics weaker and less likely to work, which means, now you've started the course, that you have to finish it or you're basically killing future generations with invisible bugs."

"Is that so?" said Stephen with a twinge of his former sarcasm.

"Yes," said Rosie. "And also, it takes five seconds for infections to take hold in poor-healing wounds, of which you undoubtedly have one. And if you want to be alone, you don't want an infected wound. Because you will be spending months lying in a bed, surrounded by old men telling you their prostrate problems and coughing all night every night."

Rosie listened to the quiet of the house for a second and took in the great piles of books around the room.

"I just don't think you would like it."

Stephen sat still, and Rosie took the plates over and put them in the dishwasher as he made a halfhearted attempt to tell her not to do that. Then she picked up her bag. Once again, she got the feeling that, although he couldn't possibly articulate it, he would rather she didn't go—better a bossy, judgmental presence in his kitchen than no one at all.

Rosie turned toward him, just at the same moment as he turned toward her, and they found themselves in awkward proximity. It had looked like Stephen was about to say something, but instead Rosie took a step back and he stopped himself. So Rosie leaned toward him instead.

"This…hiding up here," she said softly but clearly. "It won't make it go away, you know. There are ways to make it go away, and I can help you with them, but you're going to have to reach out to somebody. At some point."

Even as she said it, she didn't quite know why; after all, she'd be gone in a few weeks, once she'd sorted out the shop and gotten someone else to run it. Lilian was looking better already. Gerard needed her…well, maybe not needed her exactly, but missed her. She missed her home. She needed to go home, not waste time here.

Anyway, it hardly mattered, as he didn't even bother to reply.

There is no doubt about it. With the possible exception of rock, which is unpleasant in any case and only truly useful as a sword substitute for small boys, peanut brittle really is a killer as far as teeth are concerned. Which would be absolutely all right, if it wasn't such an average slice of confectionery. Its continued existence in a world of Reese's Peanut Butter Cups, possibly the only good invention to come out of America since the potato, remains a mystery, perhaps a nostalgic throwback to predecimal money. The crunchiness of the toffee is liable to send shards into the gums or at least make the experience painful, while the peanuts have the ability to root in between the teeth and nest there, attracting bacteria like a coral reef for weeks on end. Peanut brittle, as well as being slightly unpleasant to eat, is possibly solely responsible for more dental visits than any other sweet alone, with the possible exception of the unwisely bitten molar-cracking gobstopper. Still, what is life without a little danger?

1943

If there were a worse way, a worse possible way for Lilian to see Henry Carr again, she couldn't begin to imagine it. It was horribly, gruesomely, disgustingly horrible; the connection forever in her mind between the man she loved and the brother she had lost would, whenever she looked back on it, make her burn with shame.

Three days after the telegram, the shop was still shut, the drapes down. The people of Lipton, whether they had a penny to rub together or not, had been by, leaving pies and cabbages on their doorstep; letters and notes of condolence were arriving. Alerting Gordon and Terence Junior was a horrible task made worse by an army bureaucracy that, despite having to do the same thing thousands of times a day, still endeavored to make it as soul sapping and difficult as possible. Finally, in the private phone box at the post office, she found a kindly woman who promised to link her message through to Tripoli, where Gordon was stationed with a cavalry unit, but had less luck with Terence, shepherding the navy on the Atlantic, impossible to contact in any way. After an hour, Lilian stumbled out into the street, shocked, suddenly, to find it the same street as always, the same town, the same villagers going about their business, when she had been trying to connect to an entire world, a world in torment and disarray. Of course, Lipton was affected by the war. They all were. But until now, it had been possible to carry on, to take up the slack left by the men, to husband the land, to feel the sun on your face, to think about the normal, everyday events of living.

Until now. Now everything was rotten and stupid and changed, and no one appeared to be paying the least bit of attention. Didn't they KNOW? Didn't they know there was a war on and anyone could die, anything could happen, and everything was awful? Suddenly, in the middle of the street, without thinking how it would look, Lilian spontaneously burst into heartrending sobs.

Henry was the first to notice. He had seen her in the post office and had hovered, long past his dinner hour, to see her when she came out. Ned and he had been in the same class at school; Ned had always laughed at his jokes and pranks, joined in good-naturedly at sports, and been completely equanimous whether he won or lost, sharing his good fortune—his prewar hearty collection of sweets and chocolate—happily with winners and losers alike. He had liked him without knowing him very well; he couldn't imagine how Lilian, who had already lost a parent, could cope with his loss.

And there she was, sinking to her knees in the middle of the square, passersby looking uncomfortable. A young woman displaying emotion so publicly; although most people knew the family, it was still an awkward situation. After all, everyone had sons at war.

Unthinking and furious, Henry rushed forward, appalled no one was looking after the girl.

"Darling," he said, putting a strong arm around her and leading her away. "Darling. Hush."

Lilian barely knew who had picked her up or where they were going till she found herself behind the churchyard, where the village shaded into the woods—Henry thoughtfully kept them well clear of the graveyard—in a shady knoll underneath a huge spreading oak, away from the main street and the post office and kindly but officious women doing their best on the far, far end of a telegraphic wire, and guns and mortars and sweet boys who got out of trucks at the wrong moment. She threw herself into Henry's strong arms and wept and wept and wept.

• • • •

2012

"So where have you been, fannying about all day?" said Lilian.

"Did you say fannying?"

"It's a perfectly normal word, thank you, been around for donkeys."

Rosie boiled up the pasta and started grating all the parmesan cheese. Lilian would get the larger portion, she arranged. It seemed a bit unfair that her job at the moment seemed to be feeding everyone else. And what had Stephen meant about her "sweetshop figure"? Rosie knew she wasn't a supermodel, nor ever likely to qualify, but men had always complimented her curvy hips and little waist and liked the fact that she was short, even though she hated it.

So anyway. Less pasta for her, more for everyone else. She hoped Lilian appreciated it as she led the old lady to the table.

"Actually, I've been seeing YET ANOTHER MAN. All on his own! In his house!" said Rosie in mock-shocked tones. "I am going to get a name for myself as the village tart, Great-Aunt! You will have to send the vicar around to give me a stern talking to."

Lilian snorted. "That vicar makes you look like Julie Andrews. Liberal vicars."

"Why, what's he done?"

"What hasn't he done? Oh, it's all right: do this, disbelieve that, divorce that, marry your farmyard animal of choice."

Rosie let her mutter on as she put down the tea things, then served up the Bolognese.

"Foreign food now, is it?" said Lilian. Rosie was so astonished that someone would think pasta was foreign food that at first she couldn't figure out what she meant.

"Hmm," Lilian said.

"Do you not really like foreign food then?"

Lilian sniffed. "I have never," she announced, in a tone that suggested she was about to discuss her Nobel Prize, "bought garlic in my life!"

"Umm, well done," said Rosie. "Doesn't it grow out in your garden? Wild garlic is just amazing."

Lilian sniffed. "Oh yes, there's some. I usually throw it away."

"You do NOT."

Lilian looked defiant.

"Okay," said Rosie, feeling pleased. "You are going to stop eating all the stock, and I am going to introduce you to all sorts of good things."

"I won't eat them," said Lilian.

"No, I can see that," said Rosie. Lilian had already scarfed up half of her spaghetti Bolognese. Rosie watched her and realized for the first time how difficult life must be when you couldn't even lift a pan for boiling water. How hard it made things. How, even when Lilian was being rude to her, it was better, a million times better, than having no one to talk to at all.

"So it's not SO bad I'm here, is it?" she ventured.

"Well, as long as you're happy," sniffed Lilian, letting Rosie inwardly roll her eyes and remind herself that Lilian pretending she was here for her own good was all part of getting better.

Suddenly, out of the blue, the telephone rang. It was an old-fashioned ringer and made a noise like a fire alarm going off. Rosie jumped six feet.

"Christ," she said when she came down.

"Must be one of your admirers," said Lilian. "Darling, I know Angie didn't raise you in a barn. Where are the napkins?"

She leaned over and picked up the telephone.

"Lipton 453? Oh, hello Angela darling. We were just taking about you."

Rosie picked up some napkins from Lilian's very tidy linen cupboard. Staying in Lilian's house had definitely made her decide to get more organized at home. There wasn't loads of space, but everything had a definite place, and it obviously made Lilian's restricted life a lot easier when everything was tidy and handy. It remained a complete mystery to Rosie how she managed it; all she seemed to do was eat and sleep. Putting the napkins on the table, she began to eavesdrop shamelessly.

"Yes, well, she seems to be doing all right," said Lilian. "She is sleeping around the village, I will say. But young girls don't really mind getting a reputation these days, do they? Positively welcome it."

Rosie harrumphed loudly. Lilian affected not to have heard.

"So all in all she's getting some color back in her cheeks…it's obviously doing her good to get away."

Rosie stopped short. What on earth did Lilian mean?

As soon as she could, Rosie wrested the phone away from Lilian. "MU-UM?" she said.

"Mmm-hmm?" said Angie, sounding a bit distracted. In the background, there was at least one fight going on and two children screeching their heads off.

"Did you tell Lilian I really needed to get away from London?"

"Well, darling, I needed to get her to accept some help, and…"

"But did you think I needed to get away from London?"

There was, just suddenly, a tiny fraction of a pause. Rosie felt completely wobbly.

"But…but why? I mean, everything in London is great!"

"No, no," said her mother. "It was just that Lilian needed someone. And you were between jobs. That was all it was. Definitely. That's all."

"Are you sure?"

"Definitely," said her mum.

"I mean, you like Gerard, don't you?"

Gerard and her mother had met when she was over at Christmastime. He had been cute and cuddly and flirtatious and delightful with her, just like he was with everyone. Everyone liked Gerard; of course they did.

"This is a very bad line," said her mother. "Darling, Meridian needs me. I have to go now."

True enough, there was a loud screaming that, even all the way from Australia, was making its presence felt very clearly.

"Okay," she said. "Bye."

Rosie found she was feeling a bit shaky and handed the phone back to Lilian without complaint.

• • • •

Sitting in the living room, trying to tune the ancient television, Rosie wondered what her mother had meant. Surely it was just a sop to Lilian, to let the proud old bird stand on her own two feet, think she was taking care of her rather than vice versa. That must be it. It must be. On the other hand, Rosie vowed, she was going to get Gerard to come visit sooner rather than later. Then they could be back together and still in love, and she wouldn't have to worry about a thing. Not that she was worried. Definitely not.

Distracted, she hardly noticed the rap on the door. It came again, louder. Rosie got up, wondering if it was Hetty around to give her some grief on something or other, but to her surprise it was Jake, looking a little pink from the sun.

"There you are," he said.

"Well, where else would I be?" said Rosie.

Jake smiled. "Of course. I've just finished work. So come on. Saddle up."

"I am NOT getting on that bicycle again," said Rosie. "No way."

"You need milk for the morning, don't you? Old lady's bones and all that."

"I do not have…oh yes." Rosie saw what he meant. "Anyway, no. I'll get it from the store. I do NOT want to run across Mrs. Isitt again, thank you."

"Oh, she's not so bad," said Jake. Then he reflected. "Okay. She is very, very bad. But she's had a hard life."

"Sitting in her big house drinking milk," said Rosie. "Yes, I see it."

"No, more than that…" Jake's voice trailed off. "Anyway, don't worry about that. You have to come with me now. We have stuff to do."

Rosie faintly protested, "But I'm…" and she turned her hand toward the sitting room. From indoors came the mournful wavering tones of a soap opera. Outside, the sun was gently cresting pink down over the hills, with the faintest touches of indigo just beginning to lick the very edges of the sky.

Jake looked at her with his eyebrows raised. "Yeah?"

"I'll get my coat," said Rosie resignedly.

• • • •

Jake went easy on her to begin with—he was completely amazed to find out she'd never ridden double before—and rode up and down the streets a few times to get her used to it, Rosie sitting on the seat, the wind in her hair, the warm summer air hitting her skin, the sensation of traveling quickly in the open air exciting and new. She found herself starting to giggle then laugh out loud as Jake went faster and faster (waving, she found herself noticing, in a friendly fashion to the vicar as he went past—more grist to the gossip mill she supposed). Then they were taking the slope down to the Isitts' farm, gathering even more speed, but this time with a very clear sense that someone was in control, that this machine could cope with how fast they were going. Rosie let her head tilt back and she let out a happy yelp, amazed at herself—she certainly wouldn't have ever done this at home—war-whooping down the rutted track.

Jake dismounted safely at the bottom, grinning widely.

"Are you always that noisy?" he said. Then he looked suddenly embarrassed, as if he'd asked something cheeky. Which, of course, he had. Rosie was saved from having to answer by noticing the line of gardening instruments lined up against the wall.

"What are those for?"

"For us," said Jake. "You hammered Peter's vegetable garden. We have to put it back together. Or rather you do, but I figured if I left it to you, you'd try sowing packets of chips and chocolate cake and things."

"Ooh, a chip tree," said Rosie. "That's a wonderful idea."

Jake didn't say anything but handed her a hoe and gave her instructions as to what to do with it. Together, in the fading sun of the day, they worked over the patch, raking it and setting it into tidy rows, whereupon Jake let her pop the seeds in—for cabbages, potatoes, and purple sprouting broccoli—at regular intervals. Rosie found to her surprise she rather enjoyed the tidy work, setting up the strings and sticks to guide the growing patterns, then labeling each patch at the end of the row. After an hour of warm work, the entire thing looked much better than it had before.

As the two of them stepped back to admire their handiwork, the very last rays of the setting sun alighted from behind the house, resting on a heavyset woman who was carrying out a tray as if she held a grudge against it.

Mrs. Isitt looked at the new vegetable patch, sniffed, then, without a word, set down the tray and turned back to the house. Jake inspected it. "I think," he said, "that's her way of saying thanks."

On the tray sat two foaming mugs of beer and two plates with gigantic slices of buttered fruitcake alongside a large, pale yellow hunk of cheese. Jake and Rosie sat down side by side on the edge of the grass.

"I don't think I'm going to like this," said Rosie, picking up the tankard. "I'm not really a beer drinker. More rosé."

"More rosé," mimicked Jake. "Well, I am sorry, your majesty. I'll have yours." But when Rosie tried the beer—dark, not too fizzy, not too cold—she found it bitter and a bit peculiar at first, but by the third sip, she was a convert.

"This is GORGEOUS," she said.

"And about the same proof as a bottle of wine," said Jake. "Go easy on it. Old Mr. Isitt has been felling the men of the village with that stuff for years."

Rosie stuck her tongue out at him, took another long draft, giggled, and sank her teeth into the melting, tangy fruitcake.

"Oh God," she sighed. "I am going to get as fat as Mrs. Isitt if I hang around here. This is amazing."

Jake smiled.

"Maybe it's just being outdoors," he said.

"No," said Rosie. "It's because it isn't a kebab or KFC."

"What's KFC?" said Jake.

"Shut up," said Rosie.

"No, I mean it. I've heard of it, but I don't really know what it is."

"Well, you know a chicken, right?" started Rosie. Then, halfway through her beer, the thought of following through the sentence sounded too stupid for words, and she started to laugh.

"Right," said Jake, laughing because she was so helpless.

"And you know frying, right?"

"Right," said Jake.

"Okay," said Rosie, breathless with laughing over something so stupid. "Well, it's just the Kentucky bit you're having the trouble with. Ahahahaha!"

Jake shook his head and munched on his cheese. "You're mad, you are," he observed.

"Who eats cheese with fruitcake?" Rosie wondered, then took another bite of cake, quickly followed by another bite of cheese and a slug of the beer.

"Oh," she said. "Oh, wow."

Jake took a long look at her.

"I think I'd better get you home," he said, neatly gathering up the cups and plates. "Before you start blundering around and muck up that bloody veg patch again."

• • • •

Up the hill, Rosie found the pushing of the bike hilarious for some reason, and when Jake dropped her off at the house, she found herself inadvertently leaning on him.

"Whoops!" she said. Then she leaned in. "But I have…I have a boyfriend, you know. He's not got as many muscles as you though."

Jake moved away as if he'd been scalded.

"I didn't know you had a lad," he said, scowling slightly. Then he looked at her. "Why did you move here without your lad?"

"Umm, it's only..." Rosie suddenly sobered up as she realized that what she had taken for daft flirting might have meant something more.

"Umm, I'm not...I'm not here for very long."

"Oh no?" said Jake, temporarily brightening. "Well, maybe we can still have some fun then."

"Oh...Oh."

Rosie was completely mortified. She hadn't really expected her silliness to mean anything.

Rosie was used to, in London, a world of high-achieving, glamorous women. She never felt in step with them, never felt she could keep up. She was never the one picked on in bars, chatted up on the Tube. There was always somebody younger, more gorgeous, more exotic, wherever she went or turned. Maybe, she wondered deep down, maybe here, where people stayed for a long time, where a lot of young people left the village as soon as they were college age, maybe here, she was the exotic.

Jake was looking at her with a definite spark of interest in his eye. And there was no doubt, she thought regretfully. No doubt at all, he was absolutely gorgeous, blue-eyed and straw-haired and firm-muscled. If she took him to London, he'd be snatched up by some long-limbed, blond-haired Chelsea clotheshorse in about ten seconds flat. She was so used to there being no men around, or at least none she particularly liked or who liked her. She'd been single for two years before she met Gerard. She was out of practice. She smiled anxiously.

To her complete and utter horror, Jake took his hands off his thick blond mop of hair, reached out one thickly muscled arm, and put his hand on her face, gently drawing her toward him.

"What are you doing?" she spluttered, although a part of her found she was curious, smelling his fresh hay scent and feeling the rough calluses of work-hardened hands on her face. But she wasn't crazy, even with the soft golden light of the evening and the faint, slightly sexy scent of the beer on his breath.

"I have a boyfriend! I just told you about him!"

"Yes, in LONDON," said Jake, in the same way you might say "on MARS." "Come on, lass, you're in the country now."

"I very much am NOT!" said Rosie, scrambling backward.

Jake winked at her.

"Oh well," he said. "Worth a shot."

Rosie changed from feeling indignant to feeling slightly peeved. "And that was it? That was your shot?"

Jake shrugged.

"Well, I'm not going to kiss a girl who don't want kissing, am I?"

"It wasn't exactly romantic," complained Rosie. "You could show a bit of dedication."

Jake smiled at her.

"Well, you know where to find me if you want to pedal over…"

Just then, thankfully, in reach of a signal for once, her mobile rang.

Apologetically, she pointed to it, but Jake was already wheeling the bike around the back of the cottage and back into the shed.

"Hey," she said into the phone.

"There you are!" came Gerard's familiar voice. She was ecstatic to hear from him. "It's impossible to get hold of you, you know. Are you switching your phone off?"

"Of course not!" she said. "The signal up here is appalling, that's all."

"Really?" Gerard sounded dubious. A world without consistent mobile signal—he was wedded to his iPhone—seemed very strange to him. "Hmm."

"So," said Rosie, hoping she didn't sound guilty. Because she wasn't guilty. So why did her voice sound so guilty? It was very annoying. "How are you? I haven't had the chance to speak to you properly in ages."

"Oh, you know, babes," said Gerard. "Desperately sad without you."

"Good," said Rosie.

"In fact," said Gerard, "I was wondering if maybe you fancied a bit of..."

"A long weekend?" said Rosie excitedly.

"Phone sex?" said Gerard at precisely the same moment.

"Umm, yes, well..."

Jake came around the back of the house.

"I'll be off now then," he said, but the query was clear in his very loud voice.

"Who's that?" said Gerard.

"No one...just Jake."

"No one?" said Jake. Rosie wanted to shush him but couldn't figure out a way to do that without (a) being hideously rude, and (b) making Gerard very suspicious.

"Jake and I have been planting a vegetable garden," said Rosie in as dignified a manner as she could muster when she was half-pissed, had just been propositioned, and had a horny boyfriend on the phone.

"Yeah," said Jake. "Shall we go get another pint?"

Rosie cursed inwardly and tried to cover the speaker with her hand. "I can't," she said. "I'm taking this very important call."

"Who IS that?" Gerard was yelling.

"I can wait," said Jake, smiling at her again.

Finally, Rosie took the initiative by waving sternly to Jake, going inside the cottage, and closing the door. But with Gerard, the mood was most definitely gone.

10

> Younger children often disdain boiled sweets in favor of a more instant hit, and they are quite right to do so; the boiled sweet is the sweet of the older connoisseur, one who knows that it releases its pleasures slowly. Boiled sweets—particularly boiled butter sweets—are a sweet of contemplation; the relaxed pleasure of the cigar, as against a quick rush that doesn't last and needs to be immediately replicated. So keep the originals, the gobstoppers, the pineapple chunks, and the Red Hots for your slower, more fruitful years. They will repay you in kind.

1943

When there was no one, Lilian felt, to hold on to that autumn, the house was a dismal place. The shop was all but closed; her father, sitting at the scrubbed kitchen table, stared into space; Ned's letters—daft, most of them, full of silly little pictures of dogs and birds—were piled up on the dresser with some stupid, useless medals. And they had no body for burying, nor would ever have, and no brothers home to mourn him. So Lilian had nothing to do but escape, hour after hour, the friendly, pitying faces of the villagers—or worse, the sobbing heartbreak of other families who had suffered their own losses. Lilian had absolutely nothing to give Mrs.

Archer, who had lost her darling only son, with four little girls after that, who would launch herself at near total strangers, talking about how her boy could never sleep at night without her there to tuck him in, that he must not have been sleeping right—he needed his mother, he couldn't do without her, he wasn't himself—which is why he got shot.

She was deranged by grief and threw herself on Lilian as a fellow passenger on this ghost train, this awful ride into oblivion, where everyone else was on another track, but you were shunted off into a siding that went nowhere. Lilian couldn't bear that either.

Henry, though, did nothing, and it was everything. He didn't say anything, didn't mention Ned, didn't engage her in conversation. He just came away as often as he could from the farm, at lunch or in the evening, and let her lie there, her head on his shoulder or sometimes by his knees like a child, and weep till it was out. Then she could go home and make supper and try to get her father to eat and answer questions from the ministry and fill in papers and orders and sometimes—not often, but sometimes—get some sleep.

One morning, just before the dawn, she lay there trying not to think about Ned, sleepless, her eyes gritty, her head feeling like it was an endless loop. The same thoughts, the same fears kept going around and around again, until she couldn't think straight. She was such a mess of exhaustion and fear and horror and gloom that she wanted to black herself out completely, felt like literally hitting her head against the narrow iron bedstead, just to get it to stop for five minutes. As she turned under her hot bedspread once more, she heard the rattle of a little stone against her window.

At first, she got a shock of terror—she had been thinking so strongly about her brother that she thought it was him, summoning her. But as she jumped up, heart pounding, and went toward the front dormer, she saw in the early dawn light a figure wearing brown canvas trousers held up with braces (one of which, she noticed, was missing a button) and a collarless shirt that was open at the neck and had been washed so often that the thin stripe had faded to almost nothing. His throwing arm was behind his sunburned neck, his other supporting his bike. Nothing else stirred in the village, except far away over the hills, where a kite circled lazily.

He looked up at her with that heart-meltingly shy smile and put his fingers to his lips to shush her then beckoned her down.

She dressed in an instant, throwing water from the ewer over her face and rinsing out her mouth, then threw on her plain, old-fashioned day dress. She'd lost all interest in clothes anyway, even though she noticed even this plain old gingham was getting too big for her. She tried pulling a comb through her hair, but without much luck, then crept downstairs through the silent house.

Henry refused to accept her demurral, insisting, all the time in silence, that she get on the bike seat. Worried that someone would see her creeping out of the house, Lilian couldn't do much else but spring on.

He powerfully pedaled off in the direction of his farm. The early morning mists of the dew ascending turned the village and the fields beyond into something out of a dream, as if they were moving through the clouds. As Henry picked up speed, Lilian suddenly began to feel something momentary—a slight lifting, a sense that there was something within her that wasn't just bleak and done and gone and empty. They went effortlessly uphill, then there was a long stretch down into the valley where the Carrs farmed and where they kept their sheep.

As the bike picked up speed going downhill, Lilian exhaled and felt the tension leave her, the resilience of youth bouncing back into her, if only for now. Sitting behind Henry, she watched his strong back, his hair whipping back from his head, and hung on around his waist as they bounced through the damp grass, the first shots of light through the hills promising another hot beautiful English day and a cloudless sky. Momentarily, she closed her eyes.

"All right now," said Henry as they clattered to a halt. He was pink in the face from the exertion.

"Here. I have to pen them this morning; they need marking. But I have a problem."

Lilian looked at him, uncomprehending.

Henry whistled, and Parr, his dog, shot out of one of the distant outbuildings like a black-and-white flash, arriving seconds later with his characteristic panting grin. He nestled his head under Lilian's hand, and she gave him a good scratch. Henry frowned. He didn't approve of petting working dogs. Lilian knew that, of course, but did it anyway. Parr was a lovely dog by anybody's standards.

"Come by, Parr," said Henry. With another two short whistles, Parr bounded off to do his duty, Henry taking to follow them.

"Why do you need me?" said Lilian timidly.

Henry took a bottle of milk from his pocket. It was frothy and warm; the cows had been turned out already.

"We've got one…she was very late," he said. "Her mother got caught on the wire. Bloody stupid buggers, sheep. Tore her own bloody throat open. And the little one…she's not adapting well. Needs a bit o' help."

Sure enough, Lilian could see just up the hill that, as the sheep started to trot along in unison to Parr's practiced maneuvers, there was a lamb, small for the time of year, trailing behind, its nose practically on the ground.

Lilian nodded. "All right."

"It will take all day to round them up otherwise," said Henry.

But he didn't need to explain himself. Not at all. Lilian understood as she picked up the little lamb—she was easy enough to catch, trailing along, bleating piteously, underweight. She knew why Henry had thought of her when he saw the lamb. And she sat on a rock in the corner of the field and waggled the teat of the bottle under the lamb's nose. At first it struggled and wriggled, anxious and frightened. Then it caught the scent of the milk: the lamb sniffed, nervously. Her little body felt heavy and warm in Lilian's arms, its white fleece still soft and pure. Finally, the lamb figured out what to do, and she felt its entire body relax as it grabbed hold of the teat and started sucking vigorously, and Lilian held her close as the sun came up. The lamb drank the bottle, and Henry and Parr got on with their days work up the valley, and Lilian felt, if not happy, then a tiny modicum of peace.

• • • •

2012

Rosie was whistling. She couldn't help it. She'd woken up bright and early, and it was a glorious day. But more than that, yesterday she'd had her first delivery for the shop. And today she was unpacking it all. The smell, even through the cardboard boxes and packaging, was light and rosy, with tinges of mint and lavender, fruit and sweet caramel escaping through the shop. With the freshly cleaned windows, the sun shone straight into the new, brightly polished jars, the washing that had taken her all morning, two breakages, and an entire bottle of dish-washing liquid. And some swearing. But now, they were perfect, clean, sparkling, and new, and ready to be filled with humbugs and jujubes and cola cubes—black AND red. Rosie had found herself adamant on this point, even though the red ones were very difficult to track down and had eventually been sourced at a small warehouse in Aberdeen. There were long red licorice laces, to be pulled out two at a time, and striped candy canes, even though they were a bit Christmassy. Rosie felt very strongly you couldn't call yourself a sweetshop if you didn't have striped candy canes.

• • • •

"AND?"

Angie had been basically relentless.

"You've got to have a business brain, my love. Any buyer is going to want to see profit and loss accounts, all of that."

Rosie had shaken her head in disbelief.

"ANGE! You sent me up here for, and I quote, 'a couple of weeks looking after the old lady.' Now you're telling me I need to apply for *Shark Tank*."

"There is not a man on *Shark Tank* I don't fancy," said Angie dreamily for a minute. "Anyway, think about it. Of course you have to know how the business works."

"I'M. A. NURSE," said Rosie.

"An auxiliary," sniffed Angie.

"I'm hanging up on you."

"No, listen."

Angie had, it cannot be denied, taken on enough temp jobs in her time. And as Rosie grudgingly reminded herself when she was getting annoying, she had worked her head off, every single day, to provide for her and Pip when no one else could have cared less.

"Now, listen to me," said Angie. "Let me try to get it through to your bandage brain how it works."

And she had explained, rather well in fact, how the business should run: what percentage she should spend on stock, what the difference was between turnover and profit, how much stock to hold. Rosie ended up grudgingly taking notes, holding the old receiver awkwardly clamped to her neck. At last it started to make a bit of sense.

"Ange," said Rosie finally, after she'd been listening for an hour. "You know when you were working your head off when me and Pip were little and we didn't have much money and stuff?"

"You never went short," said Ange.

"I know! You were amazing! I didn't even realize at the time! I liked getting toothbrushes for Christmas. Anyway. All I wanted to ask is, Lilian here…I mean, she doesn't really have anyone to spend money on. Did she ever…I mean, well, I suppose she was busy and everything, but…"

"Did she ever help us out? Is that what you're asking?"

Rosie shrugged. "I mean, it doesn't matter, everyone's busy."

She was surprised by how much emotional weight the question had though.

"Of course she did," said Ange softly. "We'd never have made it through without her and your grandpa. All the Hopkins. That sweetshop kept us afloat for years."

• • • •

Now Rosie looked around approvingly. There was Edinburgh rock in its pretty pastel dustiness, and Turkish delight by the pound set out under the glass display cabinet next to the violet creams and chocolate truffles. Rosie had started off very small on the expensive handmade chocolates, though, and had bought some tiny boxes if people just wanted to try one or two. She wasn't sure how big the market would be here. Whereas who didn't want rainbow drops? Or raisin fudge or cream-whipped caramel chews? She kept whistling happily as she donned her new apron. She'd persuaded Lilian it was an essential shop purchase, after Lilian had offered her a clean, soft, but obviously very, very old white one. This one was chic, stripy, and brand new, and Rosie kept admiring it and thinking how fond of it she was before remembering that she was a modern professional woman and liking an apron was betraying the sisterhood. Then she remembered that she was actually restarting a woman-run business, and therefore it was absolutely fine, and anyway, the new owners didn't need to keep it if they didn't want it. At any rate, she liked it enormously.

Humming happily, she tidied the boxes away neatly, making final alterations so all the jars stood equidistant in a row, their labels facing outward. She'd wanted to get Lilian to make the labels, but her fingers were so stiff with arthritis that she'd found it almost impossible, so Rosie had used her loopy writing. She'd kept Lilian's original scales, polishing them up with Brasso and newspaper till they absolutely gleamed. Even though she had to sell things metrically, she still expected everyone to ask for quarters and half-pounds and had memorized her responses precisely ("Is that 224 grams? Coming right up!"), and she was also trying to figure out a way of measuring that request of her childhood: Can I have twenty pence worth, please?

She'd also kept the antique till—even though she figured if times got really tough, they might be able to get something for it on eBay—but found a cheap electronic one secondhand. She couldn't figure out for the life of her how to work it, but she was sure it would come to her, and she'd hidden it behind the counter as far away from sight as possible, hoping to keep the illusion of the original sweetshop as intact as possible.

At last, she'd done as much as she could do. The whole place was gleaming. It was as bright as a new pin. If Rosie squinted so that the new cash till, with its little green light, was entirely out of sight, the sweetshop looked like a set from a period drama or like something out of Harry Potter. It was, to her eyes, utterly beautiful. She smiled and sighed with satisfaction.

"Lilian?" She knocked on the cottage door before she went in, even though no one else ever did.

"Lilian? Do you want to come see something?"

Lilian was dozing, slightly irritably, in her blanket. Rosie didn't want to wake her up, but she was stirring. Plus she felt that Lilian ought to be trying to stay awake a little more during the day; she was complaining she couldn't sleep well at night. It was in many ways, Rosie often felt, not unlike looking after a baby. Except not quite as adorable.

"What? Why are you always shouting at me?" Lilian squinted. "Did I give you that apron?"

"We've been through this," said Rosie. "Come on. Give me your arm."

Grumbling and reluctant, Lilian got up, even when Rosie told her she didn't have to change out of her slippers.

"Leave the house in my slippers? I don't think so. I àm old, my dear, not a slattern." So Rosie had had to kneel down and slip on her rather elegant heeled shoes with the ankle button. Lilian leaned on Rosie heavily as she left the house. Rosie had borrowed a stick from Moray but was having almost no joy getting Lilian to use it. She hoped she used it when she wasn't looking.

The day was still warm outside, although Lilian insisted on a cardigan being placed around her shoulders. Rosie hoped that if she could get a bit of weight on her, she might not feel so absolutely freezing all the time.

She led her next door. Rosie had refurbished the bell that hung above the door and had gotten so gummed up with muck and stuff that Rosie couldn't have imagined the last time it had rung. She had scrubbed and scraped and polished it with Brasso, and now it dinged out cheerfully. When she heard it, Lilian exclaimed despite herself, then as she walked forward into the new, shiny sweetshop, she let out another noise.

"OH," she said, hands suddenly grasping a shelf to keep herself upright. "Oh." Rosie watched the color drain from her great-aunt's face and redoubled her efforts to support her.

"What...what's the matter?" she said.

But all Lilian could do was point around her.

"But," she said, slightly gasping for breath and leaning perilously. "This is...this is just how it was then. Just how it was."

• • • •

When Rosie had gotten her back, as fast as she could, into bed and made her some restorative tea with three sugars, she found Lilian sitting up, still staring into space.

"Uncross your ankles," she ordered unthinkingly then sat down on the edge of the covers. "Are you all right?"

Lilian's eyes seemed a thousand miles away.

"It hasn't..." Her voice was strangulated, tight and high. "It hasn't looked like that...in a long time."

She shook her head. "Just...just seeing it again. I haven't really seen it...I haven't really been there for...maybe a while."

"Yes, I'd gathered that," said Rosie, who'd had to reconnect the electricity.

"It brought a lot of things back," said Lilian. She had been thinking of a hot summer's day, with clean, gleaming windows, when the bell had dinged and in had walked a mop of brown curly hair.

"What things?" said Rosie, glad to see some color come back into her aunt's face. She was even nibbling on the chopped up banana she'd put on a plate without much hope of success.

"Oh look," she said, "you're eating one of your five a year." Lilian ignored her, which Rosie took as a good sign.

"Tell me," said Rosie.

In Lilian's head, hearing the bright bell... It had been silent for decades—it had gotten stuck one day, and she'd forgotten to fix it, and well, maybe she had been distracted. Then time had gone on, and it didn't seem to make much sense to fix it—she could always see anyone in the shop, so why did it matter? Hearing the bright bell ring had been like a clapper tapping on her conscience, rousing all her memories.

"Someone I know," she said. "Who used to come into the shop. And when he did, the bell would ring."

"OOH," said Rosie. "Intrigue! A man! Tell me everything!"

But Lilian just looked tired. "I think," she said, "I had better have a little rest."

"All right," said Rosie, "but I am waking you up very shortly. You can't snooze the day away. It makes the nights too long."

"My nights," said Lilian faintly as Rosie closed the door. "My nights are always too long."

• • • •

Rosie wondered about Lilian all that afternoon as she handmade traditional signs to distribute around the town advertising the reopening of the shop and 20 percent off all first-day purchases. After all, she'd kept the fact that the shop was closed a secret from all of them for years. How many other secrets did she have? And it was mad to think you could get as old as Lilian, which was rapidly approaching the age of being as old as a person could possibly be, and not have had at least some intrigue. She had obviously been quite glamorous. Never left the village, obviously, but there must be someone there. The only problem was, Rosie felt, as a nurse, would she be doing the right thing or the wrong thing for Lilian's health by digging into it?

• • • •

"Aha," she said, smiling politely at the doctor's office. The door to the large house was opened by a distracted-looking receptionist. "Can I ask you to put a few leaflets out?"

Hearing her voice, a mop head popped around one of the large doors.

"I thought that was you," said Moray. In fact, he had seen her walking down the street and found himself hoping she would stop by; updating his filing was a tedious business. Also, he wanted to know why she was wearing an apron. There was no doubt about it: as a general rule, she dressed more peculiarly than anyone he had ever met. But apart from that, he liked the idea of a partner in crime.

"Hello!" said Rosie.

"Have you come to join the office?" asked the receptionist.

"Oh no," said Rosie. "I'm perfectly healthy." Moray raised an eyebrow. "And I'm NOT staying."

"No," said Moray. "Don't you want to fill in a form just in case?"

"Well, if I was staying, I wouldn't want you as my doctor," said Rosie.

"Really? Do you get lots of those really embarrassing illnesses they show on television?"

"No!" said Rosie.

"Are you sure? Vestigial tail?"

"Are you even allowed to ask me that?"

The receptionist rolled her eyes, used to Moray.

"Anyway, I wouldn't worry about it. Like all doctors, I only focus on the body part and never connect it afterward to an individual."

"Is that true or the kind of thing all doctors who work in small towns say?" asked Rosie suspiciously. She'd been privy to more than a few pharmacy cupboard conversations that did not bear out this statement. Moray glanced quickly at the receptionist in a way that confirmed what Rosie had been thinking.

"Never mind," added Rosie hastily. "I'm perfectly fine, thank you. I just wanted to put out a few of these leaflets."

Moray took them. Rosie's calligraphy teacher of long ago would have been delighted to know that he was actually quite impressed.

> Come to the grand reopening of Lilian's Traditional Sweetshop…no request too small…20 percent off on our grand reopening weekend!

There followed a list of available sweets and the promise that everything would be served with a smile and a special gift for the first fifty customers.

Moray looked at Rosie sternly. "Rosalind," he said.

"It's Rosemary, actually," said Rosie.

"Really? I prefer Rosalind."

"Okay, MORGAN."

Moray gestured around the waiting room, which was full of old toys and magazines and, on the walls, many, many bossy posters.

"What do these say?"

Rosie glumly looked at a poster of an apple and an orange wearing training shoes, bearing the slogan "We love fresh stuff!!" Next to it was a picture of a pair of scales that said "Weighty matters," and beneath it a terrifying list of ailments that would befall you if you were carrying a few extra kilos. And, worst of all, a picture of a child lying on the sofa playing computer games with the horrifying caption "Choose an early death—do nothing."

"God," said Rosie closely. "It's very perky around here. No wonder everyone is miserable and sick, staring at those half the morning."

"Hmm," said Moray. "So you don't think there'd be any conflict of interest in us stocking your leaflets."

"But these are just sweeties!" said Rosie. "They're not made of scary trans fats. We don't have to give away free toys to get the kids coming back. They're just sweets! A treat, not their bloomin' breakfast!"

"Can I give you a bit of advice?" said Moray. "Don't go into…"

"Mr. deBlaine," said Rosie. "I know. I've met him."

"If I wasn't a medical professional, I'd say keep out of his way altogether."

"Look," said Rosie, taking out her pen. "What about this?"

She quickly scribbled on the bottom, "And don't forget to get your five fruits and veggies a day too!"

"That's like people who tell you to drink whiskey responsibly," said Moray. "You do have to wonder if someone isn't having a laugh."

"Well, I think you're very not helpful about a town enterprise," said Rosie. "AND, you know, if the business works well, that will be good economically for the town, and as everyone knows, the better off everyone is, the better their health is. So actually, it would be making Lipton healthier, if anything."

"You're wasted in sweets," said Moray, "when you should really be in epidemiology."

"Yeah," said Rosie.

"Well," said Moray, "I might take a few, with your fruit and veg waiver, thank you. If you do something for me."

"Is it what I think it is?" said Rosie with a twitch of an eyebrow.

"No," said Moray. "It's to go see Stephen Mannering again. You're the only one who seems to be able to get any sense into him."

"That is EXACTLY what I thought it was," said Rosie.

"Oh, was it?" said Moray, looking momentarily guilty. "Umm, yes. I mean. Obviously. Totally. Great."

• • • •

Rosie felt bold enough, in the end, to cycle up the hill to Peak House by herself. She figured it would be just what she needed to counteract the effects of the stodgy meals, including roast pork with crackling and apple sauce, which she had guessed correctly that Lilian would be wholly unable to resist; being here was actually really helping her cooking skills. Gerard's favorite home-cooked meal was pasta with supermarket tomato sauce "with no bits."

Roads that zipped by in a Land Rover went on for bloody ages at ridiculously steep angles—why on earth people lived so far out of the way, Rosie couldn't imagine. Her rucksack weighed a ton on her back, she got a stone in her shoe, and she was cursing for once, not the rain but a hot Indian summer day that made her striped T-shirt stick to the back of her neck.

Finally, and in a thoroughly grumpy mood, thinking it probably wasn't worth all this effort to distribute a few leaflets, she dismounted, stiff and saddlesore, outside the back door.

Maybe, she thought. Maybe this time, he'd be pleased to see her. Drop the hostility. Maybe he'd realize he needed someone like her. And maybe pigs would fly.

Rosie rapped loudly on the kitchen door then marched in before he had the chance to tell her to go away.

"Meals on Wheels," she announced. There he was, still in that same seat at that same table. It beggared belief that he was still there, in the same spot, after all that time.

"Are you STILL there?" she asked, trying to keep the horror out of her voice.

"No," came the clipped tones. "Obviously I took some time off to test-drive my new rocket. Then there was the Wimbledon evening. And I spent a pretty wild weekend in Ibiza."

"You're becoming one of those shut-ins," said Rosie. "Next time I come here, you'll have sixty-seven cats."

"Next time," said Stephen. "Be still my overexcited heart." But she could see him eyeing her bag.

"What's in there?" he asked.

"Nothing," said Rosie, unpacking pork chops, half-roasted potatoes, homemade applesauce, and red cabbage on the table between them, as well as half a pound of butter fudge and a large packet of dolly mixtures. They regarded each other.

"The National Health Service is a lot more caring than I remember it," said Stephen.

"This isn't about the NHS," said Rosie. "This is about me trying to bribe people to come to my sweetshop."

Stephen looked completely bemused as Rosie turned on the oven. "Oh yes?"

"I thought you got all the gossip from Mrs. Laird," said Rosie.

"Well, she talks, but I'm not saying I listen."

"My lovely sweetshop…I mean, Great-Aunt Lilian's lovely sweetshop, is having its grand reopening ceremony…tomorrow." She showed Stephen her leaflets. "Why don't you come?"

Stephen grimaced.

"Thanks for that. Afterward, maybe I could do some basket weaving and some art therapy?"

Rosie gave him a look.

"No. You could eat a lolly, like normal people."

"Thank you for lumping me in with the normal people," said Stephen.

"Ha, you'd HATE that," said Rosie. "You'd hate being one of the normal people."

"That's not fair," said Stephen mildly but with real hurt in his voice.

Rosie loaded up the surprisingly clean grill pan and set the potatoes in to finish cooking. Already they smelled wonderful.

"So to what do I owe this munificence?" said Stephen. "Is Moray trying to poison me?"

"No," said Rosie. "Maybe yes. No, I don't think so. But there is a snag."

"I thought there might be."

"You have to let me change the dressing."

The light went straight out of Stephen's eyes. "No," he said. "I do that myself."

"God," said Rosie, "I'm surprised you're not dead of blood poisoning."

"It's fine," said Stephen.

"If it were fine," said Rosie, "you'd be sitting out in the garden, or climbing the stairs, or going to the gym, or seeing your friends, or chatting up some girl or boy, or going back to work… Stephen, where's your *family*?"

Stephen scowled.

"Can't you just keep the fuck out of my business?" he said.

"No," said Rosie. "I'm involved now. If I just wander off, I'll have to wonder about it for the rest of my life and live with the hideous mental image of you still sitting at your kitchen table or being eaten by ladybugs or somcthing."

"Ladybugs?"

"The amount you move about, it could happen."

"Seriously, ladybugs?"

"I've herbed the pork chops," said Rosie as a heavenly smell started to fill the kitchen.

Stephen looked torn, and so sad that Rosie suddenly felt overwhelmed with him. What on earth had he gone through to make him end up like this? A young, handsome, obviously otherwise fit guy…what had happened to him? She looked under the grill and turned it down.

"You know, if we start now, it will be perfectly ready by the time we're finished."

"Rosie," said Stephen. "It's horrible, you know. Horrible."

"I've seen worse," said Rosie stoically. "Honestly, until you've seen someone present at emergency with a cockroach up their arse, you haven't lived."

"A WHAT?"

"Exactly. And yet YOU'RE the one depressed. Come on."

It was the time for action. Gently yet firmly, Rosie took his elbow and steered him into what she guessed, correctly, was the old-fashioned but clean bathroom.

"Take your trousers off," she said, turning to scrub her hands. "I'm not looking. Let me know if you need me to help you."

He insisted he didn't, but she could tell by his careful movements that it wasn't easy for him.

"Are you looking in the mirror?"

"Yes," said Rosie. "Looking and giving you marks out of ten. Get on with it, please."

When she turned around, he was perched anxiously on the side of the bath, running his hands through his hair, which was now in obvious need of a cut and kept falling into his eyes.

He was wearing long white boxers, and she saw that his right leg was extremely long, muscled, still brown, and firm. His left, though, looked like it didn't belong to a matching set.

It was white and hairless and almost wasted away. Rosie knelt down and, without speaking, because she knew it would be painful, quickly and expertly unraveled the bandage. Although he didn't make a sound, Rosie could tell by the tensing in his muscles how painful it was, and his fingers gripped the side of the enamel.

Ready for something much worse, she looked carefully at the wound: a great jagged rent down the inside of his thigh. It did not look particularly nice—it still gaped—but it was, most importantly, clean; it didn't smell and there was no sign of degradation in the wound. Rosie looked up at him.

"This is clean," she said, her face furrowing.

"Hmm," he said. "I'm not a complete idiot."

"Well, apart from the fact that you are," said Rosie—she could see quite clearly where the stitches had dissolved before they'd done their job properly—"you've been cleaning this. Or someone has."

"No," said Stephen. "Mrs. Laird is nifty, but she's not all that."

Rosie followed his eyes to the medicine cabinet to the upper right of the sink. On top of it was a huge, half-empty brown bottle of surgical spirit.

"Jesus," she said. "That must hurt like buggery."

"The whiskey helps," said Stephen. "I like to feel I'm doing the job from inside and out."

"But can't you see it doesn't matter?" said Rosie. "It doesn't matter how much of that stuff you pour in; if you don't get it restitched, it's never going to get better. It just can't."

Stephen didn't say anything as she set about cleaning the area—softly—using an anesthetic cream. Then he said softly, "Could you do it? The stitches?"

"No," said Rosie. "I shouldn't even be doing this, really. Just don't slip on the bathroom floor and knock yourself out, or then we'll really be in trouble."

"You mean I'm going to have to go and see that supercilious prick Moray?"

"What's your problem with Moray?"

Stephen shrugged. "Thinks he knows it all. Likes to stick his nose in everyone's business. Goes to all the trouble of getting a medical degree then wastes it, sitting on his arse looking up old ladies' arses."

Rosie privately thought to herself, *Ladies about the same age as you*, but very wisely kept it to herself.

"Well," she said. "What about going to the nearest hospital? The emergency doctors could stitch that right up for you."

Stephen looked down at his leg as she bandaged it up. There was a long pause. Rosie sighed.

"Have you just been sitting up here like a poky old man, crossing your fingers and hoping it would get better on its own?" said Rosie with a note of tenderness in her voice.

There was a silence.

"You must know, it never, ever can."

There was another pause. Rosie could tell what he wanted her to say; he was so funny. Like a child in some ways.

"You know, I could probably drive you there," she went on.

"On your bicycle?"

"I'll figure something out."

Stephen said nothing, just sat and sighed. Then finally he looked up. "Can you get out while I put my trousers on?"

Rosie packed up her bag and turned around to leave the room. "I'm taking that as a yes!" she yelled cheerily.

• • • •

1943

Life returned to normal, or as normal as wartime life could be. Although it seemed impossible, although it seemed that no one could ever behave normally again, although every child laughing in the street, every old man saying good evening in the roadway had at first seemed like a personal affront to the heavens, to the awful destruction of the world. Pure unobstructed grief, Lilian found, was too heavy and tiresome to keep up. Little by little, the real world returned; she would find her attention distracted by a program on the radio or a pretty cuckoo in the hedgerow, or the touch of the warm sun on her skin would make her feel happy for a moment, before she would remember all over again. And although it seemed likely that her father's jaunty, energetic sense of humor may, it seemed, have gone for good, he could still make a comment over supper about how good the soup was, or how takings were up or down in the shop. And after the lamb, which they'd christened Daisy, was on to grass, bounding about happily in the field (Lilian pretended she always knew which lamb was hers), she and Henry had more time to chat and found they wanted to talk about almost everything, not just her loss: about his sister, who'd died of scarlet fever when he was nine, or how he wanted to go to technical college in Chester. He didn't want to do farmwork for much longer, but it depended on whether he could get enough money together, and anyway, he was bound to get called up before long, so he wasn't sure if it even mattered.

And Lilian found she enjoyed talking about his life, his plans and dreams; they took her away from thinking about Ned, from the sweetshop, from the stifling little parlor that held what was left of her family. So they would sit, sometimes sharing a bag of damaged rock candy, and talk about what he would do, sometimes with Henry practically falling asleep after a long hot day in the fields, sometimes sharing a bottle of cider as Lilian stared at his sunburned neck and curly, tangled hair and wondered how, for the life of her, she could ever have found him annoying, how she could ever, for a second, have found him anything but the most wonderful, kind, amazing man she had ever known. Gradually, little by little over those stolen hours, she, growing more and more bold, lay her head on his shoulder; let him, gently, take her hand as they lay and talked in the meadow; and slowly, their plans, their ideas for life, started to include both of them, started to twist around together like two plants growing side by side.

Before the war, Lilian reflected as they walked home late, the heavy blood-orange moon rising over their heads, this would have been absolutely disallowed; the scandal could have affected everything. Now, it seemed, the rules had changed. So many young men had gone, or left the village, or been killed—one thing Lilian had learned, horribly, was the amount of tragedy masked in other people's lives. From feeling herself the only person mistreated by the universe, she had realized that in fact, until now, she had been innocent and protected, that to lose a brother, to lose a son, was a common experience, that it had been as long as there had been wars. She felt as if she had joined a new group of people: those who knew how cruel the world could be and could never unlearn that fact.

They were crossing the cobbled main street together when, biting her lip, she reached out her hand, and without even breaking stride, Henry's strong, calloused fingers were instantly there to meet it as they walked entwined together down the darkening road.

Despite the fact that she knew deep down that it was only a matter of time before he got his call-up papers, that Henry must leave shortly, despite the loss of Ned and the fact that her two brothers were still at war—despite all of this, she would look back on this forever as one of the happiest moments of her life.

11

Getting bits of peanut brittle out from between your teeth requires some skill. I did at one stage suggest to the manufacturers that they include a toothpick with every package, but they were extremely rude and made remarks about having children's eyes out and so on, which in my opinion is why peanut brittle is much in decline today. But who am I to talk? After all, why would any confectionery manufacturer listen to someone who has been directly selling sweets to the general public for the last fifty years? Oh silly me, how dare I get ideas above my station, like sending helpful information about a product that causes a clear and obvious problem, as well as making your breath smell like a diabetic monkey.

TA-DA!"

Rosie stood at the bottom of the stairs. Even though it was only just past 7:00 a.m., she hadn't been able to sleep because of her excitement. She had heard her aunt moving restlessly downstairs and helped her wash and dress before heating up the pan for scrambled eggs and nipping upstairs to get dressed.

"What do you think? Too much?"

Lilian looked up from perusing the local paper.

"You're in here," she said, handing it over. On the little sixteen sheet, filled with small ads for washing machines and farm machinery, was a picture of the newly refurbished sweetshop.

"Ooh!" said Rosie. Underneath, it said, "Teeth-rotting Hopkins Family Trying Again."

"Oh," said Rosie, surprised by how much this knocked the wind out of her sails. "That's not very nice."

"No," said Lilian.

"It's actually horrid," said Rosie.

Today marks the reopening of Lipton's formerly derelict sweetshop, in the same place, returning from the grave to wreck the teeth of another generation of Lipton children.

Rosie looked up. "Lilian?"

"I think your scrambled eggs are burning."

"Okay, hold your horses," said Rosie, grating cheese into them as Lilian looked on almost hungrily. Rosie was delighted at this, as she slipped two slices of whole grain bread under the grill—there was no such thing as a toaster in Lilian's dollhouse kitchen. She added two strong cups of tea, and they sat down at the table.

"Lilian…who edits the local paper?"

"The *Lipton Times*? It's that awful charlatan deBlaine."

Rosie glanced at the other stories in the thin sheets, most of which appeared to be about tooth-whitening competitions at the local school. "So he does this job on the side?"

Lilian looked sad. "It used to be a thriving paper, the *Lipton Times*. Everyone read it, had a journalist and an editor and everything. Then, you know…"

"What?" said Rosie.

"That thing everyone talks about. The really big newspaper in the sky that came along and ruined everything else, blah blah blah."

Rosie was stumped, until light finally dawned. "You mean the Internet?"

"Well, yes. I hate that thing."

"The whole thing?"

"Yes."

"You hate the entire Internet?"

"Yes."

"Why?"

Lilian looked at her as if she was the biggest idiot ever.

"Because it took my lovely local paper and turned it into a ridiculous sticky free rag, that's why," she said. "And it shut down the ruddy post office! And I've scarcely had a letter in seventeen years! Why on earth would I want anything to do with anything like that?"

"You know," said Rosie, thinking suddenly, "if you were online, you could send sweets to anyone anywhere in the world."

"Why on earth would I want to do that?" said Lilian.

"Well, maybe people might like old-fashioned sweetshops," said Rosie. "Maybe they'd like proper humbugs and half-decent jellies and proper Turkish delight—not that weird pink stuff—wrapped up nicely and sent properly."

Lilian looked as unconvinced as it was possible for a person to be.

"Well, you're full of pep this morning," she said. "What are you wearing?"

"Well, yes," said Rosie. "I did wonder if it would be too much."

Rosie was wearing a Get Cutie dress that suited her very nicely—it had a sweetheart neckline, three-quarter-length sleeves, and a pattern of nesting birds—beneath her candy-striped apron, with a mobcap covering her dark curls.

"It's the hat, isn't it?" she said. "The hat's too much."

"I wouldn't say the hat was too much," said Lilian, a ghost of a smile hovering around her lips. "Although it does look a little bit like the theme catering staff Hetty gets in at the big house around about Christmastime or for those awful wedding things she does."

Rosie snatched it off. "It was just an idea," she said hastily. "Plus I need to wear it when I'm handling the chocolate."

Lilian snorted.

"Political correctness gone mad," she sniffed.

"I don't think it is," said Rosie gently. "I think it's just basic cleanliness and all that."

"I always kept a clean shop!" said Lilian. The women regarded each other.

"Let's not talk about the mice right now," said Rosie, who had spent several unpleasant mornings emptying traps.

"So, are you coming? I'm going to have free lollipops! And balloons!"

"FREE?" said Lilian.

"It's called marketing," said Rosie. "And I thought…if you wanted to come…Moray has a spare wheelchair in the office I thought he might lend me…"

"Absolutely not," said Lilian. "I'm not going to sit out like one of those awful war-wounded old…I mean one of those awful old crones."

"Just a thought," said Rosie. "I'm hoping…well, I'm hoping we get SOME people. Jake said he'd bring along some farming boys, and I've told the school and handed out leaflets and…"

"No," said Lilian. "Lipton people don't fall for things like that. I think you're just going to have to face it, Rosie. I do appreciate what you're kind of trying to do for me here, and it would be nice for you to find someone and let things continue, I suppose. Yes, I suppose."

"Is that a thank-you?" said Rosie.

"But we must just face things, Rosemary. These shops…they're dying. Like everything else. Like the post office. Like the newspapers. Like me, and everyone I've ever bloody known."

Lilian attempted a wry smile, but it didn't sit well on her old, too thin face. It showed off long, old teeth in sunken gums and cheeks with deep crevasses running through the middle.

"We're done. It's nice of you to come here, and it's nice of you to look after me, and if we can sell the sweetshop as a going concern, well, that will be jolly wonderful for me, I suppose, and I can find a home, I suppose, and sit in the corner of a room and watch television all day with drool hanging out of my mouth. I know what you're up to."

"We're not 'up' to anything," said Rosie. "I thought it was wrong you being left where you were, coping on your own. I still think that. And I'm trying to do the best I can for you and for the shop. And I think…" Rosie stole a glance at the large helium canister that had been delivered the previous evening, "I think we can do that."

Lilian snorted.

"I was fine, you know."

"I know," lied Rosie again for the nine hundredth time. "I know you were, Aunt Lil. We're just trying to help. I'm only trying to help."

"People shouldn't help until they're asked."

Rosie thought of someone else.

"Some people can't bear to ask," she said. "Maybe that's where I come in."

• • • •

It was another lovely September day; Rosie noticed the sweet smell of freshly cut hay in the air. The town was full of itinerant laborers, good to spend a penny or two, a few late holidaymakers, and the first rush of schoolchildren, all scrubbed and polished and wearing oversized blazers, shuffling painful shoes after a summer in bare feet or crocs. By eight-thirty, Rosie had already mastered the helium canister for the balloons (quickly passing over a small pang of loneliness that Gerard wasn't there to hear her funny voice) and stuck them up outside. Listening to the happy tinkle of the bell, she turned quickly to see a small boy wearing glasses looking up at her solemnly. She recognized him from before.

"Hello, Edison," she said.

"I'm here early," said the boy, blinking behind his magnifying glasses. "I thought if I got here early, I might be able to put away some of the sweets before the big boys take them off me."

"Tell the big boys not to do that!" said Rosie. "Or punch them."

"I can't do that," said the boy. "I'm a pacific."

"A what?"

"A pacific. It means I don't fight back, as it's morly wrong."

"Are you a pacifist, Edison?"

"Yes," said Edison. "That's what I said."

Rosie took out the big dish of old-fashioned lollipops—strawberries and cream, lemon and lime, and black currant and vanilla, each with the colors swirled around its top and tied up with a simple twist of waxed paper.

"Well, one way of looking at it," said Rosie, "is that you never start a fight, but if you get into one, make sure you fight them back."

Edison was closely examining the lollipops, picking them up and turning them over in his hands as he tried to make up his mind.

"Yes, but the thing is," he said, sounding like a very small professor, "my glasses cost one hundred and fifty-nine pounds, you see? I have stig-mis-ma. Mummy says it will make me very clever."

Rosie arched her eyebrows then glanced outside. A woman with a very severe haircut and no makeup gave her a tight smile then glanced deliberately at her watch.

Don't start a fight, but always finish it, her gramps, Gordon, had always said. He'd given her lessons on the balcony of their old flat. It had come in handy precisely once—in year four, against a gang of hard-core girls from the next estate along. The second she'd used Grampa Gordon's patented neck-whacker, the girl had staggered back, screaming abuse, and she'd never had the slightest bit of trouble from them ever again. She was tempted to teach Edison the neck-whacker right now but suspected his mother wouldn't approve. It was bad enough bringing evil sugar to town, she supposed.

"Have you decided yet, genius?" she said. Edison looked absolutely helpless. "Remember your friend who isn't allowed to eat sweets? What's his name?" said Rosie.

"Reuben?"

"Yes, Reuben."

"Uh-huh," said Edison.

"Would you like to take one for Reuben?"

"But would that be morly wrong?"

"No," said Rosie. "Not if some mean people are going to try to take your lollipop. You can offer up Reuben's, if he wasn't going to eat it anyway."

Edison's brow furrowed as he followed through the ramifications of this. Finally, his brain ended up at a solution he liked, and he smiled and popped his head back up.

"Okay!" he said. "I'll have strawberries and cream, and REUBEN would like lemon and lime. Or maybe Reuben would like black currant. I hate black currant. Maybe if some people who are mean and take Reuben's lollipop would then go bleurgh bleurgh yuck yuck, we are going to be sick, we hate black currant so much."

"That could happen," said Rosie.

Edison nodded his head, and Rosie popped them in a bag for him. "Congratulations!" she said. "You are officially our first customer."

Rosie propped the door open, where several rubberneckers, passersby, and schoolchildren were officially gathered around.

"I now pronounce this sweetshop...open!" said Rosie with a big smile.

In poured quite the river of people—little boys and girls—Rosie looked among them to see if she could make out exactly which ones were making Edison's life such a misery, but they all looked identically rosy-cheeked and adorable, a little homogenous perhaps for her eyes, but this was the country now, and smart in their little red blazers and leather satchels, all smiling and cheerful.

"I'm going to buy the BIGGEST BAG EVER IN THE WORLD and buy every sweet in this shop," announced one tow-headed chap.

"Me too, I am going to do that," said his friend. "Except mine will be the biggest bag in space and so it will be bigger than yours even, so there."

"I am going to bring all my birthday money, all the money I got for my birthday, it's a lot, it was ten pounds, yes, and I am going to buy ALL THE CHOCOLATE IN THE SHOP," said another.

"You will not," said a mother's voice, and when Rosie looked up, she realized it was Maeve Skritcherd, the receptionist from the doctor's office.

"Hello!" she said.

"Hello," said Maeve. "I couldn't resist. When I was little, Miss Lilian always used to have…I don't suppose they even make them anymore, I've never seen them anywhere…"

Rosie cocked her head, desperately keeping her fingers crossed. This was the crux of it; this was where the shop could rise again. Not from the pennies and birthday money of the children, but from the memories and desires of the adults.

"…I don't suppose you do have any mint creams?"

Rosie nearly punched the air with pleasure. They did. She had restocked as many of Lilian's originals as she could track down.

"Why yes," she said. "Of course. Would you like a big bag or a small bag?" Even though Rosie had been metric since she'd started out in nursing, she knew it wasn't the right thing for a traditional sweetshop, so she was selling small, medium, and large bags at one, two, or three pounds. You could choose all of one or, for medium and large bags, mix the sweets up two or three scoops together.

"Ooh, large," said Maeve, coloring with pleasure. "Or maybe small. No, large."

Rosie filled a large bag—her first sale—with Maeve's mint creams while Lavender, her daughter, unwrapped her strawberry lolly. (Rosie made a mental note: when offered a fruit-based choice for candy, children invariably went for strawberry. A tiny thought behind that said that knowing this wouldn't matter a bit when she sold the shop on to its real new owners, but she suppressed it quickly.) Maeve couldn't wait. She bit into one as soon as she handed over the cash and sunk her teeth into the large white round disc immediately.

"Oh my God," she said as the sharp taste flooded her mouth. "They haven't changed a bit. Not a bit." She went pink. "I used to have a big bag of these on my way home from school every day. It was where all my pocket money went. Everyone else would have something different: alphabet sweets, and whichever name you spelled out would be the name of the boy you were going to marry. But I just stuck with these; I was completely addicted to them. Every day, for about a year. Then I just kind of forgot all about them. Alice Mandon had the alphabet sweets, Carly had the sugar mouse, she was always watching her weight…you know, I must find Carly and tell her about this place being open again. She loved it. We got back in touch, you know, on Facebook…"

Then she checked her watch. "Anyway, why am I telling you this? I'll be late opening up the office, and Hye will be furious."

"I'll be fine," boomed the voice behind her, and Maeve jumped, turning around. "So this is where you're sending all the sugar addicts, is it, young lady?" said Hye. He really did look like a country doctor caricature, Rosie thought again, in his tweeds and his pink shirt. "Hmm. Got any Red Hots?"

Again, Rosie blessed her great-aunt for not throwing anything away, including her invoice records, as she for the first time used the stepladder—she hadn't thought Red Hots would be in the least bit popular—to reach the higher shelves and put a bundle of the very strong cinnamon-tasting candies into a bag.

"Terrifies the children, these things," said Hye. "Stops them stealing 'em."

Rosie had an immediate mental picture of him as a small boy with a fat bottom in short trousers.

"Hope you like them," she said, smiling.

"Hmm," said Hye. "I'm just glad you're keeping away from the town dogs." Rosie tried to flip over the paper bag so it fell into two twists at either side, but she hadn't quite gotten the hang of it yet, or of the big old-fashioned till, which she tended to jar with her elbow at awkward moments. She did both of these things now as Hye watched her in a patronizing way. Then he turned to leave, popping the red sweet into his mouth reflectively.

"That," he said, "that is not bad. Not bad at all."

Rosie smiled, genuinely pleased.

Hye pulled open the door, his crusty demeanor seeming to diminish somewhat.

"I think Moray is very grateful for the help with our little…business up at Peak House," he said as Rosie wondered for a moment what he meant. "Thank you."

The bell dinged, and he was gone. What did he mean, "business"? How was Stephen a business? Why was he such an important patient?

But suddenly she found she barely had a moment to think about it, as the doorbell rang again, and as the children melted away to school (one of them stealing one of her balloons—she wondered if this was the town troublemaker). The workers started passing by, some hovering outside looking at the window display—she had put out some of the most tempting of the beautiful chocolates on the shadier side and a sweet display of sugar mice and pigs playing on the other—or wandering in, and she greeted them all with a friendly smile. People requested the oddest things: rhubarb and custards, pineapple chunks, barley sugar, and eucalyptus—sometimes sweets that Rosie had never heard of, but often, thanks to Lilian's little book, she found she did have on her shelves, fresh and shining in the glass jars. She weighed and twisted until she got the hang of it, made change for small bags and big bags and one huge box of heart-shaped chocolates borne away by the newly married young man to his new bride, seeing as, he admitted somewhat shamefacedly to Rosie, they had had to spend their honeymoon on the harvest even though she'd wanted to go to Malaga, so he was trying to make it up to her. This charming gesture (she couldn't remember anyone ever bringing her a box of chocolates, though Gerard brought home pizza from time to time, when he was feeling really romantic) immediately made her knock five pounds off the price. Although to be fair, she hadn't really expected to sell anything much. But here they were, inundated. Novelty factor. It must be the novelty factor. Everyone would pop in for a couple of days, then it would go back to normal. Which meant, Rosie thought, measuring out a small bag of Parma Violets that immediately filled the shop with their sharp, slightly astringent odor and made two small children ask for the same thing, that she should probably get it on the market as soon as possible. Probably. That would be the right thing to do. Definitely.

Rosie bent down and offered a small purple sweet to each of the children. They looked up at her, wide-eyed, then glanced at the woman standing by the door, who nodded indulgently.

"I LIKE your shop," said the littlest.

"I'm glad," said Rosie.

"Wass your name?"

"I'm Rosie," she said, smiling.

"HEYO, MISS ROSIE. MAH NAME IS KENT."

"Hello, Kent," said Rosie. "And what about you?"

But the little girl, obviously Kent's sister, was struck dumb with awe and stared at Rosie with her eyes and her mouth wide open.

"She's very shy," said the lady at the doorway. She was slender, young, and, incongruously in Lipton apart from Lilian, beautifully dressed in a mummy style, with a soft cashmere pink pullover and expensive-looking draped trousers. "But I think she likes your shop. This is Emily."

"That's great," said Rosie.

"I like it too," said the lady, peering in. "You've done a lovely job. It looks just like a proper old-fashioned place."

"Oh well, it is," said Rosie. "This is all genuine. I didn't change a thing, just polished it up a bit."

The woman smiled. "Well, I like it. I hope it does really well. I'm Tina, by the way. Tina Ferrers."

"Hi," said Rosie. "I'm Rosie Hopkins."

The woman smiled. She had very neat white teeth, Rosie noticed. "Oh, I know who you are," she said. "The whole town knows who you are."

"Hmm," said Rosie. "Is that good or bad?"

"Oh, they all know me too," said Tina, rolling her eyes. "It's the country. It's just how it is. Come on, Kent. Come on, Emily. We should have coffee sometime and you can tell me about this place," she said to Rosie as they dinged their way out of the shop, and Rosie tried to pretend she wasn't pleased that someone was trying to be friendly without her having to save a dog first. And she seemed interested in the shop. That could be useful.

The entire morning passed busily, although at one point, Rosie was a bit shocked to look up and see Mrs. Isitt looking at her through the tiny panes of glass. She did not come in. Rosie made a mental note to herself to deliver a portion of coconut ice down to Mr. Isitt as soon as was humanly possible.

• • • •

1943

There was no denying that it helped, none at all. Gordon had a week's leave from the North African front and had fought his way home over seventy-two hours, hitching rides on supply boats and trucks and, finally, trundling over the hills from Derby in a little slow-moving, green single-story bus, his kit bag on his knee, in time for Saturday lunch. Lilian could see it in her father's eyes—the first spark that had been there for a long time. She reflected briefly on the fact that she hadn't been the one to put it there.

The two men did not hug—they didn't do that in their family—but her da held Gordon's hand for a long time and clasped his shoulder with water in his eyes. Gordon looked older, more grown-up, but there was still a spark in his eyes of mischief, although he was crumpled and weary. The men sat in near silence at the table as Lilian served up two weeks' meat ration for chops, but she could tell that, although they merely muttered and made remarks about army food, both of them were happier than they had felt in a long time. And so, inside, was she. Every time she thought about Henry, her insides lit up with a nervous, excited kind of joy; her guts twisted up in disbelief. She had planned to steal away that night to meet up with him, but now Gordon was back maybe…maybe it might be time to bring him home.

"So what's the talk of the town tonight, sister of mine?" asked Gordon. "You know, I visited that Piccadilly Circus in London."

Lilian bit her lip. She would love to see it. Maybe one day, she and Henry…but that was such an impossible dream, she brushed it off immediately and pressed Gordon on the lights—he'd been to London and was far keener on telling them about how one of the privates had had his trousers and his money stolen by a vagabond in town, and about Tangiers, the shimmering hot city of sand and bazaars and little children who ran after you shouting "Charlie Chaplin! Charlie Chaplin!" in English. It was so many worlds away. Gordon told them funny stories about their commanding officers and how clueless they were and about how their equipment broke down, but when Da asked him about any skirmishes, he went quiet for a long time. Lilian thought about Ned and turned away. But Gordon couldn't keep his natural ebullience down for long. After a long pause, he looked up and remarked, "Da, I was scared out of my bloody wits."

After a pause, Lilian's dad let out a huge guffaw of laughter, the first Lilian had heard from him in months.

"Ha," said her da. "Ha. Yes. Exactly. It's exactly like that. Ha." And he laughed so hard he had to wipe a tear from his eye and resettle himself in the old wooden chair.

"You are," he said, "you are a tonic, son. It's good to see you." Lilian had never heard anything so effusive from her dad before.

"Come on," said Gordon, after he'd had a bath and a nap. "If there's nothing going on down at the church hall, we might as well go to the Boar's Head. I'll take you to the lounge bar."

Lilian snuck a glance at her father, who just waved his hand. "Aye, on you go, young 'uns," he said. "I'll see you in the morn. Behave yourselves."

• • • •

Lilian didn't quite know how to tell Gordon, but she didn't have to; as they walked down the blacked-out road together, he quite naturally asked her, "Got a fella?" And when she paused even for the briefest of moments, he laughed and nudged her.

"Anyone decent?" he said. Lilian bit her lip. She wondered how he'd feel when he knew it was one of his cronies, the one Lilian had most disliked. Gordon had stood around many times when Henry had teased her or made comments about his sister. And he hadn't stood up for her much either. This was going to be rather sticky.

"It's…it's Henry Carr," she said so quietly it was nearly a whisper.

Gordon had to strain to hear her then translate the words in his head. Then he let out a guffaw.

"Carr! He managed it at last. By gum, I thought he'd never get around to it."

"What do you mean?" said Lilian, completely surprised.

"He always had a soft spot for you, didn't he? Terence warned him off often enough. Well, there you go. Good on 'im."

"But he was always really horrible to me."

Gordon gave her a sideways glance.

"You know, I'd have thought having three brothers would have taught you a little bit more about chaps, sure enough."

Lilian felt the blush steal up her face. Was it true? Had he always cared for her, all this time?

"Is that why you never stood up for me?" she said. It came out more accusingly than she'd intended. Gordon smiled.

"Neh," he said. "That was because you were such a po-faced wee shrew. No offense."

The pub wasn't lit, but slits of warm light could just be seen at the side, poking out of the blackout curtains, and she could hear the convivial chatter of a Saturday night at the end of a long week. She felt excited and a little bold, but mostly nervous. Then, to her relief, she saw Margaret, home from Derby and heading over from the opposite direction with an oafish big chap in a naval uniform. Seeing Lilian, she shrieked and waved mightily.

"You're out of the widow weeds!" she yelled tactlessly then gave her a hug, which Lilian found herself reciprocating. "Didn't you get my letters?" she scolded. Margaret had written to her faithfully with stories of the big city and all the fun she was having at the factory with the women and the nightclubs and the men they'd met. Lilian had found them almost impossible to read—the idea, in the earliest days after Ned's death, that someone else's life was continuing gaily on, improving if anything.

"This is George," said Margaret proudly, pushing forward the lanky chap with freckles and bright red hair, who muttered something so quietly she could barely hear it. "I brought him down to meet Ma and Pa."

With this, she winked massively at Lilian in a slightly confusing way, obviously intended to be confiding. It took Lilian a minute or two to realize the message she was trying to convey.

"Are you…are you two…"

"Yes!" said Margaret. "Isn't it the most romantic thing ever? I have to tell you the whole story!"

George did not, at that moment, look like the world's most romantic man—if Lilian had had to pick something, she would have picked him as the world's most embarrassed man—but Margaret linked her arm and they headed inside, into a warm fug of tobacco smoke and the smell of dogs and warm ale. Lilian had been inside before, sometimes, from when she was a little girl, sent down to make change for the shop in their lunchtime opening hours, but today she was going in for the first time on her own, as a woman. She felt a little exposed, and very bold, even though having Margaret clasping her elbow tightly was a definite help. Gordon was on her other side.

"Now, I have no regrets about missing out on the lovely Margaret," he said to her, sotto voce, "but there's someone I always hoped I might take a crack at one of these days."

For there, in a cozy corner table by the fireplace in the ladies lounge bar, nursing a port and lemon and deep in what appeared to be a very intense conversation, were Ida Delia Fontayne and Henry Carr, once again only a heartbeat away from one another.

• • • •

2012

Lilian found herself polishing off some scones Rosie had run up yesterday. Even though she'd always wanted to be thin, she couldn't deny that Rosie putting a little bit of meat on her bones was making her feel slightly better, slightly more able to get through the day. It felt like her joints weren't quite so stiff, her extremities not so blooming cold all the time, even when she huddled in front of the fire. She was sleeping better too, possibly because Rosie, unbeknownst to her, was bulking up her nighttime cocoa with calorie powder. And yet, paradoxically, feeling slightly better was making her feel more worried, not less, about the future. As long as she had been feeling so awful, she could kid herself that she was rundown and still a little ill after her operation. Now, she had to admit to herself that there was a possibility that this was it—little by little, she had gained energy, but there was going to come a time when that was going to stop. And whatever she was left with—her arthritic left wrist, her impossibly unreliable knees, just how damn long it took her to get going in the morning—that would be that. Rosie would go—she didn't know how to even admit to herself how much she'd enjoyed the company—the shop and the house would be sold, and she'd be packed away into some gruesome awful home somewhere to drool out of the window and be parked in front of game shows and shouted at in a room that smelled of piss. Every day until the day she died, in a piss-drenched prison, stuck in a chair, being shouted at in front of a game show. And she was only eighty-seven; she could easily live another ten, fifteen years these days. Easily. She hadn't wanted change. She was getting on all right. And now here was Rosie, poking her nose in and shaking everything up…

Shakily, reluctantly, Lilian pulled on a cardigan and applied a little pale pink lipstick in the large sitting room mirror with the rainbow rim over the fireplace. She looked at her reflection and sighed. Then she picked up her stick, pushed open the front door, and set out to visit her sweetshop, her place, once more, while she still could.

chewing gum

• • • •

What are you? A cow? A great big cud-chewing cow in the middle of the field? Or do you feel a pressing need to give yourself terrible wind and tie up your intestines? Did your nanny never teach you that it's rude to open your mouth to all and sundry and eat in public? Are you badly brought up, or a field-ridden quadruped? Which is it? I must know. Or perhaps your breath is so bad and your dental care is so appalling you have a mouth that smells like the pits of fiery hell, and for some benighted reason, you wish to advertise this fact to the world. Is that it? Perhaps you would like to snap your gum now, pull it out on a string on your fingers, or throw it in an indelible globule on the pavement. Great. Thank you.

Now, hopefully our bovine friends will have left this book behind. To all sensible people. May I recommend a mint imperial?

Rosie didn't notice Lilian straightaway for the very good reason that her view was blocked by Anton, the obese man she'd helped Moray treat. He'd arrived ten minutes before with a walker set heavily in front of him.

"Hello, Anton!" she said, delighted. "You're out of the house!"

Anton smiled shyly, his chins wobbling in a pleased fashion. "You recognized me!"

Rosie swallowed back a giggle.

"Yes, Anton. I recognized you," she said. "And well done for getting out of the house! That's brilliant!"

Anton beamed.

"Yeah, well, Chrissie said…she said it might be about time. She also said if I manage to get up and down the high street, she'll take me to McDonald's in Carnow."

Rosie looked at him severely.

"Isn't that one step forward, two steps back?" she said.

"Oh no," said Anton. "I already eat lots of McDonald's. I'm just really excited by the idea that I might get to eat a hot one. By the time they reach Lipton, they're always cold."

"Everyone needs a dream," said Rosie. "And look, this is mine. What do you think?"

Anton looked around, noticing but not mentioning that there didn't seem to be a chair, and when you were somewhere nice like this, there ought to be a chair.

"I think," he pronounced carefully, "I think it is one of the nicest places I've ever been to. It hasn't changed at all."

Rosie decided not to mention that it had changed, then she'd changed it back again.

"I know," she said. "Would you like one of our free lollies? Please have black currant; none of the children like it."

"Ergh," said Anton. "No thanks. Bit too fruity. Got any chocolate?"

"Where's Chrissie?"

"She's driving the car down to the other end of the street. She said it'll make me walk." He looked around again. "It's a shame you don't have a chair in here. I could stay all day."

Rosie made a private note not to bring out the chair.

"Also she says she has to pop into the garage and ask them something about the suspension."

Anton's eyes raised up the shelves.

"Oh wow," he said. "I don't know what to have."

There was no one else in the shop. Rosie leaned forward.

"Tell you what," she said. "Just for you—and I wouldn't do this for anyone else—how about I give you a small selection of one of each in a little bag."

"I was thinking," said Anton, "about maybe two pounds of butter fudge. And a pound of tablet. And…"

"But with this," said Rosie persuasively, "you get to try a little taster of absolutely everything. Without overdoing it. Just a tiny delicious taste, like pick 'n' mix. For after your tea."

Anton looked unconvinced and gave a hopeful-looking glance toward the Turkish delight tray.

"And some of that," he said.

"A tiny, teeny taste," said Rosie. The door clanged, and Moray walked in, his usual amused look on his face. Rosie smiled at him then remembered she'd put the mob cap back on again when she was dishing out chocolate and snatched it off her head. Moray smiled.

"I like the way you dress," he observed. "Every day is an adventure." He glanced around. "Morning, Anton."

"Miss Rosie was just saying I could have any sweets I wanted from the whole shop," said Anton.

"Was she?" said Moray with a querying look.

"Not QUITE like that," said Rosie desperately. "We're just going to have a little taste, aren't we, Anton?"

"I suppose so," said Anton, whose knees were hurting him. He hated conflict of any kind.

"You're quite the talk of the office," said Moray. "Maeve came and shared all her treats with us. Someone else I couldn't possibly mention shut his door and ate all his on his own. Anyway, I thought I'd pop in to say congratulations."

"Thank you," said Rosie. "Would you like a black currant lolly?"

"God no," said Moray. "Got any strawberry?"

"I have so much to learn," said Rosie to herself, handing it over. "Nice to see you."

But Moray wasn't looking at her; he was gazing at the shelves.

"Are those..." His face suddenly looked disarmingly young. "Are those bubble gum GOLF BALLS?"

"They certainly are," said Rosie.

Moray shook his head. "I haven't seen those for...well. For a long time."

"Would you like one?"

Moray was still shaking his head. "We used to share them at school. And fight like mad if there was an even number, or if we burst each other's bubbles."

"Who's we?" asked Rosie, but Moray was caught in a flood of reminiscence. Then he snapped himself out of it.

"Doesn't matter," he said. "No one important."

"But would you like some?"

Moray shrugged.

"All right," he said. "I'll take two."

"I always serve my sweets in even numbers," said Rosie severely. "Small, medium, or large?"

"I hate that question," said Moray flirtatiously.

Rosie grinned and made up two bags, one with a smattering of everything for Anton, which both Moray and Anton watched like a hawk, and one with some golf balls, which Rosie handed over with a smile then put out her hand for the shiny pound coins.

"Thanks," said Anton, making to turn his body around.

"No problem," said Rosie. "And Anton, please don't finish them before..."

But the doorbell had already tinged, and Anton already had his big paw inside the incongruously small looking bag.

"Oh well," said Rosie. "It's a start."

Then she noticed, where he had been, the tiny figure of Lilian.

"Lilian!" she said, delighted and worried again for her great-aunt, who looked even smaller outside of the low-beamed cottage. "I lied earlier," she said. "I do have a chair. Hang on." And she disappeared through into the back room.

"Hello, Mrs. Hopkins, how are you keeping?" said Moray. Lilian sniffed at him.

"What?" said Moray. "Come on, I'm not even your doctor."

Lilian indicated toward the back room and spoke quietly. "That's my niece in there, you know."

"I do know," said Moray, smiling.

"Well, try not to get her mixed up in any Lipton rubbish," snapped Lilian. "You know who I mean. She's not here for long and she doesn't need any of your nonsense, thank you very much."

By the time Rosie had dislodged the chair from the empty boxes waiting for the recycling run, Moray had gone.

"Where's he off to?" she said pleasantly, sitting her aunt down.

"Got more quackery to do, I expect," said Lilian, arranging herself.

• • • •

From her vantage point in the corner near the window, she had a good view of the entire shop, Lilian realized. It was truly, she saw, uncanny—these shelves she'd worked with her whole life, the big old till still there, the bags. She adjusted her glasses as Rosie served some older children on their lunch hour. With Rosie's dark hair tumbling around her shoulders, sometimes it gave her the oddest sensation that she herself had slipped back in time, that she was watching herself. How differently, she reflected. How differently she would do it this time.

"Humbugs are in the wrong place," she barked. "They go a row up."

Rosie looked around. "Yes, but I thought I'd arrange everything alphabetically, then I can find it quickly."

The children scampered out with Twix bars.

"Well, that's nonsense," said Lilian. "You have to put everything where you can easily reach it. There's no point having cola cubes on the top shelf for 'c' when they get asked for every two minutes. And you have to keep the love hearts handy; that's just plain obvious."

Rosie was stung. She was still waiting for one word of congratulations or thanks for the hard work.

"Well," she said. "Maybe what people like has changed over the years."

Lilian snorted. "Only if they're idiots. Which they are. I can see by the fact that you've ordered in chewing gum."

"What's wrong with chewing gum? The markup is unbelievable."

"Oh nothing, if you don't consider the complete decline of Western civilization a problem."

"I do not," said Rosie stoically.

• • • •

Lilian settled back with a pleasantly relaxed feeling as a sunbeam hit her chair. It was the ding of the bell and the ting of the cash register, the smell of the boiled candy and the pink candy floss ribbony top notes as, all day, people dribbled in and out to have a look, pick up a free sample, and make requests for things. (She heard, approvingly, Rosie explain in her soft voice that she was sorry they didn't have any toasted coconut mushrooms; as she, Rosie, hated them, she hadn't ordered them, but she promised to correct that forthwith.) Apart from saying hello to some of the older customers who remembered her from years ago, she let her mind wander until she was in such a haze, she half expected her father to walk in or Gordon to come try to cadge some candy cigarettes and get his hand slapped, or…

• • • •

1943

"'Ang on," said Gordon. "Isn't that the man you're stepping out with?"

Lilian couldn't say anything. The breath was sticking in her throat. Margaret clasped her arm and said loudly, "Henry sodding CARR? That eejit?"

At the sound of his name, Henry's head flicked to the side and once again took on that terrible guilty look Lilian had seen at the dance. She couldn't believe it. He was a two-timing, woman-baiting idiot, a dame teaser, and she couldn't believe she'd just fallen for it again.

Margaret, meanwhile, was looking shrewdly at a flush-faced Ida Delia with a look Lilian couldn't interpret.

For once, Lilian didn't care. She didn't care what was right and proper, whether people would talk in the village, what Ida Delia would think and tell her friends. She looked straight at Henry's stricken face, turned around, and stormed out.

At first, slightly caught up in the drama of the thing, she worried that no one would come after her. Then the gravity of the situation—what a fool she was, what a fool she must look to the world, all the private hopes and dreams she hadn't dared to admit even to herself—came bubbling up and erupted, not in tears (her tears, she felt, she had spent for Ned), but in fury, an absolute rage at the universe, at the enormous unfairness of falling in love, of finding the right man in a world with so few. She wanted to scream, to punch the stars, to howl to the moon about the absolute bloody unfairness of absolutely everything. Quiet, skinny, mousy Lilian wanted to take her knotted fists and punch down trees, trample bushes and houses and carts, kick the new pavement to dust. Her eyes blinked in frustration, as she found herself making her way to the churchyard thoughtlessly, hardly even noticing what she was doing.

Footsteps pattered to a halt behind her, but she didn't turn around. Margaret would be bad, or Gordon making some horrible joke about what lads were like, or anyone but…

He didn't even say her name. She felt, instead, a strong, tentative touch on her shoulders, which shot through her anger with temporary fear. He made a sharp intake of breath, then slowly, as if against her will, she allowed herself to be turned around. Only then did he say her name.

"Lily," he said, his face a mask of misery and desperation. "Lily, I…"

But then, like the last gasp of a drowning man, he reached for her, and she felt him reach for her and was happy as he did so and let him grab her shoulders and hold her, as she gave herself up entirely to his fierce, devastating kiss, feeling the contrast between his rough, unshaven face and his soft, pillowy lips, now hard against her own. Then she didn't think at all; she channeled her anger and her rage into passion, a huge and long pent-up passion for him that felt, once it had burst its banks, like it would never stop flowing. By the churchyard, lit only by the bright harvest moon, hard against the old oak tree, she felt herself melt into him, could barely tell where she ended and he began as they kissed on.

But eventually, gasping for breath, his whole body, it seemed, straining toward her, Henry pulled himself away. Lilian balked; was she doing it wrong? Had she done something lewd or awful? Inside she started to panic.

But it was far, far worse than that.

• • • •

Rosie was flushed with success cashing up that evening; she put all the money neatly into the nice smart little bags she'd gotten from the bank and put the figures into her laptop with a little sigh of satisfaction. It was far more than she'd expected. She was secretly rather proud of herself.

"Don't you think that was amazing?" she said to Lilian, hoping to elicit a word of praise—hoping that Lilian might congratulate her of her own accord, even say that it was just how it used to be, or thank her for her hard work, or do anything in fact but what she'd been doing for the last three hours, which was pretend to listen to Radio 4 while actually staring out of the window.

"I do," she said loudly to herself. "I think I'm amazing. Let's order in a curry." She thought about it. "Gah. Is that even possible? Is there Indian food here?"

"Is there *what*?" asked Lilian, as if this Rosie had asked her if there was any chance of getting an elephant burger to go.

"What about pizza?"

In fact, it turned out, there was pizza, a little van that parked up at the side of the school, and Rosie wandered down, feeling curiously content and like she did sometimes coming off a successful nursing shift when everything had gone well and the sun was coming up over the Thames. Except now the sun was sinking gradually over the top of the distant hills, turning them purple and pink and sending huge shadows of clouds shooting out for miles against the undulating fields. It was exquisitely beautiful, as if the country were showing off just for her, the houses of the main street turned the other way.

"Wow," said Rosie as her mobile rang, and she didn't realize till she heard it that it hadn't rung in days. She hadn't even noticed.

She snapped back when she heard it ring a second time; it was Gerard. "Hello?" she said tentatively then more fondly, "Hello, sweetie."

"Where have you been?" came the voice, sounding cross. "Every time I call, your phone is switched off."

"It's not switched off!" said Rosie. "It's just really hard to get a signal up here. Middle of nowhere and all that."

There was a pause. "Hmm," said Gerard.

"How are you, sweetie? It's amazing here, the most gorgeous sunset, wow. The sky is just totally pink and…"

Rosie sensed a pause on the other end of the line, as if he were just waiting for her to finish talking.

"…anyway, mmm," she found herself finishing. "It's cool."

"Sounds like you're loving it up there," said Gerard, a slight edge to his voice.

"No, it's not that," said Rosie. "No. No. There's nothing to do."

As if in mockery, suddenly Jake and his friends passed her by, shouting and laughing and nut-brown from the sun.

"Hey, Rosie!" they called out. "Coming for pizza?"

"I'm all right!" she waved quickly.

"Who's taking you out for pizza? I thought you were in the middle of nowhere, not Pizza bloody Express."

"It's nothing," said Rosie. "Just a van they have here some days. Nothing. Honestly."

"Where you're going with a whole load of men?"

"Gerard," said Rosie, feeling this was somehow going wrong and not quite sure how to get the conversation back on track again. "Darling."

"You didn't phone yesterday."

"Well, lots of times when I called, you were out, or on your way out."

Gerard's voice was sullen. "Well, I was just enjoying…you know, first few days of freedom and all that."

"Freedom? What kind of freedom?"

"Nothing like that. I mean, just going out with the lads and that. Then back to Mum's."

"Well, that sounds reassuring."

His voice changed. "But, you know, I miss you, Rosie. I really do."

"Now you're tired of being on the booze and have run out of socks?" Rosie teased gently.

"No! Yes! Maybe. A bit."

Rosie smiled. "I miss you too," she said. "All the time. I mean, well, I have been really, really busy and everything, but…"

Rosie paused. Something struck her. She'd been working, making friends, seeing the countryside, making an idiot of herself. And Gerard had been going out, seeing his mates, crashing at his mum's.

It hit her that someone really ought to have been missing somebody else a bit more in this scenario. That at least one of them should have been a little sad.

"So," said Gerard finally. "So I thought I'd come up this weekend!"

"Oh yes!" said Rosie, relieved. "It's market day! They have a fete! Apparently it's great. Everyone brings their cows and stuff, and there's a fair and it's going to be amazing and brilliant for the shop."

"Okay, whatever," said Gerard. "You know, this is only a temporary job, this shop thing. It's just a favor to your family. You have to get rid of it."

"I know, I know," said Rosie. The pizza smelled amazing now she was closer; the van had been outfitted with its very own brick oven.

"Well, have you advertised it yet?"

"Umm, no, not exactly. I've been really busy."

"And what about your career? Have you seen anything in *Nursing Times*? Have you spoken to your agency?"

Rosie had to admit that she hadn't done any of those things, but she was close to perfecting her recipe for cauliflower cheese, as Lilian loved it so much.

"Well, I'll drive up on Friday night," said Gerard.

"Okay!" said Rosie. "Hang on, I'd better ask Lilian."

"Ask her what, if it's all right for unmarried people to spend the night under her roof?" Gerard let out an incredulous guffaw.

"Yes!" said Rosie. "It is her roof. It's only polite."

"Yeah, whatever," said Gerard, and rather unsatisfactorily, they hung up. It was hard, Rosie reflected, to get your meaning across properly on the phone. She was sure all they needed was a proper cuddle and they'd be fine.

Jake smiled at her from over by the pizza stand.

"This is great here," he said and introduced her to some of the lads who worked with him or were down for the fair. All of them were friendly and chatty, and Rosie ordered a large ham and mushroom with extra pepperoni and cheese for her and Lilian. It was the fattiest thing she could think of; this feeding-up-Lilian project was going to have the most appalling effects on her own waistline, and that was before she took into account the odd flying saucer she snuck out the back after a break from work. She passed a pleasant ten minutes chatting and had, to her horror, almost forgotten all about Gerard coming till they were halfway through dinner, which Lilian insisted on eating with a knife and fork, at the table, from a plate. She sniffed and made some pointed remarks about the cleanliness of the pizza van and the undesirability of those who hung around it (Rosie thought she couldn't possibly mean Jake and his friends, but maybe she did), but she almost ate the entire thing before Rosie remembered to mention him.

"So," she said. "Umm, my boyfriend was thinking of coming up this weekend…" Suddenly she wasn't too sure she wanted Gerard and Lilian to meet, for some reason. She was used to Lilian's crusty ways; Gerard could get a bit grumpy and take offense easily.

Lilian was regarding Rosie with that intense beady look she sometimes got. "So is he going to marry you?"

Rosie shrugged, twisting slightly. "Ha. Well, you know, we haven't really discussed it."

"How long have you been a couple?"

"Seven years."

"Hmm," said Lilian, with feeling.

Rosie shifted in her seat. The thing was, she thought it was too long too. She had had friends meet and marry since she and Gerard had gotten together, even though Gerard had insisted on keeping it a secret for ages because they were at the same hospital and he thought it was unprofessional. Every time she came across one of those articles in magazines about "he should propose after two years," she quickly turned the page and mentally went "lalalala."

"Don't be sexist," she said.

"And how old are you?"

"Or ageist."

Lilian kept her bright bird eyes fixed on her steadily.

"I'm thirty-one," said Rosie. "That's nothing these days."

"Well, you're hardly a couple of kids," said Lilian.

"No," said Rosie slowly. "But I think we're fine as we are, thanks."

She started to clear away the dishes. Lilian looked at her, uncomprehending. Young people…didn't she realize? That if it wasn't the real thing, if it wasn't proper true love, then she was wasting her time; she was wasting her life.

"People always believe," said Lilian, musing, "that they have more time than they think."

coconut ice

• • • •

Now here is a sweet that is truly unjustly overlooked these days in favor of the gelatin and cheap, sour perfume scent of a conglomerate whose name I have been legally advised to remove. A marriage in pink and white, spring blossom and a wedding dress, powdered with confetti, a fine coconut ice is a joy for the eyes as well as the tongue. Even standard coconut refuseniks—and you know who you are—can't fail to be enthralled by the perfect match of the sweet fondant with the slightly tart coconut pieces as it melts in the mouth, like two halves of a perfect puzzle finding one another. It is both beautiful and useful.

Ingredients

- 9 ounces sweetened condensed milk
- 9 ounces powdered sugar, sifted, plus extra for dusting
- 8 ounces desiccated coconut
- pink food coloring

Mix together the condensed milk and powdered sugar in a large bowl until very stiff.

Add coconut. It will not want to mix. Make it. Use your hands. If you wear rings, take them off at this point.

Split the mix into two and knead a very small amount of food coloring into one half. Dust a board with powdered sugar then shape each half into a smooth rectangle and place one on top of the other. Roll with a rolling pin, reshaping with your hands every couple of rolls, until you have a rectangle of two-tone coconut ice about 1 inch thick.

Transfer to a plate and leave to set for at least 4 hours, or ideally overnight. These will keep for up to a month at least, if stored properly. If your coconut ice lasts for a month, you are not making it correctly.

The weather held into the weekend, and Rosie waited with anticipation for Gerard to arrive on Friday, the roar of his cool Alfa Romeo lighting up the quiet high street just after five o'clock. Rosie was waiting, nervous with anticipation, in the shop. It had been another good day, with children bursting out of school all ready for the weekend with pocket money to spend. Her steady sales were around the traditional chocolate bars, but gradually, tentatively, the children were starting to experiment, to try new things. Edison had boldly come in holding up a shiny pound coin.

"From the tooth fairy," he said, showing Rosie the gap. "I did wait up, but I didn't see it. It was good to get the money, but I'd rather have had the fairy. Hester was not happy about that. I really did wait up an awfully long time. After midnight. So I have proved that the tooth fairy doesn't come before midnight. That is what is called 'a start.'"

"It is," she said. "Now you know you have to choose what you want"—she couldn't forget the other side of things—"and make sure you brush your new teeth properly!"

Edison nodded gravely.

"And replace your toothbrush every three moths," he said.

"Months?" said Rosie, wondering briefly when she'd last replaced hers.

"No, moths, I think. When they come toward the bathroom light at bedtime? That's when you know you need a new one."

"Hmm," said Rosie. "Now, young man, what would you like?"

Edison's eyes looked enormous behind his glasses as he scanned the shelves anxiously.

"I want to try something new. I think," he added tentatively.

Rosie eyed him up and down.

"Well," she said. "Have you ever tried Edinburgh rock?"

Edison shook his head.

"I don't like rock. It's too hard. It's a little bit frightening."

"Aha," said Rosie. "Not THIS rock. This rock is soft and crumbly, like chalk. It's like delicious chalk."

Edison's face perked up. "Can I..."

Rosie bent down, her face mock-stern.

"Now," she said, "you're not going to ask me for a free sample, are you?"

Edison shook his head vigorously.

"Okay. Do you trust me?"

The shaking turned to nodding.

"Would you like me to make it a half and half, so you can have something else in there too in case you don't love it?"

Edison gave her his steady gaze.

"No, thank you," he said. "Embra rock, please."

And he stoically handed over his pound coin. Rosie was just bending down to give him the bag when the door opened with its traditional ting and Gerard walked in. For five seconds, Rosie found, blinking, that it was difficult to tell the difference between Edison's six-year-old face and Gerard's. Both had an expression of anticipatory joy. One was for the sweets and the other...something surged in

Rosie's heart then. Gerard was looking delighted. But it wasn't at her. He was scanning the shelves and the tins and bars with a cheerful, hungry look on his face.

"Hello!" said Rosie, as Edison tentatively bit into his first piece of pale pastel candy.

"Hello!" said Gerard cheerfully. "Wow, look at this place! You've got EVERYTHING!"

"And it's lovely to see you, Rosie."

"And it's lovely to…have you got licorice torpedoes?"

"I do," said Rosie.

"Wow. Can I have some?"

"You can, for a pound."

Gerard stuck out his lip.

"I don't get free sweets?"

"You can," came a high-pitched voice from the floor. "But you have to lose a tooth. And then, do you know what happens?"

Gerard regarded the boy carefully.

"Does a dragon come?" he asked finally.

"Noooo," said Edison, pleased he knew the answer.

"Is it a goblin?"

"Nooooo!"

"Is it a little mouse?"

"It's a FAIRY!!!"

"No way! Excellent!"

Rosie smiled. Gerard had always been good with kids. Well, he was one, so that helped. She reached up to the high shelf and got the licorice torpedoes, bright red little sweets shaped like a capsule. A real boy's own sweet. Classic Gerard.

"A pound, please," she said, holding out her hand.

"Or a tooth," added Edison.

Gerard grimaced then handed over a pound. "Thank you," said Rosie. "We are, of course, a going concern."

"Yeah, yeah, yeah," said Gerard. He looked, Rosie thought, a bit wobbly; he'd put on some weight, and his jowls were beginning to show. Too much of his mum's indulgent cooking or takeout, she imagined. Inside, she couldn't help but be a bit annoyed. So if she was still to find him fit and attractive, she had to moderate his diet? That didn't seem very fair. Although to be absolutely strictly truthful, her waistband had grown a bit tighter since she'd been in Lipton, that much was definitely true. So.

"Run along, Edison," she said to the figure below. "I'm closing up the shop now."

Edison looked at her, his mouth full of pink and lemon gunky stuff, the gaping hole his bottom tooth had left acting like a conduit.

"THESE," he said excitedly. "THESE are the BEST THINGS EVER. I mustn't tell Reuben about them."

"No," said Rosie with a sigh. She thought it was time to have a word with Reuben's mother maybe, whoever she was. Wasn't nice to be victimized like that for a child.

"Who's Reuben?" asked Gerard when Edison had gone, clanging the door happily behind him.

"His little mate. Isn't allowed any sweets. Edison's a good soul, keeps it secret from him."

"Well, wouldn't he be a better soul if he shared them?"

"What, and have a marauding parent down here accusing me of child murder because white sugar was involved? No, thank you."

They regarded one another. "I've missed you," said Gerard.

"I've missed you too," said Rosie, remembering back to those first chilly evenings. "Come here." She gave him a hug, smelled his familiar scent—aftershave, chips—and smiled.

"Okay," said Gerard, greedily attacking his torpedoes. "What are you making for supper? I'm starving. Or sex first. Sex then supper? Or after supper? Or both? What about now? In the back room? I like the apron."

Rosie grinned. "No, darling! I've got to lock up and cash up. I'll clean in the morning."

"Well, hurry UP," said Gerard. "Come on. Can't you do it all tomorrow? It's not really your shop."

"No," said Rosie. "But right now it's my job. It won't take long."

Gerard looked pouty.

"But please. I've come all this way."

"And I'll be ten minutes. Wait here, then we can go and I'll introduce you to Lilian. Or you can take yourself off to the pub down the road and have a pint if you like, and I'll meet you in a minute."

Rosie hadn't really meant the last one seriously, but to her disgruntlement, his face immediately perked up and he asked her for directions straightaway.

"Can you eat there?" he asked.

Rosie nodded. "Okay. Great. See you down there, yeah?"

Rosie turned back toward the cash till and started putting things away. "I really won't be long," she protested.

"Great," said Gerard, leaving her to it. "I'll order you a gin and tonic."

• • • •

Rosie was so cross she dawdled doing the books then nipped back next door to get changed.

"Isn't your young man coming?" asked Lilian by the door. She had clearly dressed up and was wearing a lavender coat dress and matching lipstick.

"Ooh, you look nice," said Rosie. She almost added "are you going somewhere?" but thankfully stopped herself just in time.

"Well, where is he?"

"Umm...he's...I'm meeting him at the pub."

"At the *pub*?" asked Lilian as if she'd said "At the brothel."

"Yes, it's all right—here, I have pie and beans for you. I'm just going to heat it up in the microwave."

With her first week's profits, Rosie had bought Lilian a microwave. Even though Lilian refused to go near it, Rosie felt better knowing it was there.

"Sorry, I know it's nothing fancy, but it's delicious and full of calories."

"He's at the pub?" asked Lilian again as if she hadn't heard her. "He didn't come to say good evening?"

Rosie tried to tell herself that Lilian was just an old fuddy-duddy caught up in old-fashioned ideas about things. That was it. She was old and set in her ways. But even so, doubt crept in. It was terribly rude, wasn't it? Not to greet someone who was putting a roof over your head for the night? Classic Gerard.

"He was really exhausted after driving up here," she said.

"So he can't stay off the sauce?" said Lilian acidly.

"No," said Rosie. "I'll...I'll go meet him. We'll see you later. Don't wait up."

"I don't like that pub," said Lilian. "Never set foot in it again."

"Again what?" said Rosie, but Lilian didn't answer.

"Are you all right?" asked Rosie, taking dinner out of the microwave, but Lilian waved her away.

"You have fun," she said.

"Okay," said Rosie. "Don't wait up."

Lilian smiled. And for the first time, spontaneously and without thinking about it, Rosie leaned over and kissed her great-aunt on the cheek before she left.

• • • •

The Red Lion was warm and busy-looking on a Friday night. Rosie had never been in there before and felt tentative at the entrance, the busy noise spilling out onto the pavement with the warm light and the smokers. There was a filled water trough outside and the sound of hearty male laughter. Rosie had noticed just how many men there were in the countryside—the farm boys, the vets, the tree surgeons, the chemists. This was probably why all her female friends were always complaining about how difficult it was to find a man in the city. Because they'd all moved to the countryside, or never left it. It was true, Lipton was full of hunks; if you let them loose on London, the women there would hold a parade. Whereas here they just carried on hauling hay, undiscovered.

Rosie checked her lip gloss—and slight sense of nerves—and pushed the door. Inside, the wallpaper was ancient and yellow, and the fire was burning to stave off the early autumnal chill; big oblong tables were positioned willy-nilly around the room, with horse brasses on the walls. And there he sat, somewhat awkward-looking, his boyish face and pink cheeks out of place among the tanned agricultural laborers, his shirt slightly crumpled. In front of him was a nearly empty pint of cider and three empty chip bags. This was her man, she thought. For the first time since she'd been so wrapped up in the giddiness of moving in together, planning their future, here he was. Not perfect. Well, she wasn't perfect. And he was her bloke. Her face broke into a smile.

"Hey!" she said. "Where's that gin and tonic?"

• • • •

Two hours later, Rosie was well into the swing of things. Although Gerard did talk about what it was like to be back at his mum's and how great it was and how he got a cooked breakfast every day perhaps a little bit too much, and he did suggest, after his third pint, perhaps a little too loudly, that he thought they should nip into the bathrooms and have sex, particularly as, aside from Jake and his friends, there were the vicar, Edison's mother, and Malik from the grocery store within a few tables.

"How do you know everyone already?" said Gerard. Rosie considered telling him it was because she'd ruined Mr. Isitt's vegetable garden and was considered by half the town as a consequence to be sleeping with the other half, but she shrugged and simply said, "Oh, you know, small towns."

"I don't," said Gerard. "It's weird. Did you say that guy runs the grocery store?"

Rosie smiled and nodded over at Malik, who was, it had to be said, remarkably sanguine about their opening and had merely remarked that as long as she stayed out of booze, cigarettes, and lottery tickets, they would get along fine. They occasionally made change for one another. They had a quick chat about how they expected to do for market day. (Rosie instantly regretted not getting an ice cream fridge—Malik sold standard ice creams, so she could possibly get in something nice like Green & Black's to appeal to older people instead...that would work well next summer.) Then Jake came over to say hi and gave Gerard such a blatant look up and down that Rosie found herself blushing.

"Who's this?" said Jake.

"This is...this is Gerard," said Rosie. "Umm, my...my boyfriend."

Gerard wiped some chip dust off his fingers and didn't get up. "Hello," he said amiably. "You're a big fella."

Jake looked at Rosie with a questioning look. She ignored him.

"There's a lot of blokes around here," said Gerard, glancing around the pub.

"Yes," said Rosie, smiling good-bye to Jake, who didn't seem to take the hint.

"We need to go and do some more gardening," he said. Behind him, his friends were nudging each other.

"What, now?" said Rosie.

Jake stuck out his bottom lip. Rosie suspected he probably found it quite easy to get women. She was just the new thing in town.

"Soon," he said.

"Yes, all right," said Rosie. "Soon."

She took a long slug of her gin and tonic, waving politely to Hye, Maeve, and Moray over in the far corner, already well into some bottles of wine. Typical doctor behavior, she thought.

"What is this, *The Waltons*?" said Gerard, turning his head. "You've been here five minutes and you know half the town."

"Well, I run the local sweetshop," said Rosie. "Of course I'm going to meet a few people. And everyone knows Lilian."

"Yes, but…"

"And I don't know everyone, anyway. There're loads of people I don't know, like them, for example." Rosie gestured at a random couple by the window. The woman smiled back at her shyly then got up and came over.

"Hello," she said. "I'm Edison's mum."

"Oh, hello."

"Well, even I've met Edison," said Gerard, throwing up his hands.

"He liked his tooth fairy bag," said Edison's mother stiffly. "I've tried to tell him it's all just ridiculous superstition, but…"

"Oh, it's harmless," said Rosie.

The woman sniffed.

"Actually," said Rosie, standing up. The woman had naturally gray hair even though she was quite young—this was such an unusual sight Rosie had to try not to stare at it—and wire-rimmed spectacles. She wasn't wearing a scrap of makeup and was very thin. Potentially she could look amazing. "I did want to ask you something. Edison talks about his friend who isn't allowed any sweets? I realize mothers do take quite a firm line on this kind of thing, but we sell fruit drops and raisins, and…"

Edison's mother smiled in a slightly superior kind of a way. "Oh gosh, no," she said. "There is no Reuben!"

Rosie squinted. Edison's mother seemed to be implying that she, Rosie, was believing something stupid.

"Reuben is his imaginary friend!" said his mother cheerfully. "He's terribly imaginative! It's a sign of very high intelligence."

Rosie stifled the unkind thought that if his mother dyed her hair and bought Edison a pair of normal sneakers then he might not have to make imaginary friends and manage to make a real one, but nonetheless she arranged her face into an expression of concern.

"You know," confided his mother as if this were a badge of honor, "we've taken him to all these child psychologists and they just don't know what to do with him."

"Loads of children have imaginary friends though, don't they?" said Rosie, stunned they would send such a small boy to see a shrink. "Maybe they just think it's perfectly normal."

Edison's mum let out a little laugh. "Oh no, you would never call our Edison anything like normal! There's nothing average about our Edison! You see, he is particularly highly intelligent. So really, it is something of a worry for us."

She didn't look like she thought it was a worry, thought Rosie. She looked absolutely delighted that she was turning her own child into the town weirdo.

But she didn't say anything—it was hardly her place—and after all, who was to say that one day, if she did have children (though Gerard had never shown the slightest indication in that direction), maybe she'd be an overprotective basket case too. She hoped not though.

"Oh," she said. "Well, good luck. He's welcome anytime. And his 'friend.'"

Edison's mother smiled. "Oh it's SO nice to have someone a little broad-minded around town," she said loudly, and Rosie smiled her good-byes as politely as she could and sat back down.

"So," said Gerard. "What about selling the shop then? Have you got it on the market? Have you had any viewings? What are you selling it for?"

"Umm," said Rosie. "Well, you know, I've been very busy getting it up and running."

"Getting it up and running?" said Gerard. "You've been here four weeks. It was only meant to be for six. You've got a career waiting for you."

For the first time, oddly, Rosie found the idea of going back to a big hospital—which she normally found buzzy and exciting and endlessly interesting, with the camaraderie, the sudden bursts of adrenaline, the occasional drama, the sense that she was doing something useful—not at all appealing. It was so unlike here, she supposed, and for the first time, instead of being anxious to get back and get started and frustrated with the pace of things here, she found herself in no hurry at all.

"Yes, yes, I know," she said. "I know, you're right."

"Well, if you know I'm right, why don't you just do it?" grumbled Gerard. "Don't just nod your head and say yeah, yeah, yeah."

"Mmm-hmm," said Rosie. "No, I will, definitely."

"Because I don't want to keep living at my mum's."

"You don't have to live at your mum's!" said Rosie suddenly in exasperation. "Why don't you live in our home like a normal, adult human being?"

"What, ha, and do my own laundry and buy my own food when I can get it all done for me for free?" said Gerard in a scoffing voice. "Yeah, right, that sounds like a GREAT idea, Rosie. Yes, brilliant."

"But don't you enjoy your independence?" said Rosie.

Gerard shrugged. "Why should I? MY mum didn't move to Australia."

"Oh, that is very unfair," said Rosie, incredibly annoyed that, suddenly and out of her control, they seemed to be skidding toward a fight. She was also conscious that, around her, people were watching them. This was a DEFINITE disadvantage, she thought, in knowing everyone in the town. It felt a bit like being famous; all sorts of people were watching them, judging her, she knew, judging Gerard. She felt incredibly irritated: how dare they? On the other hand, if Gerard had made more of an effort to say hello to people, come said hi to her great-aunt, turned up with a huge bouquet of flowers, or even a small bouquet of gas station flowers, or…well. That didn't matter.

"Shall we get out of here?"

"Where else is there?" asked Gerard slightly bitterly, looking at his pint. That was a fair point. There was a fancy hotel up the road that they used for weddings and conventions, but Rosie had never been there and didn't know what it was like on the weekends.

"Well, we could try…" Rosie looked around and took a deep breath. She was going to make the effort. They could try again. "Hey," she said. "Why don't we have another drink?"

Gerard smiled, his pique forgotten.

"Pint of Magners, please! And some chips! Then I'm going to have the scampi! Can I have the scampi?"

Rosie wondered for a second if he'd always been so young. Well, it was endearing. Of course. He was cute; everyone thought that. It's just…well, Jake wouldn't bother asking her if he could have scampi. Moray wouldn't eat it. And Stephen…well. Anyway.

"I don't mind what you have," she said, sounding slightly sharper than she'd intended. "Eat what you like."

"It's just I thought, chips AND fries…"

"Yes, they're a terrible combination."

His face fell.

"But if you want them, have them."

Gerard bit his lip.

"I won't enjoy them now you've said that."

"Well, have something else."

"But I really like scampi."

"Well, have that and I'll eat the fries."

Gerard's face relaxed. "Okay!"

Rosie went to the bar, tentatively ordering herself a salad—after all the high-calorie meals with Lilian and the two of Gerard's fries she'd probably manage to lay claim to before he wolfed them all—and, turning, looked at him, his head buried in the chip bag as he tried to get out the last few grains of salt. She smiled halfheartedly. It was odd to see him out of his normal environment. At the hospital, with his white coat on, he was important, authoritative. Nobody needed to know that he still got his mother to iron it because Rosie (a) refused, and (b) once when she offered on a Sunday night, "did it wrong." Carefully, she picked up the two glasses. The difference in her though—from just a few weeks ago. She hadn't been unhappy before, had she? She hadn't. There wasn't anything missing. Well, so, perhaps she'd been a little bit over her job. There was that. And perhaps moving in with Gerard hadn't been the dream she'd hoped it would be. There was definitely that.

It crossed her mind as she paid for the drinks (about half, she noticed, what she paid in London) that perhaps if she had been completely happy, she'd have refused to come at all.

"I think maybe I wanted the steak and ale pie," said Gerard when she got back. "Can you tell them?"

"You tell them!" said Rosie in exasperation. A good turn for the conversation right there she felt would have been for him to say something along the lines of "I've really been missing you" or "you look great" or "tell me about setting up the shop."

"Can't you?" said Gerard. "You're the local."

Rosie tried to forestall a row—why were they being so snippy with each other? Normally she found Gerard cute. She tried to remember how sweet he'd been with Edison earlier. It was nearly helping. He was already halfway down his fresh pint. Sighing slightly, she got up out of her seat and headed to the bar again, pinkly conscious of all the eyes in the room on this fresh piece of gossip, when the door of the lounge bar crashed open, and all eyes turned.

• • • •

1943

"No, no, it's not you."

Henry looked half-crazed, completely wild-eyed, as they stood, heart to heart, both of them breathless and panting.

"It's not you. It's never you. It's always been you."

Henry was holding her shoulders now, though Lilian felt that if she didn't kiss him again, RIGHT NOW, she was going to explode or die. She could barely breathe. What was he saying to her? She couldn't take it in at all.

"Kiss me again," she said, suddenly emboldened, by the great moon and the smell of him and the feel of being wrapped so tightly in his arms; she had to feel it again, she had to.

Instead, Henry wrenched himself away with a huge effort of will and gradually lowered her arms, holding her thin wrists in his huge hands.

"I don't..." Lilian's voice sounded strange, even to herself, like a child talking. She couldn't keep the wobble out of it. "I don't understand."

Henry turned his head away. Lilian wanted to force him to look at her. "What is it?"

Then from his mouth came the worst words, the words she was dreading hearing, in a voice so low she had to strain to hear it above the rustle of the trees.

"It's Ida," he muttered. "From months back. She's knocked up."

• • • •

Lilian had forced her arms from his as if they were on fire. "WHAT?" she said, thinking it was possible she'd misunderstood.

Henry crouched down at the side of the road and put his hands over his head. Then he pulled himself together and stood up. He had a look on his face that Lilian recognized from her brothers when they'd received their call-up papers—that of condemned men.

"I…I…" he started. "Me and Ida…that night. That night at the dance. I came looking for you and I couldn't find you and…oh, I was so stupid, but she was all over me and I thought that would be it, you know. I mean, I wanted to see you so badly and I thought…well, I just thought maybe I should get some practice in, and then, well…"

He shook his head.

"I've messed up, Lilian. I've messed up, right badly."

• • • •

Lilian thought about Gertie Fanshawe last year, who'd been spirited away from town and come back about five months later. Her mother had insisted it had been a bad bout of influenza and she'd been on a rest cure. Nobody said anything about it; of course they didn't. It would be unthinkably rude, to Gertie and her family, to bring it up at all. But Lilian remembered Gertie at school: wild and funny and uncontrollable, smart as a whip, but she only really loved her horses down at the Fanshawe place. Lilian remembered seeing her, flying across hedgerows whenever she got five minutes off from working the farm—which wasn't often—her long hair flying loose behind her, one time, even, with her feet bare. People talked, but Lilian had never thought Gertie cared, thought she was deaf to town gossip, only wanted to be free.

When she returned, she didn't ride anymore. She was hardly seen. When Lilian saw her, she was shocked at how thin she'd become, how meek. No more cutting remarks or the yearning looks she'd always given to the classroom window. It was as if something vital inside her had vanished; something had gone.

Six weeks after she had returned to her family, Gertie Fanshawe had left without a word, and no one had ever seen her again.

"I…I have to marry her," stuttered Henry. "You know. I have to. Remember…"

Lilian nodded. "I do. I do remember."

"I can't…I can't let that happen to Ida. It's inhuman. She'd be ruined."

Lilian shook her head. Her hands were still shaking, but she was, she knew, practical, sensible Lilian. Always ready to help. Always with her feet on the ground. That's what everybody thought.

What she felt inside was, "Get me pregnant too then. Get me pregnant too." All she said was, "Her mother is going to make your life a living hell."

Henry looked up at her from the roadside.

"At the moment, that couldn't be any worse than how I feel."

"Henry?" a familiar voice screeched down the road. It sounded exasperated. "Henry? Darling? Where ARE you? Where are you?"

"I'll go," said Lilian quickly, her mind working. This didn't need to be any worse than it already was.

Henry looked at her with desperate eyes.

"I don't…I don't want you to go," he said, furious with himself, bitter and ashamed and choked up with emotion. "I never ever wanted to let you go. Ever."

"If only…" Lilian wasn't going to say that sentence, although she would dwell on it for a long, long time. If only she had let her feelings be known earlier. If only she had swallowed her stupid pride when he'd asked her to the dance. If only she'd been bolder, stronger, more of a woman. If only, if only, if only.

The voice was getting closer. Henry stiffened and stood up to his full height, trying to look stoic in the face of what lay ahead. Lilian saw, suddenly, a glimpse of what he would look like in uniform, but it was only a trick of the moonlight and the wind waving through the trees. Then, quick as a flash, she turned around and took the back way through the woods, running until she felt as if her heart would burst, running because she wanted her heart to burst, wanted it to burst its very banks, carry her away, and let her drown in it all.

• • • •

2012

The door to the pub banged back against the stained glass siding, and everyone turned to look as cooler air whooshed in from outside. Standing, silhouetted against the dark street, white as a piece of paper, listing to the left, was Stephen. Rosie jumped forward, and Moray jumped up from the far table.

Stephen looked straight at Rosie and managed to say, "I think…I think I need…" before his head started to loll to the side.

"QUICK, someone help me!" shouted Rosie, rushing to his side. Gerard stayed put, annoyingly, but Moray was already there, and they helped Stephen to a nearby chair and put his head between his knees until he could stabilize his breathing. His left leg was an absolute waterfall of red. Moray and Rosie looked at each other with worried expressions, and the landlord indicated they could carry him into the back room. Even as thin as he was, his large frame was heavy to manhandle, and the landlord had to help. Finally out of the hubbub of the lounge (which buzzed with intrigue and excitement—at least, Rosie thought in passing, she and Gerard would no longer be the main topic of conversation), they could get some peace and quiet.

Stephen was looking around him blearily as Rosie got him a glass of water. He was still bleeding, and Moray rushed off to fetch his medical kit. The landlord made himself scarce when he worked out that there was nothing more he could do to help but that there was little more than a minor adventure to bring out the thirst in his customers. Stephen and Rosie were alone.

"What the HELL did you do?" said Rosie, close to his ear. She tied together two bar towels to make a tourniquet. There was one already—it looked like a long red napkin, obviously made by Stephen.

Stephen shook his head. "Nothing. Nothing. Accident."

"What kind of an accident?"

Stephen gulped down some more water. His face was very, very white indeed. "Stupid bloody...broke the bloody bottle..."

"You are BLEEDING OUT, for fuck's sake," said Rosie. "I'm calling an ambulance."

"They're two hours out," said Stephen. "Durn't matter." His breathing was shallow, and his eyes were having trouble focusing.

"Why didn't you call us?"

Stephen shook his head. "Reception..."

Rosie shook her head. "Ah, this BLOODY countryside."

"I am very cold," announced Stephen quietly. Rosie covered him in a tablecloth, the nearest thing to hand, and checked her tourniquet. It was holding it, but he was in a very bad way indeed. Rosie knelt very close to him to try to keep him conscious.

"It's all right. It's going to be all right," she said, her heart racing. Where was Moray? She clasped Stephen's freezing fingers between her own. "Just hold on."

Stephen's eyes were drooping.

"How...how did you get down the hill in the dark?" asked Rosie.

"Mm?" said Stephen. "Oh. Oh, they left...they left some stupid old thing...stupid really. Stupid."

At that moment, the door burst open and Moray came in with a large black bag, the landlord close behind him carrying what looked like a quadruple brandy.

"There's no time for that now," scolded Rosie, rolling her eyes.

"Not for me, for him."

"You don't keep a full medicine cabinet?"

"SOMEONE never sorted it out after the DOG thing," panted Moray, glancing back into the bar where Hye hadn't actually bothered to come through to see what was going on.

Stephen looked around him in confusion. "Where's that shyster doctor gone? Has he been drinking again?"

Rosie knelt down, holding both his hands as Moray scrubbed up at the sink. "Listen," she said, moving his head around so he could see her. She didn't like his condition, not at all. "Moray is going to stitch you up, and the landlord's called the ambulance. You need a blood transfusion really, really quickly. What type are you?"

Stephen couldn't answer.

"Okay, well, fine, I'll make sure they bring whatever they have. But listen. Moray's going to stitch you now. But I'm afraid there's no anesthetic. There's just..."

Moray was holding up a packet of ibuprofen.

"Oh, for CHRIST'S sake," said Rosie. She took the brandy off the barman. "Drink this," she said. Together, they managed to get most of it down his throat, along with a couple of pills. Then Moray ripped off the last of Stephen's trouser leg. The wound was a horrible, livid thing against the stark white of his leg.

"Okay," said Moray, breathing out.

"So Stephen," said Rosie. "You have to trust me. You have to trust me, okay?" She turned quickly to Moray. "Do you think the tourniquet would hold till the ambulance arrived?"

"I don't know when that might be," said Moray. "So no."

Rosie nodded.

"Just keep looking at me," she said to Stephen, moving to the side to let Moray work. Stephen's eyes didn't falter from hers for a moment, although they closed, briefly, when the needle went in for the first time.

"It hurts," he breathed quietly, his grip on Rosie's hands strengthening.

"I know," said Rosie as if she were speaking to a child. "You're being very brave."

"Oh, Rosie."

"I know. I know. You doof, if you hadn't been such a stubborn arse, you'd have had this done under a lovely local anesthetic."

The violet shadows under his eyes gave him a haunted look as he winced. "Christ."

"I know, I know." Rosie glanced at Moray, urging him to work faster, but he was making a careful job of it. He caught her eye.

"This appears to be our new hobby."

"I don't like it," said Rosie. Then she concentrated again on Stephen. Later, he would remember very little of it. Nothing but a tight grip on his hands that did not falter, even when he was gripping them in agony like his life depended on it, and a pair of green eyes that refused to let him look away.

In reality, stitching Stephen's leg took just over ten minutes. To everyone in the room, it felt like a million years. Stephen fell silent, the only sign he was even awake a tear he could not prevent falling from the corner of his eye and making a track down his cheek. Rosie could not remove her hands from his to wipe it away, but she moved their hands together, gently, to brush it from his cheek. Then she tried to focus on their breathing, taking deep breaths, holding them and exhorting Stephen to do the same; to breathe in time with her to relieve the pain; to keep the oxygen moving, until their breath was going in and out at the same time and Rosie, briefly, had the oddest sensation of being unable to tell quite where Stephen ended and she began.

Moray worked away accurately and intently, the only sign of pressure a bead of sweat on his forehead. The landlord brought in another brandy and announced that there was no sign of the ambulance yet and that everyone was worried. Rosie concentrated on trying to somehow compel herself into Stephen's body, to keep him with her, stop him nodding out or his blood pressure dropping too far. She tried to beam energy to him through her eyes, even though she knew this was ridiculous, willing him away from looking down or contemplating what was been done to him.

Finally Moray straightened up.

"Fine," he said. "That'll hold it. But he needs blood. And he needs to be in the hospital now."

He eyed Stephen harshly.

"If you'd gotten over yourself three months ago, we wouldn't have had all that little drama, would we?"

He went over to the sink and washed his hands then looked around at the bloodied floor.

"Sorry, Les," he called to the landlord.

"Oh, I've seen worse," said Les.

Rosie found she couldn't put Stephen's hands down. She was cramped but barely felt it. It felt as if the entire universe had contracted to the dark blue of his eyes, fringed with black, his shallow breathing, and white, white shoulders.

At last, the ambulance siren sounded, and as soon as the medics arrived, everything exploded into noisy color and action.

"Did you find out his blood group?" shouted a cross, stout paramedic at Rosie, who flushed, realizing she hadn't found out even this most basic of useful information.

"O-neg," said Stephen suddenly, as if from the bottom of his consciousness. "I'm O-neg."

They started loading him onto a gurney brought in through the back door of the pub, someone starting with a drip, someone else checking the wound area. There was a lot of yelling and noise, and the ambulance lights lit up the quiet street, attracting large numbers of the curious and the freshly awoken. The entire pub was on the road. In the back room, the stout paramedic turned to Rosie.

"Okay, let go now, ducky," she said. At first, Rosie didn't realize. Until she worked out that her left and Stephen's right hand were still completely intertwined. Stephen looked at her.

"Can you come with me?"

Rosie suddenly remembered that she was in a pub, that she was meant to be here with her boyfriend whom she hadn't seen for four weeks, that the hospital was an hour away over the dales, and she didn't even have her wallet. All of those things dissipated in a millisecond.

"Of course," she found herself saying as the pub door banged open again. There stood, once more, Lady Lipton.

marshmallows

• • • •

Ingredients

- ✶ powdered sugar
- ✶ corn starch
- ✶ 9 sheets leaf gelatin
- ✶ 16 ounces sugar
- ✶ 1 tablespoon liquid glucose
- ✶ 7 fluid ounces water, divided
- ✶ 2 large egg whites
- ✶ 1 teaspoon vanilla extract

Lightly oil a shallow baking tray, about 12 x 9 inches, and dust it with sieved powdered sugar and corn starch.

Soak the gelatin in 5 fluid ounces cold water.

Put the sugar, glucose, and remaining water into a heavy-based pan. Bring to a boil and continue cooking for 12 to 15 minutes until the mixture reaches 260°F on a sugar thermometer. This is very hot indeed. Please do not be an idiot about this; these are only marshmallows and not worth risking a trip to the hospital. I do not recommend allowing children to help in the cooking of marshmallows, only the eating.

When the syrup is up to temperature, carefully slide in the softened gelatin sheets and their soaking water. Pour the syrup into a metal jug.

Whisk the egg whites until stiff, pouring in the hot syrup from the jug. The mixture will become shiny and start to thicken. Add the vanilla extract and continue whisking for 5 to 10 minutes, until the mixture is stiff and thick enough to hold its shape on the whisk.

Put the mix into the baking tray, level off, and leave for 2 hours.

Dust the work surface with powdered sugar and corn starch Loosen the marshmallow around the sides of the tray and turn it out onto the dusted surface. Cut into squares and roll in the sugar and corn starch. Leave to dry a little on a wire rack.

1943

Down by the Salley Gardens." Lilian was humming repetitively to herself in her bedroom, finishing up on the accounts for the shop. She found the singing distracted her. Since that awful night in the woods, she had decided to focus on nothing more than putting everything behind her. Gordon had gone back to the regiment; Margaret, after begging her to come to Derby with her for the last time, had gone back to her life with her jug-eared young man, who'd managed barely a word in their three days' leave, which was all Margaret needed to know to know that they'd be together forever apparently, and she'd already booked the church. She'd asked Lilian to be her bridesmaid. Lilian couldn't think of anything she'd rather do less. She'd said yes, of course. But to stand inside a consecrated space and talk about anyone's true love and commitment to the other would taste like ashes, she knew.

She had thrown herself into the shop and was teaching herself double-entry bookkeeping as a way of taking the burden from her father a bit. Gordon had made enough nods toward the idea that after the war—if there was ever going to be such a thing, which Lilian doubted—he was never coming back to Lipton ever again, that now he'd seen a bit of the world, he wanted to make his way in it, which was fair enough, Lilian supposed. Terence was so far away it made the mind boggle even to think of it, and he wrote neat, tight little letters that didn't even need to be censored. And her Neddy was never coming home again. So she could shoulder the burden. She would have to. This was, she realized, even at seventeen years old, how it was going to be. She carefully, day by day, swallowed tear by swallowed tear, built and managed a carapace over her heart, bit by bit. When the banns went up for Ida Delia and Henry, she smiled politely at everyone gossiping about it and barely disturbed her composure. When she heard on the grapevine that Henry had received his call-up papers, she simply nodded, even though inside she was riven. There was a bit of her that thought, that pleaded, that hoped that everything was going to be all right. That he would realize the error of his ways at the last minute.

In her deepest, darkest moments, late at night, tossing in a damp bed, her mind in circles, she even thought the worst, the darkest of thoughts—perhaps the baby was someone else's. Perhaps the baby would not make it, and he would be free.

It was this last, most unspeakably dreadful thought—to wish harm on an unborn innocent—that shocked her to the core, that made her more determined than ever to display no hysterics, to do no begging, no pleading, no complaining about her lot in life. She clearly wasn't worthy. For her superior manners before, and her evil thoughts now, she didn't deserve Henry Carr, and however much she might long for him and yearn for him, it wasn't going to change a thing. She told herself that, but it changed nothing.

And now he had his papers. It felt as if, somehow, while she could still see him, there was still hope. He didn't come into the sweetshop, of course—he avoided her as assiduously as she avoided him—but she had seen him: at church, in a high collar, standing next to his in-laws-to-be, who were, town gossip had it, every bit as horrified by their daughter's farm laborer choice as Lilian had predicted. Or being tugged up and down the high street by Ida Delia, wearing a too-large dress and pretending to all and sundry that there was nothing in there and they were madly in love, that was all. Ida Delia, thought Lilian spitefully, was probably glad when his call-up papers came. It gave a little veracity to why they were getting married in such a hurry.

Glimpses as he rushed past, head bowed...they were nothing. There wasn't a note, not a word. It seemed Henry, once he had given his word, was a man of it. The fact that, as far as Lilian was concerned, he had given it to the worst person she could possibly imagine didn't detract from that.

They got married on Whitsun. It was sparsely attended; Ida Delia's mother certainly wasn't going to ask her Bristol cousins to watch her beautiful, eligible daughter settle for someone who could hardly pick the straw out of his hair. Henry had started basic training and was wearing an ill-fitting uniform in rough wool that was hot and scratchy in the heat. Lilian stayed upstairs in her room all day but couldn't resist a glimpse outside to see the procession go past. Ida Delia, wearing a rose-pink suit dress and a pink netted hat on her lavish golden curls, looked glorious—happy and radiant, rounded, her breasts full and lavish, her waist still small, her face beaming in triumph. Henry looked tall—different with his newly shorn hair and his awkward worsted uniform. Lilian had decided there and then that she hated weddings.

At around six, when the procession had long passed, her dad knocked on Lilian's door. That she wasn't crying was the worst bit. Instead, she sat, perched on the edge of the single bed with its floral duvet, not looking, not making a sound, but completely and utterly blank.

Not knowing what else to do, he took her in his arms and sat her on his knee like she was a child again—she was so thin, he felt; even for his little Lily, she had gotten so thin—and waited till gradually her rigid body bent a little toward him, and she turned and buried her head in his shoulder and made small, mewling animal noises of pain. Terence Senior stared out of the window and felt her heart break as he watched the sun go down over the blue hills and wondered why on God's earth any living creature would want to bring a child into this world.

• • • •

2012

"She was," remarked Moray quietly, "a lot quicker with the damn dog."

Rosie stared at Henrietta, not understanding. Stephen had allowed his eyes to close briefly.

"Ah," he said. "Mother."

Rosie stared at him in consternation then looked at Lady Lipton. Sure enough, the resemblance, though slight, was there. But this didn't make any sense at all. She'd been over at the big house all the time? Knowing her injured son was stuck in that cold house all by himself? Why hadn't she been looking after him? Wandering around making sarcastic remarks and worrying herself senseless about her DOG. Rosie shook her head in disbelief.

"Why..." she began then wasn't sure how to go on. If she had injured herself, her mother would drop everything, would haunt her house, drive her mental and up the wall and get in the way and basically totally wind her up until she was 100 percent sure she was better. And it wouldn't matter if Rosie said "No thanks, I don't want your help" or "Please don't visit." Her mother would have hit in the door with a hammer. And why had she spent all this time worrying about Stephen when he had half the county at his disposal and a hundred-room mansion for whenever he got bored of being petulant? She looked from one to the other.

Lady Lipton turned on her ferociously. "This is all your fault," she spat at Rosie.

Rosie started in shock.

"Up there pestering the life out of him since the day you arrived. Don't think I didn't spot what you were up to. Mrs. Laird tells me everything, you know. He'd have come back to his family in his own time. But now…now…" Her voice cracked.

"Rosie," came a weak voice from the gurney, but they were already wheeling him away, and Rosie's head was reeling. She took a couple of steps back and watched as the ambulance turned on its blue lights and, with a great commotion, took off for Ashby.

Completely shaken, Rosie tried to wash her hands in the tiny pub room sink. Moray was right beside her, packing up his used equipment.

"What the hell?" said Rosie.

Moray looked at her curiously. "Didn't you know?"

"How the hell would I have known? I've been here five minutes. Why didn't you tell me?"

"I thought he'd have told you!"

"What happened?"

But at that very moment, Gerard burst through the doors at the back of the pub.

"Where the hell have you been?" he said. He was clearly a bit pissed and had chip crumbs all around his mouth. "There wasn't any food! And you just disappeared when that guy fell over. And I had to sit there by myself for ages! And everyone was talking about that guy.

And you. And I had to sit there and listen to it! That scary woman reckons you're shagging him."

"Of course I'm not!"

His lower lip was wobbling. Rosie genuinely feared he might cry. She moved toward him.

"I'm sorry," she said. "He was sick. He needed help."

She felt, uncomfortably, that it was strange to be touching her boyfriend when she had spent the last half hour clasping another man's hand.

"Well, *he's* a doctor, isn't he?" said Gerard. Moray tried to make himself look scarce.

"Yes, but I needed to help."

"I thought you ran a sweetshop now," said Gerard stubbornly. "You made me sit out there all by myself, feeling like an idiot."

"I have no relationship with him except that he's a bleeding man!"

Gerard harrumphed furiously then turned to Moray and put out a pudgy hand.

"I guess I don't need to introduce myself?"

Moray didn't even bother to hide his bewilderment.

"Umm, no, of course not..."

Gerard looked at Rosie then.

"Well, you've told him my name?"

"Umm," said Rosie.

"Unbelievable," said Gerard. "I'm Gerard. I'm her boyfriend. Which she hasn't seen fit to mention, apparently. Fine. What a great trip this is turning out to be. I'm missing Formula One for this." He looked around. "I'd storm out, but there's nowhere in this godforsaken backwater to actually go."

"We could go home," said Rosie quietly. After the adrenaline burst of the last hour, she suddenly found she was exhausted and emotional and really needed a quiet place to sit down and think about the events of the evening. It was very unfair to Gerard—who didn't need this right now, it wasn't his fault his weekend was getting ruined—but she didn't really have the energy for him to have one of his tantrums.

"It's only nine o'clock," whined Gerard.

"We'll get a bottle of wine," said Rosie. "And I'll make you something in the house."

"Can you make scampi?"

"Of course I can't make scampi, Gerard."

Moray was keeping his head down, but Rosie couldn't help feeling herself go pink at the thought of him overhearing this ridiculous conversation.

"Can I call you tomorrow?" she said as they were leaving. "Continue what…what we were talking about?"

"Of course," said Moray.

"What's that?" said Gerard as they were leaving. "What are you talking about? Me?"

"No," said Rosie in exasperation. She'd just helped perform a medical procedure, had clasped Stephen's hand, been unjustifiably yelled at by his mother—she was exhausted. The last thing in the world she needed right now was Gerard making it all about himself. Especially when, as she suspected, there was a grain of truth in what he was saying.

Okay, so she and Gerard didn't have a massive spark in their relationship—who did? Everyone got annoying sooner or later, right? And she was hardly the catch of the century—the wrong side of thirty, the wrong side of a size two, the wrong side of a swiftly moving career.

"No. About the boy…the man who was hurt. Anyway, it doesn't matter. Just village gossip, I expect."

Gerard took on a more conciliatory tone.

"Well, no point in finding it out then. You'll be gone in a couple of weeks."

"Mmm," said Rosie. There was a very good restaurant open halfway up the high street. She'd take him there for fish and chips.

Out in the street, the crowd had dispersed; Les was having a truly fantastic night. Out of the corner of her eye, halfway up the alley that led to the back of the pub, Rosie spied something. Going closer, she confirmed her suspicions as to exactly what it was.

"Well, I'll be," she breathed. It had to be four miles up to Peak House. Severely injured, bleeding out, with a steep gradient down the road. Stephen might be an awkward so-and-so, with all sorts of ludicrous family shenanigans going on. But anyone that sent themselves hurtling down a road in the pitch dark in a standard-issue military hospital wheelchair most definitely had balls.

• • • •

Rosie was half expecting Lilian to be asleep already—it was past her bedtime—but she'd underestimated the old lady's curiosity, and there she was, in her chair, in a long flannel nightie and matching, immaculate carpet slippers, her eyes bright as a bird's. She looked Gerard up and down. Pink and smelling of beer and fish and chips, slightly sweating from the walk up the hill, Rosie had to admit that he didn't look like the most appealing prospect on first view. Well. Maybe his charm would kick in.

But Gerard looked down in the mouth, not his usual ebullient self at all. It was as if all the bounce had gone out of him.

"Hello, Mrs. Hopkins," he murmured, like a child forced on an auntie at a birthday party. "How are you?"

Lilian gave him a long up and down look then glanced quickly at Rosie. This made Rosie even crosser; it was patently obvious what she was doing. It was none of Lilian's bloody business; she knew nothing about it. Nothing about how hard it was to find a man these days. So you didn't get some prince. That was life.

"It's nice to be here," mumbled Gerard, the look on his face suggesting that being in an old lady's home in the middle of nowhere was anything but. And Rosie, too, felt sudden embarrassment, which was ridiculous—she and Gerard lived together. There was a double bed upstairs. There was nothing to be ashamed of. Nonetheless.

"What were the sirens?" demanded Lilian as Rosie went into the kitchen to put the kettle on and forestall the awkward moment when she and Gerard had to go upstairs together. She hoped Lilian would keep up the selective deafness.

"Umm. It was Stephen Mannering. His leg took a turn for the worse."

"Oh, Hetty's boy. He is just no end of trouble."

Rosie marched out of the kitchen, waving the sieve.

"Why didn't you tell me he was Hetty's son? Why does no one tell me anything? Her name is Lipton!"

Lilian shrugged. "I assumed you knew. Not much of a son he's been anyway. And she's Lady Lipton, that's the title name. Mannering is her name."

"Right," said Rosie. "This is ridiculous. Once and for all, I have to know."

Gerard sighed. "I'll just sit down over here, shall I?"

Rosie came out bearing a tray and sat next to her great-aunt.

"How?" she said. "How could Lady Lipton just abandon him like that?"

"And how," said Lilian simply, "could you ever believe that she hadn't tried?"

• • • •

"It was Felix's fault, of course," said Lilian, thoughtfully sinking her teeth into a ginger biscuit she'd softened carefully over the steam of the teapot. "Stephen's father," she added. "He was obsessed with his regiment and everything like that. He'd been quite the thing in his day. Liked to get it out for weddings, parties, any old thing—there would be Felix, polishing his medals. And so when they had a boy after Jessica, he was over the moon. Had that little boy drilled before he was five, up and down. Had little uniforms and everything."

Rosie tried to picture Stephen as a small boy. He would have been, she imagined, a particularly grave one. She also wondered where Jessica was but didn't press the issue.

"So he didn't want to join the army?"

"He did not," said Lilian. "Of course, it's very common—children don't want to do what you want them to do. Look at your Grampa Gordon."

Rosie smiled. "He didn't even sound like you."

"Of course he didn't. Couldn't put enough space between here and London. Wanted to leave it all behind. That's why we never saw you."

Rosie shrugged. "I wish we had."

Lilian muted but could not entirely hide her smile.

"Any sensible man would have waited it out, just ignored it. But have you ever met a sensible aristocrat?"

"No," said Rosie honestly.

"So there were fights, and threats, and will rewritings and all of that. Big scandal. Stephen was such a sensitive child."

"He still is," said Rosie.

"With a tendency to be an utter mule."

"And that," said Rosie.

"Wanted to do English literature at university. Felix wouldn't hear of it. No son of his doing some namby-pamby subject, not on his money, etc."

"No, really?" said Rosie. "That's just daft these days."

"Well, them lot don't necessarily live in these days," Lilian pointed out. "There's an inheritance, a big house to run and maintain. It takes hard work and duty. A lot of people rely on the estate for their livelihoods. You can't just wander off and read poetry."

"Why can't the sister do it?"

Lilian rolled her eyes. "Oh yes, well done, you are very modern."

"So, what happened?"

"Well," said Lilian, "finally…finally, they came to an agreement. He could keep his college course up if he did army training on the weekends. Felix thought it was the only way to learn discipline and restraint for when he inherited, rather than all the drug taking and loose living you need to get an arts degree, apparently."

Rosie hadn't known a single person with enough money to do much drugs or loose living during her nursing courses, but of course, things were different when you were a girl from town making her own way rather than a funded kid at university. She started to feel a bit sorry for Felix.

"So he was fine in college, then what?"

"He took himself off to Africa without telling his dad. Caused a HUGE stink, I could tell you. Giving it up to go run a village school in Namibia. He owed the army time too."

"He went AWOL?"

"Not exactly—you're allowed to defer—but Felix was utterly furious. Sent his blood pressure sky high."

"What happened?"

Lilian half smiled.

"Well, it wasn't in the least bit funny. Not at all. But I believe you might call it ironic…he was caught in a land mine blast. A piece of shrapnel got stuck in there. He ended up being airlifted to a military hospital."

Rosie took a minute to take it all in. "Whereas if he'd joined the army…"

"If he'd joined the army, he could have been part of a land mine cleaning team. Yes. Could have made things better. And of course, while he was convalescing in some hell hole in Angola…"

"His dad?" said Rosie sadly.

Lilian nodded. "Heart attack. He was getting on, of course. He didn't just shout at Stephen. He shouted at everyone. He was an accident waiting to happen."

Rosie sipped her tea.

"But Stephen didn't help."

"Your only son getting his leg half blown off halfway around the world? No, I doubt it."

"Oh God," said Rosie. "What a stupid bloody mess."

"People carry on," said Lilian. "But Hetty and Stephen...they found it very difficult."

Rosie nodded.

"She wanted to look after him, and he...I think he just wanted to wallow in the guilt. And she wanted to hand over the estate and, well, you can imagine."

"Hadn't he been disinherited?"

"No," said Lilian. "Of course, that was the thing. It was all bluster and nonsense. Felix was stubborn as a mule too, but he wasn't daft, and he loved his boy. Poor Hetty, she does such a good job of carrying on, but she needs him. Him sitting up there sulking about everything..."

"I think he's depressed."

"He owns half of Derbyshire," said Lilian sharply. "He ought to get over it."

They both glanced over at Gerard suddenly, who had fallen asleep and let out a surprised, jerking snore.

"I think you'd better get Jemima Puddle-Duck to bed," said Lilian.

"Lilian!" said Rosie. "Don't be rude."

She gently shook Gerard awake; he'd had a long day. "Come on, darling."

Gerard stumbled clumsily up the stairs. Rosie took the tea cups back into the kitchen to wash and drain them. Lilian carefully and gently, but nonetheless on her own, got up and started to make preparations for bed.

She said just one thing as Rosie passed her in the hallway, checking whether she needed any help. Lilian shook her head proudly, and as Rosie went to head upstairs, asked gently, “Do you love him?”

And for the tiniest split second, Rosie didn’t have the faintest idea who she meant.

surprise eggs

• • • •

First, we shall have a naming of parts. Anything that is more than 70 percent small plastic wheels is not confectionery. It is a choking hazard, a losing hazard, an absolute cast-iron guaranteed tantrum generator, and, frankly, an abomination in any self-respecting sweetshop.

I have absolutely no idea when it came to pass that one treat was not considered enough for a child; that on being offered chocolate, they would instantly expect to receive something else as well as a basic human right. The rise of the OPB, or Obscene Party Bag (see sections IX to XVII, and appendices 4(i) to 4(vi)), seems also to be mirrored in this obsession, to ensure children never, ever, ever learn when enough is enough.

Therefore, I shall oppose the creeping of plastic and nasty cheap choc-o-like items whenever I see fit and for as long as it is within my power to do so. The real thing is out there. If you really want to be kind to your children, let them discover it.

Rosie lay awake for a long time that night and was still upset even when she did drift off, and when she woke up again too, remembering glumly that it was market day; there was a long day ahead. She glanced over to the other side of the bed. Gerard was still out for the count, his mouth open, a small, damp patch of dribble underneath where his mouth had been. She looked at him for a long time. What had changed? In a couple of months? Was it just getting out of town, looking around a bit? Or was it something else, the idea of running her own place and doing something for herself? Even if she was only caretaking, she reminded herself. Even if it was only for a bit. She had gone from her mum's house to student halls to her and Gerard's flat without ever really having done anything by herself, not really. The fact that she could take something and turn it into…well. There was no point in thinking about that. As if on cue, her phone rang.

"Rosie? Meridian, put that down. DOWN!"

"DON WAN PUT DINE!" came the strident Australian tones distantly down the telephone.

"Hi, Mum," said Rosie, moving to the bathroom to avoid waking Gerard. Her mother really did pick her moments.

"Now, listen. How are things?"

"Things are fine, fine."

"Have you found a buyer yet?"

"No, no, but it's looking good… I'm sure it'll be really soon," lied Rosie. These things took time, after all.

"And what about a home? What does Lilian say about going into a home?" Even though Rosie knew there was no possibility of being heard downstairs, she cupped the phone to her ear nonetheless.

"Well, you know. I'm just getting her better."

"You can get her as better as you like; she's still going to be eighty-seven years old," said Ange. "What, you want to stay there forever and look after her?"

Rosie was quiet. "No, obviously not. No."

"Found any nice men to replace that fat one yet?"

"ANGIE!"

"Oh God, is he there? With or without an engagement ring?"

"Mum. Stop it. Please."

Angie sniffed. "Well. You don't know how hard it is being the mother to someone whose boyfriend thinks he's going to do better."

"He doesn't think that," said Rosie.

"Hmm," said her mother. "Well, good. I'm impressed that he's managed to make a go of it on his own without you down in London."

Rosie didn't feel quite up to answering that one.

"Well, listen. Have a great day, and I need to know ASAP when everything's sorted out, okay? And you don't want to disrupt your life for longer than necessary, do you?"

"No," said Rosie, looking out of the bathroom window, which overlooked the other side of the cottage. One of the bushes had sprouted a vibrant shimmering purple flower. Rosie couldn't name it, but she could smell the heavy, rounded scent and hear the hum of the bumblebees as they started work even earlier than she did.

"No," she said again, thinking of Tube strikes and overcrowded litter bins and queues and people, people everywhere, and lorries thundering down the road and recycling glass crushers at 4:00 a.m. and drunks on the pavements and queuing to get into bars and to get served in bars and to get into the Tube and being squashed up against the side of the Tube and...

"Sorry, Mum," she said. "I'll get on it."

"Good girl," said Angie. "Meridian, don't eat that! Is that beetle red or black? PHILLIP!!!!"

"Speak soon, Mum," said Rosie.

"Very soon," said her mum. "She'll need to sign all the paperwork and everything before...well, you know. Before she goes loopy or something."

"I don't think she's loopy," said Rosie. "Well, not by local standards."

"I'm glad to hear it."

• • • •

1943

Life went on. It had to. Lilian hurled herself frantically into her work at the sweetshop, trying to balance the books. And the long hot Indian summer finally passed, and when she saw Ida Delia in the street, she would quickly pretend to look the other way and so would Ida, so that suited them both well, although Lilian couldn't quite quell a pang every time she saw Ida's swelling stomach, her brand new, cheap but still shiny wedding ring growing increasingly tighter on her pudgy fingers, all the while thinking to herself, *It could have been me.*

It could have been her, set up in Henry's tiny freehold that Lord Lipton had granted him now he had a family coming. Lilian knew the cottage, had run past it many times on her afternoon jaunts back, she reflected, at the tender age of seventeen—when she was younger, carefree, when she could run wild, rather than sit and fill out endless rows in her double-entry book, making sure everything tallied neatly at the end before showing it to her father. It was small, but it had everything you needed, as well as a beautiful, overgrown garden, fecund with wild flowers and overgrown, sprawling rose bushes. There was even an apple tree. They had talked about it once, on one of those long hot summer evenings when she was mourning Ned and they chatted of anything and everything to take her mind off it; she had told him she dreamed one day of an herb garden and a kissing gate and honeysuckle and roses, and he had laughed and stroked her shoulder and said he didn't think the cottage was that big, and she had felt a deep inner thrill that one day she might have the run of the garden.

Ida Delia, she suspected, would fill it with tight rows of easy-to-maintain pink and yellow perennials, dump gravel on the rest, and never think of it ever again.

• • • •

"Bacon sandwich?"

Rosie vehemently hoped that Gerard's favorite sandwich would make up for the night before. They'd just gotten out of the habit, she decided. The habit of being together. They'd been together for so long, in such a rut. He was probably suffering PlayStation withdrawal. That was it. And it was just that moving had changed her perspective so much, that was all. She'd get it back.

She sat down and looked at him stirring awake, blinking the sleep out of his eyes, struggling to remember where he was. It was so like him. Suddenly, she realized she had to know.

"Darling," she said very quietly. "Can we talk?"

"That's odd," came a sleepy sounding voice from the pillow. "Because at first I thought that sounded like someone asking me if I would like a bacon sandwich." Gerard opened his eyes. "What time is it?"

"Seven thirty," said Rosie. "It's a lovely day outside."

"Seven thirty?" said Gerard. "On a SATURDAY? You've changed."

"Hmm," said Rosie.

Gerard turned over. "I'm going back to sleep," he said. "I never get up before eleven on Saturdays. You know that."

"Yes, but this is different…"

Watching him, completely oblivious to her own plans and ideas, completely uninterested as he was in anything more than when she would come back to cook his dinner and take care of their flat, Rosie realized something. Something, she supposed, she'd known for a long time. As quietly as she could, she withdrew into the bathroom, sat down on the cistern, and painfully, silently, burst into tears.

It wasn't Gerard's fault—his easygoing, laissez-faire approach to life had charmed her once. But what she'd taken as his likeable good humor concealed, instead, simple laziness. It was easier to be nice to everyone than to stand up for yourself. It was easy to find someone like Rosie to look after him and take the place of his mother. But to grow up, to actually take on the responsibilities of the things she wanted—a nice home, a family, nothing too ambitious, surely?—these were beyond him. For now, perhaps forever. Gerard just wanted to be fed and to have a quiet life. And she'd been so wrapped up in working and scurrying about and being part of London that she'd decided that was enough, no matter what her friends said behind her back or her mother said to her face.

She felt like such an idiot. Seven years of her life, SEVEN YEARS. Seven years when everyone else had been settling down and building a home and starting a life together. She didn't even know how much Gerard earned. The only reason they'd gotten a mortgage together at all was that apart, they simply wouldn't have been allowed one. Oh God, there was so much to untangle. There was going to be so much fuss. And she was going to have to sit and listen, over and over again, to everyone—even including her bloody great-aunt, it looked like, who'd met him for all of five lousy minutes—about how they'd known all along, and how was she going to find someone else now, and wasn't she getting on a bit and…

Oh God, what a mess. Rosie realized suddenly that she was crying. She simply let the tears stream down her face and stared out of the window, where even now, clouds were gathering in a far corner over by the purple hills. What a stupid mess. She'd come up here to stop Lilian from getting into trouble, and all that had happened was it felt like she'd gotten herself irrevocably into trouble. Her heart beat troublingly fast. It wasn't too late, she told herself. He didn't know anything about how she felt. Maybe she could issue him an ultimatum or suggest they take some time out, or…

But she felt, deep inside, that it was over, as surely as the tolling of the village bell. It was over. Suddenly, painfully, she had a memory of glimpsing him from a ward window, coming into work early one morning, many years ago, eating a chocolate bar and carrying his briefcase, and feeling a sudden burst of happiness and love, watching him unobserved. How could it have deteriorated from then to now? To every weekend being spent with him in bed till lunchtime then sitting in front of the TV till supper then complaining he was too tired to go out? To her shrewishly banging about washing up in the kitchen because he wasn't capable of emptying a dishwasher. It was so…so banal.

Suddenly the bathroom door banged open, and Rosie jerked up guiltily. Gerard was still half-asleep.

"Need to pee," he mumbled, his hand ferreting inside his boxer shorts, his paunch protruding. Then, rubbing the sleep from his eyes, her finally cottoned on to her tearstained face.

"Hey, what's the matter?" he said, concerned. Of course, that made it worse. Sweet to the end. Rosie found she was no longer capable of crying silently and instead let the whole lot come out in unsightly choking sobs. It was lucky there was plenty of toilet paper. Gradually, Gerard sat down on the side of the bed, concern written large all over his face.

"What's wrong? Do you really hate it here?"

"No! No, it's not that. Gerard. I don't…I don't…I mean…" She sighed. "I should probably have done this ages ago. Gerard. You have to tell me. Are we going anywhere?"

Gerard furrowed his brow. "I thought you were working."

"You and me, Ger. You and me."

There was a long pause. A long pause when, for the final time, Rosie thought he might have suddenly revealed himself, gotten down on one knee, whipped out a ring, and declared undying love. Instead, there was just a very long pause.

Rosie worried. Had she not been clear? Assertive enough? Had she just fumbled her way along in this relationship for so long that they were no longer capable of understanding one another? She felt cross with herself.

"I mean, I don't expect fireworks and flowers, but…"

Gerard's face had taken on a rather frosty look. "Well, it sounds like you do."

"We only get one life, Gerard. Is this it?"

"What do you mean? Why do girls always want to know what we're doing and what's coming next? We're boyfriend and girlfriend, aren't we?"

"Yes, but..."

"But what? You've come here, surrounded by all these blokes, and you've decided I'm a bit boring for you? Not good enough? Maybe I can't chop up a sheep? Which I can do, by the way. I've done dissection and everything."

"No, Gerard, it's not that."

"So what, the second we're not living under the same roof, you just want to go out and do your own thing? Screw half the local pub?"

"Of course not! Stop being childish!"

Rosie couldn't believe what she was hearing. She didn't expect him to be delighted, but not spiteful either.

"Ooh, ooh, let me go see that man! With that other man! I'll just leave my silly old boyfriend in the pub, will I? He won't care. All he does is look after me and hang out with me and put up with me all the time."

Rosie's eyes were wide.

"I didn't...I never did. I promise."

"You changed the second you got here," said Gerard.

"No," said Rosie. "No."

But she knew she owed him the truth.

"I think I started changing a long time ago."

"They always do," muttered Gerard.

Rosie blinked in sadness.

"Oh well," said Gerard. "Mum'll be pleased."

"Really? Didn't she like me?" said Rosie, genuinely quite surprised. "Oh gosh. Wow. I didn't know that."

"She liked you fine, but she always said you wouldn't hang about. And she was right."

"I wish you'd listened to her five years ago!"

"Plus, she didn't even know you were a tart."

"That is out of order, Gerard, and you know it."

Gerard shrugged. "Yeah, whatever."

There was a long, awkward pause while they both stared in different directions. Finally Gerard looked up from the floor.

"Ehm, I still really need to pee," he said.

And oddly, as though they hadn't peed in front of each other a thousand times, Rosie left the room to give him some privacy, as if they didn't know each other at all.

• • • •

Gerard was in the bathroom for a long time. Rosie sat on the bed, shaking, her stomach a tight knot of anxiety. What had she done? Was she mad? You heard about this all the time, people breaking up with perfectly decent guys in their early thirties, only to find there was absolutely no one else out there at all, and then in eight years or so, she'd be forty and that would be it: it would all be over, it would be too late… She tried to breathe, not work herself into a real state. It was hard. Her throat hurt.

Gerard emerged from the bathroom standing a little straighter. He'd obviously given himself a talking-to in the mirror, and he looked at her, the picture of wounded pride.

She felt, suddenly, as if she was on the very top of a rollercoaster, just the second before it plummeted.

"When do you want to collect your stuff?"

Rosie bit her lip. Of course. All of that.

"We'll need to figure it out," she said. "All of that."

"That's right," said Gerard. "Because you haven't only fucked up my personal life; you're going to fuck up where I live as well."

Rosie swallowed hard. She couldn't deny it. She had thrown a big bomb into his life. For Gerard, who hated even walking a hundred meters to the Tube station and consequently drove everywhere, it was horrible to think about having to do lots of work.

"I…I haven't quite thought about it," she said. "I might…I can maybe buy you out, or you could buy me out, own the whole thing outright."

"Oh great," said Gerard. "You leave me and charge me thousands of fucking pounds for the privilege." He glanced at his watch. "I don't even want to think about that now," he grunted. "If I leave now, I can get back to Mum's before the Arsenal friendly. I wouldn't want to hang around this shithole anyway."

Rosie smiled apologetically.

Gerard shook his head. "Well," he said.

"I'm sorry," said Rosie again. It sounded so pathetic and weak. Gerard started to get his stuff together—despite being in the room less than twelve hours, he'd already contrived to make an almighty mess—and she sat on the bed and watched him. Rosie suddenly felt panicked. Seven years couldn't just go like this, could it? Not just get thrown away so fast. They couldn't have finished talking, could they? Desperately, she searched for something to say.

"Can I ask one thing?" said Rosie. "Just so I know?"

Gerard shrugged. Rosie took a deep breath.

"Were you ever going to pop the question? Did you ever see us together forever?"

He shrugged again.

"Dunno," he said. "I'd never really thought about it."

"Really?" said Rosie, wondering if this was bravado. "What, all those weddings we went to and you never once thought about it?"

"I liked things as they were," said Gerard. "I didn't have a problem with it. I thought you were cool too."

"So did I," said Rosie, shaking her head. It had genuinely never even crossed his mind. "So did I."

They gazed at each other in mutual incomprehension.

They even managed an awkward, difficult embrace as he left, a little, kind of social kiss that Gerard tried to turn into something else.

"I can't believe I didn't even get a farewell shag," he said, which Rosie thought was encouraging. That was the thing about Gerard, she hoped—his irrepressible cheerfulness. She didn't think he'd be down for too long. But for now, prodding her heart carefully to feel the truth of the matter, it was undeniable, as she heard him gently closing the bedroom door then the front door, which squeaked, and heard the thrum of his beloved Alfa Romeo start up. However much she might regret it later, even if Gerard was her very, very last chance, she could still feel it.

Relief.

• • • •

"That was an awful lot of door banging," observed Lilian at breakfast, pained to see how pale and stressed Rosie looked. She had back that slightly drained skin she had had when she'd arrived, which a few weeks of outdoor living, early nights, and good food had put paid to. She tried to remind herself that this was the evil family stranger who was here merely to take all her money and dump her in a home, but she couldn't help being concerned for the girl.

"I don't want to talk about it," said Rosie, dourly frying up eggs. The smell made her feel slightly sick, even though they had been waiting on the doorstep and the vicar's hens had laid them just a few hours before.

Lilian raised her eyebrows. "Well, better get ready for a busy day then," she said.

• • • •

1944

You couldn't ever really dislike a child, Lilian knew. It wasn't right or fair. But still, it did seem incredible that any offspring from two such attractive specimens as Henry Carr and Ida Delia Fontayne could be so badly favored. Dorothy had a difficult birth, Lilian had heard, inevitably, with Henry far behind enemy lines in France and Ida Delia in labor for three days, yelling like a stuck pig. People told her this as if she'd be pleased—everyone knew everything, of course—but Lilian took no pleasure in it. Dorothy had been undersized and bright red, slightly boiled-looking, always looking irritated when pushed about in the smart pram that had been sent for, uncomfortably trussed up in several layers of bright yellow wool that gave her a jaundiced look, festooned with bows and ties and frills, with two tiny feet desperately trying to kick their way out and a howl or a scowl on her little features.

One day, Lilian had been cycling down to the hatters when she'd spied them, Ida Delia having trouble getting the enormous pram up off the cobbles. Lilian had searched within herself and made a decision. She'd dropped the bike, which made a hell of a clatter and instantly started the baby screaming, and ran over to help.

Ida Delia, looking older than her nineteen years, her yellow hair unbrushed and tied back with a rag, lurched the pram away from her.

"I don't want your help, thank you," she said.

"Ida…" started Lilian.

"I don't speak to people who try to steal other people's lads," said Ida. "He's mine now. You stay away. I know you wanted his brat. Well, I got her." She made an ugly sniffing noise, halfway between a laugh and a snort. "So you can keep away from our family, thank you."

"But I…I… Well, I just wanted to say congratulations," said Lilian as humbly as she could.

"Well, any time you want to come around and boil some cloths, just say the word," said Ida Delia bitterly. The baby's cries grew louder.

"Can I…"

"You'll just encourage her," Ida said and finally managed to get the pram mounted onto the pavement. The two women looked at each other. "Just stay away," said Ida, her tone full of menace. Lilian didn't—couldn't—know it, but seeing the trim, youthful, full-of-energy Lilian cycling freely down the street had filled Ida—whose letters from Henry were so infrequent and so stiff, who never passed a forty-eight-hour leave without managing, somehow, to casually bring the conversation around to the Hopkins family—with absolute terror.

Those were the last words the women ever exchanged.

• • • •

2012

Lilian hadn't undersold market day. The entire town was absolutely thronged. There seemed to be as many horses as cars, and there was so much noise from the cows as they were driven through in large trucks on their way to the Stirlings' field, where the fete would be held. Travelers had set up a large fair, and bunting was strung up all the way across the high street. Already Rosie could see the outline of a lost red helium balloon floating upward through the trees. She took a deep breath and tied on her apron.

Outside the door of the shop, her first customer was already waiting.

"Does your mother know you're here, Edison?" asked Rosie, seeing no one behind him.

Edison nodded seriously. "Yup. She said it was the best place for me. Encourage self-safishsee."

"Really?" said Rosie, slightly peeved. She wasn't a daycare center. "Why's that then?"

Edison pushed his glasses up on his nose with a surprisingly adult-like gesture. "I am most terribly afraid of animals," he said.

"What, all animals?" said Rosie, turning the heavy key and finding herself smiling despite herself.

"Yes," said Edison. "And some plants. That's why it's best if I keep myself out of the way."

He wandered into the shop.

"Hester said I should make myself useful."

"Who's Hester?"

"My mother."

"Of course she is," said Rosie. She called her mum Angie sometimes, but it didn't seem quite the same really.

"She thinks I would be a good help to you."

"Does she now? Why doesn't she take you to see the animals so you could find out they're not scary?"

"Hester thinks it's wrong that animals get killed for us," mumbled Edison. "She doesn't really 'prove."

At that moment, Hester did appear, gray hair glinting.

"Hello," she said coolly. "Now listen. I have to go distribute these vegan leaflets at the market. Can I leave Edison with you for a little while? He'll be a huge help, I'm sure."

Rosie was completely taken aback.

"Well," she stuttered. "Well, I suppose so."

"Fantastic! Wonderful! The animals will thank you!" said Hester, barely breaking stride.

Rosie and Edison watched her disappear down the high street. Then Rosie turned toward the thin boy.

"The thing is," said Rosie, "you see, everyone's entitled to their opinion. But the thing is, if you stay here, I'm going to go down later to see all the animals."

Edison looked at her, his eyes blinking anxiously through his glasses. "Oh," he said.

"You could come with me if you like," said Rosie. "I promise to protect you from all the animals."

Edison considered it. "Okay," he said.

"Okay," said Rosie. "Now, I need you to fold up these boxes very small and put them in this larger box for cardboard recycling."

"Can I draw on them first?"

"You can," said Rosie, "as long as you keep out of my way."

Edison looked at her.

"Where's the nice man who was here yesterday?"

Rosie bit her lip.

"He had to go."

"Oh," said Edison. "That's a shame. I liked him. He was nice to kids. Not everyone is nice to kids. Did you know that?"

"I did know that," said Rosie, suddenly hit with a pang and the feeling that she might have made a terrible mistake. "Gerard is very good at being nice to kids. He's very like one, in a way."

"No, he isn't," said Edison. "He's grown up."

"That's a metaphor," said Rosie. "Surely Hester has taught you about those?"

Edison nodded.

"But it's not a metaphor," he said. "It's a simile."

"Let's open up, shall we?" said Rosie. She could feel her temporary ebullience at the busy town eking out of her like air out of a balloon.

The next person she saw was hardly likely to cheer her up any further.

"Mr. deBlaine," she said. Roy deBlaine, the dentist, was standing in front of her, holding the newspaper in his hands. His own newspaper, of course.

"I have notice of an advert here," he said.

Rosie squinted. What was he talking about?

"About the forthcoming sale of a going concern…"

Rosic rcalizcd what it must bc.

"But I advertised in the Derby papers," she said.

"We share advertising," said Mr. deBlaine. "It's the same company."

"Oh."

Roy marched around the shop rather rudely, sizing it up.

"Hello," said Edison from down by the counter. He was drawing a large, very complicated machine on one of the cardboard boxes.

"You need to come for your six-month checkup," said Roy, barely drawing breath. "I haven't seen you."

"You don't need to see me," said Edison, with a bravery Rosie thought rather commendable. "Hester says we'll look after my teeth omopafica-lee."

Both Rosie and Roy rolled their eyes at the same time. "And I don't get sugar at home."

"No, just when you live in the sweetshop? So," said Roy, looking around. "It's not exactly a GOING concern, is it? Couple of months of playing milkmaid."

Rosie vowed to change her stupid apron.

"After years of neglect. Not unlike some people's mouths."

"Are you interested?"

"I might be," said Mr. deBlaine. "This might make a rather good site for my new dental practice. Brand new veneers, perfect smiles, superfast whitening, expensive fillings." He was practically rubbing his hands together. "Everyone wants that perfect smile nowadays."

Personally Rosie thought that his hyperstraight, neon-white, Hollywood teeth were absolutely creepy and weird, like a direct view of a skull picked clean by birds. But she didn't want to say.

"Yes, it's all new techniques in dentistry these days. A quaint little place like this might work rather well."

"So you wouldn't be selling sweets?"

"No!" said Roy. "I'd be selling top-of-the-range teeth whiteners at four hundred pounds a pop. So what do you think about that, snaggle mouth?"

"Did you just call me snaggle mouth?" said Rosie.

"Affectionately, of course," said Roy. He looked around greedily a little more then checked his very expensive watch. "Well, I'd better get on. Time is teeth, and teeth are money," he said with a final flash of his ghastly luminous grin. He left the shop, making the bell ring abruptly. Edison quickly made some changes to his drawing.

"I'm putting him in," said Edison. "He is a very mean dentist."

Rosie looked at him. The idea of Roy deBlaine taking over Lilian's beloved beautiful shop and turning it into some high-tech tooth emporium made her feel absolutely miserable. He'd rip out all the shelves and the benches and the fixtures and…she didn't want this. She didn't want to sell it like this.

"He is," she said. "He is a very mean dentist." She glanced down. If she had to have a six-year-old hanging around now Gerard had gone, it might as well be this one.

• • • •

The shop filled up quickly, many people who had come in to Lipton for the first time from the surrounding villages exclaiming with delight at the restoration of their beloved sweetshop, missing from so many market days past, tentatively asking for their favorite, asking after Lilian, exclaiming as to how much Rosie resembled her, and beaming when Rosie deftly twirled and passed the little striped paper bags full of memories out into the crowd.

The morning flew past, the door and the till ringing busily, the shop full of children pointing excitedly and their parents surreptitiously helping themselves to the fudge tasters Rosie had temptingly placed on the top of the glass cabinets. Things were going so well, Rosie almost forgot about her terrible start to the day, persuading Anton that only four sugar mice were more than enough to get him through the next half an hour as he waited for his wife to get back from the fete. Indeed, she popped in to fetch him and admired the shop as soon as she arrived.

"Oh," she said. "And I'm on the organizing committee for the raffle. I never thought, we could have touched you up for a donation."

"Of course you can," said Rosie. "What about a big box of chocs?"

"You're a darling!" The two women looked at each other. Anton's wife had her hands full of shopping and a steadying arm on Anton.

"Why don't I bring them down later?" said Rosie. "I'll probably need a walk."

"That would be fantastic," said Chrissie.

"You know," said Rosie to the pair of them. "You could run this sweetshop."

There was a ringing of the door right behind her. Rosie didn't even have to turn around.

"What are you doing now, Hopkins?" said Moray, sighing. "I wish you'd stop trying to kill all my patients."

"I MEANT," said Rosie, "when he's slim enough to get behind the counter. Like a challenge. What do you think, Anton?"

Anton looked thrilled, his wife less so.

"Hmm," she said. "I don't want you up any ladders."

"I would like to run a sweetshop," said Anton.

"NO!" said Moray. "Out of here."

Anton looked sadly into his now-empty paper bag. "I don't even remember eating those mice."

"Will you just get him that gastric band appointment?" said Rosie.

"No!" said Moray.

Anton heaved his vast bulk out of the shop, a tad sadly. "I only sold him three," said Rosie defiantly. "I talked him down from nineteen."

Moray checked his watch. "Well, we've been in the same space for almost four minutes, and nothing has turned up bleeding to death. A record for us, wouldn't you say?"

Rosie smiled. "What can I get you?"

"Just some mints. I'm judging the baking and some of those old ladies get a tad overenthusiastic when they win."

"I bet they do," said Rosie. Moray was looking very dapper today in his green tweed jacket and checked shirt. She was less sure about the mustard-colored trousers.

"Are you looking at my trousers?" asked Moray.

"Yes, but I'll stop before I go blind."

"They're COUNTRY," said Moray. "Anyway, you are in no position to be making sartorial comments." Which was the exact moment when, in a blinding flash, Rosie realized with a start—it wasn't like her, after all, having grown up surrounded by male nurses, for goodness's sake—that of course Moray hadn't been asking her out on real dates.

"They are a little bit country and a little bit rock 'n' roll," said Rosie, grinning at him with sudden—what? Relief? Disappointment? "Do they like you, those little old ladies?"

"They mostly like doctors who have been on television," said Moray, crunching into an imperial mint. "But in their absence, yes, sometimes I have to do."

"What's happened?" asked Rosie impatiently. "How's Stephen?"

"I thought you were going to go with the ambulance," said Moray.

"Hmm," said Rosie. "Anyway. Once that old bag was on the scene…"

"She's all right, Hetty," said Moray. "Her life is just a bit different from ours, that's all. Remember, she only lost her husband last year."

Rosie instantly felt a bit guilty. It was true; she'd been thinking of Stephen's parents, whoever they were, as awful deserters. But she'd only ever seen one side of the story.

"Anyway?"

"Anyway," said Moray, lowering his voice as Rosie served two teenagers enormous portions of candy bananas. "I called the hospital this morning. They got plenty of blood into him, and he's very weak but on a drip—he was malnourished too."

Rosie suddenly got a flashback to his pale, white chest. "Good," she said, unconvinced.

"Then as soon as they'd checked him out—I did a beautiful stitching job, by all accounts."

"Helped by me," said Rosie.

"By my glamorous assistant, yes. Anyway, as soon as they patched him up, he insisted on discharging himself. Doesn't like hospitals, apparently."

Rosie tried to think of him alone in a military field hospital in Africa. She wasn't at all surprised.

"So, just goes to show he should have done this months ago. Bloody stubborn idiot," said Moray.

"Sounds like you rather like the bloody stubborn idiot."

"Oh, Stephen was always different. Always his own man," said Moray. He wrapped up his bag of sweets. "And some golf balls," he said. "I'll drop them off at Peak House."

"Were you guys good friends?" asked Rosie.

Moray nodded.

"We were actually. Till he went off on his do-gooder jobs in Africa. Couldn't believe I didn't want to go with him."

"Why not?"

Moray snorted. "Do you? Anyway, I believe my sort isn't exactly welcome over there. No, seriously. I'd have been rubbish, no help at all. I like my home comforts too much. Just too selfish. Anyway, of course he pulled a classic Stephen, stormed off, and I didn't hear from him… I didn't even know where he got his injury. I only found that out the other day. I figured he'd been bitten by a stoat or something and was just too embarrassed to tell anyone. Or a tiger."

"You don't see tigers in Africa," piped up Edison.

"And that," said Moray, "is why I'm better off in Derbyshire." They fell quiet for a moment.

"Well, when you see him…" said Rosie. Then she couldn't think what she meant to say. "Oh, nothing. Just say hello from me. And that he's an idiot."

"Will do," said Moray. "Are you coming down later?"

"Yes, in a bit. Keep some cake for me."

"Is that really what you feel like after a morning surrounded by fudge? Cake?"

"It's for Lilian," said Rosie strictly. "Don't you start. I've already had deBlaine in here. And Hester the vegan."

Moray shuddered. "Ugh. Dentist cooties," he said and winked and turned to go. "Hi, Edison," he said, catching sight of the small figure crouched behind the counter. "How's the stress constipation?"

"Much better, thank you," said Edison seriously. "I think perhaps the yoga is helping after all."

Rosie looked at Moray.

"I suspect being here, in an environment where no one makes you do yoga, is helping after all," said Moray quietly to Rosie. "Good for you."

Rosie watched him leave, shaking her head in disbelief. The country air had clearly made her gaydar go on the blink. She was pleased too, though kicked herself for feeling that it would have been strange for such a good-looking man to fancy her. It wouldn't have been strange, she told herself, trying to make herself believe it. She still couldn't get her head around it; after being in a relationship for seven years, she was single. Single at thirty-one. It was terrifying and upsetting and oddly liberating.

• • • •

"I WAN EGG WI PRESENT!!!" a child was screeching on the floor as his mother rotated anxiously, her hands fluttering like butterflies.

"I'm so sorry," said Rosie for the tenth time. Lilian had very strong views on candy that came with toys, and after forcing her to back down on the whole gum issue, Rosie hadn't pushed it any more than she needed to. "We just don't have any."

Rosie came out from behind the counter and crouched down beside the child. Behind, a queue was building up. Rosie was used to dealing with children in the hospital—scared, in pain—and was good at coaxing. But pointless fury she couldn't really get a handle on.

"I WANT AN EGG!"

Rosie realized the child wasn't as small as she had thought before. In fact, he was a big bruiser of a boy, which probably explained why his mum was not exactly rushing to pick him up.

"Now, Nathan, they don't have any," the mother was saying anxiously. "I'm very sorry. I'm sure we can find another place."

"WANT IT NOW!"

"Mummy will get it for you just as soon as possible…"

"NOW!"

"Come now, little man," said Rosie gently. "Would you like to try our bird's eggs? They have a candy shell then chocolate then inside a little candy bird. What do you think?"

"SHUT UP," shouted the boy. Rosie smiled apologetically at the queue, who were rolling their eyes, and decided to move back behind the counter pronto, but nobody really liked to buy sweets while someone was screaming, and people quickly grabbed chocolate bars or just left altogether. Finally, Edison popped his head out from behind the counter.

"That's Nathan," he said to Rosie, who was wondering how she could politely order the child's mother to remove him without sounding like an evil witch.

"So it appears," said Rosie.

"He's the mean kid who took my lollipop," whispered Edison.

"Him?" said Rosie, surprised. "That little squirt?"

Edison nodded. He touched her knee, obviously frightened.

"But he's pathetic," said Rosie. "Go take a look at him."

Edison shook his head frantically.

"He's mean."

"He's rubbish," said Rosie. "Come on, let's have a look."

Gently, she coaxed Edison out to the front of the shop, where Nathan was rolling from side to side in protestations of agony, shouting about how it wasn't fair and he wanted his egg. As soon as Nathan felt eyes on him, however, he turned. As soon as he saw it was Edison, his eyes widened. He clearly became conscious of himself lying prostrate on the floor. The two boys regarded each other for a long time. Edison pushed his glasses up on his nose.

"Hello, Nathan," he managed eventually, his voice quavering. There was a pause.

"Is this your sweetshop?" came the voice from the floor.

Rosie nodded her head. "Yes," said Edison. "Kind of."

Casually, as if it was the kind of thing anyone might do, Nathan picked himself up from off the ground in an insouciant way.

"You've got a whole sweetshop?"

Edison shrugged. "Whatever."

Rosie looked at him.

"Did you just say 'whatever'?"

Edison got up on tiptoes to whisper in her ear.

"I don't know what it means," whispered Edison. "It's something you're meant to say."

"Okay then," Rosie whispered back.

Nathan was now rubbing the back of his shaved head. "Iss all right," he said.

"Did you want anything?" said Rosie, as if she and Edison were equal partners.

Nathan shrugged.

"Chocolate eggs please."

Nathan's mother was practically sobbing with gratitude as she handed over the money.

"Thank you so much… He's just tired, aren't you, Nathan?" she said, nervously caressing his shoulders.

Nathan pushed her hand away. "Whatever," he said.

"See?" whispered Edison.

Nathan took the chocolate bag without a thank-you. Then, turning to go, he turned back.

"Wan one?"

Edison's eyes popped behind his spectacles. Hardly daring to believe it wasn't a trick, he stepped forward very shyly and carefully. Rosie reckoned Nathan was buying his silence. But whatever was happening, it would clearly feel worth it to Edison. Rosie felt sad, suddenly, that it would make the unusual, interesting Edison happier to be part of this boy's horrible gang of screaming hooligans. Even worse, not an equal member of the gang, probably, but some kind of craven lieutenant. Even though she knew this was just how school was, it still made her sad. But this was Edison's life, not hers.

Tentatively, Edison reached out his hand toward the bag. Then, suddenly, he stopped himself.

"Neh," he said. "It's my shop. I can have anything I want. Can't be bothered."

There was a moment's silence as Nathan reassessed the skinny boy standing in front of him as though through totally new eyes. Then he nodded.

"Awright," he said. "Maybe see you down at the fete later?"

"Maybe," said Edison nonchalantly.

"Edison," Rosie said after they had left and the bell had safely dinged. "I could kiss you."

"Please don't do that," said Edison. "It would be inpropreet behavior."

Rosie smiled.

"I would not like to inflict inpropreet behaviors on you," she said. "But well done."

Edison shrugged and went back to playing with the boxes.

"Some of them are quite a handful, aren't they?" came a voice nodding down the road where Nathan had torn the bag out of the hands of his mother, who had obviously suggested he keep some for later. (She had also asked him, a six-year-old, whether he wanted the small or the large bag.) Rosie looked up; she hadn't even noticed the nice woman from before, Tina Ferrers, quietly browsing the powdered sugar sweets with the twins, Kent and Emily.

"Not yours," said Rosie. "Yours are angels."

Tina laughed, showing nice teeth.

"Ha, right. Yeah. They do show an amazing turn of being angels when promised a visit to your sweetshop though, I will say that."

Rosie smiled. "I wish all of them did."

"It's just part of the job, isn't it?" said Tina. "You can't just like the nice children. I used to work in a nursery," she added.

"Oh yes? Did you like it?"

"Loved it. Alas…" she gesticulated toward the children. "Unfortunately, the times I could work after these guys were the times other people can work too. When they need a nursery is early, late… couldn't make it fit." She looked around. "I love what you've done here though. It's brilliant. Imagine, having your own business. I'm totally in awe of that."

"Oh, it's not mine," said Rosie. "I'm only caretaking for my aunt. In fact, it's going up for sale."

Tina blinked. "Really?" She ran her hands down one of the shelves and sighed.

"What?" said Rosie.

"Oh, nothing. Just a silly idea…"

Rosie smiled. She liked this woman. "What, about this place?"

"Oh, I couldn't…" Tina looked around. "It really is lovely, you know."

"It is. It's beautiful."

"I mean, there's no reason why you couldn't sell more things here—little souvenirs. Nothing tacky, but just things to add on for holidaymakers to remember their time here—if they wanted to spend more money than a pound. And rock."

Rosie smiled.

"I mean, it's doing so well already."

She lowered her voice as Rosie weighed out some expensive fudge for a cheery-looking family.

"It sounds like you have lots of ideas," said Rosie.

Tina smiled. "Well, you know. Once Kent and Emily are at school, I have a bit of time on my hands. And I have my divorce settlement..."

"You're divorced?" Rosie said. Tina was so pretty, so obviously nice, with such nice children. Could it really happen to just about anyone?

Tina looked sad.

"Well, let's just say he preferred the bottle to me," she said. "Open secret around these parts, like bloody everything. That's why I took a final settlement in the divorce," she whispered. "In case he drinks everything else away."

She tried a half smile, but Rosie could feel a huge torrent of pain beneath the words.

"If you like," she said, "you could come around one night and I'll take you through the books."

"Really?" said Tina. "But...well, I don't know. I'd have to employ someone to help."

"Oh, it can't be done alone," said Rosie. "I'm going half-crazy here. Have to shut the shop if I'm to do anything else at all."

"But you're not shutting up today?"

Rosie hadn't stopped serving for a second since she'd unlocked the front door. "Well, I know it sounds a bit daft, but I kind of wanted to see the market day fair. I won't be here for it next year, and I thought it would probably be my only chance."

Tina's brow furrowed. "But this is one of your busiest days of the year!"

Rosie smiled. "You definitely have a business brain on you."

"You can't just shut it up and go!"

"But it's my shop! And I want to take Edison."

Tina grinned. "Okay. How about I mind the shop for you for an hour?"

Rosie was taken aback. But she considered it from all angles. Tina seemed absolutely nice and decent. She was interested in the shop. If the worst happened and she ran away with the cash box, well, Moray would know where she lived. This was a village. Nothing bad would happen.

She made up her mind. "Okay!"

"Do you have hand sanitizer?" asked Tina.

"Umm, no, just a sink," said Rosie.

"See, if we put some hand sanitizer in, you wouldn't have to run the water every five minutes."

"Did you say you ran a nursery or an international business conglomerate?" asked Rosie, joyfully taking off her apron. She watched Tina serve a couple of customers—of course she knew nearly all of them and had a friendly word for them all, including, she noticed, the couple who asked after her ex-husband sadly. Reassured that Tina knew what she was doing as well as Rosie (and possibly, Rosie thought, watching her serve a young man in military uniform and talk him into buying one of the largest boxes of chocolates they had), Rosie hauled down another box for the raffle and set about persuading Edison.

"Cows," he was explaining to Kent and Emily, who were only a very little younger than he was, "can stampeded. That's when they all run in a big line. They can kill you. Superfast."

"Superfast," said Kent.

"Nobody is going to be doing any stampeding," said Rosie. "Come on."

"Also," said Edison, "there are pigs. Pigs will eat a man if there's nuffink else to eat."

"Where do you GET this stuff?" said Rosie.

"Vegan Playbees," said Edison obediently.

Tina and Rosie swapped a look. "You know Hester then?" asked Tina pleasantly.

"Not well," said Rosie, equally pleasantly, as both women tried to avoid discussing Edison's mother in front of him. "And I've never even heard of Vegan Playbees."

"It's a vegan playgroup Hester set up," said Tina breezily. "To teach the correct lifestyle in the village!"

Rosie's cheeks hurt, she wanted to giggle so much. "And was it successful?"

"I believe Edison is the head of Vegan Playbees. Isn't that right, Edison?" said Tina. "And sole member?"

Edison nodded seriously then stood up and saluted and sang, very loudly and rather tunelessly, "Plants are our friends! Right to the end! Soya is great and our very best mate! Hummus is zoomous and kale never fails! Vegan Playbees SAVE THE WHALES!"

The two women laughed until Kent jumped up and announced, "I wan be Vegan Playbee," and Edison started teaching them the song, whereupon Rosie started to usher him out.

"Come on, Vegan Playbee. I promise only to take you to the squash-growing competition, will that help?"

Edison looked awkward. "And the cake stand. I can't have anything with eggs in."

Rosie rolled her eyes. "Well, I'll find you a flapjack then."

"And no gelatin."

"I'll read the ingredients."

"And I'm allergic to strawberries."

"How you ever get out of bed in the morning, I have no idea."

Tina waved. "I'll hold the fort. Enjoy yourself. I will!"

She was already, Rosie noticed, straightening up all the sweet jars that had been opened and not put back exactly straight that morning and turning to smile at the first customer. This could, Rosie thought to herself, just possibly work.

tablet

• • • •

Ahh. Tablet. Bonnie Prince Tablet.

Ingredients

* 2.2 pounds granulated white cane sugar. Yes, 2.2 pounds. Don't look at me like that; this is a sweetshop.
* fresh milk to dampen sugar
* 1 14-ounce can sweetened condensed milk
* 4 ounces unsalted butter

Add milk until sugar is damp but not sitting in a puddle in the pan. Add the butter and the condensed milk, and turn the heat on medium-high.

Stir for 10 minutes till it comes to a boil. If you are getting brown streaks, turn down the heat.

Once boiling, turn down the heat. Keep stirring for 20 minutes. The calories you expend you can pretend will balance out the tablet you eat.

When the mix is ready, a ball will solidify in cold water.

Take the pan off the heat, and stir extremely quickly. When the mix feels slightly stiffer, pour into a tray and let chill.

Ah. The Prince of Sweets.

Although the day was bright and sunny, there was a chill wind rushing down from the hills that made Rosie pull her cardigan closer around herself. "Autumn is coming in," she said, almost to herself. It seemed odd that she'd arrived here in midsummer—however drenching it had been—and now the seasons were changing. Or perhaps it was just because it was so much more obvious here. In London, she barely noticed the leaves drifting off the stunted little trees that grew in iron cages in the parks, spotted with disease and discolored by gas fumes and dust. Here, it was as if the entire world had been painted over. The greens and deep blues of the hills had changed to plowed-up fields and earthy browns; the huge oak trees at the end of the Isitts' lane were barely believable shades of bright red and orange, leaves everywhere drifting into huge piles by the side of the road. And the north wind was picking up, sending tiny clouds scudding quickly beyond the mountains. The air had a freshness to it, a crisp edge. Rosie could smell bonfires.

"Don't you want to kick the leaves?" she asked Edison.

Edison frowned. "Leaves are our friends," he said. Rosie smiled. He looked very anxious about the market fair.

"Don't worry about anything," she said.

In response, his little, very thin hand crept up to meet hers. Very quietly, he said, "I worry about everything."

Rosie squeezed his hand. In this sheltered vale a million miles, she often felt, from the real world, it seemed terrible that a child should worry about anything.

"You shouldn't," she said. "There's a whole world beyond here, you know."

"I know," said Edison, dragging the front of his Cornish pasty shoes along the ground. "Hester says it's full of Hoom rights Aboo."

"Well, yes," said Rosie carefully, feeling in her pocket and handing him a lollipop from the collection she had taken to keeping in there. "But there're lots of other great things you'd like too. Transport museums and railway lines and all-night supermarkets and…well, lots of things. Lots of nice people too."

Edison sucked thoughtfully on his lollipop.

"I'm glad," he said suddenly. "I'm glad you came to Lipton."

Rosie smiled, completely taken aback. She had, on balance, lost her boyfriend, her home probably, and lots of lucrative agency work. But somehow, she felt this too.

"So am I," she said, squeezing his hand.

• • • •

The main street was empty; everyone was up past the churchyard, in Farmer Stirling's large pasture, now churned up with van wheels. Over in the next field, teenagers in neon vests pointed out parking, and tinny music played through a sound system so bad it was completely unidentifiable. Edison's grip grew a little tighter. Over the PA, a man was talking so rapidly and in such a thick Derbyshire accent that Rosie had trouble following it, something about a pony parade and a cucumber competition. The place was thronged with people, all of them, Rosie noticed, without fail, wearing a waxed jacket and boots. She hadn't realized that it was going to be the kind of thing that needed boots, she realized, glancing down glumly. She was wearing wedges. They were pretty, comfortable, and good for the shop. Now, she was in severe danger of lurching into a bog. She never got it right.

There were wooden walkways, thankfully, around the main perimeter of the field, and Rosie stuck to those as carefully as she could, looking for the raffle stand. Plenty of people nodded at her as she passed, and she smiled back politely and tried to say hello to everyone while clopping along like a particularly ridiculous mare. She peered into tents—there was one full of different types of jam and some very serious-looking people sniffing and tasting them; one with huge, ridiculous vegetables that looked like they were on steroids; a baking tent, where she would have liked to have spent a little bit more time, till she overheard the PA bellow that the raffle drawing was about to take place in tent A. Tent A was, of course, all the way back around the field again, but Rosie decided not to risk cutting through the parade of lambs in her silly shoes and paraded the entire circumference, feeling silly and flustered in the process, particularly when she passed Mrs. Isitt, who simply looked at her feet and made a loud *harrumphing* noise, as if to say who could expect anything else from a townie like her. Fortunately, just after her was Mr. Isitt, walking so much better he was like a different person. As Mrs. Isitt stalked into the jam section (Rosie pitied anyone who dared to enter against her), Peter drew her to one side. "My tomatoes," he said. "Best ever."

Rosie grinned, finding it miraculous that she—well, mostly Jake, but she was involved too—could actually grow something.

"That's brilliant!" she said.

"It's because of unseasonly high temechurs," came a voice from by her side. "Mr. Isitt, do you know about the terrible threat of global warmin?"

"We must dash," said Rosie, smiling. "But you are looking so much better."

"Reckon," said Peter.

"MR. ISITT!" came a voice from inside the tent. "MR. ISITT, GET IN HERE!"

"Back to normal," said Peter Isitt.

"Yes," said Rosie, looking after him as he followed the summons inside the marquee.

Finally, they made it to the right tent, and she crashed in, holding up the enormous box of chocolates, just as the tub was beginning to spin.

"Here it is!" she yelled. "Don't start without us!"

The entire room turned around to look at her. Of course, standing up on the stage, wearing her magnificently large coat and with a rather haughty expression on her face—slightly more haughty, Rosie found herself thinking, than you might really expect in someone drawing a ticket out of a spinning box in a drafty tent in a small village—was Hetty. Lady Lipton herself.

• • • •

Rosie immediately glanced around for Stephen. Hetty saw her do it and smirked. Chrissie, Anton's wife, immediately approached and took the large red velvet box off her with sincere thanks as Hetty took the first ticket out of the box and announced to a large red-faced farmer that he had won—he looked absolutely delighted—a free fifteen-minute dental checkup at Roy deBlaine's. The farmer's face went from delight to sadness all at once.

Rosie hauled out the raffle tickets Lilian had made her buy earlier and handed them to Edison to watch for her, but the prizes came and went—a large ginger cake, an hour of free gardening, a fishing rod—and she realized she wasn't about to get lucky, even as Lady Lipton conferred effusive congratulations on the winners. Finally it came to the large box of chocolates, and a large roar of applause went up as the winner was found to be Anton.

"Now," said Lady Lipton. "I'm afraid Anton can't have his prize, as his wife is on the committee."

"Everyone's wife is on the committee," said Anton in shock, his lower lip wobbling.

"And," said Lady Lipton, "we'd like you here next year to play again. Do I have your permission to donate these to the local children's home?"

"No," said Anton.

"Yes!" said his wife and jumped up onstage before he could stir himself, shaking Hetty firmly by the hand.

"Thank you," she whispered in what was meant to be a quiet aside but was clearly picked up on the ear-shattering PA.

"And finally," said Hetty. "Our top prize."

There was a murmur throughout the room, with many people checking and rechecking their tickets. The box twirled around, but Rosie barely paid attention; she was busy thanking Anton, who looked pink but not pleased on being complimented on all sides for his generosity. So at first, when Hetty called out the number, Rosie missed it completely, and Hetty was required to repeat herself.

"Yellow 197! Yellow 197!"

Gradually Rosie became aware of a tugging at her sleeve.

"What is it now, Edison?" she asked, suddenly aware that she would probably have to take him to the toilet at some point and wishing his mother hadn't dumped him on her in such an insouciant fashion. Sure enough, the boy was hopping up and down. "Do you need to go to the bathroom?"

Edison shook his head. "No. Oh, yes, I do now. But look! Look!" He waved the ticket in the air. It was yellow, number 197.

"There it is!" shouted one of the farmers behind her. "She's got it!"

There was a general outburst of clapping and much chatter. Rosie glanced around, looking confused.

"On you go," said Chrissie. "Go and collect it. I'll keep the boy."

"Go and collect what?" said Rosie, but before she could think, Hetty was beckoning her up onstage. The man from the local paper crouched down in front of her to take a pic, and the room applauded as Rosie, feeling extremely confused, was handed a very small, very pink, very curious-looking piglet.

"What…what's THIS?" she said. The camera flashed, capturing, Rosie suspected, the most ignorant look in the history of Lipton, which would be saying something.

"It's your pig," said Hetty. "Congratulations."

"My what?"

"First prize in the raffle."

"A pig."

"Yes."

"Not a car?"

As Rosie held the pig, it started to pee on the straw and mud floor of the marquee. It didn't stop for quite a while. There was much guffawing from the floor, particularly when the pee started to flood her already muddy River Island wedges.

Rosie decided just to stand very still and pretend it wasn't happening. Hetty was laughing her head off.

"What am I supposed to do with a pig?" she hissed.

"Bacon sandwich?" said Hetty, clasping her hands around Rosie's shoulders so the photographers could get another shot. After that, the crowd drifted away, leaving Hetty, Rosie, Edison, and the pig.

Edison was absolutely fascinated with the creature. He would move within a few centimeters of her—it was a her, she had two long lines of little teats running down her stomach—and they would go nose to nose and regard each other seriously, then he would back off again.

"What am I meant to do with this?" asked Rosie. "Would the children's home like it?"

"That's a very valuable animal," said Lady Lipton. "I'd hold on to it if I were you."

Rosie looked at it very mulishly. The pig looked back and made a small grunting noise. It was, she supposed, rather cute.

Lady Lipton let out a sigh.

"So. It appears that my son, and the, ahem, the entire town think I owe you an apology."

Rosie looked at her. "But you don't."

Lady Lipton shrugged.

"I was…I was upset. It appears that…yes. Without you…well. He is up. And about. And outside. So thank you. Thank you for what you did for Stephen."

"And Bran," Rosie reminded her with a slight twitch of the lips. It was such an unusual sight to see Hetty cowed, she was attempting to prolong the experience.

There was a pause. "So how's..."

"Bran's fine, thanks," said Hetty.

Rosie smiled to herself. She had walked into that.

"My son? Well, I wondered when you were going to ask."

"I was going to ask before someone handed me an incontinent pig," said Rosie. "Then I got distracted."

The pig obligingly started peeing again. Rosie was slightly past caring by this point.

"He's fine. He's going to be fine. He's going to be all right," said Hetty wonderingly, as if she couldn't quite believe it.

Rosie bit her lip.

"But why weren't...why weren't you... Sorry, but I have to ask."

"Why wasn't I looking after my only son?" said Hetty. There was no one else in the tent now. Hetty turned away.

The raffle box stood there quietly, and Hetty flicked it, quickly, with her fingers. "You don't have children, do you?" said Hetty.

"Edison, could you go and play outside for a moment?"

Edison shook his head instantly.

"I'm not 'lowed outside. Stranger danger!"

Rosie rolled her eyes. "All right, sunshine. Go play over in the very farthest corner of the marquee."

Edison bit his lip.

"Then I'll buy you a dairy-free ice cream."

Edison scampered away.

"I do, kind of, appear to have children," said Rosie ruefully, looking after him.

Hetty smiled tightly.

"Until you do," Rosie said, sitting down. Rosie sat down too; her feet were killing her. Not knowing what to do with the piglet, she put her on the floor, where she instantly started to squeal until Rosie picked her up again.

"I definitely do," said Rosie.

"Until you do," went on Hetty imperiously, "you can't know. You can't know how much you love them."

Rosie thought of her mum, madly in love with Pip's brats, even when they treated her like a serf.

"Hmm," she said.

"And when you're a family…you just try as hard as you can to hold it all together. And when you're part of a certain type of family."

"You mean posh?" said Rosie, wondering if Hetty was about to explain away her behavior by having too much money and too big a house.

"No…I mean, having a responsibility for something. Like you have a responsibility toward the shop. In our case, Lipton Hall. Trying to preserve our heritage and not throw everything away. We got plenty of offers to turn it into some tacky hotel or horrible old people's home, you know."

"People need hotels and old people's homes," said Rosie.

"That's not the point," said Hetty. "Rosie, don't you understand what I'm saying to you—I don't even know why I have to justify myself to you. I lost my husband. And my son. Even though I bounced between them for years trying to make it right. Even though I tried everything. You have no right to march in here with your big-city ways and think you know about us. No right at all."

Rosie felt ashamed suddenly, as Hetty's face manifested how deep her grief went.

"I'm sorry you lost your husband," she said. "So sorry. But that night…I still can't get my head around how quickly you came running when it was your dog and how late you were when it was your son."

Hetty turned on her, suddenly furious once more.

"Bran loves me back," she said, imperious. Rosie cast her eyes to the ground. "And don't you ever think I stopped trying. Not for a second."

She turned and stormed out of the tent in her boots. Rain had now come on properly, and the drops trickled down her large waxed hat. Rosie watched her leave, feeling awful. She glanced down. Edison was back at her side.

"That looked awkward," he observed.

"How old ARE you?" she grumbled.

• • • •

Rosie went out in search of lunch—she felt like she'd been up for hours—and someone to give the pig to. The fete was in full flight: dogs were showing off their prowess at jumping obstacles around what looked like a miniature race course; people walked about, proudly wearing large rosettes that they'd obviously won for different events—marmalade and pickles being ones she saw displayed particularly prominently. The photographer from the local paper was taking a picture of Roy deBlaine handing over a winner's check to someone with an entire flock of lambs in front of him. Roy was doing what he obviously thought was a lovely smile and displaying all his gnashers in full view of the camera. It was lucky the sun had gone down, thought Rosie savagely. He'd blind half the crowd. It occurred to her that she hadn't had enough sleep.

She found him—and realized instantly it hadn't really been lunch she'd been looking for after all—in the corner of the flower tent, of all places. It was practically deserted, and a shocking display of incredibly neon and vulgar gardenias had taken first place. But on the floor was possibly the most even surface in the entire place: green Astroturf. Stephen was crossly, and painfully, inching his way up and down it with a large wooden stick.

"Nice stick," she said. Stephen's back stiffened, then he turned. Rosie realized she'd never seen him standing up before. He was taller than she had thought he would be.

"Nice pig," he said. Then he sniffed. "Can I smell..?"

"It's the pig," said Rosie.

"Well, that's good."

"There're flowers everywhere. That should mask it."

As if in response to this, the piglet leaned over and started eating one of the more gaudy arrangements.

"So, how are you?" Rosie asked carefully. "Were they happy to discharge you?"

"I'm not in the business of making nurses happy," said Stephen, a fact with which Rosie could not disagree. "I'm fine, I'm fine. I'm pretending I'm Charlie Chaplin. Plus, they gave me the good drugs."

"Well, that's good," said Rosie. Even so, she saw him wince and look around for a chair. "I saw Hetty."

Stephen winced again.

"Oh yes? Did she tell you all about her hideous ungrateful son who killed his own father? I kind of liked it better when you didn't know who I was." He sat down. "Do you have any sweets?"

Rosie nodded and felt in her pocket. The piglet immediately started snuffling at her hand.

"Stop it," she said. "Naughty girl."

"Is that really your pig or did you put a magic spell on my mother? It's true," he said. "I did like it when you didn't know. You can't imagine what it's like around here, everybody knowing everyone else's business. And now the news is out—ooh, Stephen's okay again. The jags will be out in force."

"What are JAGs?"

Stephen looked at her wryly.

"You don't know? Umm. They're like WAGs, wives and girlfriends of sports stars. But for chaps they think have big houses."

"Really?" said Rosie. "I'd never heard of them."

"You're lucky," said Stephen, grimacing. "Neither side tends to come out of it well."

Rosie shot a look at Edison, who was touching a cactus. "I can imagine," she said.

"Sometimes it's easier to have secrets," Stephen mused. "I mean, you might have disliked me because I was an oaf, but you didn't dislike me because I killed my dad."

"It was definitely the oaf thing," said Rosie. "But Stephen, you didn't kill your dad."

"She thinks I did. So I imagine half the town thinks I did. And look at me now, still not facing up to my responsibilities." He bit his lip. "He was meant to disinherit me anyway."

Rosie absentmindedly ate a marshmallow. It helped her to think.

"Did you love him?" she asked finally, swallowing. She gave the piglet one too.

"Of course I did!" said Stephen. "I loved him however he was. Unfortunately, he didn't extend the same courtesy to his son. You can't make people be how you want them to be!"

They both looked at Edison, who had pricked his finger on the cactus but was trying to cover it up and not cry in case he got a telling off.

"And she backed him all the way." Stephen rubbed the back of his head then smiled cynically. "Just because they were right doesn't mean I'm not still pissed off about it."

"How were they right?"

"Because if I'd been clearing land mines, it could have saved my leg and…and…" His voice trailed off.

"Did you like it in Africa?" Rosie asked him gently.

"Some of it," he said thoughtfully. "Well, I stayed eight years. I loved the people—no jags!—and building the school, and the children…the children were so amazing. They didn't care that they didn't have big houses or computer games or fucking liberal arts degrees… all they wanted to do was learn, and play, and be kids. I didn't want to stay there forever," he said. "But yes. I was happy. I didn't want to think about bloody Lipton and bloody Lipton House and all the dreary day-to-day penny-pinching STUFF of it. Paintings and rugs and roofs and taxes and all of that. Out there, we hardly had anything, but it was still life, you know?"

In a funny way, even though their experiences couldn't have been more different, Rosie did know. To leave behind everything you had in the world—your home, your friends, your job. It was something she knew a bit about too.

"I would have come back one day," said Stephen. "You must think I'm such a child."

"Families are families," said Rosie. "Always complicated, no matter how old you are."

"But to get stretchered back here in disgrace, without Feli...Dad. Without Dad." Stephen stared at the floor. "I think anyone would have found it difficult."

"I agree," said Rosie.

"But if I'd been better suited to the army, I'm sure I'd have gotten over it a lot quicker."

Rosie shook her head. "You know, when I was in emergency, we got a lot of poor sods and drunks in. Half the poor broken-down creatures we saw in there were ex-military men. They feel it too. They're just not allowed to show it."

"Whereas because I'm a spoiled sissy with a free house, I am?"

"Yes," said Rosie. Then she tried to put the piglet down again. "I wish they all were."

• • • •

The fete was quieting down outside, the overloud PA finally stopping. Stephen looked miles away.

"Akibo," he said "And his brother, Jabo. Akibo was really serious, all the time. Had a million questions about all sorts of things. Was obsessed with Manchester United. There was one TV in the village, but it didn't show football, of course. But sometimes I could get up to town and go to an Internet café, and I'd check out the scores for him. He was delighted. Once a charity sent us down some clothes, and I got a shirt out for him. It was like I'd gotten the whole team to stop by and do a kickabout with him."

"Probably better," said Rosie. "They're not that nice."

"He was thrilled. Didn't have a clue, really, what it meant or what it was. Just something to be obsessed by."

"I think I know someone he'd have gotten on with," said Rosie. Edison was playing a very complicated game involving leaf spaceships dive-bombing over the cacti.

"Yes," said Stephen. "I bet. And Jabo was just the most beautiful thing ever. So cute. All he wanted to do was whatever Akibo was doing. He'd sit with a piece of paper and a stone and pretend he was writing letters. And you'd say 'Are you doing your sums, Jabo?' and he'd say 'YESSUH! NINE! SEVEN! SIXTY!'"

Rosie smiled.

"Akibo wanted to come with me to get—God, of all the stupid things—a frog. I was going to dissect a frog with them. I wasn't meant to, but I thought it would be a useful exercise, something good to do. I'd learned all the parts and everything. And Akibo came to help because he was useful for that kind of thing, knew a lot. And Jabo came because...because Jabo did whatever Akibo did."

He stuttered.

"There wasn't...I don't know. But I don't think there would have been enough left for their mother to bury."

• • • •

Suddenly, there was a shriek from the opening to the tent.

"WHAT is going on here? What are you doing with my gladioli?" came the high strident tones of Mrs. Isitt. Behind her marched in Roy deBlaine.

"Those are MY cacti," he enunciated very clearly. "Grown in the sterile and unique environment of my dental office. They are NOT a toy."

Edison jumped up, quivering with fear.

"Are you responsible for this child?" said Mrs. Isitt.

"Yes," said Rosie. "I'm sorry. I didn't realize."

Mrs. Isitt let out a sniff.

"Can I pay for the damage?"

"Can you go to one of your fancy schmancy London shops and just BUY your way out of trouble, you mean?" said Mrs. Isitt. "Those took a year of hard work."

Rosie felt pink and confused. She stood up. As she did so, the piglet gave a scream and went tearing toward Mrs. Isitt's ankles.

"Call your pig off!" she screamed. "Call it off!"

Rosie looked helplessly at Stephen, who finally, it seemed, had a smile back on his face.

"So you see," he said, "why I was so desperate to get back here."

"Can you sort this out?" she asked him desperately. "Can you talk to your mum?"

"She doesn't know anything about catching pigs," said Stephen, looking puzzled.

"I don't mean the blooming pig, you divot," said Rosie. "I mean you."

• • • •

Rosie went back to the house. Peter Isitt, thank God, had offered to take the pig away and look after it for her (Rosie could see a spark in Mrs. Isitt's eye that made her think the pig obviously was worth something), and she crept back through what was now substantial rainfall and early falling dusk with a lovely set of lamb chops she had felt only momentarily squeamish about buying from the butcher's tent—perhaps she was turning into a country girl after all—and some new potatoes, green beans, and fresh mint from the produce stands, all still covered in earth. Edison's mother picked him up at the gate and thanked Rosie.

"I know adults enjoy his company. He's so intellectually stimulating, so far beyond the boys his own age."

Rosie, who was undoubtedly fond of Edison, still bristled at the concept that Hester was doing her an enormous favor.

"Well, a boy still needs friends," she said. Then she knelt down. "It was lovely to see you, Edison," she said.

"Thank you," said the grave little boy.

"Can I give you a hug, or would that be inpropreet?"

Edison glanced at his mother.

"Best not, eh?" said Hester in a jaunty tone. And Rosie was left staring after them as they walked off, shaking her head in total disbelief.

Tina had not only scrubbed the whole shop from top to bottom, she'd helped the sweetshop have its best day ever and cashed up perfectly. Rosie couldn't believe it and insisted on paying her. Tina looked at the money. "Wow," she said. "It's like having a real job again."

Rosie looked around. Tina had moved the chocolate teddies right to the very front, near the till. It was a good strategy. Few small hands could resist wanting a chocolate teddy, and few grandparents could resist buying one.

"You know," said Rosie. "There have been expressions of interest…" She thought again of Roy deBlaine's terrifying image of rows of bright gleaming gnashers. "…but why don't you see…talk to the bank or someone…"

She looked around the soft lights of the sweetshop illuminating the ancient jars; the neatly stacked piles of candy-striped paper bags that needed to be pulled off a piece of string then looped over, twice, to make a secure carrier; the big brass scoops for the shards of cough candy that reflected the lights through the jar and turned them into a kaleidoscopically colored prism.

"I mean," she said, "if anyone has to take it over, I'd really like it to be you."

• • • •

The second she walked in the house, unlocked as ever, she knew. Not a light was on; neither was the perpetually-tuned-to-Radio-4 wireless set. The fire wasn't lit and there was an odd smell in the air.

Rosie rushed to the bedroom, cursing herself for being absent for so long. Her great-aunt was sitting up, shaking and staring straight ahead. There was something wrong with the left side of her face, Rosie noticed with a sinking heart. And there wasn't a second to lose.

barley sugar

• • • •

Barley sugar is nature's way of making sure you don't feel too guilty when you are unwell and want to eat sweets. The concept of barley as a healthful, life-giving cereal, albeit found in confectionery as more of a trace element, should help you with your mood. And under the circumstances, when you're feeling poorly, the best possible remedy is to improve your mental attitude, which means eating a sweet that feels like on some level it might be good for you is surely the way forward.

Plus as long as you suck and don't bite (as a qualified professional, may I repeat that you should no more bite hard candy than you should shut yourself into a wardrobe), the barley sugar will release a comforting, slow-burn sweetness that will alleviate your mood, make you feel cozy and safe, and set you on the road to health again. Frankly they should prescribe it with aspirin.

So you're her caregiver?" the snappy nurse had asked, not very kindly. Rosie couldn't blame them. She of all people knew that when someone had a stroke—or a ministroke, as seemed likely; Lilian had come around and, although a little confused, seemed basically all right—speed was of the essence. Moray had helped give her aspirin then driven them the long, long way to the hospital, and now Lilian was being helped into a robe—Rosie had packed her favorite nightgowns, delicate shades of lilac and pink, and unearthed a soft, practical, unattractive dressing gown that still had "Merry Christmas '04, love Angie" on a card attached to the bag. She didn't want Lilian confused and frightened in a strange place with her bum hanging out.

"Yes," said Rosie. "But I have to look after her business as well." She said this, feeling horribly guilty in the pit of her stomach, knowing she had taken the afternoon off. If she hadn't, if she had been just next door...maybe that would have made a difference. Maybe not. She'd tried to interest Lilian in a mobile phone, but Lilian had looked at her as if she'd suggested she start carrying around a shark in her pocket, so she hadn't insisted. And she had a panic alarm but hadn't used it, for whatever reason. It was entirely possible, Moray had assured her, that she could have been in the shop all day, rushed off her feet—it had been so busy—and wouldn't have gotten there any faster. It didn't really help.

"She needs someone watching her all the time," scolded the nurse. "If you can't look after her, she'll need to be in a place where people can."

Rosie nodded. The fact that she knew this was coming—it was, she supposed, inevitable—didn't make up for the fact that she couldn't bear, suddenly, to have to tell Lilian that she'd have to move. Move out of the cozy cottage, with its beautiful pictures and little ornate grate. The house, indeed, she'd been born in with the high attic room and the garden. Her beautiful, beautiful garden. How could she tell her to give that up? What would Roy deBlaine do to it? She knew the answer instantly, of course: he would turn it into a parking lot.

Oh God, why were things so complicated? Rosie rushed into the little side ward. Lilian was sitting up, looking around her.

"Henry?" she said only once as Rosie came through the door.

"Umm, no," said Rosie. "Of course it's me, Rosie. Who's Henry?"

Lilian shrugged, and her eyes blinked.

"Rosie," she said. "What kind of a hellhole is this?"

"Umm, it's the hospital," said Rosie. She didn't think the local cottage hospital was bad at all; she'd seen a lot worse.

"It's horrible. Can I go home? I'm hungry."

"Well, that's a good sign," said Rosie. Behind her, the nurse was shaking her head crossly. "I know, I know," said Rosie. "You can't go home quite yet," she said. "They have to keep and check up on you. But I'll stay with you. We'll play Scrabble; it'll be good."

Lilian's face looked perturbed.

"But who's going to mind the shop tomorrow?" she asked.

Rosie didn't want to pick a vulnerable moment to remind her that before she'd arrived, the shop hadn't been open for years. "Umm," she said, taking out her phone. The nurse gave her a warning glance, but Rosie knew full well absolutely nothing was going to happen to the machines if she used it, so she scrolled through it defiantly. "I might have someone in mind."

The nurse sniffed. "Well," she said. "You might have gotten away with it *this* time." There was no doubt in Rosie's mind, two days later, when she took a chastened, frightened Lilian home, exactly what she meant.

• • • •

Tina was absolutely delighted. And as soon as they got Lilian home and comfortably ensconced, Rosie offered her a job. Rosie knew full well it was only a temporary solution, but she had placed a baby monitor next to Lilian, taken the other end into the shop, and scared Lilian half out of her wits by talking into it every so often to check she was okay. Lilian got her revenge by listening to Rosie advising customers on the sweet choice and vigorously advising them some other way. It took a bit of getting used to, not least by the children startled by the disembodied voices, but after a while, it became obvious to Rosie that Lilian was absolutely loving being involved in the life of the shop and had started turning down Radio 4 (except for *Gardener's Question Time*) to take part, through her monitor, in the life of the shop.

Tina dropped Kent and Emily at school then worked a long lunch so Rosie could go sit with Lilian, organize her prescriptions, and do the messages, while Tina served the lunchtime rush and helped in myriad other ways—stock control, product suggestions, and some gentle marketing tips. Then she would leave at three and Rosie could finish up the day and make supper for Lilian, who, while technically recovered, was still rather wobbly.

So life continued, the year moving deeper and deeper into the autumn. It wasn't like the city, where you hardly noticed the seasons come and go, merely adding or removing a jacket as needed and complaining about the bits in between, when it wasn't clear whether you could go bare-legged or not and ended up leaving the house in flip-flops and a raincoat.

Here, the colors of the hills changed so magnificently, the whole world gone russet. Rosie woke one morning to the very first frost on the ground and, just by the door, a huge basket of apples. At first Rosie was overwhelmed and touched, until she started to receive, every couple of days, more apples, and realized it was simply a bumper crop, sweetened by the Indian summer, too many for people to sell or eat. She made apple jam and apple pies and roast pork with apple sauce and compotes and juice until Lilian begged for mercy.

Every morning now, as Rosie looked from her window, she would see an odd mist curling off the grass, the precipitation of the night before turning to frost then gradually melting under an occasional autumnal sun.

Some mornings, the skies outside her window were black as pitch, and the rain and the wind howled down the vale, and she could only just make out, in the far distance, tiny blobs of white that must be sheep, which meant, she knew, that moving among them would be Jake and Farmer Stirling and Will. Everyone was out—the dairy boys even earlier—on a morning when the only conceivable thing she wished to do was huddle under her duvet. Even the locals, coming in to pick up their white mice and Saturday night bonbons, talked of it as a shocker for the time of year, cold beyond memory. Which is how Rosie found herself, one lunchtime, as Tina was hand crayoning their half price offer on candy floss, down outside Lipton's only clothes shop.

She stared in the window. This was the place, on her first day here, she'd sworn never ever to come into. Now, she had been here for a lot longer than she'd expected—and hadn't even heard from Gerard. For all she knew, he'd burned all her clothes in a large bonfire on their tiny balcony. On a whim, she took out her mobile and called Mike, her best mate back at the hospital.

"Yo!" she said, checking her watch and hoping he wouldn't be up to his elbows in something, or someone.

It took Mike a second or two to figure it out. But when he did, his pleasure was gratifying.

"ROSE-OH!" he yelled. "Where the HELL have you been? You've just totally disappeared off the face of the planet."

"Off the face of London, you mean," said Rosie.

"Yes," said Mike. "The planet. Like I said. What are you up to, you lazy old witch?"

"I know," said Rosie. "You won't believe this place. I get lunch breaks and everything."

"No way," said Mike. "And don't tell me, no one ever pees at you or hollers abuse."

"Hmm," said Rosie, reflecting. "Nope, I'm afraid there is both pee and hollered abuse."

"The world of sweets is more cutthroat than I thought," said Mike. His voice softened. "When are you coming home, love? We heard about you and Gerard."

Hmm, Rosie thought. They'd heard about it from Gerard. Which meant it probably didn't reflect well on her. Still. That wasn't really her business, after all.

"What did he say?"

"He said…" Mike paused.

"What?"

"Oh nothing. He said you'd just gone a bit mental in the country."

"He said WHAT?"

"And that he thought maybe the sugar had gone to your head. And that you're living with a mad old spinster lady and turning into her." Mike said the last bit in a rush, as if he were trying to get it all out.

"Okay, okay, that's enough," said Rosie crossly, looking in the shop window. Everything in it seemed to be waxed, even the skirts. Or worsted. She sighed.

"As it happens, my aunt is really quite ill."

"Duh," said Mike. "Surely you knew that before you went racing off?"

Rosie considered it. "I…I mean, sure, but I didn't think it would be so long."

"Are you sure? Are you sure you didn't just think it would be a convenient way of dumping Gerard?"

"No!" said Rosie, stung. She thought about it. "I thought it might be a convenient way of getting him to unload the dishwasher by himself. I think it kind of spiraled down from there."

"Okay, good," said Mike. "It didn't sound like you."

Rosie sighed. "How is he?"

She hoped he wasn't moping too much. Well, maybe a BIT, obviously. She didn't want him to be dancing about, delighted to be free from her, the stupid cow. On the other hand, she hoped he'd restore his natural exuberance. Rosie bit her lip. "How does he seem?"

Mike paused. Rosie didn't really like the pause. "Umm. You are totally over him, right?"

"Well...you know, we've only been broken up—what, a month?"

Standing shivering in the cold shop doorway, it was hard to believe only a few weeks had passed since that sunny weekend.

"Hmm," said Mike.

"Tell me!"

Mike sighed. When Rosie had left, he'd thought she'd be back in five minutes; he never thought she'd be cut out for country life. Not only that, but he didn't think she could separate herself from that wee bloke she seemed so inexplicably keen on. The fact that she was handling both of these things, he assumed, was positive. Yes. She could take it.

"Well," he said. "I did see him."

"Uh-huh."

"At the Bears."

That was the local hospital pub.

"With his arm around the neck of Yolande Harris."

• • • •

Rosie was so surprised she nearly tripped up. She couldn't believe what a strong reaction she was having. After all, she'd dumped him, hadn't she? It was she who had called it off?

But really, how had he managed to get over her that fast?

Rosie realized she wasn't thinking about Gerard specifically. It wasn't him. It wasn't him she was missing. It was the horrifying realization that seven years, seven years could become meaningless in a flash. And everything she had told herself—that he had loved her really, that they'd been in love and it just hadn't worked out—instantly became meaningless in her eyes.

"Yolande HARRIS?" she managed to gasp out. "How does he even get up there?"

Yolande Harris was about six feet of gorgeous, imperious attitude. Rosie was amazed she'd even look at a jerk like Gerard.

"Oh, you know what he's like," said Mike. "He's been doing all the running. I think he just wore her down in the end."

Rosie swallowed hard. She did know what he was like. When he turned on the charm full beam, when he brought out the romantic gestures and the love poems and the...well. It was a long time ago now.

"She'll eat him for breakfast," said Mike.

"I hope she'll make him breakfast," said Rosie, a little stutter in her voice. "Otherwise he'll starve to death."

"Darling, I'm sorry," said Mike, who had a relationship with a very histrionic Italian boy and always gave off the impression that if plates weren't being thrown and people weren't being devastatingly kissed in airports, it didn't really count as a relationship at all.

"No, it's all right," said Rosie, meaning it. "It's good...it's good. I should know. It means I can stop worrying about him."

"You think? You know Yolande though, right? If anything, this is just the start of his problems. She'll eat him alive."

"Good," said Rosie, feeling miles away. Mike kept on talking, something about a birthday party for Giuseppe that she absolutely couldn't miss, but she had drifted off and was barely listening, even when Mike was insisting she come back and spend the weekend in London before they rescinded her transit pass.

Rosie blinked as she hung up. It was odd how these things could come back and affect you, completely unexpected. She hadn't thought about Gerard, not really, not with Stephen getting ill and her aunt getting ill and all the business and work of the shop. But it was obvious that he had been not-thinking-about-her a lot more than she'd been not-thinking-about-him and that hurt her, terribly. As well, she reflected grimly, as really giving her nowhere to live and no home to go back to. She gazed at herself in the shopwindow. Was this it now? Might she just as well give up and start dressing like a fisherman?

And she felt a stab of crossness too. It wasn't exactly easy for her, was it? The nicest man in the village was gay, and the grumpiest one hadn't called her or been in contact at all since she'd told him to speak to his mother. From which she could only wonder if they'd had some enormous falling out and were furious with each other, and her too.

"Hello," said a busty lady with tiny spectacles on the end of her nose, coming to the door. "You're Lilian's girl, aren't you? Did you want to come in and look at our autumn specials? We have some truly spectacular kilts."

Rosie smiled as nicely as she knew how. "No," she said firmly. "No, thank you."

It was true. She wasn't ready quite yet. Not ready at all. Other people were getting on with their lives. She had to too. She couldn't hide away up here forever. Otherwise, her life was going to slip through her fingers.

• • • •

"How are you doing, Lil?" she said, sitting next to the old lady on the bed, sharing the freshest buns from the bakers. Lilian had deliberately requested corned beef, which Rosie privately thought was disgusting.

"I miss Chewits," grumbled Lilian. "And don't call me Lil."

"Oh well, mustn't grumble," said Rosie. "You know," she said, "Tina might buy the shop. What would you think about that?"

"Hmm," said Lilian, feigning disinterest.

"The thing is," said Rosie, "I have to go back to London. At some point. I do. I have a whole life there...well, I don't really. I have a kind of ruins of a life there. I'm not explaining this very well. But the thing is, I need to go home. At some point. Some time."

Lilian looked at her. "Well, people do leave," she said faintly.

"I wouldn't be 'leaving' leaving," said Rosie. "I wouldn't want to do that. I'd want to come up and make sure you were okay and pop in and check on the sweetshop and that."

Lilian fixed her with a gimlet eye. "Mmm-hmm."

Rosie took a bit of her bun and chewed thoughtfully.

"I mean, I can't stay here forever. And you need proper care. I thought I might hire a car, and maybe we could travel around a bit and maybe look at some...some homes."

Lilian was silent.

"Some...some old people's homes," she said finally. "Lilian," said Rosie, "you are old."

"My body is a bit rubbish," said Lilian. "But I'm not OLD old."

"You're eighty-seven."

"Not in my head," said Lilian defiantly.

"How old are you in your head?" said Rosie, genuinely curious.

Lilian stared out of the window. In her head, forever, she was seventeen. And there was a handsome young man coming down the lane at the end of the day. And even though there was an ache in her heart, an ache for Ned, still, when she saw this young man, his curls lightened in the evening sun, then her heart would soar and leap, and even though he was tired, he would rub down the back of his neck and come toward her, his handsome face full of concern and tenderness, and they would walk to their special place around the back of the churchyard and...

Lilian smoothed down her coral pink dress carefully.

"I feel...I feel young," she said. "Just like everyone else."

"I see," said Rosie. They sat in silence for a while. "The thing is," said Rosie, not sure how she could broach this. "The problem is, well...Lilian, you need someone to look after you. And I know this is selfish, and I do...I am really, really fond of you..."

"It's all right," said Lilian. "I know. You're young. You really are."

"I don't feel it," said Rosie.

"Can I take it that that young...'gentleman' was not the man for you?"

Rosie smiled ruefully.

"Yes. You can take it like that. Yes. I suppose. And..." The sentence lingered in the air. "And I kind of feel…I kind of feel—at SOME point—that I need to get back to London. Sort my life out a bit. I sometimes feel that everyone else is moving on miles ahead of me, that they all know what they're doing while I'm just floundering on in the slipstream. Do you ever feel like that?"

Lilian squinted at her.

"All my bloody life," she said. She sat herself up to be more comfortable. "I know," she said suddenly. "I'm being selfish. You can't stay and devote your life to a silly old woman. You have to go. I realize that. I'll go…"

Suddenly she looked very tiny on the bed.

"I'll go wherever you like. I don't suppose it matters."

Rosie felt awful.

"I won't…I mean, we'll get the best price possible. Even if I have to sell to that dentist arsehole," she vowed. "And you'll go to the nicest room in the nicest place with the nicest people…or if you like, you can come down to London and I'll find a lovely home there, and I can come see you all the time, and when Angie comes home, you can meet your hideous great-nieces and great-nephews, and…"

Lilian patted her hand.

"Don't worry about me," she said. "You find your own life, and live it."

"But it's in London," said Rosie.

"London, London, London," said Lilian. "Now darling, if I have a little midafternoon nap, do you promise not to call an ambulance?"

"If you nap now, you'll get grumpy tonight when you can't sleep," threatened Rosie.

"Then I shall listen to the shipping forecast," said Lilian. "Everyone needs a hobby."

Rosie kissed her soft white cheek.

"Sleep well then. And if you feel the least bit strange…"

Lilian patted the panic button on her chest.

"I know, I know. I'm very tempted to let this off in the middle of the night every night. Just to keep you on your toes."

"They're going to love you in the home," said Rosie, smiling sadly. She turned out the light.

"Oh," said Lilian, turning over in bed. "I almost forgot. The postman came for you."

"For me?" said Rosie, puzzled. Nobody had her address but Gerard, and he was almost certainly currently wrapped around the burnished form of Yolande Harris.

"I believe so."

• • • •

The large cream-colored envelope was sitting on a little table by the entrance to the sitting room that normally held keys; Rosie realized she must have been very deep in thought coming in to miss it. It was made of heavy laid paper, properly stiff. On the front, in old-fashioned script written with a fountain pen in slightly faded blue ink, the card was addressed to "Miss Rosalind Hopkins, The Sweetshop Cottage, Lipton." That was all. And a stamp, at perfect right angles to the top right-hand corner.

It was the most beautiful envelope Rosie had ever received.

Carefully, she unstuck the back and pulled out a stiff white card. At the top was a little golden crest and a coat of arms. Rosie gave herself a stern talking to about how ridiculous it was to be impressed by this kind of thing. Nonetheless, she couldn't help it; it was pretty impressive.

Lady Henrietta Lipton
invites you to the Lipton Hunt Ball Meet
Saturday, October 29, 8:00 p.m.
Lipton Hall

Carriages: 1:00 a.m.
Dress: black or regimental tie; hunting colors

Ooh, thought Rosie to herself. It was the first thing that had perked her up all day.

liqueurs

• • • •

Something unexpected on the inside is always welcome. This can go too far—witness the Name Deleted for Legal Reasons, a chocolate noisette product clearly marketed for whores by whores and bought only by professional whores, or "sex workers," as I believe we must call them these days. (Note to legal: this is not disrespectful to the brand. It's disrespectful to whores, if anything.)

But a liqueur chocolate—out of fashion since the young decided that the only way to sample alcohol was to drink nine bottles of blue synthetic gunk and hurl up their innards into the nearest hedge or, if that is not available, my front garden—is an overlooked pleasure. For once, the dark chocolate is appropriate, as it does not jar too strongly with the sharper taste of the alcohol within, both held back from one another by a delicate candied mesh that melts on the tongue then vanishes, allowing the inner flavor of the spirit and the outer of the chocolate to join one another in a transcendent depth and strength of flavor. Cherry is the best, followed by raspberry. Honey is to be avoided at all costs. If you can't handle your drink, leave well enough alone.

The harvests were gathered in, great sheaves tied up in fields, just as the rains came tearing down the mountains from across the Irish Sea, freezing and soaking anyone unwise enough to step out of doors. Lilian's garden was a sea of mud, the petals from the roses long since washed away, and getting down the street was a constant kicking of leaves.

Although some mornings felt sharp and frosty, fresh and different, Rosie felt the encroaching dark, the wheel of the year turning. She wasn't sure if it was because the summer had seemed to last so long, or because, for the first time in her life, she was fully aware of the changing of the seasons, since it was happening so clearly all around her. The stars from her bedroom window, without the distraction of light pollution from the city, were clear and huge, the Plough looming into view as the Virgoan sky took over from Castor and Pollux. It was the first new season in such a long time that she was alone, she thought, wondering what stars her mother and brother saw on the other side of the world.

The one thing that kept her cheered was the sweetshop, of all things. It was small enough that, with a little heating, it was very cozy in there. She and Tina got on very well, and it was lovely to have a friend, and she was hopping up and down the ladder to the topmost jars. Jake did come in once and repeatedly asked for mint toffees, which were kept on the very highest shelf.

"Are you doing this to see up my skirt?" she'd finally managed to ask. Jake had smiled, utterly unembarrassed.

"Come on, love," he said. "What else am I meant to do for fun around here?" Tina had chuckled.

"That's not funny," said Rosie. "That's harassment."

"You're the one in the short skirt."

Rosie rolled her eyes.

"No more mint toffee for you."

"I'll have some sweetie bananas."

"JAKE!!!"

"Also your gorgeous assistant," he bowed. "Hello. I'm Jake."

"How come she gets bowed to like you're a highwayman and I get leered at like I'm Barbara Windsor in 1965?" grumbled Rosie, marching up the steps in an awkward sideways movement so as not to let any snatch of thigh get noticed.

"Because Tina's a lady who doesn't throw it about," came the voice over the baby monitor.

"Thanks, Lilian," said Rosie.

"Maybe that's just because I never get the chance," said Tina, rolling her eyes. "Children and an evil ex and a mortgage I can barely pay."

"Don't be daft, you're still young and gorgeous," said Rosie. "And as soon as you hear from the bank, you're about to become an entrepreneur."

Tina smiled. "Oh, yes. I hope they hurry up with that." She let out a sigh. "It's a big ask."

"You'll do it though," said Rosie. "And you'll have help."

"Did you mean that in a sarcastic way?" came the voice from through the intercom.

"Noooo," said Rosie. "I said 'help,' not 'constant shouted instructions.'"

"Have you taken the rhubarb and custards through from the back?"

"Yes! It's like living with a particularly bossy Jesus," explained Rosie.

"I heard that."

Jake wasn't listening, however. He was looking at Tina with a little smile on his face.

"You and that doof finally broken up then?"

Tina looked a little pink and shrugged.

"If he asks if you would like to go out on a bicycle," said Rosie, "don't go."

"You're coming to the pub this weekend, aren't you, Rosie?"

"No," said Rosie. "I'm going to Kuala Lumpur in a private jet."

Jake ignored this.

"Why don't you bring Tina?"

Tina went slightly pink and started stuttering. "Oh, I…I mean, I'd have to find a babysitter…"

"Couldn't your mum do it?"

"Yes, I suppose…"

"Amazing how everyone knows everyone's business," said Rosie.

"And useful too, sometimes," mused Tina. She did, though, still look terrified. Rosie decided to take over.

"She'll call you," said Rosie practically. "Or send a badger or whatever it is you country folks do to communicate."

Jake smiled his slow, handsome, Brad Pitt smile and held up his sweets. "Well, give me an answer quickly before I turn into Anton."

Rosie smiled as the doorbell tinged and he left.

Tina turned, cheeks pink. "Well!" she said.

"I think," said Rosie gently, "without wanting to be a killjoy AT ALL, and to say you know you are completely gorgeous in every way, but I will say that when I arrived…"

Tina grinned.

"Oh, you don't need to tell me. I was at school with Jake Randall. Always got through the womenfolk." Tina smiled. "I was a bit older than him. Never thought he'd get around to me."

"He'll make you plant vegetables."

Tina picked up her feather duster—Rosie had been completely unaware that it was still possible to buy such a thing—and started to dust the top shelves again, something, Rosie had realized, she did when she was nervous.

"When Todd…when Todd got really bad. And he had good days and bad days. But, well. You can't imagine how far away from…from going out. For a drink. With anyone."

"And?"

"And..." Tina smiled and bit her lip. "Do you think I should go?"

"Of course!!!!" said Rosie. "Go out and get back on the horse."

"The horse you didn't want?" said Tina mischievously.

"Well, I was in a relationship then."

"Ha! I'm still married. Technically."

"He's all yours," said Rosie. "I saw the way he was looking at you."

"Honestly?"

"Honestly."

"Just get over yourselves and step out with him already," came the wobbly but opinionated voice over the intercom. "You girls don't know you're born. There's no point messing about with these things at all."

"Would you like a shot at him, Lilian?" said Rosie into the speaker.

"Be quiet," came the voice. "I'm very busy listening to the *World at One*."

• • • •

That Saturday, Tina came over to Rosie's to get ready. She oohed and aahed at how sweet the cottage was—she lived in a modern house behind the main street. Although, as she pointed out, she could let the children run wild on the scrubby grass, whereas here the front door opened straight on to the main road and the children would utterly ruin the beautiful back garden, vault the fence, and never be seen again. But the first thing she jumped on was the invitation.

"OOH!" she said. Lilian had propped it up on the mantelpiece, even when Rosie had wanted to stick it in a drawer somewhere. She was sitting by the fireplace. Rosie had insisted on getting her a DVD player, even though she couldn't work it at all. Then she'd ordered a cheap job lot of DVDs off eBay with names she'd only ever heard of distantly: Errol Flynn, Rita Hayworth, Esther Davis, Joan Crawford, Douglas Fairbanks Jr. As the evenings had grown longer and the rain hammered down ever harder, she'd pretended she wanted to watch them, and sure enough, Lilian had come around, sometimes, in fact, gasping in recognition of something she hadn't seen for over a century or taking against someone—Ava Gardner, for example—for reasons completely lost in the mists of time. Rosie had originally done it to help her aunt, but soon realized she had completely selfish reasons for losing herself in these wonderful old black-and-white movies...*It Happened One Night*, *The Philadelphia Story*.

By the time they got to *Brief Encounter*, both of them sniffling quietly by the fire, she was completely hooked on the dramatic romances, self-sacrifice, and real men wearing proper hats with their clipped accents and deep devotion. Part of her knew that hiding herself away here next to the fire, with a small bag of lemon bonbons for her and a very few marshmallows for Lilian (as long as she'd eaten her shepherd's pie), immersing herself in other people's romances, was not exactly conducive to the vow she'd made to be getting on with her life. But as she waited for Tina to work out the details of purchasing the shop—and for anyone else to come forward before the end of the month—well, she knew what she should be doing. She should be sorting out a new place in London. Finding a home for Lilian. Making sure all the paperwork for the shop was totally in order. Preparing herself to leave. Not making herself comfortable by the fire. It was as if there was a whole real life clamoring at her door, but she wasn't able to open it up quite yet. The total silence—apart from the occasional hooting of a lonely owl—of the country, its all-encompassing dark blanket, felt peaceful. There was money coming in from the shop—not a fortune, but certainly enough for them to get by; the fire was cozy; Lilian, if even more restricted in her movements, certainly didn't seem much worse in the head following her stroke.

Now, she turned around as Tina entered the sitting room.

"A woman?" she said loudly. "Have you managed to make a female friend, Rosemary? I thought it was just every boy in town you were touting yourself around."

"This is my great-aunt," said Rosie.

"Yes, we've spoken on the intercom," said Tina. "Hello."

"You're Todd's wife. His father was no good," said Lilian.

Tina looked taken aback.

"Sorry," said Rosie. "It's like Tourette's, only she does it on purpose."

"Did you know Harold?"

"Everyone knew Harold," said Lilian. "Always stumbling out of the Lion whenever he had a free five minutes."

Tina smiled ruefully.

"Like father like son, I'm afraid."

Lilian blinked.

"I'm sorry to hear that. Man hands on misery to man."

"Uh, yes," said Tina. "Anyway." She looked suddenly nervous. "I've always loved your shop. When I was little, I always used to hang about for ages before I could decide what to buy."

Lilian took off her glasses.

"I never forget a child," she said and peered at Tina closely. Then she sat back. "Christina Fletcher," she said with evident satisfaction. "Candy shrimps and gobstoppers. But you always spent a long, long time in deciding. Then chose the same things, every Saturday."

"That's amazing," said Rosie. "Your mind is like a steel trap."

"Yes, well, it is now," said Lilian. "Wait till I've been in that home you're dumping me in for five minutes. It will have turned to mush, and I'll be dribbling and crying and wetting my chair at the same time. While listening to popular music that they'll pipe in at a ludicrous volume."

"Yes, yes," said Rosie. "Do you need to go to the toilet?"

"Yes please," said Lilian.

• • • •

Once they were back, Lilian relaxed a little bit.

"You were such a quiet little thing, Christina," she said. "Not like Drew, that brother of yours that liked the fizz bombs."

Tina nodded. "I know. He went off to York, got into finance. He's done really well for himself. I suppose… I didn't really know what I wanted, not really. I just kind of bobbed along, played it safe."

"With the gobstoppers and the shrimps," said Lilian. "One hard, one soft. Covering both bases."

"Yes, I suppose so," said Tina, smiling. "Just to be on the safe side, you know?"

Lilian nodded.

"I do," she said.

"Married the first guy that came along…mind you, he gave me Kent and Emily. I'm happy about that."

Lilian nodded.

"And they like sweets?"

"Of course. Emily is just like me. She gets Hello Kitty flumps and a Chupa Chups so she has a bit of everything. Kent wants to try whatever is the latest thing."

"Funny," mused Lilian. Then, catching Rosie glancing at her watch, said, "All right, all right. I like her."

• • • •

Upstairs in the bedroom, Tina opened the bag she'd brought with her.

"Oh my God!" said Rosie, her eyes hungrily taking in the logos—Zara, Topshop, even Reiss—and pretty fabrics and colors.

"Look at all your amazing clothes!"

"My amazing clothes I NEVER WEAR," said Tina. "Since I had the twins, I dress exactly like them. Jeans, T-shirt, flat shoes."

"You always look immaculate though," said Rosie loyally.

"I'm a mother, not a—" Tina smiled. "Okay. Dive in!"

"Nothing you have will fit me!"

"Of course it will," said Tina. "Well, the pinafores and stuff."

"Okay, okay."

Tina came back to the invitation, which she'd carried up the stairs. "But look at this!"

Rosie shrugged.

"I just assumed everyone got invited."

"Everyone does NOT get invited. Why do you think Lilian has it hanging out to impress everyone? Lady Lipton's hunt ball is, like, the talk of the county."

"The whole county?"

"Yeah, yeah, very sarcastic. But it's, like, all the landowners and aristocracy from all around the place, and she really does it all up and makes it all fancy..." Tina's voice trailed off. "I kind of hoped...well, it's silly. But last year when I broke up with Todd, I wanted to go so badly. Anyway."

"Maybe Jake will be going."

Tina snorted.

"Yeah, to park the cars, maybe."

"Really?" said Rosie. "Well, actually, this sounds a bit shit now, the way you're talking about it."

"It's the only time of the year the house is really open, apart from tours in the summer and weddings and stuff," said Tina, her eyes gleaming. "They light the whole driveway so you can see it from all over the village, and you can hear them all night. Plus there's always some posh loony who drives his Land Rover into someone's house on his way home."

"This sounds AWFUL," said Rosie. "I'm not going."

Tina gave her a knowing look.

"Not even to see your patient?"

"I haven't heard hide nor hair from my EX-patient in weeks," said Rosie, realizing as she said it how irritating this was. She thought they were becoming...well. Maybe not close. Stephen didn't really seem to do "close." Intense and quite often irritating he could manage. But not a line, not a phone call, not even a proper thank-you—would a bunch of flowers have been so out of the question? It stiffened her resolve.

"I don't think I really want to go to some poshos throwing themselves about thing," she said. "Plus I don't know those weird dances they do, and I won't know anyone except Stephen, who will probably be sulking, and she's not inviting any of my friends, and anyway, she's totally rude to me all the time."

"She's only rude to people she likes," said Tina. "To everyone else she's just kind of distractedly polite. You should be flattered."

"And yet I'm not," said Rosie. "ARGH!" She was trying to zip up a dusty pink sleeveless party dress. It was beautiful, but clearly wasn't going to fit.

"Bum, this is annoying. Running a sweetshop is doing nothing for me."

"It's still pretty," said Tina. "Try this."

And she handed over a top in the same color, which did fit, and made Rosie's dark hair and pale skin look like Snow White.

"Gorgeous," said Tina. "Although you'll need some lipstick."

"Always," said Rosie. "Where do you GET all this stuff?"

"Mail order!" said Tina. "It arrives off the Internet. It's like somebody sending you a present."

There was a silence.

"Does that make me sound really lonely?" she said.

"No," said Rosie immediately.

"Well, that's good," said Tina. "I am really lonely though."

Rosie glanced out at the moon rising in her window.

"Oh fuck," she said. "Me too."

The two girls dissolved into laughter.

"Come on, let's go out and get a bit drunk," said Rosie. "I believe it's medically necessary." She reached under her bed.

Tina's eyes widened as Rosie pulled out two packets of Refreshers, some sherbet powder, and a large bottle of vodka.

"What the hell is that?" she said.

"Aha," said Rosie. She'd already put the ice cubes in her sink with the cocktail glasses. She dissolved the sherbet powder in the vodka, added ice cubes and sugar syrup, and topped it off with a refresher.

"You're joking me," said Tina. "Sweetie cocktails?"

"Fabulous, non?" said Rosie. "I just made it up. If it weren't so gosh-darn illegal, I'd sell them in the shop." The girls giggled and chinked glasses then sipped slowly.

"The weird thing is," said Rosie, "the first sip is a bit odd. But the second is AMAZING."

"If I have a third," said Tina, "I'm going to fall out the window."

Rosie shrugged on a dark red bolero over the shoulder-ruched top.

"Ooh," she said. "What do you think? Too sexy señorita? Should I be wearing a rose in my mouth?"

"I think what Lipton needs is a sexy señorita," said Tina. "That is the ONLY thing lacking from this town."

Finally, shushing each other as they crept past Lilian and giggling their heads off, they headed down to the Red Lion.

• • • •

"All right, girls," said Les as they pushed open the door. "Ooh, look at you two, going somewhere fancy?"

Tina started to sigh, but Rosie said, "Of course! Here! For you, Les!" Amazingly, this made him smile and the normal residents grin. One of the farmers came forward and asked to buy them their first gin and tonic, and from then on, they were happily ensconced by the fire.

"This," said Rosie, "is because of my terrible reputation."

But it wasn't Rosie in fact who was getting all the attention—it was Tina.

"We never thought we'd see you out again since Todd left," said Rodge, the vet, who was enjoying a rare and well-deserved night off.

Tina smiled. "Well, you know, it's been hard."

"Why didn't you come out, see some people?" asked another. "We're always here."

"Yeah, ALWAYS here."

The farmers were good company, cheeky and funny and flirtatious over the course of the next few hours.

When she got up to go to the bathroom, Rosie realized instantly that she was drunk. Well, not drinking much for months then making up ridiculous cocktails out of vodka and whatnot would do that to you. She found herself making a silly face in the mirror then putting her lipstick on slightly wonky. Oh well. They were having fun. And it was nice to see Tina happy again. It couldn't be easy looking after twins on your own. She wobbled slightly coming out of the toilet. Then she blinked, and blinked again, just in case her eyes were deceiving her. They weren't. Sitting in the corner with his back to her, his stick on the floor, his face filled out, his hair desperately in need of a haircut, was Stephen Mannering.

Had she not had some vodkas, and gin and tonics, and unwarranted admiration by Lipton's many single menfolk, Rosie would probably have thought twice about what she did next. Instead, emboldened and in a foolish mood, she marched straight up to him.

"Hey!" she yelled. "Not a phone call? Not a word? What kind of a grateful ex are you?"

She meant, of course, ex-patient. But it came out wrong. Stephen, startled, turned around hastily, and Rosie noticed that the other person at his table was a girl.

And not just any girl. A long-haired, very slender, wide-eyed, blond girl, with a flick to her hair. She flicked it now then glanced up at Stephen. It was not a friendly glance. It was a "Who the hell is this?" glance.

"Hello?" she said inquiringly. She wasn't local, Rosie noticed straightaway. She was southern, just like her. It came to her suddenly. She must be a jag!

Stephen looked uncomfortable immediately and ran his fingers through his hair. "Umm," he said. "Hi. Hello."

Even in her fuddled state, it was obvious to Rosie that something was up. She felt like she was intruding on something. And worse, she realized, in a horrible, blinding flash, that whatever she'd said to Tina or told herself she believed, she did have feelings for Stephen. Not pity or tenderness or proper professional feelings of a caregiver taking care of a patient. Nothing like that at all. Proper, real feelings. Real feelings that were suddenly being whipped into a frenzy of jealousy by this woman here with the flicky hair.

"Umm," said Stephen. Rosie wondered about this too. He was obviously uncomfortable. But why? If she was just a nurse to him, then he wouldn't feel embarrassed, would he? He'd be perfectly happy to introduce her. The fact that it was awkward…a tiny pilot light lit inside her. If he…if he…

"This is Rosie," said Stephen. "She was my nurse."

The light inside Rosie sputtered and died. His WHAT?

"Umm, Rosie, this is CeeCee."

CeeCee? The girl gave her a tight social smile that basically said, "Back off, I am chatting up the hot young aristocrat." She reminded Rosie of the girls you saw on TV at Formula One. All blond and skinny and identical—and DESPERATE to hang around the rich boys.

"Nice to meet you," drawled CeeCee in the most languid way imaginable before picking up her iPhone. She put it down to add, "Oh, darling, Kibs and Francesca have also been DYING to know what you've been up to."

"Oh, yes, well," stammered Stephen. He really wasn't himself at all. Rosie hadn't felt so ignored since the last time she tried to rouse a ketamine addict in the emergency room.

"Uh-huh," she said. "Well, I didn't mean to barge in. Bye!"

She started to retreat to her gang when Stephen turned to her. CeeCee busied herself putting on more lip gloss.

"Umm," he said, his face going bright red. "Thank you. Again."

"All part of the nursing service," said Rosie tightly.

Stephen blinked a couple of times.

"Uh. Oh," he said. She had never known him to be lost for words at all. "I meant, thanks for telling me to talk to Mother."

"Mother?"

"Yes, Mother. Female thing. Gave birth to me." Well, the old Stephen hadn't disappeared completely. "Anyway. We've been getting on a lot better. Thank you."

"Who's that?" said Rosie bluntly.

CeeCee looked as out of place in the cozy confines of the Lion as a tropical fish in a goldfish bowl. Her shoes had red soles. She was talking loudly on her iPhone.

"Umm, it's an old friend of mine…"

"Oh, it was so nice of her to spend so much time with you when you were poorly," said Rosie. "Still, now you're on the mend and set to inherit, it's lovely she's made the trip."

Stephen gave her a sharp look, and Rosie knew she'd gone too far. "I'd better go," she said.

"Maybe you had," he said. "You're not being very nice."

"Maybe I'm not very nice."

Stephen half smiled. "Well, neither am I."

"I bet she isn't either," said Rosie, really knowing she'd gone too far this time. There was tension in the air as they looked at one another. Then Stephen laughed.

"Are you coming to Mother's—sorry. Ma's or Mummy's or Lala's or whatever they use around your way, obviously the only acceptable way you can talk about the person who gave birth to you. Are you coming to the ball?"

"No," said Rosie. "I won't know a single person there. There's not one single nice person I like from the village going. It'll be full of people like CeeCee, and your MUM treats me horribly. But thanks for asking."

Rosie felt her walk back over to the other side of the pub would have been a lot better if she hadn't accidentally stumbled over her shoes before she got there.

• • • •

The fun had gone out of the night, and they all knew it. Tina wanted to head home anyway; the twins would be up at seven whether she had a hangover or not, and that was the end of it. Rosie trailed up to bed alone, taking off the pink ruched top—what had she been thinking? She looked like she was dolled up for flamenco fancy dress. Stephen and CeeCee were probably chuckling about it right now. Rosie groaned in embarrassment. Oh God. Did he know? Of course he knew. She must have made it so obvious. But how hadn't she known?

She had, of course. A bolt of electricity had shot through her when she saw him there. She couldn't help it. And he was going to think of her as such an idiot, chunky little curly-haired London girl, against a slender, lissome creature like CeeCee. It probably happened to him all the time before he cut his leg open. Handsome aid worker, posh family, big fuck-off house… God, what an idiot she must seem to him. It probably happened all the time. He probably felt sorry for her, like George Clooney did every time he got gushed on by a TV reporter.

And she realized something worse: that when she had ditched Gerard, a perfectly nice man, she had obviously, on one level, hoped there might be a chance with Stephen, that she might have a shot. What a totally stupid thing that had been. Of course, now he was on the mend, he'd have bees around the honey pot. She was lucky he had even remembered her name.

"Bugger," said Rosie out loud, her voice resounding in the silent country night air. BUGGER, BUGGER, BUGGER.

Dear ignoramuses, Hallowe'en is not "a Yankee holiday" celebrated only by gigantic toddlers wearing baseball caps back to front and spraying automobiles with eggs. This is ignorance.

Hallowe'en is an ancient druidic holiday, one the Celtic peoples have celebrated for millennia. It is the crack between the last golden rays of summer and the dark of winter; the tiny balanced tweak of the year before it is given over entirely to the dark; a time for the souls of the departed to squint, peek, and perhaps travel through the gap. What could be more thrilling and worthy of celebration than that? It is a time to celebrate sweet bounty, as the harvest is brought in. It is a time of excitement and pleasure for children before the dark sets in. We should all celebrate that.

"I'm not going, so stop it."

It was 4:00 p.m. on Saturday, October 29. The shop had been almost entirely overrun all day, with Hallowe'en lollipops, white chocolate skeletons with raspberry icing, gum balls that looked like eyeballs, gobstoppers with teeth, large bags of economy sweets for people expecting huge parties, and lollipops of every conceivable flavor and hue. Tina had had the idea to make up special Hallowe'en bags with a few sweets in them to be handed out easily without mess, and these had proved highly popular. Edison had sat in the corner putting the sweets into bags.

"Hester doesn't believe in Hallowe'en," he said sadly. "She said it's commercialized tooth rot and encourages loutishness. She says if I like, I can come to her druidic festival next week. But it always rains, and I don't like all the men with beards who hit trees."

Rosie and Tina swapped worried glances. "Would you like to come out with us?" asked Tina hurriedly. "Kent would love to go with you, I think."

Kent and Edison had become friends, which Tina mostly approved of, although she worried about Edison filling Kent's head with nonsense. Rosie had pointed out that Kent was absolutely robust enough to figure out the world for himself, and ever since they'd started playing together, Edison had hardly mentioned Reuben, his imaginary friend, and Tina had been mollified after that. It was a little hard on Emily though.

"YES YOU ARE," came the crotchety voice over the loudspeaker. "Tina, you tell her."

"I would love to go," said Tina. "Jake and I supposedly have a date, and I can't seem to get further than the bloody Red Lion!"

Rosie stuck her lip out.

"It is going to be full of bloody snobs, all of whom will look down their noses at me—you wouldn't believe what the woman was like in the pub with him—and go 'HWA HWA HWA' when they laugh and dance with swords and talk about horses. Of course I'm not going. I'm staying in to watch *The X Factor* and Tina is going to come over and we'll put the kids to bed upstairs and it will be lovely."

"Did you ever go to those balls, Mrs. Hopkins?" asked Tina.

Lilian was silent for a while. Then, "Not at first. Of course, she was the girl of the big house, and I was just the sweetshop lady. But then the world changed, and changed, and changed, and lots of new people moved into town, and it suddenly didn't seem to matter quite so much anymore exactly who your parents were, and then we somehow...we became friends somehow. We'd had a lot of people in common growing up. But it was too late for me by then!"

"Too late for what?" said Rosie. "If you say 'to find a husband,' I'm going to put you in a dog home."

"To really enjoy the dancing, of course. And the beautiful gowns, and the champagne that flows all night, and the wonderful food, and the romance of it all, the men so handsome."

"ARGH!" said Tina. "Honestly, I am going to go and just say I'm you. They won't care."

"You should," said Lilian.

"I won't," said Tina. "Someone would hand me a tray of empty glasses before I'd been there five minutes, I know it."

The bell tinged, and Lady Lipton breezed in, imperious as ever. "Ah!" she said. "It's the little scarecrow. How are you?"

She eyed Rosie.

"Still not got any clothes sent up for the winter?" she said, looking at Rosie's floral frock. It was freezing outside now, incredible given that it wasn't even November. The ground was frosted over every morning; Lilian's garden looked like a twinkling fairyland.

"I'm fine, thanks."

"But what are you wearing tonight?"

Rosie looked at the ground.

"Not that, I hope. You know, it is formal."

"Umm," said Rosie.

"Well, come on, spit it out. Also, you." She meant Tina. "I need all the eyeball gobstoppers you have. I think it will be HILARIOUS for my guests."

Tina jumped to it. Rosie couldn't bear the rudeness.

"I'm not coming," she said quietly, but she knew she could be heard.

"What's that?" Lady Lipton looked like she couldn't believe her ears.

"I'm not coming. Tonight."

"Whyever not?"

Rosie was on the brink of making up a good excuse—she would keep her manners even when Hetty didn't—when the voice squawked again from the baby monitor.

"Because she's a bloody idiot!"

Hetty looked all around her in surprise and consternation; it did sound like Lilian was booming out of nowhere.

"Lilian? Where are you?"

"She's on the monitor," said Tina shyly.

"WHY isn't she coming?" continued Hetty.

"Ask her yourself," said Lilian. "Because she's a bloody idiot."

Because I fancy your son and he thinks I'm a servant and you think I'm a gold digger, thought Rosie bleakly.

"Why not?" demanded Hetty, red in the face.

"Because I have nothing to wear, and I won't know anyone there," mumbled Rosie.

"What's that? What NONSENSE," said Lady Lipton. "Invite some friends; we always get some people passing out from drink before dinner. What about you?"

Rosie would have pointed out that Hetty and Tina had lived in the same tiny village for thirty-five years, had Tina not immediately looked absolutely delighted and barely stopped short of clapping her hands together.

"Ooh, yes please!"

"And you can bring that dirty Isitt laborer if you must," sniffed Hetty. "A bit of what I believe you call 'eye candy.' Not quite so broken-veined as the rest. And I've invited that poofy doctor. Isn't that enough chums?"

Rosie felt her face flame.

"And I'll lend you a dress!" Hetty boomed.

Rosie couldn't bear to think what that might consist of. Did they even make waxed dresses?

"I have a full-length kilt I'm sure will look splendid on you. Of course Bran used it as a blanket, but it looks absolutely fine."

"I'm sure I can find something for her," pleaded Tina.

"Jolly good!" said Hetty, handing over a twenty for the huge bag of sweets. "See you at eight, trippety-trip."

And the bell clanged and she was gone.

• • • •

"Eek!" said Tina, turning to Rosie to give her a hug. "Now it'll be great! What's up?"

"Nothing," said Rosie.

"What?" said Tina. "Don't hide it from me. OOH," her excitement got the better of her. "I wish Todd could see me now. He would be LIVID. Do you know how many times I've been to something like this? Never!"

"Me neither," said Rosie.

"Well, we can make idiots of ourselves together…what's up?"

"It's stupid," said Rosie.

"What?"

Rosie was torn. On the one hand, she couldn't bear to reveal what an idiot she'd been. On the other, if she didn't tell someone, she thought she was going to burst.

"It's Stephen," she said. "I fancy him."

Tina stared at her for a few seconds then burst out into peals of laughter.

"What? Why's that funny?" Rosie was genuinely stung.

"Oh no, it's not, it's not, it's just… Oh," said Tina. "Back when we were at school…he didn't go to our school, of course."

"Of course," said Rosie.

"He was sent away. But when he came back in the holidays…oh wow. EVERYONE fancied him."

"You don't say."

"He was always slouching around the village with a book of

poetry, in a furious mood because he'd just had another big fight with his dad."

"Oh yeah? Did anyone ever catch him?"

"Oh God no. What, him mess with the likes of us?" Tina grinned. "It wasn't for want of trying though. Claudia Mickle once cycled her bicycle into a wall, craning her neck to take a look at him. She needed four stitches."

"Okay, okay, okay, I get the message," said Rosie.

"Then he went all weird of course..." Tina suddenly looked stricken. "I mean, I'm really sorry... There's no reason he wouldn't fancy you back, none at all!"

"There are a million reasons he wouldn't fancy me back," said Rosie, starting to clear up. "All of them tall and blond and rich and posh and bearing iPhones."

There was a silence.

"Well," said Tina, "I know you're the boss and everything, but not for long. So I order you to come with me. Just because you fancy someone is absolutely no reason not to let me go to the party of the year. It wouldn't be fair. I'm going to text Jake and Moray right now and order them to come pick us up, and we will go and get drunk again and ignore all the stupid posh folk and have a brilliant time, the four of us. It'll be great. And that big stupid pouty Stephen won't know what he's missing."

"I can't say no to that, can I?" said Rosie. "I'd be ruining everyone's night out."

"EXACTLY," said Tina. "FREE CHAMPAGNE."

"Can I be your footman?" asked Edison hopefully.

"No," said Rosie. "But you can come to our next *X Factor* sleepover."

"Don't tell my mum it's television."

"I'll tell her it's chromosomes," promised Rosie, as Hester came up the path, as usual looking as though she was carrying the world's problems on her shoulders. "Okay, scurry off, footman."

"You will look very beautiful at the ball," said Edison seriously as he grabbed his coat and cap and left the door. "Both of you."

Tina and Rosie looked after him.

"You know, it's not an expression I use very often, and I mean it in its original sense," said Rosie, "but that is a very queer little boy."

"Neh," said Tina, already making arrangement calls on her phone. "He's right."

There was a happy snuffle from the baby monitor. "LILIAN!" said Rosie warningly.

"I am happy you are going to the dance, that's all," said Lilian.

• • • •

1944

The news from everywhere seemed to be getting slightly better; even Terence, on his leave, had seemed more cheerful. The tide was turning, everybody said. The Germans were in retreat. The war was going to finish. It was.

Lilian couldn't believe the war would ever be over. She had been a child when it started. Now, she felt about a hundred years old. People were lost, people moved—she had taken a bus, four hours, in to see Margaret's baby, and they had discovered, once she had oohed and aahed at his little fingers and toes and round chunky cheeks, that they had very little in common anymore.

Margaret kept asking her if she was stepping out with someone, and Lilian didn't know how to answer: that the very thought of it seemed unbearable. Not that men didn't ask, didn't come in looking for sweets on the very top shelf to make her climb up or casually ask if she wanted to go to a dance. But having refused that very first dance, Lilian didn't know if she ever wanted to go to another. They seemed to cause nothing but trouble. Margaret urged her to find a beau—"There's no men left, you know, ducks," she said. "There's going to be a right scramble once this is all over."—and pushed her in the direction of all the new American GIs, who seemed so tall and exotic and handsome. "Go wi' one of them," she said. "You'll get a whole new life." Gerda Skritcherd was talking about going to America; it sounded thrillingly exotic.

But Lilian didn't want a whole new life. She wanted her brothers back around the table, and her da happy, and the shop, and Henry back. The fact that these were impossible wishes from an impossible heart didn't seem to have any bearing on the way she felt about it at all. And she knew Margaret was giving her good advice—good within the ways of her world. Bert was a decent enough chap too, she knew. But it was as if she were frozen; she could feel all this good advice, but she couldn't seem to move, to take it.

Gordon came home one honeysuckled spring evening—Henry had now been away for one year and four months, or 432 days. Rosie assumed Ida was getting word of him; she never heard and was far too proud to ask. She hoped he wasn't scared out there. She hoped he wasn't seeing terrible things. She wondered if he thought of her as much as she thought of him, while knowing, deep down, that that couldn't possibly be the case. But she had changed now. She knew he wasn't coming back to her; he couldn't, possibly. Dorothy was toddling about now, while remaining quite the most recalcitrant child anyone in Lipton could remember. Her mouth was a permanent kidney bean of dissatisfaction. Ida was developing frown lines between her eyes. Rosie had seen Henry once, on leave. The family was walking down the high street. Ida was obviously displeased at something; she was clearly shouting at Henry, who had lost weight and gained muscle and looked tall and rangy and somehow older in his army suit. He wasn't saying anything. Lilian had hidden behind her bedroom curtains until he'd gone away.

But now, she told herself, all she cared about was that he was safe.

That he wasn't bleeding in a field somewhere, or with half a leg missing like Dartford Brown's youngest, hopping about the streets, trying to make jokes about how it could have been worse, but with an ocean of pain behind them. Still. All she cared about, Lilian told herself, was that Henry came home safe. When the war finished. If it ever did.

"Look what I have for you," said Gordon, ebullient as ever, dragging his huge heavy kit bag over the flagstones of the kitchen floor. Their da looked up from his account ledger.

"What's this then, son?"

Gordon flashed his cheeky grin. He'd been promoted, twice, and was now a lance corporal, but to Lilian he was still a fat-bottomed boy in short trousers, getting away with murder.

Gordon drew two bottles out of his kit bag, and their da wolf-whistled. "Is that..."

"Certainly is," said Gordon. "It's pure champagne. From the vineyards of sham-pag-en itself."

"I've never even seen it," said Da, shaking his head. He picked the bottles up very carefully.

"You carted these back all the way?"

"Slept on them like a pillow," said Gordon. "Case anyone nicked 'em. I've been doing a bit of, well, nod nod wink wink on the side for the men, like. Make sure they get some decent grub. And these came my way. Thought I might need 'em for a bribe coming home, but I forgot what a straight old place England still is. So here they are!"

Da sent Lilian down to the dairy for an ice block. Then he insisted they lay a bottle in it for an hour to keep cool. Mostly, they sat around and watched it.

"Put the other one away in the larder," said Da. "We'll keep it for a special occasion."

Lilian tucked it right away at the very back of the top shelf. "For when Henry comes home," she said to herself.

• • • •

2012

They decided, wisely, to stay clear of the vodka experiments this time until they were sensibly at the party. To let Lilian join in, Tina brought half the contents of her wardrobe over, and they tried on everything.

"When did you even NEED a cocktail dress?" said Rosie.

"Well, you never know," said Tina.

Rosie raised her eyebrows.

"Okay, okay," said Tina. "So when Todd was going through his worst phase, I maybe became a bit…shopaholic-y. Apparently it was my way of getting him back for his illness. So his counselor told me."

"REVENGE cocktail dresses," marveled Rosie, pulling them out. They really were beautiful. But however many they tried on Rosie—Tina was insisting on a little black sleeveless number that looked amazing with her blond hair—none of them were quite right. Most of them fitted okay—Rosie's bust and little waist worked very well in a frock—but none were perfect.

"Oh well," said Rosie, coming and going for the sixth time. "The black one with the little bit of lace at the top—that's probably the best we're going to get, I think."

"If you'd asked Lady Lipton before, we could have gone shopping," said Tina reproachfully. "In Derby, they've got an Arndale."

"I don't think you need to do any more shopping," said Rosie, looking at all the shoes.

"No," said Tina. "I just need to go to more parties. Hurrah!"

Lilian sighed. "The black is no good. It works on little Tina, but…"

"She's not six anymore!" said Rosie.

"She is to me," said Lilian.

"Thanks, Mrs. Hopkins," said Tina.

"But it's no good for you. You need something to make you stand out. Make him notice you."

"Yes," agreed Tina. Rosie felt herself grow uncomfortably hot. She'd forgotten Lilian would have overheard the entire conversation she and Tina had had about Stephen.

"Well, he won't," she said.

"Why not?" said Lilian. "Stranger things have happened. Sometimes the handsomest man in the village DOES notice the girl with the dark hair."

"Not to me," said Rosie.

"I think Jake's the handsomest man in the village," said Tina.

"Yes," said Rosie, "closely followed by Moray."

"Yup."

But they're not the ones I like, Rosie found herself thinking. *They're not the ones I want.*

"If Hetty thinks her son is too good for my great-niece, she's got another thing coming," said Lilian. "Go into my bedroom. The large armoire."

"The what?"

"What DO they teach you at school these days? The wardrobe. Tch!"

Rosie did as she was bid. It was a huge old thing. Inside, it smelled of camphor and beeswax. The clothes were packed so closely together it was hard to see what was in there.

"Count six from the far right side," said Lilian. "No, seven."

Everything was in dry-cleaning bags, immaculately ironed and hung. Rosie gasped as she started to leaf through them. There were beaded gowns in jewel shades, bright hot fuchsias, a jacket with a proper fox trim. Tina came charging in and her eyes widened.

"Oh my God, LOOK at this stuff."

She popped her head back into the sitting room.

"No wonder you always look so immaculate. This is a treasure trove in here."

Lilian shrugged and tried not to look pleased.

"Well, everyone needs a hobby," she said.

Tina pulled out things here and there, unheeding of Lilian's commands not to. But it was the dress seventh from the end that drew the eye. Lilian had been absolutely right.

• • • •

There was a faint, not unpleasant hint of perfume as Rosie pulled the cool green silk over her head. It shimmered, almost iridescent. It wasn't a forest green, or a racing green, more of a dark emerald, but the material itself was so light it seemed to dance before the eyes. Rosie was convinced it would be too small, but there was ruching along the back, cleverly concealed at the base of the waist.

"It's to allow room for dancing," grumbled Lilian when she saw her. "Of course, you stretch it out."

"You were bigger then though," argued Rosie back.

"I was," said Lilian. "You'd think you'd be happy that being terribly old helps you lose weight. I assure you, you won't be."

Finally, however, Rosie wriggled and shrugged and felt the material flow over her hips with a soft swooshing noise. She could tell by the way Lilian and Tina had gone silent that they approved.

"What?" she said.

Lilian suddenly, quickly, found herself wanting to look away. Rosie was a softer-looking girl than she had been, not so angular, her nose not so long, her shoulders not so pointy. But something in the long, dark curling hair and the wide, pink mouth caught and tugged hard on Lilian's memory—the memory of a hopeful young woman in front of a full-length mirror, waiting and waiting, until there was no point in waiting anymore, and then continuing to wait, in pretty dresses, even when she no longer knew what she was waiting for but had simply formed the habit.

"You look AMAZING," said Tina. "That color is gorgeous on you!"

Rosie dashed off to the full-length mirror over the bath. She couldn't help smiling at what she saw there. Odd, really—and, frankly, annoying when you thought about it—but a few months of staying off the late nights, and getting a bit of fresh air, and not eating takeout, or nicking all the chocolates patients brought into wards, of not working nights, or wrestling catheters at 4:00 a.m., or blearily making her way home through the dawn and trying to sleep through car alarms and buses and parties and deliveries and noises in a busy London street—it had changed her. She could see it. Her skin looked soft and creamy, with a pink blush in her cheeks that she identified, correctly, as excitement. Her eyes were clear, and the green in the beautiful shining silk dress brought the same color out in them. Shed of her practical clothing and slouching demeanor, she felt…

Well, beautiful would be silly, she told herself. But really. This was clearly as good as it was going to get.

She went back into the sitting room, grinning.

"All right, all right," said Tina. "Look at you, cat who's got the cream. Okay, so you look lovely."

"Sorry," said Rosie. "I will go back to being my normal grumpy self immediately."

She caught sight of her great-aunt's stricken face.

"Lilian," she said, darting forward. "Lilian! Are you all right? Are you feeling all right? Show me your left hand." She turned her head back to Tina. "I'll have to stay behind. I can't go."

"Stop being daft," said Lilian. "I was just thinking how nice you look. Now, go into the larder and look behind the mustard box on the highest shelf. Carefully."

• • • •

They put the ancient, dusty, exquisite bottle of champagne into the freezer, on Tina's advice.

"Probably ruin it," she said with a nervous giggle.

"It was probably ruined a long time ago," said Lilian. "Will be the most undrinkable muck, probably."

"Stop being such a pessimist," said Rosie. "I can't believe you've had that there all this time. It's probably worth a fortune. Can't you sell it?"

Lilian shrugged. "It won't be worth that much. Anyway, sell it so you can pack me off to a home? Not bloody likely."

"Actually, I was thinking we could use the money to hire a nurse for a bit, SO THERE," said Rosie.

"You'd never guess you two were related," said Tina.

"Well, it doesn't matter what Miss Green Dress says," said Lilian, undaunted. "That is my bottle of champagne. Your grandpa Gordon liberated it during the war and brought it all the way back to Derbyshire. He brought two actually. We drank the first one to celebrate Gordon being home—he said it would be like drinking stars. I thought he was talking rubbish myself. But by his second glass, my da was singing a stupid song about blackbirds I hadn't heard since my ma died. We spent the whole afternoon just laughing and talking about Neddy—that was my brother, he died in the war—and...well. It was the first time I'd been happy in a long time. And then we were going to keep the second one for Terence coming home, but then we weren't all there together, and he was always so low-key anyway, hated any fuss, didn't even invite us to his wedding, the bugger. So we never drank it. Then your grandpa went off to London and that was the end of THAT branch of the family, till about two months ago."

"Sorry," said Rosie, listening intently.

"And well, me and my da kept waiting for some great occasion to drink it, and it just never arrived. We were working when the war ended. Everyone came in and spent all their coupons on as many sweets as they could manage, and we were rushed off our feet. And then after Da died, well, I never thought to drink it after that. I never was much for the drink."

Tina and Rosie swapped glances. Rosie squeezed Lilian's hand. "Thank you," said Lilian.

"That's all right," said Rosie gently. Then, more awkwardly. "Also, would you mind squeezing back please? Just so I can check?"

"Ah, away with you!" said Lilian, giving her a hard squeeze that involved digging her beautifully manicured nails into Rosie's hand. Rosie jumped up, laughing, and went to get the glasses and fetch the bottle out of the freezer. But it wasn't that funny, she thought. A life should have more opportunities to drink champagne than that.

Tina carefully peeled back the ancient, brittle foil and untwisted the wire.

"Oh God," she said. "I can't pop this. Honestly, if it all goes wrong, I'll be a mess."

Rosie took it from her.

"I will now try to look like I do this every day of the week," she said, smiling. "Okay, everyone cover their eyes and stuff."

And she very carefully and very slowly twisted the ancient cork out of the bottle. It eased itself out with a gentle pop, no great crack at all, and the women held their breath in case it had gone off or flat. But it smelled good, a deep, viney scent, and when Rosie poured it, very carefully, into Lilian's immaculate, heavy, pure crystal glasses, it made a satisfyingly fizzy noise. It was darker than champagne Rosie had had before, but when she took her first sip from the thick-edged glass, it still burst onto her tongue.

"Not so fast!" commanded Lilian as if she drank champagne every night and this was a terrible breach of etiquette on Rosie's part. "This is special, and we must have a toast."

Tina giggled nervously.

"Oh yes! To…to…hmm. Babysitters! And big posh nights out! And…"

"Your friend is very noisy," said Lilian.

"You're not allowed to be rude to Tina," said Rosie. "I won't allow it. Say sorry."

"That's all right," said Tina.

Lilian raised an eyebrow.

"I'll make the toast. To exciting nights out, when anything could happen. How when you're young and in a pretty dress, you should always say yes to a ball."

Rosie rolled her eyes.

"This is pretty much just what I said," whispered Tina.

"To grabbing what you want, Rosemary. As quickly as you can. And to love…"

"Hurrah," said Tina.

"…and to family," concluded Lilian. And then they chinked the heavy glasses.

Rosie smiled.

"That was a lovely toast," she said. And Lilian had been right about something else: it was like drinking stars.

• • • •

Tina had not lied about the size of the affair. The entire driveway to the great house was lined with braziers lighting the way up the side of the moor. Rosie couldn't resist a shiver of excitement. The weather had turned suddenly vicious, colder and colder. There were mutterings that it might snow. And then, just as Moray and Jake had turned up, honking loudly in the Land Rover—Jake looking big and uncomfortable in his hired dinner suit, Moray looking like a totally at-home smoothie in his—"of course it won't matter," he'd said. "All the real poshos turn up in their pinks."

"In pink?" Rosie asked innocently. The other three all tutted.

"No," said Tina. "They're red, of course. Red hunting jackets. They're called pinks."

"Of course," said Rosie. "How clever of posh people to come up with their hilarious codes."

Lilian had insisted they hurry up and be off; they were going to be terribly late—but insisted they take the champagne with them. She said this was because it was wasted on her when they could share out the good stuff among them. She did not add that she could not bear to spend the evening sitting staring at the bottle and thinking of things that were past long ago.

"Are you sure we can't persuade you to join us, Mrs. H.?" said Moray with a twinkle in his eye. "I promise not to swing you too fiercely around the dance floor."

"All those ghastly old hooligans yelping and barking at each other till three o'clock in the morning? Oh, no, thank you," said Lilian.

"That was exactly what I said!" said Rosie.

"No, no, you young folk go and have fun."

And she ushered them out the door. If that great-niece of hers saw a tear in her eye, she'd cancel her entire evening, sure as eggs were eggs. And they could snuggle up and watch television together and it would be like having a daughter, or a really good friend, or both, and then Rosie would cook them something nice and it would be lovely.

Lilian hardened herself. She would not be selfish. She would not. She would not. She would *not* stand in Rosie's way.

"Out!" she barked at them. "Out of my house immediately!" And she shut the door behind them as the young folks exchanged glances at the grumpiness and irascibility of the old.

• • • •

Out in the deserted main street of the village, as they walked companionably up to the car—Moray gallantly put his coat around Rosie's bare shoulders, whereupon Jake, walking behind with Tina, started fumbling and wondering if he should be doing the same—they passed the bottle between them, Moray whistling at the vintage. As they did so, the very first flakes of snow began to fall.

"It's OCTOBER," said Tina. "Where IS this global warming?"

"It's nigh on November," said Jake, looking up in a worried farmer's way. "This is going to play pure havoc with my cabbages."

But Rosie didn't listen to either of them, just stared up into the freezing night sky, stars sharp and ice-cold among the clouds, the flakes beginning to whirl now in the streetlamps, and with the champagne coursing through her veins, she smiled broadly. The little sleepy village looked like something from a Christmas card, the cobblestones dotted here and there with tiny specks of white. She felt giddy and excited, despite the disappointments of the day and the knowledge that she didn't have a chance with Stephen—well. Who cared about that? Who cared about any of that? She WAS still young(ish); she did look, as both the men had pointed out, very pretty in her green dress. Even though it was silly, and old-fashioned, and pompous, and kind of ridiculous—

"I'm going to the ball!" she announced loudly.

"SO AM I!" hollered Tina, her happiness much less complicated than Rosie's at that moment, as Jake's fumbling hands attached his coat around her shoulders.

Moray bowed low in front of the door of his Land Rover. "Your carriage, Mesdames."

And laughing and yelling, they took off up the hill, along the driveway of flaming torches, to the great house at Lipton.

20

turkish delight

• • • •

Turkish delight has had a bad reputation since that man C. S. Lewis—a positive genius in other ways—associated it forever with one of the most terrifying creations in literature, the White Witch of Narnia, and that naughty, sticky, traitorous Edmund. But there is sensuous pleasure imbued in its melting, gelatinous texture, and when made in the proper way—delicately perfumed with rose petals, flavored with oils, and dusted with sugar—it reclaims its power as a sweet as seductive as Arabian nights, as succulent as the dates of the country it comes from. The fact that it now carries with it, too, a whiff of danger merely adds to its pleasure. It is not, truly, a sweet for children. They shall simply complain and get the almonds stuck up their noses.

Who even ARE these people?" said Rosie, still nervous and exhilarated from the champagne and their snowy drive up the mountain. "And are you sure the area's only non-mad health professional should be stepping out of the driving seat of a car slugging from a bottle of champagne?"

"Ask the local police superintendent," said Moray. "He's over there."

Truly, the place was thronged. Up close and floodlit from below, so it could be seen from miles off, Lipton Hall was truly imposing, built in the Queen Anne style, with red sandstone, gargoyles on the upper reaches, and rows of windows stretching along either side. The windows were brilliantly lit with chandeliers, and noise and candle smoke and rowdy laughter poured out from each of them. Rosie felt her ebullient mood shrink a little.

"How does she pay for all this," she wondered aloud. "I thought they were all broke."

"Oh, she is, completely," said Moray. "People pay a fortune to come."

"They PAY?" said Rosie. "Do we have to pay?"

"We do NOT have to pay," said Moray. "We are Lady Lipton's guests. But you'll see big tables full of the Rotary Club and the Masons and all sorts."

"But why do they want to pay?" said Rosie, completely confused.

"To rub shoulders with the haut monde of course," said Moray, as if talking to a slow child.

"They pay to do that?" said Rosie.

"Could you just get inside, before I take you home? And if you start singing 'The Red Flag,' you'll be in serious trouble."

Inside was a seething mass of people, all hailing one another and looking slightly pink in the face. Many were at the window, marveling at the snow. Rosie paused at the huge door, up the enormous flight of steps, then hopped over the threshold. The main hall was enormous and paneled, with large creatures' heads attached to the walls. A huge grandfather clock, just like the one in Peak House, stood at the end. Teenagers in white shirts and black trousers were taking coats or scuttling about with drinks. "I always wanted to do that job," whispered Tina.

"Why didn't you?" said Rosie.

"Oh, it's notorious," said Tina, as Jake sniggered. "They drink all the leftovers and get into TERRIBLE trouble later on. Getting off with guests, getting off with each other. My father wouldn't hear of it."

Jake smiled again.

"You did it though?" said Rosie.

"Oh yes," said Jake.

Tina grinned. "Course 'e did."

"And was it as bad as what her dad thinks?" said Rosie.

"Well, let's put it this way," said Jake. "With the absolute and definite exception of us four, it's those kids in the black and white who are going to have the best time out of anyone at this party tonight. *And* they're the only ones getting paid."

Moray smiled nicely at one girl wearing a black skirt that was obviously her mother's. She went red then immediately brought them over some glasses of champagne.

"Thanks for what you said when I came in last week," she whispered—although loud enough for the others to hear—as she brought the drinks straight over.

"What was that for?" asked Rosie.

"I have absolutely NO recollection," said Moray. "No one ever believes me, but it is true. Can you keep us all topped up, sweetie?"

The girl smiled and nodded eagerly.

Looking around, Rosie thought she could see what Jake meant about not everyone having a good time. They moved to the left, where, opening off the great hall, was a ballroom, not paneled but instead with a parquet floor, pastel-colored walls, and, at the far end, large sets of French windows leading out onto a balcony overlooking a sunken garden. Despite the cold outside, the heat in the room was immense, and the doors were open, people standing there, smoking cigarettes only just outside.

There were stony-faced women in bejeweled boxy jackets over black dresses, looking disapprovingly at their red-cheeked husbands if they accepted another drink or guffawed too loudly at a story. There were old chaps half dozing on the little antique chairs that lined the wall, jauntily patterned waistcoats stretched to bursting. Hye Evans was telling a loud story to a group of men, all of whom were laughing heartily. Next to him was a very skinny woman, looking anxious in a tight column dress and lots of gold jewelry, her eyes skittering around the room.

But there were happier groups too: young farmers out for a night of frivolity, fervent horse freaks in their smart red coats huddled in groups discussing fetlocks and farriers and all sorts of technical terms Rosie couldn't understand as her party threaded themselves through the crowd to have a look around. Tina wanted to see everywhere and everything—even the bathrooms! She was to be disappointed in this, as there was a large set of port-a-potties—the most lavishly appointed port-a-potties Rosie had ever seen, it had to be said, but port-a-potties nonetheless—lined up discreetly in the courtyard at the back of the house. Tina scuttled off to explore, Jake keeping closely behind her—it made Rosie smile to see it. Good. Tina deserved a good man. Moray was waylaid almost immediately the second they entered the room by dozens of people he knew and, with his affable manner, immediately fell into conversation with most of them.

Unfussed, Rosie wandered alone out to the balcony at the end of the French windows. The cold had driven most people indoors, and the hubbub dimmed behind her as she gazed out at the garden beyond, clear beneath the full moon. It was almost incandescently beautiful, the snow falling on the knot garden beneath the shadow of the house, falling on the hedges, neatly trimmed borders, and raked gravel, and tumbling down the ridge of the land below.

She felt suddenly as if she were being watched and turned swiftly. Just inside the doors, at the corner of the ballroom, was a dark corner filled with sofas and chairs. She had barely registered that a large group had moved there, but she saw it now and was just in time to catch Stephen's eyes on her. He glanced away quickly as she gave a slightly awkward smile through the open door. He was surrounded—not just by CeeCee, who looked unbelievable in a cutting-edge, metallic silver dress with fierce studded shoes. On anyone not tall and skinny and incredibly stunning, it might have looked a bit scary. On CeeCee, it looked incredibly scary, but also utterly amazing. There were other girls there, many blond or with thick sheets of straight hair that covered their eyes and dresses in pale nudes or sheer fabrics or plain unadorned black. Suddenly Rosie felt a little silly wearing green, like a little girl in her party frock.

And there were other young men, Stephen's age, obviously his friends, laughing and drinking his mother's champagne and flirting with the girls and teasing each other. One was wearing the most ludicrous pair of tartan trousers imaginable.

Where were they? Rosie found herself thinking. Where were they when he was sitting by himself in the kitchen, pouring whiskey down his throat?

She composed herself to give the coolest, most distantly polite hello she knew how—it was, she knew, the only way. She risked another look, but of course his attention was elsewhere. How foolish, she knew, once again, remembering how she'd looked at herself in the mirror. As if she compared to these model girls. But she knew that already. She was not going to be downhearted.

To her delight, Moray came toward her, waving madly.

"Dinner!" he said. "You have to be quick—the food is terrible, but there's more of it if you rush."

"Excellent," she said, proffering her arm. He might be the only gay man in the village, but Stephen's stuck-up chums weren't to know that.

"Hello," she said to Stephen politely as she passed by.

"Hi," said Stephen shortly. Rosie hoped he remained as rude and as grumpy with CeeCee until the day he died.

"Hi, CeeCee," she said. CeeCee looked up from a conversation with a friend and did absolutely nothing to disguise the fact that she had absolutely not the faintest idea whether she'd ever seen or met Rosie before.

"Oh yeah, hi," she said then turned back to her conversation.

"That's CeeCee," said Rosie to Moray, loud enough for Stephen to hear. "She's very special."

Stephen didn't react.

"Well, it was nice of your mother to invite your nurse," said Rosie. "I'm going to find her to say thanks."

"I don't—" Stephen started but then couldn't go on.

"What?"

"I don't think of you as my nurse," he said.

"You just call me it."

"No. No."

"LIPPY!" came a loud voice. An enormous pack of rugby players was crossing the floor. "YOU WEAPON!"

Stephen looked crestfallen. "Oh God. Umm."

"DINNER!" said Moray.

"YOU UTTER WEAPON!" shouted the rugby boys.

Rosie waved her hand.

"I'll just…"

Stephen was engulfed as Moray walked her across the ballroom and in to dinner.

"Well, well," he said.

"What?" said Rosie.

"How long have you had a little soft spot for our lord of the manor?"

"I do NOT…" Rosie felt herself turn pink. "Never mind. I know everyone fancies him."

"Christ, yes," said Moray. "Oh well."

"Is that why you never wanted to look at his leg?" said Rosie.

"No, that's because he's an irritating arsehole obsessed with the moral high ground," said Moray. "It was miles easier just to get a pretty girl to do it."

"Aw, thanks." Rosie slumped.

"You need more champagne," said Moray, though even before he did so, his little acolyte had appeared, bearing more glasses.

"Thanks," said Rosie. "Oh, sorry. This is lovely. It's all just silly bollocks, that's all. I'm like a teenager with a crush."

They both looked in the young girl's direction, who blushed bright red when she saw Moray's eyes on her.

"Christ," said Moray, "let's get into the dining room immediately."

"That's exactly what Stephen thinks about me," said Rosie. "Bugger it."

The dining room was more of a dining hall, with round tables set up with autumnal leaf arrangements and bright red poinsettias. Each table, too, had a little pumpkin on it. Most people were already seated, the men smart, even Rosie had to admit, in their bright red hunting jackets, the women wearing all their jewelry, with their hair done and their lipstick bright. It was a nice sight, after all, made even nicer when they found their table was full of other fun young people from the village, the farmers and their wives, who outdid each other with filthy stories and silliness. Rosie could see that they got out so seldom, and their lives were full of such hard work that they were determined to enjoy their night to the full, and they heckled the speeches, imitated the hunting horns that were blown to announce each course: mulligatawny soup, roasted pheasant with autumn vegetables and game chips, and a splendid rhubarb crumble made from rhubarb from the gardens.

"There is NOT," announced Rosie, "enough ruching in this dress."

Tina and Jake were nowhere to be seen. Someone announced that they'd noticed them in the orangery—a long, low conservatory running along the back of the house on its south face—and Rosie decided to leave them to it. She couldn't even see Stephen and did her best to forget all about him—helped by the tremendous food and a story about pig insemination she suspected she wouldn't be able to forget even if she tried.

• • • •

The noise in the great rooms grew louder and louder as dinner finally ended and everyone repaired next door while the tables were cleared. One room was to have disco dancing, the other proper reeling. Rosie wanted to stay in the disco room, but Moray was adamant.

"No way," he said. "How many times are you going to come to a thing like this if you piss off back to London?"

"Are you sure you don't want to come back to London with me?" said Rosie. "I think you'd like it."

Moray gave her a look. "I do better here in Lipton than you will ever know, love. These farmers play a good macho game, but…"

Rosie laughed.

"What is it we say in the emergency room…"

"Be safe darling!" they trilled together, as she let him lead her back to the original ballroom, where a band with a fiddle player, an accordionist, and a bodhrán drum player were all ready to go.

"Good GOD, what is going on?" she asked, as several men—including the one in tartan trews—and one unlikely but rather touching middle-aged couple, he in a kilt, she in a white dress wearing the same tartan as a sash, all took to the floor.

"It's easy," said Moray. "You just fold your arms behind your neck like this."

"How is THIS easy?"

"Now take your partners for the Gay Gordons," the leader of the band announced.

"Oh well, I see why you like this," grumbled Rosie. Moray ignored her and lined her up with everyone else, as the band leader walked them through it. And sure enough, once she'd done it a few times, she got the hang of it and found herself enjoying the rhythm of the music. They bumped into a few people, but that was all right—everyone else bumped into them too—and Moray was a skilled partner, his hands always there to catch her as she twirled. And the green silk dress made such a beautiful twirl. It was made for it. Made to be danced in, on a dark night in early winter, where the snow whirled in time in front of the great window panes in the big house.

After the first dance, Rosie found she wanted to dance another, and another, and she found no shortage of partners. Gasping with thirst, she drank plenty of water—but plenty of champagne too—then allowed herself to be carried off into a dance that involved two partners. With Jake, who had reappeared, and Frankie, one of his farmer friends, and her head spinning, she danced and bowed and shimmied, lighter and more gracefully, she knew, thanks to the green dress, than she had ever danced in her life. The skulking corner of silver-clad, model-type wraiths with pouty mouths and tight half smiles ceased to bother her completely.

Traversing the room, floating in a huge bubble of champagne and company and the sheer pleasure of being "out" again, being out with friends, and laughing and dancing and having a good time, she barely noticed when Frankie spun her around then deposited her not two feet from where Stephen was sitting, still perched awkwardly on the sofa, his stick resting in his left hand. She made an involuntary gasp of surprise to find herself so close to him, especially so flushed; her hair had fallen out of the clasp Tina had found for it, and her curls were tumbled around her face, her breath coming in gasps from the exertions of the dance.

"Oh," she said.

Stephen's face was like stone.

"Oh," he repeated flatly. There seemed nothing more to say.

"Is there anyone in this town you DON'T let yourself get manhandled by?" he barked suddenly.

"WHAT?" said Rosie, unable to believe what she'd just heard.

But Stephen didn't repeat himself; instead, he hauled himself up and, as fast as he could manage, which wasn't very, started pushing his way through the hordes of people dancing, right across the dance floor to the door.

The spell of the dance broken, all Rosie could do was stand there, staring after him, mouth open in fury.

There were mumblings around but not for long, as the band played on and people restarted the steps. It was not, Rosie reflected, probably any surprise to the people in this village to see Stephen Lipton have a big sulk about something. It was to her though.

She stormed through the ballroom after him. CeeCee was there, walking unsteadily back from the bathroom. She was running her tongue around her teeth, and her eyes were glazed.

"Hey, you seen Lippy?" she asked Rosie, but Rosie didn't bother to answer. Outside, the snow was thick and still buffeting it down, but Rosie didn't feel a thing. Without thinking twice, seeing one car roar away into the distance, she jumped into Moray's Land Rover. As usual, he'd left the keys in the ignition. Regardless of the weather or how much she'd had to drink, she turned the key.

• • • •

She was going to tell him a thing or two. About rudeness, and how just having a bit of a lame leg was absolutely no excuse for behaving like a total arsehole, and how what he REALLY needed was therapy.

It was utterly freezing when she got out of the car. Rosie pushed open the door without knocking; she knew it wouldn't be locked. He was sitting upright in the chair, stick to one side. She could see his jaw twitching with tension. His eyes darted to her when she walked in, but he made no other signal that he was aware of her presence in the room. The lamp on the table shone onto his profile.

Rosie stopped short. She thought, suddenly, of how many times she had waited for things to happen in her life, how she had waited for a man to grab her then settled for Gerard, how she had waited for a job to consume her then settled for agency. Before the sweetshop. Waiting for life wasn't going to work any longer. Anything she wanted now, she was going to have to take with both hands. Was going to grab for herself. And if she was being totally honest with herself, she didn't want to tell him a thing or two. She didn't want to say a single word. That, she realized, wasn't why she was here.

Rosie stepped forward into the dimming light toward him. He was gazing into the fire, hand clutching an empty whiskey glass.

"Stephen," she said. He didn't answer. Until she decided to take another step forward, she wasn't 100 percent sure if she wanted to kiss him or slap him. For some reason she didn't understand, she found herself thinking of Lilian.

She took the next step forward. "What the fuck was that?"

He wouldn't meet her eyes.

"I'm sorry," he said. "I was feeling stupid and useless and jealous. It was dumb. I'm sorry."

"But...but..." Jealous?

Rosie decided, right then, that she didn't want to talk anymore.

Fortified by the champagne, shc was almost unable to believe she was being so bold.

Almost.

Without saying a word, Rosie knelt before him and carefully, decisively unzipped his black trousers. He didn't move a muscle to stop her. Agonizingly slowly, she maneuvered them downward. He was wearing Calvin Klein briefs, but she ignored those for now and carefully, without pulling, drew as much of his trouser as she could down his left leg.

The light from the lamp shone upon the white and puckered skin, the scar disappearing down his long leg into the shadows. The leg was plainly paler and thinner than the other one, and the long seam was hairless and shiny.

Yet it was not at all repellent. It was cleanly healed, simply a mark on the man, nothing more, nothing less. If she was to love this man, she would love all of him, and that was that.

Agonizingly slowly, she lowered her head and gently but firmly kissed the very top of the scar, halfway up the warm inside of his thigh, once, twice.

For a moment, there was silence. Then above her she heard a very low groan, and then a long exhalation. She kissed the scar once more then rose up. Stephen's eyes were closed now, his expression completely unreadable.

Rosie felt her heart pound, felt the adrenaline course through her body; her tongue, inexplicably, suddenly felt too large for her mouth. Was he trying to think of a polite way to tell her to get the hell out? Had she mistaken an angry passion for genuine pique? Had she just made a terrible, terrible error? She blinked rapidly as she tried to read his expression—but suddenly ran out of time.

Stephen's eyes snapped open, and before she could respond, he grabbed her upper arms with his strong hands and pulled her toward him, kissing her fiercely and fearlessly. The clumsiness of their position—he already had his trousers halfway down—meant Rosie threw caution to the wind, threw up the chiffon layers of her skirt, and simply clambered onto the chair, both of them still kissing passionately, and wrapped her legs tightly around his waist. Instantly, she could feel that her instincts had been the correct ones.

"Christ," said Stephen, exhaling into her hair. "Christ. It's been… it's been so long."

"Well, it is now," said Rosie, trying to lighten the mood. "Shhh. Shhh."

Stephen held her face between his hands and gazed fiercely into her eyes. "And so hard," he said finally, a spark of mischief flickering across his face. They stared at each other for a second longer, then suddenly he was unzipping her bodice at speed, with the fumbling excitement of a man coming back to life, and she was pulling up his white shirt, desperate to put her hands and her mouth on the flat stomach and muscled chest she'd been dreaming of.

Neither wanted to mention whether or not he would be capable of moving them both to the bed—Rosie didn't want to move too much, in case it caused him pain—so instead they stayed exactly where they were, grinding close together, pressed tightly back onto the high-backed chair, the winter light turning to black, the snow falling silently on the little house, the fire blazing then eventually dying. The heat from their two bodies rose and fell and rose again, both of them pink and sweating from the extraordinary deferred pleasure, the motion made more delicious by its necessary slowness that went on so intensely and so long. Finally Stephen couldn't stand it one second longer and, all thoughts of pain to himself forgotten, he pulled down hard on her shoulders, pressing her so tightly in to him that she felt they were one person. He bellowed, loudly and suddenly, and almost without warning, her back arched, and she lost herself in him. When she came back to herself, she found to her complete and utter astonishment that she was crying.

21

> Sour cherries are an awkward taste. One would want to keep an eye on the child whose tastes run to these sweets. Harsh and chemical, they spill their secrets gradually.

Later, Rosie could never remember how long they had stayed afterward.

"I thought you thought I was a prick," whispered Stephen into her hair.

"To be fair," said Rosie, "that was only after you'd been a complete prick."

"Oh yes," said Stephen. "Did you think I was a total whiner?"

"Noooo," lied Rosie. She looked up into his face. "You are the first total whiner I have ever fancied, you know."

"Umm, good."

Rosie squirmed and wondered where her panties were. "I have to ask though," she said. "That night in the pub."

"Where you were completely hammered."

"For the first time in about sixty-five years!" said Rosie. "I'm a very cheap date. DON'T say it."

Instead, Stephen gave a kiss, which started getting out of control a little, until he winced. "Maybe we could…move?"

"Yes," said Rosie. "But first…why did you tell that lanky blond girl I was your nurse?"

Stephen bit his lip.

"Honestly?"

Rosie nodded. "Yes! You made me feel like some awful below-stairs…well. I don't know."

"Because I didn't know where I stood with you," said Stephen. "Well, I did. You were always giving me trouble for this and that and telling me off for things."

"Oh," said Rosie, stung. "I was trying to help."

Stephen stared deep into her eyes.

"You think you weren't helping?"

"No."

"But I thought…I thought I was just a kind of project for you. Professional boundaries and all that."

"Is that why you never phoned me or asked me out for a coffee or anything?" said Rosie, still slightly disgruntled.

"Can't we just say I'm out of practice?"

"Oh, I don't know," said Rosie, still pink. "And what about all those people who are suddenly hanging around all the time anyway?"

"Well, word went around that I was 'back'…the jag grapevine moves pretty fast."

"Where were they before?"

Stephen looked uncomfortable.

"This is a lot of questions. I thought we were going to bed."

Rosie tried to bite down her concern. It wasn't attractive, she reminded herself, showing off her insecurities. She looked at his gorgeous, stern head and lean, pale physique and decided to count her blessings instead.

"Let's," she said and stood up, feeling confident in the gentle light coming from the fire, her hair tumbling down her back.

Stephen smiled. "God," he said. "You are LUSH."

It was such an unlikely thing to hear him say that Rosie burst out laughing. Stephen laughed too and pushed himself up and out of his chair.

"I think I can still outrun you," said Rosie.

"Not for long," said Stephen with a wolfish look on his face, lurching for her. She screamed—and then screamed again as, suddenly, she was blinded by enormous beams of light shooting straight through the kitchen window. At first, she was completely frozen, unable to tell what was happening. Then she realized that, of course, it was another car coming back. Suddenly she could hear voices and barks of laughter in the air and realized, to her utter horror, that it was all of Stephen's friends, arriving home from the ball.

• • • •

It probably wouldn't have been so bad if Stephen hadn't found it so funny as she scurried about the kitchen, desperately trying to find something to cover herself with, giving up on the idea of shrugging herself back into Lilian's tight green gown. When she came up with Mrs. Laird's flowery apron, she thought he was about to bust a gut.

"Stop laughing and HELP me," she said, conscious of the sounds of people crunching on gravel and making a lot of noise.

"But you don't need anything! You look incredibly beautiful as you are."

"FUCK OFF!!"

"Sorry, sorry," said Stephen, hurling her his jacket.

"I'm going to run away upstairs," she said.

"Don't!" he said. "You look…you look lovely. And I thought you wanted to be introduced properly."

"Stop it," she said. "I'm going." But it was too late.

Rosie should have run and hid regardless, she figured later. They might have sniggered, but at least it would have been behind her back. If she could have been more decisive about it…but.

First to come in were two wide, red-faced rugby-playing gents.

"Way hey!" they leered straightaway. "Sorry, mate, should have knocked."

"Yeah, whatever," said Stephen. He could see Rosie was desperate to get away and pulled her close to him, holding her hand. Rosie thought this was even worse, like she was some undignified doxy, half covered up.

"This is Rosie," he managed. "We weren't expecting you back so soon."

"Obviously!" said the taller of the rugby boys. They didn't even bother introducing themselves, simply turned around, looking for wine. There was a bottle of claret open on the big kitchen table, and they grabbed that. Rosie felt herself go a bright, hot red.

Then through the door walked CeeCee. What would it take, Rosie wondered, to jerk her out of her near unconscious levels of coolness?

"Oh yeah, hi," she said, sweeping Rosie with a glance that implied that she, Rosie, was still below notice.

"Stephen, DARLING. I can't believe you deserted us."

"Uh…" Stephen stuttered again. Rosie shook her head. "Well."

CeeCee accepted a glass of wine from one of the rugby boys.

"Not to worry. I see you were having a spot of local fun." Venom dripped from her voice.

Rosie had had enough. She looked around the room to see if there was a way to reclaim her dignity. There wasn't.

"I'm going," she said to Stephen, whispering in his ear.

"Don't," he said. "Please, don't. You can stick on my pajamas; they're in my room."

Rosie shook her head. "Umm, no. I need to get Moray's car back. Truly." Stephen blinked. He wondered if she were already regretting it.

"Okay…sorry. This lot are staying here tonight…"

The other three simply sipped their wine, completely unperturbed.

Stephen saw her to the door, Rosie fully conscious that she was wearing a ridiculous apron and a too short dinner jacket. She found she wanted to cry again, but for very different reasons.

"Don't you want to get dressed?" he said.

"No," said Rosie, her face flaming. She wanted to get as far away as fast as she could.

"I wish you could stay," said Stephen. "I know there're guests, but…"

"No, thank you," said Rosie, realizing her attempt to be as cool as CeeCee was just coming across as silly.

"Okay. Okay, then I'll call you."

Rosie shrugged. "If you get a signal."

"Umm…" CeeCee paused, as if she had been about to use Rosie's name then realized she couldn't remember it. "Umm, don't you want to take your panties?"

Burning with frustration and embarrassment, Rosie didn't answer, just tried her hardest not to flip her off on her way out.

Stephen stood in the doorway, his untucked shirt hanging out of his black trousers, looking at her car for a long time as she drove away down the long steep road. Rosie didn't even notice him; she was looking at the other three, outlined in the kitchen windows, laughing their heads off.

• • • •

Fully sober now, she caught up with the other three marching down from a now darkened Lipton House.

"Hurrah!" said Moray. "I thought it had been stolen."

Rosie opened the doors.

"Do NOT say anything," she ordered as they all got in, Jake with his arm tightly around Tina's shoulder, something that made Rosie go all tight-lipped. They were all giggly and happy and loved up.

"But," said Tina.

"NOPE!"

"What on EARTH?" said Moray.

"Not you either!"

Moray and Tina exchanged worried glances. Jake tried to hide a smirk and failed.

"NO SMIRKING," said Rosie. "Otherwise I will cry, and I mean it." There was a long silence.

"So," said Moray finally. "You made out with him then." The rest of the car collapsed in laughter.

"It's not funny," said Rosie.

And Moray heard it in her voice, just before she started to cry.

"Don't worry, girl," he said. "Don't worry. He's just some posh nut job with a hole in his leg. He's an idiot."

"He just let them laugh at me," sobbed Rosie. "Like I was some stupid tart he'd picked up somewhere."

"Did he really?" said Tina. "That sounds horrid."

"Arsehole," said Jake. "Would you like me to punch him for you?"

"I would like that," said Rosie. "On his leg."

Her sniffs turned to hiccups.

"Oh GOD. Why did I shag him? He'll be having such a laugh about it with his mates. We never even had a cup of coffee. Not a date or anything. Nothing. I'm just some slutty nurse who went around his house and did him. They'll all be having such a laugh."

"No, they won't," said Tina unconvincingly. "Or okay, even if they are, that means they are all pathetic idiots and fuckwits and horrible twats. So it doesn't matter."

"No," sniffed Rosie. "It doesn't matter."

They all came back into the cottage, and Tina made tea and toast for Rosie, who was still torn between thinking how sweet a moment they'd had and how quickly it had all gone horribly wrong. Moray brought the empty champagne bottle in from the car.

"Don't rinse it," he said. "It'll be nice to smell for your aunt."

Rosie nodded, now changed into her super-sensible, big furry pajamas. The tip of her nose was still red, and her mascara had run, but she felt much better with friends around her.

"At least you never have to see him," said Moray. "Whereas if I have to give him another fricking tetanus shot, I'll tell him it's the one that has to go right into the tip of his penis."

"Ha," said Rosie. Then, "I don't suppose he'll be here for much longer anyway. Now he's got all his posh townie mates back again. He'll be off with them."

"If he can get a job," said Tina. "Which he won't, because he's a useless fuckwit."

He's not, a part of Rosie was thinking. He's a teacher.

"Well, I am SO GLAD I managed to let everyone convince me into going to the ball," she said. "But I think I want to get back to being Cinderella."

"Cinderella of the Sweeties," said Tina. "That doesn't sound so bad."

"It's all right for you," said Rosie. "You've already found your prince." Jake rolled his eyes. Tina giggled. But neither of them contradicted her.

• • • •

Things are meant to look better in the morning, grumbled Rosie to herself as she woke up to a world where the snow was already turning gray and melting, and the lane looked dreary. The mountains loomed, seemingly closer than ever, but large clouds in the sky threatened more snow yet.

Lilian glanced at Rosie quickly and declined to ask. This was a mistake.

"So, has the news reached you?" said Rosie, more sharply than she would have liked, mostly because she was nursing a horrible headache that had less to do with the champagne and more to do with reliving every second of the nightmare from the moment she'd woken up.

"No," said Lilian pleasantly and sipped her tea, complaining bitterly about the news in her *Sunday Express* (when Rosie had suggested she change her paper, she had harrumphed and pointed out that she needed something to complain about, otherwise her life would be just too perfect).

"Well, good," said Rosie. "Never mind then."

And they spent the day like that. Except Rosie couldn't help it. She spent a lot of time up by the highest front window of the cottage. If she leaned her arm out at a dangerous angle, it could just about get a mobile phone signal. Once, the idea swept over her that CeeCee and her friends would drive by, see her arm, and know immediately what she was doing and piss themselves all over again, and it made a cold sweat pass over her, but she maintained the stance defiantly. All the while, she was thinking he wasn't like them. Was he? Was he?

Had she known it was the exact same position Lilian had sat in nearly seventy years before, she would have been horrified.

• • • •

Just after four, she heard a bang downstairs. At first, she thought it might be the door and Stephen striding manfully through it…of course not. That was ridiculous, a completely stupid thought. Then panic hit her, and she couldn't believe she'd been so selfish.

"LIL!" she yelled, charging down the stairs. "LIL!!!!!"

Lilian was lying there, thankfully conscious, but with her ankle at a strange angle.

"What the hell…what on earth were you doing?" she said.

Lilian blinked up at her, confused.

"I…I…" She looked down to where she had urinated on the floor. "Oh," she said.

"Don't worry about that," said Rosie. "Don't worry about that for a second. Come on, let me get you to a chair."

She weighed little more than a child, even with all of Rosie's feeding up. She wasn't putting weight on as she should, Rosie realized. She wasn't…she wasn't good enough for Lilian. She wasn't doing it right.

Lilian was confused and tearful.

"I just…I just wanted to get to the bathroom."

"I know, I know," said Rosie. "Why didn't you call me?"

"Because," said Lilian. "Because it is utterly ridiculous I can't make it to my own bathroom."

"I know," said Rosie. "I know it's ridiculous. Doesn't make it any less true. I had the monitor upstairs."

"I hate…I hate being a stupid old woman," said Lilian, her face crumpling. "I hate it. I hate it. I hate it."

"I know," said Rosie. "I hate it too."

"I'm all covered in pee and I can't garden and I can't cook and I can't run my shop and I can't do anything. ANYTHING," she said fiercely.

"I'm here," said Rosie. But they were empty words, and they both knew it.

"You can't be here," said Lilian. "I won't let you."

"I don't have much else going on," said Rosie ruefully.

"Don't you ever say that," said Lilian. "Don't you dare ever say that to me."

• • • •

Moray came, clutching his head and looking very under the weather. Rosie cleaned up Lilian in time, and together they ascertained that it was a sprain, rather than a break, but that she needed to be careful.

"I need to be somewhere with soft walls," said Lilian, sulking. Rosie let her eat a packet of caramels for supper, while Moray handed her a leaflet.

"It's time," he said. "You know it's time."

"But she's so sharp in herself!"

Moray shrugged. "I'm sorry, Rosie. Old age is an absolute bitch-fucking motherfucker."

"Is that your professional opinion?" said Rosie.

"As a doctor, yes. I believe it is accepted fairly widely among the medical profession."

"Bitch-fucking motherfucker," said Rosie. "Yes."

22

Please let me clear this up once and for all: "Life is like a box of chocolates; you never know what you're going to get," is a quotation of the highest nonsense. Every box of chocolates comes with a handy and clearly stated pictogram relating the shape of the chocolate to its flavor. Also a box of chocolates is always welcome and delicious. Life is in fact like a bag of revels. You never know what you're going to get, and half of it you won't like.

Monday morning had gray, lowering skies that perfectly suited Rosie's mood. She checked her phone (inside and outside to make sure she was getting a signal). Nothing. Nothing at all. What kind of a prick was he? Presumably just because she turned up there, offering herself on a plate... She gulped. That was it. She was just a cheap date, that was all. Probably happened to him all the time. She sighed mightily. Stupid girl. She had rung Mike, who had laughed his head off and congratulated her on ending her dry spell. It was quite something to have sex with someone else after such a long time.

"How was it?" he said.

"That's not the point," snapped Rosie.

"Oooh, AMAZING," said Mike. "Wow. Don't let that go."

"I don't think I have the slightest choice in the matter," she had sniffed.

"Look," said Mike. "Stop beating yourself up. This is good. And funny. Everyone else spent the whole of their twenties having one-night stands with unsuitable men. God, I know I did. You spent your entire twenties convincing yourself you were ready to settle down with Captain Pie. It's all right to make a few mistakes along the way."

"Mmm-hmm," said Rosie.

"Did you really like this bloke?"

Rosie considered it.

"Well, he's really annoying and full of himself and cranky, and he sulks all the time..."

"You've got it really bad," said Mike.

"He's the bravest man I've ever met," said Rosie. "Pigheaded. But..."

"Brave and fantastic in bed?"

"And a lord."

Mike really was laughing now.

"Well. Good for you. You always set your sights too low."

"I honestly, truthfully do not give a shit about him being a lord," said Rosie. "I'd rather he had a job."

"And wasn't surrounded by jaghags," observed Mike helpfully.

"Yes," sighed Rosie. "That too. Anyway. Not to worry. I have a business to sell... I wonder if Tina will let me keep some of the jars?"

"You'll miss it," said Mike. "Incredible. I can't believe you're not desperate to get back to mopping up puke and blood all day."

Rosie looked around the little shop. "Yes," she said. "I will miss it."

• • • •

But the weather seemed to be affecting everything, when Tina crashed in at ten thirty that morning. They were selling a lot of chocolate; something about the weather coming in made people want to snuggle down on their sofas with big slabs of Lindt and Dairy Crunch, the purple jackets of the sweet white Swiss Lindt or the dark red of Bournville, and, for the more daring—Rosie often felt she should keep them under the counter—the higher count dark chocolates, 75, 85, and even 95 percent cacao, which didn't taste in the least sweet to Rosie. They were selling a lot of the premium chocolate, so much so that Rosie was taking down a whole new order before the end of the week.

"Rosie," said Tina, coming in from out of the rain. Rosie looked up and saw her distressed face.

"What's wrong?" she said. If Jake had done anything to hurt her friend, she vowed, she was going to whack his and Stephen's heads together. "What's the matter? Is it Jake?"

Tina's face temporarily cleared.

"Oh. Oh, no, it's not Jake. No. God. He's amazing."

Rosie didn't feel quite tough enough to hear about the amazing Jake quite yet. "Oh well, that's good," she said quickly. "It's not…it's not Kent and Emily, is it? There's nothing wrong with the twins?"

"Oh, no," said Tina. "No, thank God. No. Knock on wood. No. But oh, oh Rosie." She dissolved in floods of tears."It's the shop."

• • • •

Once they sat down with a cup of tea, Tina could choke out the story. It turned out, in fact, that her serious Topshop habit had in the end proven to be a serious problem; her credit rating was nowhere near good enough to take out a business loan. She had tried to raise the money to buy them out, but…

"But didn't you tell them?" said Rosie. "Didn't you tell them you were married to an alcoholic, and you had to cope somehow, and this was the best way, and…"

"No," said Tina. "I think that would have just made it all worse, don't you?"

"But we gave them all the books and projections and everything!"

wailed Rosie. "It's so obvious you're doing great things for this place! And turning it into a real business!"

"It was always a real business," croaked Lilian over the baby monitor. Rosie had placed her on the sofa with her ankle raised. She should have been walking around on it, to get it moving again, but no one wanted to risk that. Moray had popped by with a walker—Lilian didn't mind her stick so much, but there was absolutely no way, she warned them, she would be seen dead in that awful thing, hauling herself along like a zombie, and Rosie didn't want to press the issue. Still, they had appointments made for that afternoon—Moray was being generous with his Land Rover once again—and that was that. Or they had. Now this was throwing a kink in the works.

"And there's no one else that could help?" said Rosie. "Your ex? Your parents?"

"I haven't heard from the ex in months," snorted Tina. "And my parents run a strawberry farm. What do you think?"

"Oh, Tina," said Rosie. "Oh, I am so sorry."

Tina shook her head, completely unable to hide her disappointment. "Those stupid bloody cocktail dresses," she said bitterly. "What was I even thinking?"

"You were thinking, *one day I want to wear beautiful dresses to look lovely for my total hunk of a boyfriend*," said Rosie, trying to be encouraging. It wasn't Tina's fault. But she hadn't had a sniff of interest otherwise. Nothing at all. Except for…

As if reading her thoughts, the little bell rang and the two women turned around to see Roy deBlaine standing there.

• • • •

He smiled unpleasantly, his ridiculous teeth glinting off the subtle lighting. "So," he said, seeing them both there. "I heard the news."

"How did you hear about it?" said Rosie crossly.

"His brother's the bank manager," said Tina.

"No way! Small bloody towns!" howled Rosie. "Is that why he turned down the loan? That's totally illegal."

"No," said Tina. "They hate each other."

Roy shrugged.

"It really was just the computer saying 'no.' Because of my 'bad credit history.'" She dissolved into sobs once more.

"Well, I have a perfect credit history," said Roy. "There's a reason dentists pay very, very low car insurance."

"They're too stupid to drive?" asked Rosie.

Roy's lip curled. "I think you have some early onset gum issues in your upper bicuspid," he said. "I can see it from here. Doesn't bode well for the future. You'll look like one of those horses with the great big, long teeth."

Rosie shut her mouth with a click.

"Well, you have my offer," said Roy. "And for the back too. I'm going to add some huge signage then just tarmac the lot for easy parking."

"Into the garden?" said Rosie.

"Well, it's just weeds in the end," said Roy. "Anyway, won't matter to you. You'll be hot-footing it off back to London the second you can. Not a lot of gardening down there, I hear."

Rosie didn't quite know what to say to this, so she kept quiet. Roy took one last look around and sneered.

"Well, anyway. I'm making my offer. Valid till the end of the week. Then I'll go elsewhere. Had lots of other interest?"

He paused.

"Thought not. Well, up to you. Spend your whole life buried here then. Doesn't mean anything to me."

And he was gone.

• • • •

"He's doing it on purpose," said Tina. "He didn't really mean that end of the week stuff. It's not like he's going to go anywhere else. Nobody else likes him."

Rosie shrugged.

"But he's right though. Apart from you and him, no one else has shown the least bit of interest at all."

"Do you know what sweets Roy deBlaine used to eat as a child?" came the voice crackling over the intercom.

"No," said Rosie. "Poison frogs?"

"None," came the tired-sounding voice. "None at all."

• • • •

Moray had come through with the Land Rover again thankfully. Squinting at the map, Rosie settled Lilian in carefully, propping her up on cushions; otherwise, she was barely large enough to see over the windshield. She looked utterly tiny in Moray's huge car.

In fact, as it turned out, the map was almost unnecessary. Lilian knew everywhere they were going: the home that had once been a cottage hospital where half the babies in town had been born, the old hotel, the army training center. It felt as if every home that once had a purpose and a heart and a reason for existence had been turned over into a holding pen for the elderly, as if the ancient were spreading over the country, swallowing everything in their path like a slow-advancing tidal wave.

"No wonder Hetty doesn't want to convert Lipton Hall," said Rosie after their third visit. Rosie had decided to start at the bottom and go up. The first two were absolutely horrible, degrading places that smelled so heavily of disinfectant and sadness. In one, a woman with almost no hair sat in the front room by herself, tears coursing down her cheeks, like a child abandoned by her parents. The woman showing them around didn't even notice. In the second, the rooms were tiny dark cupboards; even though the building was set in the countryside, there were no views anywhere.

"There are some rooms with views at the front," said the stout woman when she saw them looking at the tiny cells. "We give those out on a rotation basis."

"You mean," said Lilian, "as someone dies, you get a bit closer to the front." The woman ignored her.

"We also have children come sing at Christmas," said the woman. "People like that."

Rosie and Lilian swapped glances. "Children HATE that," whispered Lilian when they were back in the car.

"I remember," said Rosie. "All those old fingers wanting to poke at you." They both shivered.

"I wouldn't put a fox in there," observed Lilian after a while.

"Neither would I," said Rosie. "Don't worry."

But inside, she couldn't help worrying. This was just about what they could afford if they rented out the cottage and let Tina keep running the shop, which covered its costs and paid for staff and made about five pence more after that. She just didn't see how it could be done. There wasn't any money. There just wasn't.

The next two were similar, and Rosie felt herself panic a little. Every time she seemed to be moving on with her life, it all came pouring back in again. This "little job" her mother had sent her on had turned out to consume her utterly.

The last place on her list, Honeysuckle House, had had a very bare website—all the others were full of jaunty promises their premises hadn't even looked close to being able to fulfill—and an imposing prospect. But as they drove up toward it, they saw that the gardens were tended, and there were even a few people out in the grounds, gardening—old people, not staff. Rosie snuck a look at her great-aunt, who was affecting not to have noticed them at all.

A tired but pleasant-faced woman met them at the door. "Hello," she said. "Come on in."

As they walked—slowly, of course—the lady, whose name was

Marie, didn't stop doing other things for a second: checking on a light bulb, answering queries from a junior, straightening a painting, smiling at everyone she passed, pulling up a cleaner on her uniform. Rosie recognized the style immediately. It was the style of the most successful of the hospital matrons, those for whom nothing escaped their gimlet eye. The house, once a barracks, was unfashionably furnished, but its parquet flooring gleamed, and although there was a faint trace of disinfectant, it was almost entirely overpowered by the scent of beeswax and the autumn grass cuttings coming through the open windows. Lilian was very quiet as the tour continued; the rooms were simple but comfortable, with lots of space for photos and clothes.

"This is the first place I've seen," said Lilian, when Rosie asked her what she was thinking, "that has the windows open."

The residents were having lunch. Rosie sniffed. "Is that..."

Marie checked the schedule. "Coq au vin," she said. "The residents complain something awful. A lot of them don't like foreign muck," she said then lowered her voice, "but they still clean their plates. Sometimes people like to have things to complain about. And I don't blame them. But we do try our best," she said.

She didn't have to say it. It was obvious. It was far and away the nicest place they'd seen. And far and away the most expensive. And it was only affordable on Roy deBlaine's money. That was that.

The tour complete, Rosie and Lilian paused by the front door; on the left was a large and pleasant day room, without the enormous blaring televisions they'd seen elsewhere—televisions were kept in rooms and used with headphones, Marie had explained carefully, for the comfort of all residents. Here they encouraged reading, talking, a daily crossword competition, and board games, although if you wanted to stay in your room and watch television and eat Caramacs, that was also completely fine.

Inside was a small group of residents playing what looked like bridge, as well as a woman sitting by the window. Her hair was bright white, and while very thin, the woman still wore it long, curled around the nape of her neck. She was dressed in a pale pink dress with a ruffle on the front, and she sat perfectly still, an abandoned magazine on the table in front of her.

Lilian froze.

Rosie immediately panicked and felt desperately for her aunt's left hand, begging Lilian to speak to her. But Lilian couldn't hear her; she was many miles and many years away, her vision absolutely fixed, completely frozen.

"LIL!" shouted Rosie desperately. "LILIAN!!!"

Finally Lilian seemed to come back to them. Marie was anxious that Lilian come sit down in the office and be checked over by a doctor, but Lilian point-blank refused.

"Let's go," she said in a tone that brooked no argument. "Rosemary. Take me home. Now. Now."

As they left, negotiating the ramp down the once-imposing steps, Rosie got another shock—leaving the car, in their usual positions of her stomping up front and poor Peter trailing behind, were the Isitts. Peter stopped to say hello; Mrs. Isitt marched straight past with barely a sniff in their direction.

"There's Mrs. Isitt," said Rosie in surprise.

Lilian looked at her furiously. "Well, aye," she said. "It would be."

"What do you mean?" said Rosie.

"Well, her mum's in there," said Lilian, nodding back toward the house. At the window, the woman sitting there began to move as she saw her daughter.

"Ida Delia Fontayne. She's Dorothy Isitt's mother."

• • • •

Tina shut up the shop. Rosie made macaroni and cheese, the easiest, most comforting thing she could think of. Lilian had stared out of the window the entire way home and refused point-blank to discuss things. Rosie was determined to get it out of her. Macaroni and cheese—and some violet creams for dessert—was simply the only way she knew how.

She bent over carefully and lit the fire. Lilian was sitting back in her chair, but her fingers were wavering lightly on the side of the arms, as if they wanted to say something. Rosie snuck glances at her. She looked like she was about to say something any minute but didn't know how to begin. Her mouth would open and close. Rosie concentrated on taking the dish out of the oven then set it down with salad and a large glass of water. She'd have been tempted to take out the gin at this point, but she didn't want to give her position away to Lilian. The only way, she knew, to hear this out was to pretend she didn't want to.

Finally they were both sitting at the table. Lilian pushed her dinner around the plate and sighed like a grounded teenager. After about five minutes of this, Rosie could take it no longer.

"Okay," she said. "Who was that woman?"

Lilian heaved a great sigh. But she did, she realized. She wanted to tell it. And it was important that Rosie know. That Rosie didn't let things go by her like she had. It seemed to her that Rosie was at a crossroads. If Lilian could have had her time again, she wouldn't have taken the same path. Not by a long shot.

She sighed again. It was hard, to talk about this. Everyone who knew her—or had known her for a long time—knew the story. They would probably have been surprised to discover she ever thought of it at all; it was so very long ago, and she had only been a girl.

"Once upon a time," she started. "There was a boy called Henry. And a girl called. Umm. Me. And another girl. She was very pretty then. Very."

"So were you," said Rosie loyally, looking at the portraits of Lilian here and there.

"Well, I think Henry thought so," said Lilian. "Although he was the only one."

• • • •

The fire blazed as the darkness crept around the tiny cottage in the middle of nowhere, as Lilian told Rosie about Henry and how much she had loved him. And how she didn't grab her chance while she had it.

"What happened to him?" asked Rosie quietly at the end, their tea cold.

Lilian shrugged.

"Oh," she said. "The same thing that happened to all of them. All the good ones."

Rosie turned the cup around in her hands.

"It was in North Africa," said Lilian. "That Rommel. That bastard…well. They didn't…there was nothing to send home. His dust is African now. Has been for a long time. I wonder if he liked the desert. He was such a boy of the soil, always in the fields…" She smiled to remember it. "Always grubby. He was always a bit mucky." She smiled. "But in a good way, you know. Well, I liked it, anyway."

Rosie blinked several times. "Uh-huh," she said.

"Oh, you know," said Lilian. "I know what you must think. That it was so very long ago. How can I still be thinking about it now? But you know. It doesn't feel long ago to me. It doesn't feel long ago at all; it feels like yesterday."

• • • •

1944

Everyone heard it, they said, or knew someone who did. Ida Delia's screams had filled the entire town, closely followed by Dorothy's.

"That bastard!" she was rumored to have shouted when the telegram came. "That BASTARD! How DARE he?"

• • • •

2012

"What was it like when he died?" asked Rosie quietly.

Lilian looked at her quizzically, as if trying to sum up the best way for Rosie to take it in.

"Well," she said. "It's like the most final thing you can ever imagine…think of something definite, something happening that you couldn't change…"

Rosie thought of Gerard and Yolande Harris, but somehow that didn't really bother her. Then she remembered taking her mother to the airport when she left for Australia and the horrible stone it had left in the pit of her stomach, even though she was a grown-up and not supposed to mind.

"Okay," she said.

"And take away every possibility, every semblance of doubt that anything might be any different."

She looked at her.

"Were you thinking of Ange?"

"You're spooky," said Rosie, trying to smile.

"Imagine if Ange was never coming back, was never going to call, was never going to find her way back to you. And there was no one you could tell, not really. Your granddad, Gordon, he would just have laughed; he thought I should have gotten over it years ago. My dad…"

She smiled.

"I suppose you would say these days in that modern way that I loved my father very, very much. But you have to remember, he was born in 1896. He was, absolutely literally, a Victorian."

Rosie nodded.

"And it was…Henry and I had so little time together."

"That probably made it worse," said Rosie, thinking of Gerard. "Maybe if you'd had a few years washing out his dirty socks, it wouldn't have been so awful."

"Maybe," said Lilian. "Or maybe we'd have settled into this little house and worked hard and raised our children and we'd have been looking after one another right now. And he would still look as young and handsome to me as he did then. It does happen, you know. Maybe it would have been that."

They both fell silent for a moment. "But after…" said Rosie.

"Oh, there was such a big fuss," said Lilian. "Ida Delia was in such a state. I'm sure they'd give it a name now: call it postpartum depression, get her sorted out in a hospital. You were just left to get on with it then. Poor Dorothy."

"I can't believe she was Henry's daughter," said Rosie.

"There wasn't much of Henry in her," said Lilian. "And the raising of her was a mess, a terrible shame. She was terribly beautiful though as a young girl, extraordinary."

"Mrs. ISITT?" said Rosie.

"Ask Hetty," said Lilian. "She was something else. Peter Isitt had been in the village all his life, of course. He knew what he was getting into, and he still couldn't help himself. Amazing what blond curly hair will do to a chap.

"But her mother blamed her and she blamed her mother and they both blamed Henry for dying and…I'm amazed," said Lilian, her eyes watering. "I'm truly amazed. I had no idea Ida Delia was still alive. She moved out of the village when Dorothy left home. She was still a young woman, young enough, she must have thought."

Lilian shook her head.

"And for you, there was never anyone else…"

Lilian gazed into the fire.

"Well, first off, a lot of men didn't come home. And the ones that did, they couldn't stomach village life; they couldn't believe we'd been here all quiet and safe all the time after what they'd been through. Like your granddad. He had it figured out. Life was short, and he was going to go and make the most of it. So a lot of them never came home, for one reason or another. And there weren't a lot of men about. And then, of course, I had to help Dad, and he was getting older."

She paused.

"And, you know. It wouldn't have been fair. I had this big lake of unhappiness inside me. Anyone would have been second best. It would have been unfair on some poor sod if I'd hurled myself at him."

"And did you never regret that?"

Lilian shook her head.

"I only had one bad year," she said. "Nineteen sixty-nine. The year of the new divorce act. I couldn't help thinking…I don't think they'd have stuck it out, those two. Not in the end. Not with Ida so highly strung and him so…so decent. I reckon she'd have pushed him too far. So. That was hard. Apart from that…"

She gave a half smile.

"I haven't been idle, if that's what you mean."

"I don't think I need to know about that," said Rosie.

"I took Felix off Hetty's hands for a few years," said Lilian. "Oh, don't look so shocked," she said, seeing Rosie's face. "It was the sixties. Everyone was at it. Hetty didn't mind a bit; she was getting tupped by the under-gardener."

"If you tell me you are really Stephen's mother, I am going to kill you," said Rosie.

"Oh goodness GRACIOUS, no, don't be absurd," said Lilian. "No, no. I was just helping Hetty out. Felix was so terribly demanding."

"You ARE good friends," said Rosie. "Please don't tell me any more."

"And there was…"

"Okay, okay. I get it." Rosie looked at her. "When I was little, I thought you were just some old lady who sent us cough drops."

"Did you now?" said Lilian.

• • • •

"This has been a good life," said Lilian later. It was getting late, but it was so cozy and easy in front of the fire. Rosie had poured them both a sherry. She'd always thought she hated sherry, but it appeared that she didn't mind it after all. "Honestly."

Rosie looked around at the lovely, cozy sitting room with the fire still crackling away merrily.

"I meant to ask you," she said. "How do you keep this place so nice? You can hardly move and I'm out all day and the garden is always immaculate and the logs are always chopped. I know Hetty comes in, but…"

Lilian smiled. "AH, my elves," she said. Rosie nodded.

"Pretty much everyone comes by once in a while," she said. "When you've served every child in the village, they don't forget. They remember. And they drop in. A bit of wood chopping here, a bit of cleaning there."

Rosie looked at her straight on. "Amazing," she said.

"Well, there are some benefits to living in the same place for a long time," said Lilian. "Don't pity me please."

Rosie shook her head.

"Not in a million years," she said, though she wasn't quite speaking the truth.

"I've had a happy life here," said Lilian. "I have a lot of friends. A lot of people who help take care of me. A good job. I never lost a son to war, or a man to the bottle, or a baby. I've never been rich, but I've paid my way—well, almost," she laughed ruefully, "and I've had some adventures and kept safe and sound and lived in a beautiful place and enjoyed every season of it. This has been a good life."

Rosie let out a great sigh. It did sound like a good life.

"I know. I know. But me—I've made such a fool of myself."

"Oh, you've been making a fool of yourself since you arrived," said Lilian. "Why stop now, I say."

Rosie bit her lip. "Bed," she said.

• • • •

Next morning was bleak; a gray Tuesday morning for Rosie after a sleepless night thinking of everything Lilian had been through. She made a decision. It was the right thing to do, she was sure of it. She needed, she knew, to make a call. It was just, the very idea of it made her feel sick. Lilian, conversely, slept very well and woke up feeling rested and calm, as if something had been decided for her. Which in a sense it had. Angie had rung in the dead of night Australian time, when she knew Rosie would be at the shop, and had let the phone ring till even Lilian had picked it up.

"Aunt Lily," Angie had said in her no-nonsense tone with its new Australian twang. "You know what you have to do."

"Of course I do," Lilian had grumbled.

"She's a good girl, you know. She's my good girl."

"She is, she is."

"But there are limits, you know?"

"I know," said Lilian crossly.

"Will you miss her?"

Lilian sat up straight on the bed.

"I do not for the life of me know how you can bear to be apart from her," she said in a tight voice.

Angie smiled ruefully.

"Me neither. Listen, don't tell her, I'm going to come back for a bit. Just for a bit—the little ones need me, you know. But I want to visit. Come see you all. It sounds like you've been getting up to all sorts."

"We've been doing nothing of the kind," said Lilian stiffly.

"Ah, you would say that though, wouldn't you? Always been a dark horse."

And Lilian's mind was made up.

• • • •

"I think," she said at breakfast, "I think maybe, perhaps, maybe I might like to visit Ida Delia."

Rosie looked at her, bleary-eyed. She knew this was coming. She knew what it meant.

"Sure," she said, carefully.

Lilian smiled.

"She's probably senile," she said, almost to herself. "Probably won't remember me at all."

"Maybe," said Rosie. "Maybe not." Something else struck her. "How could you have been getting milk from Mrs. Isitt all these years and never ever asked after her mother?"

Lilian shrugged.

"Well, you know. We respect privacy around here."

"Ha!" said Rosie. "My bum. Anyway."

She had decided in the night. She was going to do it. She was going to make the call.

"I have to use the phone."

Lilian raised her eyebrows and looked at her. Rosie would not be drawn but instead went upstairs and crouched by the window, near the only place with a signal. Lilian wanted her to use the home telephone, but Rosie didn't want to be overheard. Plus she didn't like the heavy old rotary dial; she kept dropping numbers with her fingers.

Her heart quaking in her chest, slowly she scrolled through her address book and pressed the button. She tried to imagine what he'd be doing right now and found, somewhat to her surprise, that she couldn't. However, he answered right on the second ring. Rosie felt her heart leap in her chest.

"Hello?" came the voice. He sounded busy and preoccupied.

"Hello," said Rosie, finding herself shaking. "Hello, Gerard."

peanut brittle

• • • •

Oh well, all right.

Ingredients

* SOME TOOTHPICKS. Keep handy.
* 4 ounces unsalted peanuts
* 4 ounces light brown sugar
* 2 ounces butter
* pinch salt
* 4 teaspoons water

Spread the peanuts in a single layer on a buttered oven tray. Put the other ingredients in a saucepan and start to heat very slowly, stirring all the while. When the sugar has dissolved, increase the heat a little and stir more vigorously until a caramel is formed. When it reaches the correct color, according to taste, take off the heat, pour over the peanuts and leave to cool.

After breaking the news to Lilian, Rosie decided to walk down the high street even though the weather was horrid; she layered up her cardigans and borrowed Lilian's umbrella, which was a ridiculous lavender froufrou number with fringing that only Lilian could conceivably pull off, but it did the job. Even the lowering clouds that touched the top of the hills and the sucking mud that sunk in by the side of the road couldn't daunt her spirits. Halfway down, she caught sight of Edison, kicking his away along the road by himself as usual.

"Hello!" he said cheerily when she caught up with him.

"What are you doing?" she asked, looking around for his mother. As usual, she was nowhere to be seen. Ghastly woman.

"I'm mingering," said Edison proudly.

"You're what?"

"MIN-GER-RING. It's when something bad has to happen but you don't want it to happen so you walk about going 'hum, hum, hum,' hoping that it will happen later."

"Malingering?" said Rosie.

"What I said," said Edison.

"I'm not sure that's quite right," said Rosie.

"Yes, it is," said Edison. "I am very smart and have a huge cablary."

Not for the first time, Rosie wanted to wring his mother's neck. "Okay," she said. "What are you mingering about?"

Edison blinked sadly behind his enormous glasses. "I have to see Dr. Roy."

"Who's that?"

"For my teeth."

"He's not a real doctor."

"He likes to be called Dr. Roy," said Edison. "He thinks it's friendlier."

"I think it's fraudulent," said Rosie. "Hmmm."

"He will say 'no sweets,'" said Edison sadly.

"Well, do you have any sore teeth?"

Edison shook his head.

"Open your mouth."

Rosie looked around thoroughly. A more perfectly healthy set of straight white teeth and healthy pink gums was hard to imagine.

"Dr. Roy said he was sure he was going to find lots of cavays because he sees me in the sweetshop," said Edison mournfully.

"Where's your mother?" said Rosie.

"She sent me by myself. She says she needs to do her meditates and that I am a big boy and she will be over in ten minutes."

"Well," said Rosie. "As it happens, I'm going that way myself and I'll take you." She marched up with him into the dentist's, absolutely furious.

"Ah, the young sugar addict," said Roy, his sparkling gnashers on display and his pristine uniform buttoned up to his neck. "Your mother said she'd be in in five minutes."

"She's doing her meditates," said Edison.

"Very good, very good," said Roy.

"I'm here though," said Rosie.

Roy looked at her.

"Here to accept my offer?"

Edison jumped up on the dentist's chair.

"I am going into space," he announced loudly. "Hello Space. Countdown is progressing. We are okay to go."

"Don't touch anything," said Roy.

"I'm just going to stay for Edison's examination," said Rosie. "He wants me here."

"Ten," said Edison. "Nine."

Roy's face fell immediately.

"Just to make sure he doesn't get any unnecessary work," said Rosie, staring him straight in the face. "You hear a lot about that from dentists these days," she said. "Of course you would never do that."

"Eight…seven…"

"I'll be a lot happier when you're gone and no longer around here making trouble," said Roy. "Miss Hopkins."

"Well, I don't know about that," said Rosie, as he picked up his little mirror and tiny pointed probe. "You see," said Rosie. "I've had a little stroke of luck. Finally."

"Six…five…"

"My ex is selling our flat and moving in with his new girlfriend."

"Aww, you can't hold on to your man," sneered Roy, moving around.

"Four…three…"

"And he's giving me my share of the proceeds. Very, very fairly, in fact. He didn't have to."

Gerard's grace, in the end, had overwhelmed her. She knew it had a lot to do with him not wanting confrontation and to get on with moving in with Yolande, who, it turned out, had a proper little house with a garden in Bow and cooked an absolutely mean chili con carne, and his mother absolutely loved her. She had been happy for him. But for him to give her a share of the profits, rather than just what she'd put in, was more than kind. It was charming. And him. And all the good things she knew she'd remembered, not just his annoying habits that had worn her down. She had been right to love him. He was worthy of it. She didn't set her sights too low. Not at all.

Finally, Rosie swallowed and said what she had come to say.

"So, I'm buying the shop. I'm buying the shop and running it, and I'll rent half the cottage, and that will be enough to cover it all and get Lilian into the nice home. If she wants to go. She doesn't know she wants to go, but she does really. So you can't have it."

"Two…one…"

Roy looked at her, startled.

"You can stuff your new office. I'm keeping it."

"BLASTOFF," shouted Edison, spraying a whole load of spit over Roy's face and glasses. Rosie smiled at him.

"Get down," barked Roy. "There's nothing wrong with your teeth. Tell your mother I'll send her the bill."

Edison jumped off and, pretending he was in space, careered around in orbit. Rosie couldn't help giggling as he knocked into trays of instruments.

"Careful! And you too," she said with a backward glance at Roy as she left the office. "There're a lot of these overcharging dentists doing unnecessary work these days. I'll be telling everyone to keep an eye out for it."

• • • •

Rosie ran into Hester in the street outside. She was wearing her usual expression of smug calm.

"Sorry," said Rosie. She pasted the biggest, brightest smile on her face so Edison, still careering up and down being in a spaceship, wouldn't see what she was saying. "I don't mean to be rude. But if you let your gorgeous, charming, delightful six-year-old roam the streets alone one more time instead of behaving like a proper mother, I'm reporting you to social services."

Hester took a step back, her mouth falling open. Rosie ruffled Edison's hair and marched back on up the street.

"Come visit me soon," she hollered to Edison. "We'll watch *Star Wars*."

"What's *Star Wars*?"

"You'll like it."

• • • •

Up toward the turnoff, Rosie spied something that at first didn't make sense. It looked like two old men walking…but also someone very familiar…it took a second for her vision to crystallize and then she realized who it was. It was Peter Isitt, walking along… with Stephen. They both had long walking sticks carved with something that looked ancient and were accompanying each other very slowly up the road. Rosie looked around. She could either slow to a crawl, which would probably mean Roy coming out of his office to harangue her again, or run past them, which would be weird. London was always full of people hurtling down the streets, whether they were jogging or mugging or trying to catch a bus. Here, nobody ran. Everyone ambled; there was no point in running if you were going to get caught up behind a flock of sheep, and anyway, what was the rush? There was always work to be done, and it would keep. The rhythm of the earth was more important, the seasons and the weather. So Rosie tried to keep up her normal pace, hoping she wouldn't get noticed. As usual, living in a village, this didn't exactly work for her.

"Hi Rosie!" called Anton cheerily from the top of the high street. He held open his trousers.

"Look! Look! I have space in my trousers!"

The two men turned to look as Rosie felt her face redden. "I…I…" She hurried toward Anton. "That's great news."

Anton beamed.

"And it's down to you! I decided just to eat one of everything! So on Monday, I just have one fish and chips, and on Tuesday, I just have one fish and chips, and on Wednesday, I just have one chicken and chips, and on Thursday, I just have one sausage and chips and…"

He was continuing, but Rosie hushed him.

"That's not exactly what I had in mind," she started, but then, seeing his falling face, consoled him.

"Well, if it's working for you, that's fantastic," she said.

"I know," said Anton. "Can I have some fudge?"

"When you're in trousers you can buy from a shop," said Rosie. "A real shop. With buttons."

"I think I've forgotten how to do buttons," said Anton sadly.

"I'm sure you've forgotten how to do a lot of things," said Rosie, winking at him. "But I suspect it's all about to come back to you."

Anton was giggling smuttily when Peter and Stephen reached them.

"Hello," said Rosie.

Anton smirked. "Rosie and I were just discussing...BEDROOM MATTERS," he sputtered out. Stephen raised an eyebrow.

"All part of the service?" he said, and Rosie wanted to kick him. Instead she smiled tightly.

"Hello," she said. "Glad to see you're both out and about."

She hadn't, she realized, seen Stephen properly outside before. She couldn't help but admire how tall he was—and now how straight his back was. Then she told herself to get these ideas right out of her head. She'd been a passing fancy for him, nothing more. She steeled herself not to think about it.

"You both look much better."

Peter smiled at her. How odd, she thought, that he had spent his entire life married to the daughter of Lilian's great love. Did he know? He must. Was he happy?

"Well," he said, as Anton lumbered off in the direction of Malik's. "I'd better get back. She'll be on the lookout for me."

"Heh," said Stephen. "Thanks for the walk. It's hard to find...well. People who understand."

Peter looked at him for a long moment.

"People do understand," he said strangely. "More than you think, young man."

Stephen blinked.

"What do you think he meant by that?" he said as Peter turned down his lane. Rosie didn't answer. "Is it one of those things about me being a spoiled idiot again?"

Rosie shrugged and didn't laugh. He looked at her curiously.

"So have your friends left?" she said for want of something to say.

"Yes," said Stephen carefully. "They have. They've gone back to London. But I've been thinking..."

He paused. Rosie couldn't help it. She couldn't help the little excitement that leaped inside her now they were gone. It was stupid; he'd been awful and he hadn't contacted her or anything to apologize or to mention it or—it was all too embarrassing for words. She kept her eyes on the ground.

"I was thinking about what you said...you know, I do need something to do. Something practical to do with my life instead of sitting around moping. I see that now. So I've decided."

At once, Rosie knew what was coming. Unbelievable. Although, in a funny way, what would have been worse? Living in some rotten squat in London, starting over from the bottom, going out on hideous dates while knowing all the while that he was wandering around town living it up with CeeCee and Weapon and God knows who while she worked? Well, no. At least she wouldn't be doing that.

"You're going down to London," she said, her voice sounding choked and husky.

Stephen nodded. "Get a change of scene. It'll be good, don't you think?"

His voice betrayed a hint of nerves. Rosie felt herself go shaky too.

"Well, that's good," she said, trying to sound cool and poised. "I'm sure it will be great."

Stephen looked at her questioningly.

"I'm staying here," she announced very quietly. She almost couldn't believe the words as they came out of her mouth.

"You're what?" said Stephen.

"I'm staying here. I'm buying out my great-aunt so she can get looked after properly. Well, buying the business and renting the cottage; I'll have to get a tenant. Then when Tina gets more together, she can buy in too. We'll be an employee-owned village sweetshop. But I've decided. I don't...I don't know if it will be forever. And I don't know if I can make a go of it. And I don't know if it will make me happy. But..."

She looked around her, the frosty fields light in the morning mists, the sun glinting off the icy tips of the mountains.

"I...I like it here. I'm happy here. I have friends here. Some friends here. Some people who hate my guts, but I can live with that. And family. I have family here, and I don't really have that anywhere else. So I'm going to change. I'm going to stay."

Stephen looked completely taken aback.

"Oh," he said. "That's a shame. That's...oh. I thought maybe, you know. You'd show me around London a bit."

"I think the London I would show you and the London CeeCee will show you will be very different things."

Stephen smiled.

"I thought I was meant to be the grumpy one," he said sadly. "But I'd hoped..."

"What did you hope?" said Rosie, suddenly furious. "That I'd do a naked dance in front of your chums? That I'd come up and give you a few handy shags before you got fully back in with your London set? That you could pick me up and drop me down whenever I'm of use to you?"

Stephen's brow furrowed.

"What are you talking about?" he said.

"You used me," said Rosie. "You used me when you were sick and you used me when you were getting better, and I fell for it every fricking time."

"You can swear," said Stephen. "We are grown-ups."

"You're not worth it," shot back Rosie, feeling furious. "I wasted... oh. It doesn't matter."

"Wasted what?" said Stephen, cross. "Wasted what? Sorry, was I wasting your time as well as the rest of the fucking town's? Oh God, how long do I have to limp around being sorry? You seemed to be quite happy at the time."

"And now it's done," said Rosie. "Well, thanks very much. It's fine. I don't need you and I don't need anything. It is VERY unclassy not to call a girl. Very. Although I'm sure those tarts in London won't give a toss."

Stephen looked at her in disbelief.

"Who uses a phone around here? Have you seen anyone use a phone around here? If you need something around here, you go and get it. And get ignored and left in the lurch," he added pointedly.

There was a silence. Nothing happened between them and nobody moved. "I have to be getting on," said Rosie stiffly.

"Fine," said Stephen. He started stomping off the other way, his limp pronounced but, oddly, rather suiting him. Tears stinging her eyes, it took everything Rosie had not to run up the high street in hysterics. She had the awful, awful feeling that this was the last time they would ever speak. That she had blown it, if she'd ever had it in the first place. She couldn't think now of the night at the ball, how exciting it was and how poundingly, devastatingly attractive she'd found him. How much she'd wanted him. Still wanted him.

Well. He was going away. Good. Better to crush her hopes now than run on indefinitely. Her heart, though, felt in her boots. Was this how Lilian had felt when Henry went away? Worse, she supposed, because Lilian knew she might never see him again. But something told Rosie she'd never see Stephen again. Not the real Stephen, the funny, cussed, brave Stephen she'd gotten to know. She might see a polite stranger, swishing past her in the pub or coming home at Christmastime, CeeCee tapping her foot impatiently till she could get the family visits out of the way. But seeing Stephen again? Seemed unlikely.

She burst through the doors of the cottage, the first sobs already on her lips. "Lilian!" she howled. Lilian was sitting up on the sofa and, like a child, Rosie threw herself down next to her and burst into tears.

"There, there," said Lilian. "There, there."

"He's going away," howled Rosie. "He's going away. I thought it wouldn't matter and I wouldn't care and I'd be all grown-up and graceful. But it does!"

It was only gradually that Rosie realized there was someone else in the room. Sniffing, Rosie tilted up her head, horrified to see Lady Lipton standing in the shadow of the kitchen door, two cups of tea in her hands. Rosie didn't even care; she was so red and damp and her face was a mess and the tears wouldn't stop dripping down anyway, and there was snot too. It didn't even matter anymore that she was such a mess-up. Hetty would be pleased, presumably, that she wasn't going to go near her beloved son anymore.

"Oh, for GOODNESS' sake," said Hetty, looking her up and down. "This HAS to stop. You must be freezing in that jacket." Rosie hadn't even noticed what she was wearing. "If you're going to live here, you'd better get yourself sorted out once and for all."

She brought up a paper bag from her feet. "Here," she said. "Lily told me your size. I thought you might like these."

Inside was a pair of boots. But not just any boots. Around the top was a little stripe of material. And the motif on it was little wrapped sweets.

"Pulled in a favor from Hunters," sniffed Hetty. "It really was getting beyond a joke."

Rosie wanted to laugh and cry at the same time. Instead, she took Lilian's proffered cloth handkerchief and blew her nose.

"Here," said Lilian. "Have my tea."

Hetty looked at her. "And I suppose you'd better have these. They've been cluttering up my son's kitchen for days now while he's looked at them and hummed and hawwed. I suppose they're for you. Well, he's never going to give them to you, so I suppose you'd better have them. I can't handle you BOTH mooning around; it's bad for my angina."

She handed over a box of sweets, something Rosie didn't recognize immediately. Then she cottoned on that they were love hearts. She opened them with fumbling fingers. Instead of different messages, on every single one was a single word: Rosie. Rosie. Rosie. Rosie. Rosie. Rosie gasped and looked up.

"I need to tell you something," said Lilian. "Last night, when we were talking. I lied. Well, I mostly told the truth. But I lied too. I have had a happy life, mostly."

Lilian took a deep breath.

"But," she said, "if I…if I…if I had the chance to do it again, if things had been different…"

"Mmm?" Rosie couldn't take it all in. Hetty had turned her head away.

"I would never have left that bloody dance," said Lilian proudly. Her voice sounded stronger than it had in months. "And I would have grabbed his other arm. I wouldn't have walked backward. I would have kept on walking forward and kept on dancing, and I would have done everything in my power to make sure he didn't get near that other girl. And kept him on bloody farming duty when I was at it, and I wouldn't have cared twopence for what anyone else said; I'd already sacrificed as much as anyone else in that damn war."

Lilian gave one of her looks. "Do you understand what I'm saying?"

Rosie squirmed.

"It's not like that," said Rosie. "Henry chased you. It's nothing like that with Stephen."

Hetty harrumphed.

"I am not going to sit here and tell you that Stephen Mannering isn't one of the awkwardest buggers ever to walk the face of the earth," said Lilian. "He's ridiculously proud and needlessly difficult. But he's a good boy," she added. "He's decent. And he's kind. And I think if you want him…I think if you want him, you should go get him."

"But he's supposed to do the chasing," moaned Rosie, fingering the sweets, torn absolutely.

"Men are meant to do all sorts of things," said Lilian. "Doesn't mean they ever bloody manage it."

"Amen to that," said Hetty.

But already Rosie was on her feet and heading out the door.

"STOP!" said Hetty. "I cannot bear you going out looking like a farm animal one more time. ESPECIALLY if you are taking my son off my hands." Her tone was crusty but her eyes were twinkly.

"Get the dress!"

Hetty held her and brushed out her hair with a thick brush, and Lilian tried to paint on this ridiculous black mascara, and Rosie pulled on a thick sweater over the ridiculously unsuitable green dress for the middle of a winter's day, but finally they judged her ready. Rosie's heart was fit to burst, and she was at screaming point before they let her go. For speed, she leaped on the bicycle and threw herself down the hill as fast as she could manage. Was she too late? Had her words hardened his heart? Had he made up his mind once and for all? Maybe—she panicked at this—maybe he was just going to get into his car and head south straightaway. No. No, that couldn't happen. In her head, she had so many panicking scenarios looming up closer and closer that she let the bicycle go once more, faster and faster, till she realized she couldn't stop it—then she spotted him, on the flat part of the road leading back up to Peak House. He must be trying to walk it. To see him valiantly marching onward with his stick distracted her for a second, and as she skidded around the corner, she realized suddenly she had absolutely no chance of stopping at all.

"GET OUT OF THE WAY," she screamed at him. The bicycle made almost no noise on the paved end of the road. "MOVE!"

He tried to move around, but he was too late, and she saw his eyes widen as she remembered, at the very last minute, to jam on the brakes. Then, gracelessly, she felt herself, as if in a long, slow moment with the stretched-out sensation of a dream, fly over the handlebars and crash, headlong and with painful slowness, into his arms.

Gradually, they both fell back, the stick clattered to the ground, and they found themselves caught in each other's arms, squelched deep into the soft, forgiving mud at the side of the track, love hearts scattered all around.

At first, they stared at each other, absolutely shocked and appalled. Then, almost inexorably, Stephen and then Rosie started to laugh. And then, finally, filthy with mud and wet with newly falling rain and fueled by adrenaline and happiness, they kissed each other once again, as hungrily and as passionately as the young of the village had kissed each other by the side of the harvest fields, witnessed only by cows, and owls, and deep swooping birds, for hundreds and hundreds of years.

• • • •

The snow had fallen so hard the cottage looked like something out of a Christmas tree advertisement the day they loaded up the Land Rover—Stephen's this time, not Moray's. Stephen and Moray had grudgingly made up, Stephen admitting it was hard to see his contemporary fit and well and wandering about when there was so much need in Africa, Moray sniffing loudly and saying he was probably also jealous of his good looks and how much everybody liked him, but Stephen had ignored that.

They had packed all of Lilian's photos, her cushions, and as many of her dresses as Rosie could get into the car.

"Why will I need those?" Lilian had said, not displeased.

"Because there'll be a different social occasion every night," Rosie had said. "You'll be tea-danced off your feet."

Lilian sniffed.

"Not with my hips."

"Don't be daft; they've all got dicky hips. They play the music at thirty-three and a third. And you'll be by far the best-looking woman there."

"Well, I can't deny that," said Lilian. She was full of nerves for moving from the only home she'd ever known. But in a funny kind of way, she was excited too—excited to be doing something new, trying something different. The idea of room service and games nights and someone to play Scrabble with...well, she couldn't deny it sounded a little interesting. Although the presence of Ida Delia made her slightly nervous, but it couldn't possibly be the other way around. Ida Delia would have forgotten her long ago, or gone senile or something.

But the best news of all was Rosie. That Rosie would still be near; that she could visit the shop whenever she chose, come to the cottage, or pick up the phone; that this was going to happen without ruining Rosie's life; that Rosie WANTED to do this—these things made her feel safe and content inside.

Rosie looked at her, sitting like a queen with a blanket over her knees in the front seat. Stephen was driving. She looked at him. She still couldn't believe it. That he was there, and that he was hers. The last few weeks had been a blur. Gerard had been unimaginably decent; mind you, when she'd gone to see him, his shirts were perfectly ironed and his hair had been cut.

"Yolande likes me to look my best," he'd said when she mentioned it. "She loves doing all that stuff."

He looked even more well fed, if that were possible, but undoubtedly, in Rosie's eyes, happier. Gleeful, in fact. She was slightly sad—she was human—that after all those years, it had been somebody else, but she couldn't deny it was right.

"I'm so glad," she said. "Does your mum like her?"

"She LOVES her," said Gerard. "Well, there are a FEW things she doesn't do quite right, but I'm sure Mum will sort her out."

Rosie smiled to herself. Finally Gerard's mum had someone to spar with. She must be delighted. She had given them the most enormous box of chocolates, which made Gerard light up with glee, just like a boy, and thanked him profusely for his check; Yolande had a lovely little three-bedroom house on a nice estate with a little patch of garden. It was perfect for them, although Rosie couldn't help but look at it and compare the tiny square of green scrub and what it had cost to her wide open spaces and vast country vistas. How could they bear it? How had she borne it for so long? Then she realized that she was going native and smiled to herself.

"Thank you," she said to Gerard from the bottom of her heart.

Gerard shrugged. "Mum said it was the right thing to do," he said.

"It was," said Rosie. "Even though I didn't deserve it. Thank you." And they hugged, tentatively and awkwardly.

"And if you're ever in…"

"The wilds of rural Derbyshire? I know, I know."

"There's a big box of sugar mice with your name on it."

Gerard smiled.

"I'll remember that."

• • • •

She had had to tear herself away from Stephen to look after Lilian. It had been a struggle. Thankfully Tina had agreed to take on longer hours in the shop, but even so, Rosie found it incredibly difficult to leave Stephen's old cast-iron bed in the high, pale bedroom in Peak House, with its view of nothing but sheep all the way down the valley, the clouds so close it was as if you could touch them. As the winter gales and rains blew in down from the mountains, they felt as close and elemental as the weather.

But life had to be planned, work had to be done, arrangements had to be made. Tearing themselves away every day made their separations more painful, more urgent, so they had a perverse pleasure all their own. But inch by inch, things started to take shape. The deeds were signed over by a sweet, quiet notary.

Lilian insisted on signing over power of attorney to Rosie (Angie, from Sydney, was utterly bemused by the entire business, but took it in her stride), who was on the point of looking for a tenant without wanting to be too obvious about it when Stephen, with his head in her lap in front of the fire one evening, talked about how he was getting sick of Peak House. His mother needed it back to rent as a holiday cottage before she went bust again, and he'd been thinking for a while of moving to the hustle and bustle of the village, and Rosie had teased him and said what about London.

"I hate London," mused Stephen. "I was only moving there because everyone here thought I was a dingwad. Correction: YOU thought I was a dingwad."

"Yes, but I never said I don't LIKE dingwads. Anyway, you'd have been a dingwad in London too. Just a posh one."

"The worst kind," said Stephen, rotating his leg out in front of him. "But you know. Fair-weather friends were better than none at all."

Lilian woke up from the sofa where she'd been pretending to have a snooze. "So what are you going to do, Lipton?"

Stephen shrugged.

"I'm not sure," he said. "I'm sure my mother will rope me into something or other, trying to make the estate make money. Which it cannot do and will be even worse when I get my paws on it."

He sighed. "I just wish there was something more useful."

Rosie froze. She was terrified, every day, that he would say he wanted to get back to Africa. Even though, one night when he woke, wild-eyed and covered in sweat from a terrible dream, she had held on to him tightly and assured him, promised him, that he would never have to go back there again. His sorrow and guilt—that he wasn't brave enough to go back there again, that he never could—had only made her love him more, for owning up to it, for not pretending everything was fine and ballsing it out. That's what got people killed.

Lilian sniffed.

"You know they've just lost one of their teachers down at the school?" There was a silence.

"Was this about five minutes ago?" said Rosie. "Lilian, really, you've practically invented Twitter all by yourself."

"I would say it's imminent," said Lilian. "If you were looking for a job to annoy your mother and that makes even less money than a sweetshop owner…"

Stephen thought about it for a while. "Hmm," he said. "Hmm."

He glanced up at Rosie. "Posh enough for you?"

"Perfect," said Rosie, her heart brimming. "Perfect."

• • • •

And now today was the day. Stephen drove slowly, being careful over the icy bumps and ruts in the road, up the winding road to the home. As they crested the hill, Lilian let out a sigh. Rosie was leaning over from the back seat, holding tight to her hand.

"Don't worry about it," she whispered. "We're here."

Lilian nodded.

"I know, my dear. I know."

But her voice quavered. After an awkward hour spent settling her in and unpacking her things—it had seemed so much in the car—it helped a lot to humanize the spotless, cozy, but bare little room.

Finally, it became obvious that the head of the facility was gently hinting that they make their way out so she could introduce Lilian to the other residents.

Rosie turned toward her.

"I…" then she didn't know quite what to say.

Lilian shook her head.

"Don't…"

Both of them stood there for a moment. Then, for the first time, Lilian stepped forward and took Rosie in her arms, and they stood there in an embrace, Rosie enveloping Lilian's fragile frame. She felt so small, Rosie thought.

"You've put on weight," she whispered.

"Shut up," said Lilian. And then, after a pause, very quietly, "Thank you, my darling."

"We'll see you in the shop next weekend," said Rosie. "And if you learn how to use that mobile phone, you can put it on speaker and shout at us all day."

Lilian indicated Stephen who was lounging by the door.

"From one wounded bird to another then?"

"I heard that!" said Stephen. Rosie grinned and blushed.

"All right," said Lilian. "Off you go, the pair of you." And Rosie kissed her again on her soft white cheek.

Then they did go, hand in hand, walking gently through the falling snow, stopping out of sight of the house to have a quick snowball fight. Rosie screamed as Stephen chased her, her boots full of snow, up to the side of the avenue of trees.

"I can't believe you can finally outrun me," she said, her face pink from the wind, her mouth laughing wide. He grinned full at her.

"Ah," he said. "I don't want to. In fact, I faked the entire thing."

"Piss off!"

He laughed and put up his hands.

"Okay, okay. I didn't. I didn't, obviously. But Rosie..." His tone turned serious for a moment. "I never thought...I never in a million years thought that out of something so awful would come...something so sweet."

And Rosie thought of her life and how terrible she had thought it would be, to be buried alive in the country, looking after an elderly lady, and how selfish she had been.

"I got lucky," she said. "God, I got lucky."

"So did I," said Stephen fervently. And beneath the freezing gray sky, the cloud cover that wouldn't lift for another six months—regardless of the windy weather, they kissed until it got dark. Which wasn't very long. But they kissed on anyway.

• • • •

Lilian was tired after being introduced to a long line of old women mostly, all of whom seemed nice. Ida Delia wasn't there, but after supper, Lilian made her way, timidly, to the games room. Sure enough, sitting in the elegant salon, looking out into the darkening evening, was Ida Delia.

Lilian, taut with nerves, cleared her throat.

"Ahem," she said. Ida Delia looked up through thick pink-rimmed glasses. Then she nodded.

"Lilian Hopkins," she said. Then a pause. "It is Hopkins, isn't it? You didn't get married and change it?"

Lilian felt a shot of frustration bolt through her.

"No," she said. "I did not get married and change it."

Ida Delia nodded. There was a long silence; much left unsaid sat between them.

"Well," said Ida Delia finally. "I have an open box of dominoes here, if you're interested."

And after an equally long pause, Lilian shrugged.

"All right," she said. She sat down quietly, and they began to play.

• • • •

The letter was tearstained and rain-stained and goodness knows what else; it was hard, after all this time, practically on the edge of destruction, to make anything out on the yellowing paper that had come back with his watch and his medals and been saved, many years ago. It said, in Henry's very recognizable handwriting, just one thing—notes, perhaps, for a letter never sent, or simply an affirmation in some way.

Ida had kept it all this time, almost convincing herself over the years. If she screwed up her eyes, or pretended otherwise, or was talking to people who had not known them both, that the ink had run in the rain, or the sweat or the blood or whatever it was; that where it said, "I will love you always, L," that it was not an "L" but an "I"; an "I" caught in the rain. That was all. She had never shown it to anyone, not even Dorothy, who would snort at anything romantic anyway. She could never, ever entertain the belief that it said "L" and not "I."

But maybe, just maybe, thought Ida Delia Fontayne, it was time.

• • • •

"Are you a sweetshop or a bookshop?" asked a curious Edison one sunny, frosty Saturday morning. "I think you should be both. That would be good."

Rosie looked up from where she was unpacking the box of Lilian's self-published books she'd found in the bottom of her wardrobe, propping them up beside the ancient cash till.

"No," she said. "Not a bookshop. We've only got space for just this one."

• • • •

People think love should be popping candy—always surprising and exciting and fresh to the mouth. Or like dark chocolate—mysterious and adult and bitter. Or the tough candy shell of a minstrel, waiting to be cracked; the friable crumbling burst of a honeycomb, spiky as peanut brittle, as painful as a sharp shard of toffee.

I think love is caramel. Sweet and fragrant, always welcome. It is the gentle golden color of a setting harvest sun, the warmth of a squeezed embrace, the easy melting of two souls into one, and a taste that lingers even when everything else has melted away. Once tasted, it is never forgotten.

And that is all I have to say about that.

Read on for an excerpt from *The Loveliest Chocolate Shop in Paris*

Available now from Sourcebooks Landmark

The really weird thing about it was that although I knew instantly that something was wrong—very, very wrong, something sharp, something very serious, an insult to my entire body—I couldn't stop laughing. Laughing hysterically.

I was lying there, covered—drenched—in spilled melted chocolate and I couldn't stop giggling. There were other faces now, looking down on me; some I was sure I even recognized. They weren't laughing. They all looked very serious in fact. This somehow struck me as even funnier and set me off again.

From the periphery, I heard someone say "Pick them up!" and someone else say "No way! You pick them up! Gross!" And then I heard someone else, who I thought was Flynn, the new stock boy, say "I'll dial 911" and someone else say "Flynn, don't be stupid; it's 999. You're not American" and someone else say "I think you can dial 911 now because there were so many idiots who kept dialing it." And someone else taking out their phone and saying something about needing an ambulance, which I thought was hilarious as well, and then someone, who was definitely Del, our old grumpy janitor, saying, "Well, they're probably going to want to throw this batch away then." And the idea that they might not throw away the enormous vat of chocolate but try to sell it instead when it had landed all over me actually was funny.

After that, thank God, I don't remember anything, although later, in the hospital, an ambulance man came over and said I was a total bloody nutter in the ambulance and that he'd always been told that shock affected people in different ways, but mine was just about the differentest he'd ever seen. Then he saw my face and said, "Cheer up, love; you'll laugh again." But at that point I wasn't exactly sure I ever would.

• • • •

"Oh, come off it, Debs, love. It's only her foot. It could have been a lot worse. What if it had been her nose?"

That was my dad, talking to my mum. He liked to look on the bright side.

"Well, they could have given her a new nose. She hates her nose anyway."

That was definitely my mum. She's not quite as good as my dad at looking on the bright side. In fact, I could hear her sobbing. But somehow, my body shied away from the light; I couldn't open my eyes. I didn't think it was a light; it felt like the sun or something. Maybe I was on holiday. I couldn't be at home—the sun never bloody shines in Kidinsborough, my hometown, voted worst town in England three years in a row before local political pressure got the show taken off the air.

My parents zoned out of earshot, just drifted off like someone tuning a radio. I had no idea if they were there or if they ever had been. I knew I wasn't moving, but inside I felt as though I was squirming and wriggling and trapped inside a body-shaped prison someone had buried me in. I could shout, but no one could hear me. I tried to move, but it wasn't working. The dazzle would turn to black and back again to the sun, and none of it made the faintest bit of sense to me as I dreamt—or lived—great big nightmares about toes and feet and parents who spontaneously disappear and whether this was going crazy and whether I'd actually dreamt my whole other life, the bit about being me, Anna Trent, thirty years old, taster in a chocolate factory.

Yes, actually. While we're at it, here are my top ten "Taster in a Chocolate Factory" jokes that I get at Faces, our local nightclub. It's not a very nice nightclub, but the rest are really much, much worse:

1. Yes, I will give you some free samples.
2. No, I'm not as fat as you clearly expected me to be.
3. Yes, it is exactly like *Charlie and the Chocolate Factory*.
4. No, no one has ever done a poo in the chocolate vat. (Though I wouldn't necessarily have put it past Flynn.)
5. No, it actually doesn't make me more popular than a normal person, as I am thirty, not seven.
6. No, I don't feel sick when confronted with chocolate; I absolutely adore it. But if it makes you feel better about your job to think that I am, feel free.
7. Oh, that is so interesting that you have something even tastier than chocolate in your underpants, yawn. (N.B.: I would like to be brave enough to say that, but I'm not that brave really. I normally just grimace and look at something else for a while. My best mate, Cath, soon takes care of them anyway. Or, occasionally, dates them.)
8. Yes, I will suggest your peanut/beer/vodka/jam-flavored chocolate idea, but I doubt we'll be as rich as you think.
9. Yes, I can make actual real chocolate, although at Braders Family Chocolates, they're all processed automatically in a huge vat and I'm more of a supervisor really. I wish I did more complex work, but according to the bosses, nobody wants their chocolates

messed about with; they want them tasting exactly the same and lasting a long time. So it's quite a synthetic process.

10. No, it's not the best job in the world. But it's mine and I like it. Or at least I did, until I ended up in here.

Then I normally say, "Rum and coke, thanks for asking."

"Anna."

A man was sitting on the end of my bed. I couldn't focus on him. He knew my name but I didn't know his. That seemed unfair.

I tried to open my mouth. It was full of sand. Someone had put sand in my mouth. Why would anyone do that?

"Anna."

The voice came again. It was definitely real, and it was definitely connected to the shadow at the end of my bed.

"Can you hear me?"

Well, of course I can hear you. You're sitting on the end of my bed shouting at me was what I wanted to say, but all that came out was a kind of dry croak.

"That's great, that's great, very good. Would you like a drink of water?"

I nodded. It seemed easiest.

"Good, good. Don't nod too much; you'll dislodge the wires. NURSE!"

I don't know whether the nurse came or not, because I was suddenly gone again. My last conscious thought was that I hoped she or he didn't mind being yelled at by people who sat on other people's beds. And I couldn't remember: Had my parents said something was wrong with my nose?

about the author

Jenny Colgan is the bestselling author of more than eleven novels, including *The Loveliest Chocolate Shop in Paris* and *Meet Me at the Cupcake Café*. She also writes regularly for the *Guardian* and the *Times*, as well as the BBC's *Doctor Who*. She is married with three children and lives in London and Cannes, where she bakes, drinks pink wine, and plays the piano to an extremely disappointing standard.

MEET ME AT THE CUPCAKE CAFÉ

A NOVEL WITH RECIPES

Jenny Colgan

International Bestseller

A sweet and satisfying novel of how delicious it is to discover your dreams.

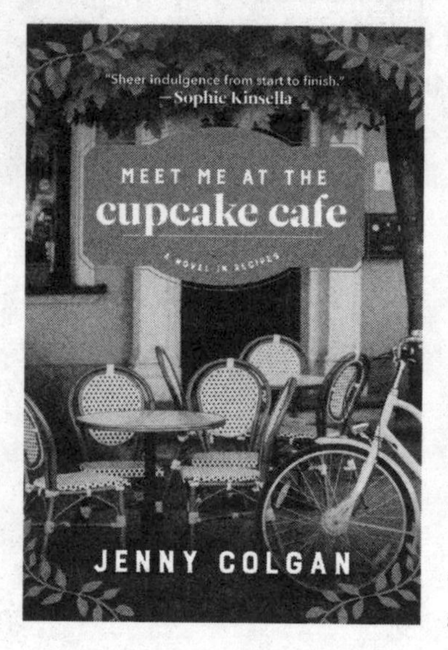

Issy Randall can bake. No, Issy can create stunning, mouthwateringly divine cakes. After a childhood spent in her beloved Grampa Joe's bakery, she has undoubtedly inherited his talent. She's much better at baking than she is at filing, so when she's laid off from her desk job, Issy decides to open her own little café. But she soon learns that her piece-of-cake plan will take all of her courage and confectionary talent to avert disaster.

Funny and sharp, *Meet Me at the Cupcake Café* is about how life might not always taste like what you expect, but there's always room for dessert!

Praise for *Meet Me at the Cupcake Café*:

"Sheer indulgence from start to finish." —Sophie Kinsella

For more Jenny Colgan books, visit:

sourcebooks.com